THE LAST HORSE

The Ninth Century Book III

M J Porter

Copyright © 2020 M J Porter

All rights reserved

The characters and events portrayed in this book are fictitious. Any similarity to real persons, living or dead, is coincidental and not intended by the author.

No part of this book may be reproduced, or stored in a retrieval system, or transmitted in any form or by any means, electronic, mechanical, photocopying, recording, or otherwise, without express written permission of the publisher.

Cover design by Flintlock Covers

ISBN: 9798669323387 (paperback)
ISBN: 9781914332302 (ebook)
ISBN: 9781914332258 (hardback)

For A.S.P

On her 18th Birthday.

How did that even happen?

Welcome to the world of 'adulting.'

CONTENTS

Title Page
Copyright
Dedication
Map of Mercia in AD874   1
Prologue   3
Part 1   8
Chapter 1   9
Chapter 2   16
Chapter 3   22
Chapter 4   34
Chapter 5   39
Chapter 6   65
Chapter 7   74
Chapter 8   82
Chapter 9   95
Chapter 10   104
Chapter 11   111
Chapter 12   123
Chapter 13   135
Part 2   146
Chapter 14   147

Chapter 15	177
Chapter 16	184
Chapter 17	197
Chapter 18	206
Chapter 19	233
Chapter 20	238
Chapter 21	253
Chapter 22	260
Chapter 23	273
Historical Notes	276
Cast of Characters	279
Meet the Author	283
Acknowledgement	287

MAP OF MERCIA IN AD874

M J PORTER

****

PROLOGUE
AD874

I feel him faltering beneath me, and I'm not surprised.

We've been riding for so long, the attackers behind us, fierce and unrelenting. I wish I could jump from his back, allow him the time he needs, but neither of us has that option.

My eyes have been searching the horizon for all that time, just hoping to see the banner displayed so proudly by the men inside Northampton. I need to see it. He needs to see it, but it feels so far away.

Even my warriors are gone, their mounts fresher and more able to take the punishing pace that Jethson has set from the front of the group.

My warriors were lost, but I found them.

I've had no time to mourn the fresh losses and the reason for their delay.

I might never need to.

But no, Haden's gait lengthens beneath me, as the ground suddenly flattens out, and there, before us, I can see the promise of survival and hope on the horizon. I never thought I'd be so grateful to see my Aunt's banner.

All of the other horses, riderless or ridden, stream away, far in the distance. I can just determine that Edmund has reached the river crossing. I watch almost despairingly, as Jethson disappears, no doubt taking steady steps down the sharp embankment, the promise of a swim across the expanse of the Nene perhaps not the temptation it might once have been.

But the sound of the chase reaches my ears, and despite Haden's best efforts, I know I need to stand. I need to face the Raiders, even if it is for the final time, if only to ensure my men and horses make it back to safety.

I should not have stirred the hornet's nest. I should have thought more before I risked everything just to have the comfort of enjoying the coming winter nights without fear of attack from the Raiders.

My tenure as king will have been brief but filled with acts of bravery, or so I hope they might record it.

Others, Edmund and my Aunt amongst them, will berate me for my foolishness, and rage will mark their grief, keeping it at bay. That brings me some comfort.

I watch as more and more of the horses flee down the steep riverbank, the hope of survival beginning to thrum through my body, in time to the elongated stride of my sweating mount. He'll run himself to death, but it still might not be enough.

Horses and men disappear, although, for each of my saved warriors, it seems as though more and more Mercians flood onto the battlements of Northampton, because I can see it now. It's so close, and yet so bloody fucking far. Men watch, weapons ready, although there's nothing they can do from such a distance other than encouraging me, their words failing to reach me, even as their intent does, their arms raised high in the air.

I strain to hear, but the only sound is that of the thudding hooves coming from behind. Fucking bastards. I've killed so many of them, and yet it's never enough.

I notice that Haden's ears flicker, he hears the encouragement as well. From somewhere he dredges more speed yet, and I consider that it's not the pursuers who drive him on, but rather the hope of a warm bed and plentiful hay. He will always prefer comfort to hardship.

And then I see it. Pybba, not realising quite how far behind I've fallen, turns and falters, trying to bring his horse under control. Brimman, desperate to be with his stable-brothers, races on, even though Pybba tries to pull him back, come to my aid. I can see his mouth opening and closing, although no words reach me. No doubt he rebukes those who've gone before him, perhaps even trying to call them back, to mount a defence until I'm safely amongst them. But it's too late. I know that, even though Pybba and Haden seem determined to ignore the undeniable logic.

I wish I had the air to shout to Pybba, tell him to get across the fucking river. My death here is almost inevitable, but his doesn't need to be. And even Haden might make it across the river when I fall from his back, and he can race on. The Raiders do not need another horse.

I hope Haden will leave me. Such constraints have never prevented him from abandoning me in the past. He better fucking not decide to be loyal and protective now. It'll kill him if he does.

From the top of the rampart that crowns Northampton, I see Ealdorman Ælhun watching me, easy to see from such a distance, rimmed as he is with his beard of frost. He, like the other men of Mercia, bellows for me to hurry, to survive, to make it to the river. Or that's what I assume he shouts. I can't hear his words. The wind rushes fiercely beyond my ears, and there's nothing but the drumming of hooves.

I wish I'd fucking left open the gateway into Northampton. Perhaps then I'd have stood more chance of survival. Would the Raiders have risked coming close to the gate when there were so many warriors just waiting to take their lives?

But I take comfort in seeing that Northampton is reinforced. Whatever the Raiders attempt when I'm dead, they'll not claim the settlement for themselves again. It will remain Mercian. It might have been birthed by the Raiders two decades ago, but it will become Mercian, and it will remain Mercian.

My gaze flickers over bows and arrows, spears and even rocks and stones, being held menacingly by those men on the ramparts, visible more by the stance they've adopted than by what they hold. It makes me smile to see my proud Mercians.

Fuck, it makes me so bloody proud.

I didn't make them like this, that part of their nature was always inside them, but I've been the one to unite them to one purpose, to assure them that King Burgred and his craven ways with the Raiders was not the only way to defeat our enemy.

I've shown them how to win, and to keep winning, because this war will go on and on, unfortunately. But each win brings them a step closer to the final victory. I believe that. And now, so do they.

I hope they carry on when I'm dead. I don't know who'll lead the Mercians, but it'll need to be a man with the guile to turn every defeat into a victory, to accept mistakes and learn from them. I don't think it'll be one of the current ealdormen. They've spent too many years being told what to do by King Burgred and his Wessex allies.

It will need to be a better man than I.

And then Haden stumbles on the rugged terrain. I knew he would.

And I'm flying through the air, my feet coming free from the stirrups in a well-practised manoeuvre, my hands soaring above the reins. I'll not take him with me; neither will I wound him when I fall.

Haden will recover his footing, continue his journey to the river. He knows where he wants to go.

For what feels like a long time, I see the darkened earth coming toward me, the recently forged trackway, already tangled with winter roots and the hint of a hard frost. My head flicks upwards, catching sight of Haden, his pace once more stable as he races to the river crossing without me. At the last possible moment, I roll myself tightly, hands to either side so that my weapons don't forge the final wound for the enemy. I'll let the Raiders do that.

The air is knocked from my body as I hit the hard ground, but I don't have time for such niceties as breathing. I roll, jump to my feet, turn, hands raised, to face the oncoming Raiders, chest heaving.

And fuck, there are so many of them. I hardly know where to

look.

I did this. I forced the Raiders from their lair at Grantabridge.

I antagonised them by killing their scouts, one by one. I led them here. I taunted them. I made them worry that they weren't as secure as they thought they were.

I did this.

And I'll meet my death as payment.

But the warriors of Mercia, behind their newly built defences, will witness it. I'll not die a coward, skulking and hiding from the Raiders, I'll not choose my life over that of the people of Mercia as King Burgred did.

No, I'm the king of Mercia, and I'll use my death to show just what can be accomplished, even by only one man, against a hundred mounted Raiders.

I grin, ensure my helm is firmly wedged on my head from my fall, and then, because to be the legend that Mercia needs to survive, I must, I run at the Raiders, seax in hand.

I'll not wait for them.

The damn fuckers.

PART 1

CHAPTER 1

Torksey
Summer AD874

Torksey is a burnt ruin. I'd like to state that it's a burning ruin, but there was too little of substance there in the first place for it to still be burning. My horse is weary. I don't know how to describe how I feel. Hollow, as though I'm hungry, and yet with a burning rage at my very core.

Icel.

He should have been here to witness the victory, and his absence clangs louder than the largest church bell, more thunderous than two thousand warriors on the march. He is everywhere, and also nowhere.

"My Lord King," a harsh voice is the first to hail me, and I nod, pleased to see that although it's a ruin, Edwin's warriors guard it fiercely and it's Æthelwig who demands my attention.

"Hail," I respond, horrified by the exhaustion thrumming through my voice. I squint, feeling the lines around my eyes draw tight under the relentless beating of the sun. I thought it was hot yesterday. Today, I fucking swear, I could melt iron without the need for the blue flames of the forge.

The thought brings an unwelcome smirk to my face. Perhaps, I could remove all the impurities and rework myself into something harder, less likely to fracture, remove all the nicks and barbs that pierce my soul. Remove this newest cut that threatens never to heal.

"Jarl Halfdan has escaped, more's the fucking pity," I complain, answering the unspoken question rather than dwelling on my melancholy thoughts. I'm the king. I'm the victor and yet I feel as though I've lost far more than I was ever willing to give up to win.

"His men are dead," I offer, as though that makes up for the fact that Jarl Halfdan has evaded me and Icel is dead.

"No one lives here, either," Æthelwig confirms, and I try to find a smile from somewhere, and when that fails, the will to look pleased. But there's nothing. The silence stretches, as uncomfortable as my tunic. It's been wet and dry so many times in the last few days, I know it's both shrunk and billowed into something that sags where it shouldn't.

It falls to another to speak the words that should have easily slipped from my tongue.

"Well done, men," Edwin is riding high on the success of our strategies. And of course, these are his men who guard Torksey.

"Did you find anything valuable?" Only now do my nostrils scent the acrid smell of burning bodies, and I flinch at the too obvious illusion to the dead. It's too soon. Far too soon.

"Some. It can be melted down," Eadric offers, a shrug of his shoulder showing that he doesn't genuinely approve of the sparse pickings. The Raiders come to make their riches in Mercia. I've ensured they die with little more than the tunics on their backs.

"How many?" This is important to know, and I perk up at the question. How many have we killed that night? I don't see how it can be the two thousand that Pybba calculated yet lingered in Mercia. Neither does it seem the lower number that Rudolf hoped there would be.

As much as my body aches, arms trembling with the exertions of facing the Raiders, I know we can't have taken the lives of that many men. Not with such a small force.

"We pulled those from the river that we could, and added

them to the funeral pyre." Æthelwig indicates with his head both the sight of the river, and the funeral pyre, but I don't need his assistance. I can smell the one, and almost see the other. But he gives no number, and I assume he doesn't know it. Not yet.

A nicker greets my arrival, and I glance upwards, unsurprised to find Haden watching me. The beast is less battered than I am, and I can tell, in the reach of his neck, that he demands to know what horse I've ridden. I pat the animal's shoulder. He's been good to me, but he's not Haden.

I slide from the back of the horse, hand the reins over to Rudolf. The loss of Icel cows Rudolf. He'll probably feel it even more keenly than I do. The two of them tolerated one another. That might have been more important than genuine friendship: my oldest warrior, and my youngest. Perhaps I should have realised the natural line of succession when I allowed Rudolf to join my men. The thought infuriates me.

I go to Haden then, running my hands along his pie-bald shoulders and back legs, needing the reassurance that he's not been injured in the fight. His black and white nose is inquisitive, and yet for once, he doesn't demand more from me than I can give. Could it be that my horse and I have finally reached some sort of new understanding, even after all these years together?

I see that my men's mounts have all be rounded up from when they were abandoned, as we streaked upriver in our stolen ship. That ship has been making its way downstream, but I know it'll be some time behind us. Bodies are floating in the water, beyond reach of the riverbanks. They need dredging before they contaminate our water with the stink and filth of corrupting bodies. I've given the task to Scef and those of Edwin's men who help him row the ship. They seemed keen on the role, but I wouldn't have been so enamoured of it.

I've seen my fair share of water-slick, marbled bodies. They're a bastard to catch.

The horses are gathered close to the landward side entrance. I quickly realise why, as I gaze at the scene of utter desolation. Out there, amongst the broken-down ruin of the tents and half-hearted wooden structures, thick grey smoke billows. The funeral pyre. Best to have the horses clear from the reek. It's typically enough to send them wild.

With a hearty smack on Haden's rump, I turn to make my way to where the dead burn. I need to see for myself. I need to start to convince myself that the sacrifice was worth it.

The ground beneath my feet doesn't give up its story of the passage of a hundred feet and hooves. No, it remains hard-baked, cracked in places, as though just daring rain to fall and fill it once more.

I look around with the eyes of someone waking from a dream, only to fall into a nightmare. Yet, this is of my doing. I fucking thrill to see it. The listing wooden poles of destroyed buildings. The hastily trampled pieces of discarded clothing. Even the splashes of red where blood has inevitably leaked into the parched ground. A pity it wasn't enough to sate the thirst and heal the fissures.

Then my eyes are drawn to the smoke, and the pile of grey and white flesh still visible on the bodies that have yet to begin their final journey. I would choke on the fumes, but instead, I inhale deeply. This is the scent of victory, and I must revel in it.

"How many?" I direct the question to the man standing watching with just as much satisfaction as I do. Perhaps he knows, whereas Æthelwig did not.

Æthelwulf makes no response, and I turn to him, only then appreciating the extent of his wounds. A bloody linen is held tightly around his head, and I can see where a blade sliced deeply into his left cheek. It doesn't gape open, but it would do, without the linen: a nasty wound, but the sort to leave a scar to thrill the women.

Not only that. His right arm is held in another piece of linen, this one closely tied around his right shoulder, where his hand hangs limply. I swallow. I know the price of war.

"How many?" I ask a little louder this time, and Æthelwulf startles and then turns pain-filled eyed my way.

"My Lord King," his voice is deep with the ash from the fire.

But also slow.

"How many of the Raiders are dead?" I phrase the question carefully.

"I kept a count. At least three hundred and eight-four met their deaths here. They all burn. Or at least what's left of them."

The number staggers me.

"So, fucking many?" and a tremor runs down Æthelwulf's face.

"You doubt me?" he demands heatedly, but I'm already shaking my head.

"Not doubting. I'm amazed at how well the small force did against so many."

Æthelwulf seems to relax at the words, but I know our conversation isn't over yet.

"How many men did we lose?" But a roar of flame fills the air, a hot blast as though from the sun itself, and I appreciate that Æthelwulf uses it to mask my question. It seems I'll have to find another to ask.

The fact Scurfa is not standing with Æthelwulf troubles me, only then it doesn't. The sound of a body dragging over the ground is unmistakable. From the grey tendrils that cover the high lying land, two figures appear, head first, as though creatures from the otherworld. Between them, they drag yet another naked body, the flaccid manhood almost making me look away in sympathy. But I can't pity these men. Who fucking knows how many women he's raped with it.

Scurfa is one of the men. I'm pleased to see him unharmed, if soot-covered and smeared in the rust of death.

"My Lord King," only when the body is dumped as close to the super-heated flames as it's possible to get, does Scurfa lift his eyes and recognise me.

"It's good to see you," I confirm, but Scurfa's eyes rest on Æthelwulf.

"I told you to rest," Scurfa levels at the other man, and I can see why. Æthelwulf sways alarmingly from side to side. Yet, he stubbornly shakes his head.

"I will watch until every last bastard has been sent tumbling into the sky."

"Then at least do it on your arse," is Scurfa's disgusted response.

"How many did we lose?" I call to Scurfa. I hope he doesn't remind me of Hereberht. It might break me. Instead, he beckons me with a sharp nod of his head, and I follow him, beyond the curling smoke, and back out into the carnage of Torksey.

It's as though I step from night into day, and I blink, cough and spit all at the same time.

"Not many," Scurfa acknowledges. "Two that we've found." His pause assures me that Hereberht is included in that number. I nod, appreciating his tact. I also grasp that he continues to speak as a quest for some sort of normality in the face of such tragedy. "Although another three are missing, so far. But the wounded are a cause for concern. It's too hot to be about with such injuries. Any cuts will fester and turn rank."

"I agree. When the ship returns, we'll load the injured and send them back toward Repton."

"Good," Scurfa states, wiping his hands down his body, although it seems to do little to clear the filth and muck, and his nails that are imbedded with grime.

"He fucking escaped then?" I can hear the disappointment in Scurfa's voice.

"Yes, he did." I don't want to say more. The fury threatens to send me rushing after Jarl Halfdan, but I know I have more pressing concerns within Mercia itself.

"Were they all Jarl Halfdan's warriors and adherents?" It's this that concerns me. If these were Jarl Halfdan's men, then what's happened to Jarls Anwend, Guthrum and Oscetel? Are they somewhere else within Mercia? Have they run from Torksey and found a new home elsewhere?"

"Impossible to fucking tell," Scurfa acknowledges. "They're all fucking dead. That's all that matters." He strides from me then, and I'm aware that Pybba and Rudolf have snuck up behind me, well, as quietly as the two of them can ever be when they argue, even now, about something that I don't quite catch.

"Are they keeping the spoils for themselves?" Rudolf's attempt at his usual post-battle cheer almost makes me smile.

"I doubt it. But maybe. Don't we have enough of other men's trinkets?" The words echo my exhaustion, and Rudolf wisely stays silent.

"A fucking mess," Pybba announces, and I don't know if he speaks of the ruin of the campsite or Icel's loss and Edmund's part in the matter.

"As long as the bastards are all dead," I announce, echoing Scurfa's sentiment too closely for my liking. I wince as I speak, forgetting the half-healed injury to my left leg, as I dig at the dried grasses with my toe, the glittering object flashing onto my face.

I bend, quest with my fingers, and then stand, turning the broach with its depiction of a wolf etched into it, between two of my fingers. I don't need the reminder that Mercia's enemy is still at large. There's no guarantee that Jarl Halfdan won't try and return to Mercia. None at all.

"Right," I huff, turning to hand the silver piece to Rudolf. His tongue sticks through his lips as he appraises it, testing it for weight, and then shrugging one shoulder.

"Not the fucking best," Rudolf mouths, an echo of my thoughts on finding it. "What now?" Rudolf asks as I peer all around me, hands on my hips, surveying the carnage.

I know what I want to do, but it's so fucking different to what I have to do, that I almost can't believe the thoughts are mine.

"We return to Repton," I announce. "The wounded can go by ship. The rest can take the horses."

Whatever Rudolf's response is, I hear it cut off with a gurgle and cry of outrage, and know that Pybba has silenced the younger man. He knows me far too well.

CHAPTER 2

Worcester

Bishop Wærferth's soft sigh reaches my ears, even though it's not supposed to. I would say something to the bastard, but now really isn't the time.

Instead, and I don't know why I bother, I hold myself tighter, try not to think of the tedium of the service, but instead of what it means for me.

That lasts for all of thirty heartbeats until I catch the eye of Edmund.

The smug shit watches me, along with the rest of the congregation, with a wide-beam across his face that only serves to highlight the gap where his flashing green eye should have been.

Fuck.

What point is there in enduring this damn tiresome ceremony, when there is the enemy to hunt down, Mercia to keep safe, and Raiders threatening to undo all that I've fought so hard to achieve?

Only then do I realise that Bishop Deorlaf has paused, his mouth open, but the incantations he recites seem to hang in the air, more substance to words than I would like to admit were ever possible.

My eyes swiftly swivel to him, and indeed, it seems that many in the church are roused from their stupor by this unexpected interruption.

A hiss from Bishop Wærferth and Deorlaf seems to shake all over and then resume as though nothing's happened. I would seek our Wærferth's eye, demand to know what the fuck that was all about, but Wærferth is busy doing something else, and when he stands, he refuses to meet my eyes. Sensible man.

I endeavour, once more, to concentrate on what's happening to me, on what I'll be able to do once I wear the ceremonial helm of Mercia on my head. Only my thoughts scatter away from me once more, just like candlelight over polished silver, or water falling over pebbles. There's no substance, only missed opportunities.

What use is a piece of gold when I need hard iron and sharper blades to prevent Mercia from being overrun by Raider bastards?

This time I feel the edge of someone's focus, and I turn, meet the steel eyes of my Aunt, and struggle to sit even taller, even more to attention. But no matter what I do, I know her gaze is riveted on me. Do I disappoint her so much that she daren't take her eyes from me? Does she do it because she knows the power she holds over me?

If her character had been embedded in my father's body, my family would never have fallen as low as it did. Never. She's a fiercer warrior than I am, and she does it all without recourse to flame-forged iron.

I swallow, taste only the sticky scent of the incense and wish heartily that this farce was truly not necessary.

I don't need to endure a coronation to make me king of Mercia. I already am. I've proved it by banishing the Raiders from Repton and then from Torksey, scouring the vast expanse of the River Trent to ensure there are none of the shits hiding away somewhere, hoping to escape my wrath.

I've lost men in doing so.

Mercia has lost men as well.

Bishop Deorlaf moves aside, his incantations done with, but Bishop Wærferth replaces him. With his back to those watching me being raised to the kingship, he pauses before speaking, his wise eyes intent as they offer me the smallest hint of a smile on his intelligent face.

Damn the bastard. He knows how hard this is for me. I'd sooner face fifty warriors, alone, their intent to kill me, with little more than a single knife to hand, than sit through yet more gabled words, the Latin a litany I find impossible to understand. The words reverberate in my head, each one buffeting me as though a gale blows through the church. Some find comfort in the sound, but the ancient language has only ever given me a headache and made me question my faith.

"*Rex*," that's as far as my Latin goes.

What use is Latin when there are Raiders to destroy?

I grit my teeth, set my jaw, and then incline my head the smallest amount to assure Bishop Wærferth that I understand.

I just wish they'd hurry up with the fucking thing.

I don't need to be inside a church. I need to be instructing my warriors, having the borders checked, reinforcing the shaky alliance I already have with Lord Cadell, and by association, his mighty brother, Rhodri Mawr, king of the Welsh kingdoms. I need to be thinking about bolstering the borders with Northumbria, East Anglia and even Wessex. Wessex was once Mercia's ally. It isn't anymore. They've made that very fucking clear.

I need to be considering the best way to patrol Mercia's many rivers, to stop the Raiders making use of inland waterways to get to the heart of our mighty kingdom.

I inhale, try not to choke on the fug of the incense and centre my resolve.

"It's only a day," those were the words that Pybba flung at me as I paced earlier, frustrated to be confined when there's so much that needs doing.

"Only a day," I'd roared, my hand covering my eyes, outraged that even he would make so small of my concerns.

The pain on his face had restored me to the realities of what was demanded.

"Only a day," I'd repeated, my words softer, the hint of an apology in the words, if not on my lips.

For all that, I know how much can happen in one day, and no matter what, I don't believe that this is the best use of my time.

The weight of the silver and gold helm placed over my head forces me to return to my body, and to what's happening to me.

Bishop Wærferth had explained the whole process to me, as quickly as he could, three days ago. Not that I needed to be spoken to like a belligerent child. I understand the process of becoming a king, but I'd sooner just be a king without all the ritual.

In the front row, Ealdorman Ælhun watches me keenly. He and Bishop Wærferth have united against me to ensure the rite is undertaken as soon as possible. The leaves have only just begun to turn, and I should be riding, not hunkered inside a draughty old church, the hopeful eyes of a generation nestled on me.

And then I understand.

This farce is nothing to do with me. The bishops might tell me that undergoing the ritual lifts me above all others, makes me holier, allows me to ascend closer to God, but really, it does none of those things. This service brings hope to all who watch, and all who hear that Mercia has a new, warrior king, and not the weak older man, reliant on the power of his wife's family in Wessex to support him; the man who gave Mercia away rather than risk his life.

With the helm on my head, a sword in my hand, and a flashing ring on my finger, placed there by Bishop Eadberht, I am the embodiment of what Mercia is and what it will be. Mercia will be restored to its lost greatness, and I'm the man to ensure it.

Why these people can't accept the tribute my seax claims, I do not know. But they can't. This ritual means more to them than the hundreds, if not, thousands of lives my relentless drive has gifted to the rich Mercian earth, or released to flutter on the wind, a grey haze of butterflies.

I allow the royal helm, sword and ring to festoon me in glittering jewels, gold and silver, and I stand, the three bishops rushing to one side so that all can see me within the church.

I face my people, wearing the items that mark me as their

king, the holiest of all within Mercia.

I shimmer beneath the flames of a thousand candles, I stand tall, my chin jutted out, my legs wide enough to support me easily, and I gaze outwards.

No one meets my eyes. No one. They have lowered gazes, as though I'm too magnificent for mortal eyes.

And then I do see an eye, and I smirk, the half-smile unusual on my face that has grown taciturn since the jaded victory at Torksey.

Edmund.

He doesn't flinch or look away from my gaze. I hold steady. I'll not look away. I don't expect him to either. We've become enemies, not allies, our combined grief making us each blame the other. It has made my warriors uncomfortable. It has made every act since Torksey intolerable. My rage, his fury, both are combining to show that we are merely men who lost a great friend and ally. Two men, the one blaming himself, the other condemning the other. It can't go on.

Edmund wears clothes I've never seen before. They gleam brightly, the golden threads depicted around the collar, a huge silver cross around his throat, the bright broaches that hold his cloak in place, winking at me as though they're the sun rising from a misty horizon.

Do I look like him in my kingly clothes, carefully chosen by my Aunt? She had insisted on the purple cloak. And the vivid blue tunic, more burdensome than my byrnie, with the weight of intricate stitches, applied to collar and wrist. But not only that, it is covered with the vivid shimmering of my family emblem, the two-headed eagle, that I also wear around my neck and my wrists. If I glanced in a looking-glass, I would not recognise myself.

I hope I don't look like Edmund, and yet I can't help but consider that I gleam even more luminously than he does, and I detect the work of my Aunt in his clothing.

We are bloody warriors, not made for pomp such as fucking this. I imagine she enjoyed herself far too much.

Edmund meets my interested gaze brazenly. An impasse perhaps.

Edmund's wounds have matured him. Or perhaps the passage of time has merely aged both of us.

I exhale slowly, feeling the weight of my responsibilities settle on me.

Are they truly any different to those I've known before? Perhaps not.

Am I truly more skilled than I was before? Assuredly not.

Am I truly more suited to lead Mercia against the Raider attacks? Against the incursions of the damn Welsh? Against the pretensions of sodding Wessex and her weak king who commands battles but takes no part in them?

No. I am not changed.

But to everyone else, I am transformed.

I see it now.

I grin at Edmund, shrug my shoulders to show the disdain I hold for my new position.

He returns the smirk, an appraising arch of his sighted eyebrow.

Our reconciliation, accomplished over the bowed heads of hundreds of men and women of Mercia, almost makes me howl with laughter.

Only then the moment is gone, a hundred pairs of eyes raised to finally gawk at me, awe reflected in the gasps of admiration, the hope of a generation threatening to skewer me more successfully than any spear ever could.

I absorb it all, and I take the acclaim as is my due.

I am King Coelwulf. King of Mercia.

Now, can I fucking go to war?

CHAPTER 3

"My Lord King," the title sounds correct, the voice does not.

I know my mouth drops open in shock, and for perhaps the first time in my life, I see a twinkle of amusement in my Aunt's eyes. She's always been so implacable, so hard, and so steady.

I want to berate her, force her just to call me Coelwulf, but immediately I realise that's what she wants.

"My Lady Aunt," I dip my head, dredging courtly manners from somewhere deep inside me, some half-remembered memory of when my father yet lived and he took me to meet one of the Mercian kings. Not Burgred, another one of the imposters, many years ago, when I was young enough to be overawed by such things.

I'm rewarded by the tightening of her already thin lips, and I almost laugh with delight.

"You should have cut your hair before you were crowned," is her acerbic response, and immediately I realise that she'll never let me win even if I am now her king. I consider if she ever harboured the hope that I would become king. And then I dismiss it. She would have hoped that Coenwulf would become king. Not me. Never me.

She's dressed in the finest attire I've ever seen. Not for her the workday clothes of a woman with an estate to run. Instead, she's adorned in exquisite pale blue linen, intricate detailing around the neck and along her sleeves, depicting the two-headed eagle, in sharp white thread, perhaps even silver. But not gold. That doesn't surprise me. The two dogs are docile at either side of her, and from behind, I'm aware that Edmund watches her intently.

Whatever it is between the two of them, I both don't want to know, and equally, hope it hasn't been compromised because of Edmund's changed state, and what happened to Icel. My Aunt had a healthy respect for Icel. They were of a similar age. I know full well that she enjoyed having someone to share stories of her youth on dark winter nights when there was nothing to do but listen to the howl of the wind, and the drumming of the rain on the roof overhead.

I'm standing outside, thankfully freed from the confines of the incense-laden church, the air clear of that stink, although the breeze is not quite as fresh as I might have liked. Bishop Wærferth assured me that Worcester didn't always smell. Maybe it does, and he's grown so used to it, he doesn't even notice anymore.

The immediate lull in conversation is far from unusual. We've never been the most vocal. We both know the duties the other expects the other to fulfil.

"Your father would be delighted," my Aunt's words involuntarily bring a tightening to my throat. I've never thought that I would want to hear that. My father was a weak man and yet to know he would be proud of me is somehow important.

"It should have been Coenwulf," I offer as a soft reply.

"It would never have been Coenwulf," she replies just as softly. "He would not have been able to accomplish all that you have." Her left-hand grips my forearm as she speaks, the firm touch a reminder that she's always been physically strong, as well as emotionally.

I wince to hear the unexpected criticism of my long-dead brother. I glance to ensure that Edmund hasn't overheard the words. Why I should be so fucking mindful of him, I don't know, but we're barely reconciled to each other. I would not have that jeopardised. Not now.

My Aunt links her arm through mine, and I begin to walk, as she directs. This is her moment. I'll let her have it. I owe it to her.

There's a mass of people who've come to witness my coronation, many of them unknown to me. I recognise some of the ealdormen, Ælhun, Æthelwold, Beorhtnoth and Ælhferht, his right arm still tightly bound against his body, the paleness of his lips against his bushy black beard and moustache, attesting to the constant pain he must feel. I'm surprised my Aunt has not taken him to task for failing to care for himself adequately. The three bishops are there as well, Wærferth, Deorlaf and Eadberht. They've accomplished the task of ensuring Mercia's king is rightfully acknowledged by God and the Mercians.

These are the men who supported me, even if grudgingly at first. It was these men who first believed the fiction that Bishop Wærferth created that I could be the new king of Mercia. It's they who sent their warriors to Repton, and then on, to Torksey, or about other tasks I set them outside Repton's crumbled gate and they who exude satisfaction at a job well done.

But these men are almost all West Mercian. There's another part to Mercia, jutted up against the kingdom of East Anglia, and these men are yet to be convinced. And I know that they're not happy that I personally killed Ealdorman Wulfstan, even if he was a fucking traitor and deserved to die. They're also unhappy that Ealdorman Wulfstan's son and successor is dead. Not that it's my fault. He died fighting for Mercia, which is more than they've done. Still, it's messy.

Ealdormen Beornheard and Aldred mingle with the other ealdormen, but their faces don't show the relief of the others. I know who they are because it's impossible not to realise they're ealdormen, but also because Rudolf, with his usual skills, has already determined who everyone is, and he's been generous to share.

I'll have to bring them round to my way of thinking. Either that, or it will happen through necessity, if the Raiders ever return. I hope they won't, but all the same, it would be nice to have the support of each and every ealdorman within Mercia.

I catch sight of Ealdorman Ælhun.

"My Lord King," he beckons me closer, and I go, reluctantly. "These are ealdormen Beornheard and Aldred."

"Well met," and I reach out and grip the offered hands firmly. I scrutinise them. Are they warriors or politicians? I have no time for politicians. I determine a lot just from their return grip. Perhaps neither of them is a politician after all. There's hope for them.

"You hold land, to the east?" Beornheard is quick to nod.

"Yes, Ealdorman Wulfstan was our neighbour. It's a pity his son is dead, and his daughter missing." I didn't know about the daughter. I did about the son.

"We'll find someone to replace him," I pledge, although who, I'm not yet sure.

Aldred seems less inclined to speak with me, his eyes focusing on something occurring over my shoulder.

"Mercia needs a strong king. Provided that's what you prove to be, you have my support." His words surprise me, but Ealdorman Ælhun nods, and I imagine, I have him to thank for making it such an easy conversation.

I turn aside, thinking to escape before Ælhun embroils me in another discussion about taxes, only to be greeted by a new group of powerful men. The bishops.

Three of them have conducted my coronation service, uniting in Worcester to bring about the culmination of Bishop Wærferth's outrageous plan, but there are others. Bishop Ceobred of Leicester is so ancient, that he sits, while one of his monks attends to him. I doubt he knows where he is, but I'm grateful that he's come. The others are far more alert, both Bishop Burgheard of Lindsey and Bishop Smithwulf of London.

They stand with the three bishops who support me. The angle of Bishop Smithwulf's lips assures me that he's far from sure he agrees with their decision, and he played no part in the coronation, other than to observe it. I think Bishop Burgheard would have happily taken his role in the coronation ceremony, had he been invited. After all, Torksey was part of the diocese he administers to, and Torksey is now free from Raiders. His eyes are by far the friendliest of the men, as they seek me out.

Bishop Wærferth wants me to walk amongst the men who are yet to know me by more than just reputation. He wants me to speak with them, win them to my cause, but if killing a shit load of Raiders hasn't won me some damn respect, then I sure as shit don't think a little conversation will accomplish it.

But, it seems my Aunt agrees with the bishop.

"Shall we?" It's not an offer to be refused, even though I would sooner be doing anything, even digging a grave to house the remains of dead Raiders. Perhaps digging a grave for rotting corpses, bloated with maggots, and stinking of fish.

"If we must," I curb my temper, aware that to speak as I usually would in front of her will only bring me more considerable pain in the future. She knows who I am. She knows my personality. All the same, she's made it clear that it's not tolerated in her presence.

With her dogs at her heels, I hope not to have to name them publicly, although I'm sure she would have no fucking problem doing so, we walk toward the group of bishops. Bishop Wærferth sees me first, and a small smile touches his lips. A caution, or a sign of his amusement, I'm not sure. I don't know him well enough, but it seems he knows me better.

"My Lord King," Bishop Wærferth inclines his head as I join him, mirroring his action.

"Lady Cyneswith," I almost startle at the use of my Aunt's name, only just not turning to see who Wærferth greets. I just call her 'aunt.' I always have. I'd almost forgotten she had another name that everyone must use.

"Your holiness," the edge to her voice softens, but only a little. It's similar to watching two warrior's eye each other up, still undecided as to whether they're enemies or allies. I almost smirk. I thought my Aunt would be pleased that Bishop Wærferth has finally brought about what she's longed hoped for; the restoration of my family's honour. But maybe not.

"This is Bishop Smithwulf of London."

Ah, London. I think to myself. Just another fucking place that needs my immediate attention. The Raiders have a thing for London. And London is Mercian. Although every fucker seems to forget that; especially the bastard kings of Wessex. They've had their eye on London for a long time. Sometimes, I think they forget a fucking great big river divides Wessex and Mercia. I wish I could make the Thames wider and more challenging to cross. There are too many bridges, and too many fucking fords, and too many who think the river is nothing but a fucking open invitation.

I appreciate London as a source of great trade and wealth, but I don't value its exposed position. Anyone with a damn ship can reach her.

"We've met," I offer, aware that Bishop Smithwulf won't remember.

The look of surprise on his face quickly smothered, assures me that he doesn't remember, but that now he perhaps has. It was not an unpleasant meeting, but it was bloody awkward.

"My Lord King," I admit, he covers his slip well.

"Bishop Smithwulf," I confirm, keen to be gone from the conclave of the holy men. I'm sure they've done more than enough for one day. But it seems they don't agree.

"I would speak with you, if you would permit, about matters in London."

I stifle my frustration, feel my Aunt's tightening grip on my arm.

"Is London threatened?" I ask, trying to keep the edge from my voice. "Are the Raiders there?" I need to know where all my enemy has gone. I can't imagine they've chosen London. If they couldn't hold Repton and Torksey, then they can't hold London either. Of that, I'm sure. Just as I'm also aware that I only faced Jarl Halfdan's warriors and camp followers at Torksey. Where he has gone, and where the three other jarls are torments me. I need to know.

"No, no, well," and here Bishop Smithwulf's face undergoes so many changes, I hardly know what to think of his thoughts.

"London was calm and well-ordered when I left," Smithwulf finally settles upon, and I nod, pleased to hear it. "But," and I wait. "There's the matter of defence to speak of, and also how London will protect itself in the event of a future attack. Of course, there's Wessex to consider as well."

"I hope you don't invite such an attack with your words," I caution, trying to make light of the matter. Yet my words are greeted with a gasp of horror. Now even my Aunt huffs in annoyance, and Bishop Wærferth looks stricken.

With wisdom I didn't know I owned, I hold my tongue. I'm a fucking warrior, not a politician. It's their damn fault for putting me in such a situation. I'm way out of my depth.

London played host to the Raiders the year before they came to Torksey. I know that. Everyone does. I went to London to determine the scale of the attack. I sent word to my king. But of course, King Burgred ignored the problem until the Raiders were at Torksey.

I wish someone would rescue me from the awkward conversation. I even peer into the distance, hoping against hope that some messenger will arrive with news of some great Raider attack. It would be preferable to being here, enduring the scrutiny of the holy men. They proclaimed me as their king because I defeated the Raiders, not because I have the required skills to manage men who desire peace and are fearful of more attrition.

Bishop Wærferth seems to take pity on me.

"The king has ordered that all the dioceses submit reports of how their settlements fare, now that the Raiders have left Mercia." Bishop Wærferth directs this at Bishop Burgheard but seems to include Smithwulf as well. I wish I knew how to do that.

I haven't, but I appreciate the attempt to smooth the meeting. I even dredge half a smile from deep inside me, as though in agreement.

"Then, I'll ensure the king is aware of my concerns. All of them." Bishop Smithwulf's voice has dropped low, as though he means to threaten me. Bishop Burgheard nods, his hand rubbing his chin in thought. I think he's about to say something to me, only my eyes have been caught by a figure trying to worm their way to my side through the press of bodies.

With a tight squeeze on my Aunt's hand and a quick incline of my head for the sake of the sensitivity of my bishops, I slip free.

"What is it?" I demand of Rudolf. Someone, either Pybba or my Aunt, has attempted to dress Rudolf in something befitting a royal coronation. It hasn't entirely worked, and the red marks around his neck attest to his dislike of the high collar, and the scrapings on his face, where he's tried to shave away the thin tendrils of facial hair. I almost smile to see him looking as uncomfortable as I do, only there's something about his face that drives all such joy from my mind.

"What is it?" I ask again, having taken his elbow, and steered him away from the press of bodies. So many people, in such a small space. I don't like it. It feels more constricting than being in a shield wall and without the advantage of being able to sever the head of those that come too close.

"A rider, from the east."

I nod, waiting for more information. When it's not forthcoming, I almost shake Rudolf to hurry.

"Reports of the jarls. They say they're to the east."

I rack my mind, trying to determine where they might be.

Rudolf's huff of annoyance, yet another in such a short space of time, infuriates me.

"How the fuck did they get there?"

Rudolf's glare almost makes me regret asking the question.

"There are rivers," he eventually capitulates, as though speaking to a child. "The fuckers must have sailed to the Humber and then chanced upon one of the other rivers that leads into the east, maybe the Granta, maybe the Ouse, maybe the Welland. There wasn't a lot of information."

"Fuck." I don't know what else to say. I'd hoped the bastards gone from Mercia. But it seems not.

"How do you know so much about Eastern Mercia and its rivers?" I ask, but I get no reply. I should perhaps warn the ealdormen and bishops, but I don't know anything, not yet.

"What are you going to do?" By now Pybba has reached Rudolf, his eyes keen as he licks his lips, his left hand held tightly over his missing right one. He doesn't appreciate the looks from those who notice the injury. I think it's the pity he hates, but I might be wrong. He too is dressed in clothes I've never seen before. Has every one of my fucking warriors made the time to commission new clothes, or is this, once more, the work of my Aunt? I imagine it's my Aunt. My men don't care what they wear provided it fulfils the required purpose.

"The king will need to speak to his advisors," Pybba states, without any preamble, in reply to Rudolf's question. I feel my eyes drawn back to the group of bishops, and beyond that, to the one consisting of the ealdormen, some I know, and a few I don't, and of course, the ones I don't know are the ones with ealdordoms in the east.

The east is far from the heart of Mercia. But it's still a fucking outrage, and one I need to counter. But Pybba is right. I am the king now. Whereas before, when I went to Repton, it was my initial decision, and just happened to fall in with the plans of the others, the situation is different now.

But there's something that neither of them is telling me. I can tell from the way Pybba won't meet my eyes and the fact that Rudolf hops from one foot to another, just like the child he used to be.

"What is it?" I demand to know, even though I'm sure the answer won't surprise me.

"Edmund has gone. He's taken half the men with him. He said it was your orders."

"Fuck," I nearly shout, only just remembering to lower my voice when I hear, rather than see, heads swivel my way. "Of course, the fucker has," I say more softly, wishing, in all honesty, that I could do the same. Yet my rage wins. I'm furious with him. He's been skulking like a beaten dog since Torksey. Only during the coronation ceremony did I feel as though we'd reached an understanding. I'd assumed he felt the same way.

But Rudolf hasn't finished.

"The messenger said there was a Mercian with them. Beaten and bruised. The size of an ox." My heart stills, and then beats far too fast, the sound pounding in my head. Now I understand.

I hear Pybba's soft exhalation of breath. It seems he didn't wish me to know that. For a moment, I'm incensed, and I want nothing more than to take him by the neck and swing him from side to side.

"The messenger did not say any of that," Pybba quickly corrects. "He spoke only of a Mercian with them. Beaten and bruised, yes, but not the size of an ox. Edmund heard what he wanted to hear, and so did you." Pybba's frustrated by this turn of events.

I run my hand through my hair, forgetting that I still wear my ceremonial helm, and it slips from my head, only for Rudolf to swiftly catch it. His eyes are filled with astonishment as he feels the weight, and examines the intricate pattern etched onto it.

I flex my neck, welcoming the release from a pressure I'd not realised was even there.

The ceremonial helm of Mercia. I eye it with apprehension, while Rudolf still handles it, turning it from one side to another, the flicker of sunlight causing it to flash, and leave a shimmering, trailing wake on Rudolf's face. I'm unsurprised by his reaction. It's a beautifully crafted item. Entirely unsuitable for wearing in an actual battle, but perfect for giving the impression that the wearer is first and foremost a warrior and only then, a king.

There are panels of intricately worked gold along the side of the helmet, running in a band from above the eyes to the back of the helm. Above these panes, gold and silver panels are interspersed, highlighting the wealth of skill lavished on the design. I'm amazed the helm wasn't taken by the Raiders, but it wasn't. Bishop Deorlaf was inordinately pleased with himself when he presented it to me. I wonder where the wily old fox had stored it.

In fact, I don't. I don't need to hear that it was in a fucking latrine ditch or some such, and has only been rescued for me to wear on this one occasion.

Not that the gold and silver plating is the end of the design. No, the nose guard carries a detailed pattern, as though of writhing serpents, and the eye-pieces themselves are picked out in silver. They don't shield my eyes, but rather highlight them further. They leave me feeling exposed, rather than protected.

The cheekpieces are close-fitting, slithers of silver threading through the gold. And then, of course, there's the crowning piece of the helm — the red horse-hair crest. I watch as Rudolf almost runs his hand through it, only to snatch it back, as though fearful it will burn him with the brightness of dancing flames.

I would marvel along with him, but my thoughts have turned to Edmund, and also to the unwelcome news that the Raiders haven't left Mercia, as I'd hoped. And then, of course, there's the problem that I'm no longer my own man. I have my warriors, as always, but I also have responsibilities I could never have imagined having in the past.

I wrench my eyes away from watching Rudolf's reaction and meet the steady gaze of Pybba. He holds himself well, his missing hand still hidden, aware that we're the objects of the gazes of many. We're no longer what we used to be, and yet we are. If we weren't who we used to be, then we'd never be who we are now. It's fucking vexing.

"Did Hereman go with Edmund?"

"Yes," a quick response. I can determine nothing of Pybba's true feelings from such a reply.

"Did the other men go willingly?"

"Yes. But they believed them to be your orders."

"Fuck," I speak the word quietly enough, but Pybba still hisses. I almost smirk at his outrage at my reaction. What did he expect? I'm hardly going to welcome this new development.

Once more, I seek out my Aunt in the crowd. She speaks with the bishops, engaging them in some detailed conversation, ensuring old Ceobred is well-tended. I admire her skill at conversing with such men, but then, she was raised at the king's court. This is merely a return to what should always have been, for her.

It's entirely new and completely strange to me. I'd sooner run my sword through the necks of ten different men than face the scrutiny of the holy men. And the ealdormen? Well, they've proved themselves willing enough to send their warriors into battle with me, but I know there are expectations that they'll be rewarded, and rewarded well.

They demand a return to the previous status quo, and I had thought to give them that. But it's not possible. Not now.

"I have to attend a feast," I can't believe I'm speaking those words aloud.

"And then you must address the bishops and ealdormen." It seems that Pybba knows my new responsibilities too well. Yet he offers nothing further, his keen eyes looking anywhere but at me. I know what I want to do. He knows what he wants to do. Neither of us says the words though.

"I would speak with the messenger." Pybba glances at Rudolf when I speak, but Rudolf is no longer listening. He's still turning the ceremonial helm one-way and then another, the depictions of warriors in the silver and gold panels seeming to spring alive. They stand, with shields and helm, as I wish to, ready to face all foes.

Such an image strikes deep inside me, and I sigh heavily. I know what I need to do. It's probably going to be received poorly, but they made a warrior their king, they'll have to live with the consequences.

If they want to govern in Mercia, they'll have to continue to fight for her.

If they want me as the king, they'll have to support me.

Because sure as shit, I'm going to fight for Mercia.

CHAPTER 4

As usual, Haden makes his unhappiness apparent as I ride from Worcester. The damn beast is never content. I thought he'd appreciate being allowed a few days of doing nothing, but it seems he hasn't. He rushes forward, only to stop abruptly, almost throwing me from my saddle, only to start up once more, and all without my input. Or rather, ignoring every single one of my commands, no matter how much I try to control him. The damn bugger.

But, I allow him his head because I know how he feels.

The ealdormen took the news of the new infiltration poorly, especially the eastern ones, the bishops with more acceptance. Bishop Smithwulf was the one to look most concerned, even though I imagine the Raiders will have chosen somewhere other than London to renew their attacks.

"Bastards," he'd muttered, surprising his fellow holy men, but earning my respect with just one word.

"London is close to the east," he'd muttered.

"But not on the same rivers?" I'd prodded, just to ensure my conclusions were correct.

"No, not on the same rivers. The Thames runs to the sea, not to East Anglia." Who'd have thought I'd ever be such an expert on bloody rivers!

"But if they take horses, it could be an easy two-day ride, if that."

I'd nodded at that, pleased to have some specifics.

Ealdorman Ælhun had grunted, as though somehow, he'd expected the news of fresh assaults.

"Take my warriors. They know the land better than any others, and they're here." I'd accepted his offer, although I'd have sooner taken Edwin and his men, including Æthelwulf and Scurfa. Only, they remained in Repton, following initial orders I'd given them, and now reporting directly to Bishop Deorlaf. I'd pretended not to notice that the two other ealdormen didn't so much as offer me their warriors, although their faces reflected concern.

"I'll send news as soon as I have it," I'd confirmed, once more leaving Ealdorman Ælhun to rule in my name, only this time with the aid of Bishop Wærferth, and my Aunt, as opposed to all of the ealdormen. While I didn't yet know everything that happened at Repton in my absence, I'd learned enough not to allow too many ealdormen to take control of Mercia. It seems they'd been too keen to fight amongst themselves, and then fuck all was accomplished. With the arrival of the two new ealdormen, I imagined it would only get worse, not better.

Along with Edmund, the men who'd ridden with him along the southern bank of the Trent to Torksey, had already left Worcester minus Icel but adding Hereman to their number. It meant Edmund had a force of eleven men, including himself. That left me with my usual men, apart from Hereberht, dead at Torksey, but including Gyrth, who'd insisted he'd recovered enough from his wounds to join me, as well as Lyfing and Ordheah. I would have argued with the three of them, but it seems that I needed all the men I could get.

Fifty or so of Ealdorman Ælhun's men led by Wulfsige, ride with my smaller force. His warriors are well provisioned, and I know they supported Edmund and Icel well. They also fought bravely at Littleborough, even though I was insensible to their presence until the end of the battle and the Raiders dead, or fled. The details of what happened have only slowly become clear to me.

We fought all summer long, and now, as the hint of a forceful wind shivers the empty fields, making the falling umber leaves dance and skip to the ground before the horses' crunch them beneath their hooves, I find myself riding to do battle once more.

I can't think that my journey will end with a pleasant conversation and a shared cup of ale. It would be foolish even to consider such. And I don't crave any sort of accord with the Raiders. Not as King Burgred did. I want them gone, preferably dead, but certainly departed from Mercia. Let them plague somewhere else, or even better, let them return home, to their women, ale and treasures.

"Come on, you daft sod," I knee Haden to greater speed, keen to be gone from the confines of Worcester, determined that he will follow my instructions, for once.

Rudolf rides easily beside me, his mount as eager as Haden, even if Dever only has half the reach. I think to pull Haden in, I don't want Dever to wind himself, but the open expanse calls to me, and so I allow my mount to amble to a full gallop, finding it impossible to deny myself such freedom.

The trackways are well known to me, even if the last time I left Worcester, it was on board a ship. It's beyond Warwick that I don't know the landscape at all well. Rudolf has told me of three vast rivers, and I've been warned that they're all open to the Raiders from the expanse of the grey Whale Road to the east. They could be anywhere along any of them.

The worry of not knowing more than the words of the ragged messenger who brought the news, gnaws at me. I wish I could absorb the news with the same calmness I would have done so with before I was proclaimed a king.

But then, before I was a king, five of my men hadn't died within as many weeks. And as much as I feel the ache of the loss of all of them, it's Icel's death that drives me on. I want to be the man to kill Jarl Halfdan. I can only hope that the fucker is one of the Raiders trying to make his home in the east of Mercia.

Eventually, with sweat beading both mine and Haden's long neck, I rein him in and take the time to look around. My warriors are following, some with wild abandon, such as Dever and Rudolf, others more sedately, Pybba amongst them. From Worcester, it seems, I've not only recovered Gyrth, Lyfing and Ordheah but also two of my squires. My lips twist in consternation, but I try and think without my king's helm. The boys are a part of my warband because they wish to learn the skills of a warrior. If I persistently leave them behind, they'll never fulfil their potential.

Wulfhere and Hiltiberht ride well, even if their horses are lighter boned than the mounts of the seasoned warriors. At least, I think, they don't ride with the terrible skills of a fucking Raider.

Ealdorman Ælhun's warriors' journey in tight formation, in total contrast to my men. I would wish my men and I were as well ordered, but with such regulation comes a failure to act on the spur of the moment. I'd sooner have men with intelligence than only those who can follow a directive. Although, I confess, having men who could occasionally follow an order would make a fucking pleasant change.

I wait, all the same, turning Haden in a loose circle to cool him, keen to speak to Wulfsige about the journey ahead of us.

Wulfsige rides a high-stepping white mare, green eyes flashing in an intelligent face. I feel Haden still beneath me. No doubt he feels the judgement emanating from the two as clearly as I do.

"Tell me of the path we'll take," I ask before Wulfsige can open his mouth. He has a tidy beard and moustache, clearly well-groomed, and his hair is kept short, curling behind his ears. Everything about him is understated, apart from his horse. She seems to resent Haden's proximity, side-stepping whenever she can. Wulfsige's hands are tight on the reins, and I almost smirk to see the animal misbehaving. Wulfsige is the sort of man who'll take such matters harshly.

"First to Warwick, where we cross the Avon. Then we'll ride ever eastwards. There are three rivers where the Raiders might be." He speaks succinctly, even if seeming to resent being forced to share such thoughts and knowledge with me.

"The first river, the Welland, is not far from the end of the

Avon. What do you plan to do?" The question is asked without any inflexion, almost as though he doesn't wish to know the answer.

Still, I consider my response. Without more details, it's challenging to know what my specific plans are. Do I need to follow the length of each river back to the sea? It will take time if I need to do that. And I don't have the men to chase down potential Raider forces along three long rivers.

"I plan to find the fuckers and kill them," I announce, a slither of unease that my intentions can't be more clearly defined. "It's always best to be alert to everything. If I decide to go to only one place, and the Raiders aren't there, I might have missed an opportunity to find them somewhere else. No. We'll keep alert, battle-ready, as when my men and I first travelled to Repton. These bastards are sly, and they know the rivers too well."

At Repton, the Raider camp was temporary but consisted of St Dystan's, a ditch, a rampart and of course, the Trent at its back. We had to use guile to gain admittance. I know I'll never be able to do that again. Not if the jarls are the same as those I met at Repton.

Torksey was a more open site, and yet it still made good use of the natural surroundings. These damn fuckers like their rivers and using the barrier of water to aid them. They must feel secure with water at their back. I suppose it makes sense.

Wulfsige absorbs the news with only the slightest trace of annoyance. I imagine he's not one for being spontaneous. Well, he's about to discover that I fucking am.

CHAPTER 5

We arrive at Warwick at the end of a long second day of riding. I'm not complaining, but my legs and arse are. Haden has set a fast pace, and I've allowed those who accompany me to follow on as best they could.

We're thinly stretched, a long snaking line, but it doesn't matter. Not in the heart of Mercia. Kyred, leading the men supplied by Bishop Wærferth, and using some of my men from Kingsholm, comprehensively staked out this area while I was riding to Torksey. A contingent of them remains alert, hunting down all possible sightings of Raiders. It thrills me to know that after my men and I killed so many of the Raider scum, that they've not risked returning to the area I consider mine.

I admit that I'll have to be less impetuous as we ride further east. I know that Kyred didn't travel this far. It was Ealdorman Ælhun's land to secure. He assures me he's done so, but of course, in our jubilation, we've all overlooked Ealdorman Wulfstan's betrayal and subsequent death, and what might be left in his wake. It's a mistake I won't be making again. Ealdorman Ælhun won't be either.

Of course, Wulfsige and his men have maintained their tight formation throughout the last two days. I'd prefer to deride them for juddering along at the fastest pace the slowest of the horses can manage, but I'm envious. I can't deny it.

Warwick, of course, hasn't changed in the time since we were last here, and we're allowed inside the makeshift defences to camp for the night. I spare a thought for Eowa and the other forest dwellers. It was Eowa's skill with healing that saved my men, both in the woodlands close to Warwick and then on the way to Torksey. If I thought he'd take it, I'd find Eowa and offer him a position with my Aunt. She'd welcome his skills. But instinctively, I know he wouldn't want that. His home is the woods.

I make my way over the wooden bridge, when the sunlight is no more than a thin thread on the far horizon, listening to the gurgling of the Avon beneath Haden's heavy steps. Another bridge. Perhaps Warwick will thrive because of its proximity to both a river and the Foss Way. Or perhaps it will gutter and die without ever really catching fire. While the Raiders are so prolific, road and river sites should probably be avoided.

I'm keen for Wulfsige to lead from Warwick, but he seems strangely reticent, and I notice that his gaze is more often than not drawn over his shoulder. Ealdorman Ælhun thought to send me with someone who knew the land well, but maybe Wulfsige knows it too well.

I'm forced to take the lead, even though I don't know the way, and I'm pleased when we do happen upon the Foss Way.

Here, the summer vegetation has been beaten back by the passage of many, many feet, hooves and wheels, and for a moment, I pause, gazing both north and south.

The temptation to return to Gloucester suddenly overwhelms me. The thought of shutting myself inside Kingsholm and ignoring everything happening in eastern Mercia, a weakness I don't anticipate finding in myself.

"Should we follow the Foss Way?" I call to Wulfsige. He's finally taken his position at the front of his men and stopped looking over his shoulder.

"No, it'll take us north, not east. I'll lead from here, with my men. You and your warriors can take the rear."

I don't much appreciate his tone, but I can't deny that I have no idea which way to go. With Haden restless beneath me, I allow Wulfsige and his force to ride on, and over the Foss Way, Rudolf's open jaw mimicking my shock.

"Stuck up arse," he complains, and I smirk, my lips tight, as I replace my water bottle in the saddlebags having swilled my mouth clear of the taste of Wulfsige's words. Rudolf's voice is far from quiet, and I almost hope that one of Ealdorman Ælhun's men hears and informs Wulfsige of what's been said.

"He's all we've got," Pybba adds, his voice doom-laden, more of a question than a statement, as he rides passed me on Brimman. Even Brimman looks unhappy, his eyes seeming to glower at the more pliant animals he has to follow.

"Worse luck." I offer, beckoning my men forward. Wulfred passes me, and his words bring a full smile to my face.

"Fucking tight arsed bastard. Needs someone to fucking relax him."

Eoppa is more pensive, and I confess, it will always feel strange to see him alone, and without Hereberht at his side. The two were made to go together. Eoppa has grown quiet and taciturn since Torksey. I wish I had Rudolf's skills with inane conversation to draw him out of his sorrowing, but I don't. Instead, I find myself trying not to be left alone with him, and hate myself for it.

Gyrth spares me a grin. It's clear to see he's fully recovered and pleased to be on the road again, and I don't even notice his missing finger as he holds the reins. He and Sæbald are as ill-tempered with each other as ever, but all of it is good-natured.

Wulfhere, his eyes rarely focused on anything other than Rudolf and his accepted place as one of my Raiders, follows with young Hiltiberht. The two lads are so desperate to follow Rudolf that I feel a pang of pity for them. I remember what it was like to not quite be counted as one of the men yet. But, I can't speed the process. Only time will give them what they want. Time and experience.

I take the rearmost position, behind Ælfgar, Wulfstan and Ordlaf. I'm not surprised to find them lingering at the back. Not all of my warriors are keen to engage the enemy. They will, but it helps if others have already taken some lives first.

From the tail, I can monitor the situation carefully. I can't see that Edmund and Icel would have approved of Wulfsige's tone and attitude. I can only see that it would have caused problems, and yet no one has mentioned any to me. Although, of course, few have spoken of that journey along the Trent. The loss of Icel weighs too heavily on everyone. Not that my warriors are more likely to talk about our journey. The betrayal of Lord Osferth and the death of Hereberht carries its own wounds.

Perhaps Wulfsige was less rigid when he rode with my warriors and not his anointed king.

I consider sending Wulfsige back to Worcester or even having him remain in Warwick, but I need the numbers he commands in Ealdorman Ælhun's name. There are few enough of us as it is, even with Gyrth, Lyfing and Ordheah included in the number. I have no idea how many Raiders have infiltrated the eastern lands. Once more, I know too little, and there's too much at stake to risk losing men I'm going to need when it comes to the fight.

I can hear Rudolf and Pybba at their usual game of counting kills.

"We killed three hundred and eighty-four of the fuckers at Torksey, and at least two hundred and sixty-four at Repton." It seems that Rudolf is determined to win the argument. He babbles, not wanting to allow Pybba the time to interrupt.

"Three hundred were killed before Repton, and at least eighty at Littleborough. Then there's the hundred or so that were killed either at the ships or in the woods."

But Pybba is quick.

"These might not be the same warriors. They might have had reinforcements from Denmark. Or, this might be an entirely new collection of warriors."

The numbers seem too huge to comprehend. How many have I personally killed since they tried to take Repton? Far too many.

I try not to focus on the increasingly heated debate, but all have heard Rudolf's words, and now my warriors discuss it amongst themselves.

"They're like ants." Without Hereman to keep me sullen company, it's Gyrth and Sæbald who ride closest to me, turning back to ensure I'm not exposed at the back. I don't invite conversation with them, but neither do I insist they remain quiet. The words distract me, as we pick a more careful path ever eastwards.

The Avon is our constant companion, a rush falling away to just a trickle, almost too faint to hear as Sæbald and Gyrth carry on their conversation.

"We could move away from ants," Gyrth complains to Sæbald. "They wouldn't follow us."

"No, but they would follow the honey," Sæbald insists, and I agree with him. The Raiders are akin to ants. They want the sweetness of Mercia and without the effort of having achieved it with more than blades and brute strength.

"How many ants in a nest? A hundred? Two hundred? There are thousands of Raiders." I'm unsure of Gyrth's point. I thought he believed they weren't similar to ants. Now he seems to be saying they are worse than ants.

"Too many. And these fuckers are too many as well. Every time we kill one, it's as though they're replaced with another two. Someone needs to tell their women to keep their damn legs closed."

"Or we need more Mercian children born, to counter their numbers."

"A long thought out counter-measure," Sæbald chuckles.

"Not really. What? They've been coming here for decades now. What do you think, Coelwulf?"

It feels nice to be called by my name, and it pleases me that Gyrth hasn't become all 'my lord' and 'my lord king' like some of them, even if it's only to antagonise and not through reverence and respect.

"It would be easier to drain the rivers," I half laugh, thinking it would undoubtedly cause the Raiders problems if they couldn't use their ships to penetrate quite so deeply into the Mercian kingdom.

"Less enjoyable," Gyrth comments, a wry grin on his face, quickly replaced by a wince of pain as his mount makes a halting half step onto an unseen stone, and he grips the reins too tightly.

I do not comment. No doubt the movement jars the hand with the missing finger. I've always allowed my men to decide when they're ready to return to my service after an injury. I can only do so much to stop them, and it helps if they're half-unconscious. Damn fuckers.

None of them is currently half-conscious, although I wish I'd made sure Edmund was. Then, while we would be racing to the eastern part of Mercia, it wouldn't be with only half of my force. Last time we were divided, I lost Icel and Hereberht. I can't shake the feeling that something equally calamitous might befall my party this time.

There are only eleven men out there. They're hardly a nest of ants, and yet they might come upon one. I can't see it ending well, not at all.

I keep hoping to see some sign of Edmund's passage, but from the back of the line of horses, it's impossible. The impact of so many hooves has churned the damp earth so that it appears as though prepared for seeding.

I think back over my meeting with the messenger who sought me at Worcester. He was no more than a youth, younger even than Rudolf when I first allowed him to join my warband. No one had sent him to find me, but rather, he'd come on his initiative, face streaked with mud and sweat, his clothes none too fresh.

His thin face had revealed all the angles of his jaw, and before I'd even allowed him to speak, I'd sent for food from the feast I should have been attending. Instead, my Aunt sat in my place, her silence when I made the request impossible to interpret, as usual.

When the chicken and baked fish had been more inhaled than eaten, the youth had begun once more.

"Raiders came down the river, over there. There were many of them." I'd tried to get an idea of numbers. But the youth, while far from stupid, had only been able to describe them as 'many,' and the place as toward the east, where he pointed his finger.

"There was someone with them who spoke our tongue. I heard them, from where I hid, on the banks of the river."

THE LAST HORSE

It was far from a great deal of information, and his directions had been even less helpful.

"To the east, along the river, we call it the 'beck.'" He'd cackled as he'd said that, but the joke had been beyond me.

"It's wide. Really wide." He'd explained, wide-eyed when I hadn't reciprocated his amusement.

"And did they attack your settlement?" A shake of his head and a swift look of unease in his eyes had alerted me that the youth had secrets of his own and wouldn't be very forthcoming. But I'd insisted he remained in Worcester, all the same, under the watchful eye of Bishop Wærferth. I didn't want the lad getting injured. He'd seemed too simple to defend himself, and yet he'd found me. The two facts didn't exactly add up, but I'd been forced to dismiss them because there was a much bigger problem.

What did it matter where the information came from, provided I had it and could save Mercia?

"My Lord King," Wulfsige's voice interrupts my musings, as I turn and realise we no longer follow the banks of the Avon.

"Come on," with encouragement, Haden is quickly at Wulfsige's side, and I turn to where he wants me to look. Unknown to me, we've been riding steadily uphill, and I can see a small vista of where we're heading. It doesn't tell me all I need to know, but I take some comfort from the lack of smoke hazing the distant horizon, now etched with the cold blue of a very late summer's day.

Only that doesn't seem to be what Wulfsige wishes to show me.

"There," I peer into the distance, wishing once more that I benefited from Edmund's excellent eyesight, even minus one of his eyes.

In the middle distance, visible more as a movement against the backdrop of the densely packed woodland beneath me, I can see the ancient trackway of Watling Street, with riders rushing along it.

I close one eye, hold my hand across my forehead, but I still can't see enough.

"Which way are they travelling?" I ask, frustrated that I just can't determine as much for myself.

"South," is Wulfsige's immediate reply.

"Can you see who they are?"

"No, My Lord King. Nothing."

"It could be Edmund and his men."

"It could be, My Lord King. Equally, it might not be. They may have followed the Welland and then happened upon Watling Street. They could know the landscape well enough to know that Watling Street leads to London."

"Fuck." I wish I could see more, but even Rudolf, his eyesight the best of us all, shakes his head when I beckon him to join me.

"Sorry, My Lord," his voice is filled with contrition, and I'm impressed he's remembered to call me 'my lord' in front of Wulfsige and his pompous ways.

"Fuck," I complain again, Haden turning beneath me so that I see much of Mercia spread out before me. From here, it all seems too open, and all too liable to be overrun. The ripples of blue that ribbon across the landscape only serve to highlight the vulnerabilities of being faced with an enemy who might not know these rivers, but who can sail them anyway.

"We follow them," I announce, aware that I need to decide.

"But what of the Welland?" Wulfsige's words recall me to my priority. I need to find the Raiders, not Edmund. Not that I think it's Edmund who rides far below us. I'm sure that I'd recognise him, even from such a distance. And certainly his bloody horse, Jethson.

"There's only a handful of them. Even if they came from the Welland, it seems there aren't many of them."

"It could be a scouting party." I can't deny that logic, nor the need in Wulfsige's eyes to go to the Welland, rather than follow the riders down Watling Street.

Only, I don't want to divide the force. Splitting my men has only caused problems when I've tried it before. I want us to stay together. Equally, this allows me to rid myself of Wulfsige without sending him back to Warwick and upsetting Ealdorman

Ælhun in the process.

"Take half of your men. Seek the Welland. If, or when, you find it devoid of Raiders, follow us along Watling Street. Equally, if we find they aren't Raiders, we'll come to the Welland." I have no real intention of getting lost in the tightly packed woodlands I can see to the far side of the road. Somehow, I know the Raiders lie further east.

"My Lord King," this seems to please Wulfsige though, and quickly half of his men peel away, and I'm left with my warriors, two squires and twenty-five of Ealdorman Ælhun's mounted men. I recognise none of them, but they do seem as relieved as I am to be free from Wulfsige's uptight character.

Before I can watch Wulfsige and his men, in their tight formation, heading off toward wherever it is that Wulfsige believes he needs to go, I turn Haden.

"We're going to Watling Street," I command. "Be alert. There might be Raiders on the road, or hiding in the woodlands, or just pretending to be Mercians."

With my instructions given, I knee Haden to as high a speed as it's possible on such a steep incline. I want to reach Watling Street. I want to know if it's fucking Edmund or the Raiders that streak along the road toward the south, but I don't want to injure my horse along the way.

I hear, rather than see, the rest of my men following, my eyes trained on the movement in front. Only as we dip lower, do I realise it's going to be impossible to keep them in my sight, as hazy as it is.

"Bastards," I complain, but Haden is keen beneath me, and his long gait stretches and stretches, as I crouch behind his neck. The sound of my warriors fades away, and although my thoughts return to the man I chased along the banks of the Trent, when my warriors believed me dead, I dismiss it. This time they can all see me easily enough. I can't be feared dead. They'd have to ride over my lifeless body for that to happen.

The ground gently undulates, sometimes higher, sometimes lower. The dense woodlands loom closer and closer, easier to see than Watling Street itself, and I try to gauge how near or far I am from it. But it's impossible. I'm a stranger to this part of the kingdom. For a moment I wish Scef was with me, but of course, he was a resident of the Trent, not this part of Mercia. He'd have been as lost as I am.

And then the hard-packed earth and stone road of Watling Street is before me, and so too are the surprised backs of a mass of Raiders.

"Fuck." It seems I've not found Edmund. Not at all.

Instead, I'm alone, and twenty or so Raiders face me. I swivel my head quickly, but there's no sign of my warriors. Haden has excelled himself with his speed. But he's left me entirely exposed.

Cold eyes greet mine, the unhappy movements of uneasy horses assuring me that these Raiders, like so many others, are not comfortable on horseback.

"Who are you?" the man who speaks almost does so with a Mercian accent, only his littering of poorly concealed inkings showing beneath his tunic and cloak, show that he's not a Mercian.

"Who are you?" I retort, hands calm before me, resting on the reins, aware that I'm perilously exposed, and likely to be rebuked by Pybba once more when he arrives, if not the rest of them as well.

"We are Ealdorman Wulfstan's men." The man indicates his tunic, and I hide my smirk at such a blatant lie, although Wulfstan's sigil is evident in the rumpled fabric visible just below his byrnie. I shouldn't have been surprised to discover that Ealdorman Wulfstan was such a sly bastard when he took a fox as his sigil.

"You're a long way from home?" I taunt, purposefully evading the question.

"He's sent us to London. To speak with Bishop Smithwulf."

It would almost be a plausible excuse; only I know that Ealdorman Wulfstan is dead.

"Who are you?" the man asks once more, but I shake my head

at his words. I've been trying to assess the men who face me.

They're certainly equipped well for a journey from the northern ealdordom of Wulfstan to London. They fairly gleam with iron, and not one of them rides without his byrnie in place.

"Were you expecting trouble?" I indicate the clothes and weapons with a sweep of my hand.

"It's best to be prepared, just in case we meet any Vikings on the road." The use of the word Viking is another clear indicator that the men are not from Mercia, if any further clue was needed.

"And what is it that Ealdorman Wulfstan wanted with the bishop?" It's evident that some of the warriors don't understand our conversation. It's clear from the side-ways glances they keep giving the man who seems to lead them. I can almost see their thoughts whirling. While they might not know who I am, they're becoming concerned by the length of our conversation.

I consider what they see when they look at me. It's self-evident that I'm a warrior. The shield over Haden's rump is evidence of that, even without the weapons littered around my waist, and the scars that line my face. Do they fear me? Would they ever fear just one man when there are so many of them?

"It's a private matter. A family matter," the man states, a forced grin on his tight face. He shrugs his shoulders, as though to imply it's unimportant, unaware that in doing so, he reveals more of the inkings that run down his right arm.

"And there are twenty of you? No more, and no less?"

"What business is this of yours?" the man tries once more, his tone uneasy. I force Haden forward, bringing him almost within an arm's reach of my enemy. The stench of fear from the man is practically palpable, polluting the air with the scent of sweating horse, and unwashed warrior. I was led to believe the Raiders liked to be clean. This man isn't, though. And beneath it all, the lingering scent of salt and rust can be detected.

These men have fought for their horses. It might be that they've even killed a stray party of Ealdorman Wulfstan's warriors, not yet aware of their lord's death. The only other conclusion I can reach is unappealing, although the most likely; that they were always Ealdorman Wulfstan's men.

Holding the man's eyes, I reach for my seax, carefully palming it into my right hand. I don't care that I'm alone, and my warriors far behind me. I don't even consider that we'll be outnumbered, even when, or if, they do catch me. These are Raiders, and I'll kill them.

"I killed Ealdorman Wulfstan," I breathe into the man's face, enjoying the flicker of shock in his green eyes.

"Coelwulf?" the question dies on his lips, as I stab with my seax, burying it deep within the exposed chasm beneath his chin, enjoying the well of heat over my gloved hand. And then chaos erupts.

The dying warrior slumps forward, as I snatch my seax clear. His mount, nostrils flaring, rears, the body slowly tilting to the right-hand side. Before I can watch it fall to the ground, a cry of outrage reaches my ears.

I turn, smiling, the smell of fresh blood inciting me to yet greater violence.

"*Skiderik.*" The man spits at me, his blade following the spittle, only I'm turning Haden, and the blow lands harmlessly on the shield, held tightly against Haden's back leg, causing the man to overbalance.

Before my opponent can recover, Haden has completed his turn. I stab down with my seax, aiming for the artery at the top of the man's legs, but only managing a deep gash as Haden is bumped from the other side by a horse.

My grip almost fails me, but I tighten it, and my thighs, kicking out with my right foot so that the leering enemy there has his advance arrested for just long enough that I can reach for my sword, the double-headed eagle a welcome weight in my hand.

I'm at the centre of a maelstrom of fury, all of the dead man's comrades wanting to kill me.

I find laughter pealing from my throat in pleasure. None of them will give way to another. So, more than anything, and even at the heart of nineteen men seeking my death, I'm safer than anywhere else.

"You couldn't make a killing cut if your lives depended on it," I roar, aware that they might not understand the words, but hopefully the intent is indisputable.

The man to my right tries to get closer to me again, encouraging his horse more by luck than any skill. Although I don't like to wound an animal, I reach out with my sword, having replaced my seax, try and make the cut as shallow as possible, but deep enough that the horse rears. The helpless passenger flails as the animal shrieks in distress, turning to escape the press of other horses and weaponed warriors.

The thud of the man falling does nothing to dissuade the others from trying to reach me. Neither does the unmistakable sound of a hoof caving in the man's skull. His shrieked cry cuts off, and ends only on a garble of blood and expelled air, the crack seeming to echo louder than falling stone.

But I've returned to the second Raider. His trews are sheeted in blood, a flap of pale skin evident beneath the slashed fabric. I might not have killed him quickly, but slowly the blood is leaching from him. Only he seems unaware.

His eyes are bloodshot, his mouth open in a howl of pain or fury, I can't fucking tell, and it doesn't matter as I lift my elbow and hammer it into the empty maws. His mount, terrified by what's happening, shifts forward and then backward, and then, in the small gap that opens between the surging warriors, the horse careers through, sending clods of damp earth high, so that men don't know if blades hit them or not, as they fumble for weapons.

The man seems to hold on, despite all the odds, only then he too slips free, his injured leg unable to hold him. I know he'll be dead before his head hits the ground.

"Who's next?" I bellow, keen to make another kill. My blade glistens with the ruby of death, but I thirst for more.

It seems my enemy feel the same way.

The next warrior, complete with shimmering helm and leather byrnie, rushes toward me. I note the dun-coloured animal, eyes wild and yet obeying all the same. It's a rare sight to see a

Raider able to control a horse with such aptitude, and that's not the only talent they have.

Rather than raising a sword and charging me, this warrior keeps his weapon hidden from sight. Only at the last moment does he swirl his war axe behind him, and then thrust it directly at my exposed leg.

I counter the move with the seax in my right hand, straining my muscles as I try and keep the sharp blade from reaching my skin. It's an effort, and all the time, I'm aware that I face more than one foe. The hot breath of those that surround me seems to fog the air. I could sever it with my blade; only my hand is trapped by that war axe.

Lifting my left hand clear of the reins, I snatch for my sword once more, not looking at where it goes, but instead threatening with it. This damn fucker tests my strength, and I won't allow another to take advantage of my distraction.

Haden is restless beneath me, the press of other horses far from ideal, as he bares his teeth, sinking them into horse flesh or human flesh, whichever he finds.

And then I sense a lessening in the strength of my opponents.

"Bastard," I mutter through clenched teeth. I don't move my seax, but my sword is suddenly slicing through the air, angled flat, and although my entire left side twinges at the unnatural movement, the blade easily slices through the warrior's exposed upper arm. The air fills not just with the hot stink of fetid breath, but the iron of blood as well.

"Fucker," my warrior fumbles his war axe, his hand falling open at the same time as my sword strike. Quickly, I snatch my seax tight to me and thrust it upwards, reaching for my enemy's throat. Only my blade passes through nothing, the warrior veering away from me, as he twists to find another weapon from those arranged on his belt.

"Shit." Quickly, I redirect my aim, hoping to catch his neck, but the man must anticipate my action, and again, he evades the shortened reach of my seax.

Bloodied teeth glint at me, from a horse's length away, but no matter the man's talents, it isn't enough.

A rumble of hooves roars in my ears, and I know my warriors have finally caught me. Their shrieks and roars of battle rage assure me that I no longer face the Raiders alone as do the reciprocal cries of fury from those focused only on me. They didn't know I travelled with others.

The press of horses is suddenly a swirling mass of confusion, and I can hear Pybba's shouts for Mercia, even as I lick my lips, pass my sword and seax from one hand to another, and again go after the man.

His eyes haven't left mine, and the length of our altercation has allowed me to notice the unusual grey eyes and the lack of facial hair. Either a youth or another woman, I decide. Neither would surprise me, and if it's a youth, it'll account for the horse-riding skills. The young learn much quicker than the more mature. I've long realised that.

The strength stumps me, though. The slight are usually no match for my years of training and killing.

Yet, I still have more than one enemy trying to kill me, and I twist my lips in thought, before kicking Haden to high speed. I feel the strength of his hind legs bunching, and then we fly through the air, my sword outstretched, my intention clear to see.

My opponent grins, a small tight thing, pulling on the cheek guard, allowing a flicker of chestnut hair to be seen.

The confidence is their undoing, as Haden comes to an immediate stop, rearing backwards, as I hold tight with only my knees.

The sound of a hoof impacting the hastily flung up shield echoes more ominously than thunder before a summer storm, but I expected as much. Instead of striking out with my sword, I hold it tight, wait for Haden to regain his balance, and then encourage him once more to great speed. As we flee beyond the shield, I stab with my blade. The grating of iron over leather is momentary, and then I feel it bite into the skin.

My sword trails behind me as Haden fights free from the horses that yet linger, a bite here and there to show them that he means it. As soon as we're clear, I turn Haden tightly, a smaller horse probably using more room, and then we rush back into the fray.

My men have each taken one warrior each, and the sound of ringing iron on shields fills the air, but I only have one object in mind.

My warrior sways in the saddle, although I can't see any blood, their movements slow and laboured in comparison to mine and Haden's.

I don't like to take a warrior in the back, but there's no choice when that person doesn't turn to face me.

With a grunt of effort, I force my seax through the leather, the feeble moans of my opponent encouraging me to act more quickly. My enemy should die, but not necessarily in agony.

"Bastard." Finally, the head slumps forward, the horse, unhappy with the unusual movement, thrusting forwards as yet another body tumbles to the floor with a resounding thud and subsequent crunch.

I rein Haden in, viewing those around me, determining my next opponent.

Only my men, and Ealdorman Ælhun's, have done their work well. Few yet live, and those that do, won't for much longer. Pybba and Rudolf, as so often the case, work together, the older man with his years of experience and the younger with his quick reflexes. Even Gyrth has managed to take a kill for himself. He bends over the prone warrior, pulling silver rings and armrings from the lifeless body.

I jump from Haden's back with a slap for his rump. He repays my kindness by following me, and as I bend to check whether I killed a youth or a woman, his hot breath is loud in my ear, as he nips at it.

"Get away with you," I huff, affectionately pushing his face away. He whiffles at my hand, as though I have a treat to share with him. I hold my empty hand out.

"Nothing. You'll have to wait," I advise him, a flicker of betrayal in his bright eyes.

I turn the wilted body, trying not to notice the splayed arms and legs, or the bloody blow on the head from falling to the hard-packed earth. Pulling the helm loose is an effort, the collision with the ground bending it so that it's no longer round. But I persist, and then a tumble of auburn hair spills from the helm, but it's not a woman, merely a young man with unbound hair.

I grunt, eyeing the clothes carefully, seeing the flash of a silver Thor's hammer on the cord tied around the man's neck. I heft it in my hand. It's heavy, but far from delicately wrought and I can garner no inkling of the man's wealth from it.

Standing, I survey the rest of my men. In the distance, the sound of rushing hooves can easily be heard. I glance southwards, even my poor eyesight picking out the backs of five horses.

I'll chase them, just not yet.

"Who were they?" Rudolf asks the question, as he runs a handful of grasses over his blood-drenched blade, having leapt to the ground as well. Dever tugs at the roots stuck in the old guttering that runs beside the road. In a moment, Rudolf will be picking and prodding the dead, perhaps even commiserating with those who took the life of a poor Raider and have little to show for their victory.

"They told me they were Ealdorman Wulfstan's men. But only the one spoke our language."

"Where were they going?" Pybba joins the conversation. I've been waiting for him to berate me for rushing off without the rest of the men, but perhaps he won't. Not this time.

"They mentioned London. But I'm not convinced."

I look northwards, the welcome sight of an empty road assuring me that the group consisted of only a small number. But it sits ill with me.

"We ensured there were no Raiders left along the Trent, or in Repton and Torksey. Lord Cadell and Bishop Deorlaf's men confirmed the rest of the Trent was clear. Kyred has been busy around Worcester and Gloucester. So where did these fuckers come from?"

"Maybe Wulfsige will know?" Pybba offers. I feel my face twist at the answer, even as Rudolf scuttles away, keen to claim prizes from the men he's killed. I know he'll share his spoils with Pybba.

"Perhaps he fucking will," I agree, even though I think it unlikely.

"Why would so few bastard Raiders be riding this way?"

I'm almost pleased when Pybba's question echoes what I'm thinking.

"That's what fucking worries me," I concur. I can't help but peer down Watling Street, to where I know London must be. But more, to where eastern Mercia waits. I shouldn't have neglected it in favour of my coronation. I should have fucking insisted that the push to drive the Raiders from Mercia wasn't yet complete.

I shouldn't have let the ealdormen and the bishops dictate my policy. I fucking should have known it wasn't over. Far from it.

"Wulfred, get your arse here," I call the man to me, his lips already forming his usual response.

"Will you ride north, keeping to the treeline if you must? Find Wulfsige and his men and have them follow us along Watling Street. Take one of Wulfsige's men with you."

Wulfred still limps, and I can already see him opening his mouth to question my orders.

"Fucking bastards," he mutters, kicking at one of the corpses. "What the fuck they playing at?" but he says nothing further, and instead moves to find his mount, Cuthbert. The animal is almost as festooned in blood as his rider.

"Is he wounded?" I demand to know, already deciding who to send in his place.

"No, the fucker's been rolling in it." Wulfred indicates the mess on the floor, and I almost gag at the thought, but Cuthbert seems content enough, as he too dips his head to nip at the straggling grasses. For a horse who carries the name of one of the most famous saints on our island, he goes the extra length to dispel any suspicion that he might be possessed of a similar life path.

"Be wary when you get to Northampton. I think we're going to find Raiders there. Don't get caught by them, and whatever you do, don't fucking get killed."

I issue the instruction and watch him as he hauls one of Wulfsige's men into line beside him. Wulfsige's men have done well enough, and already five of them are piling the bodies to the side of the road. Another grizzly scene for some unsuspecting trader. Only Wulfstan and Eoppa are busy at work, harrowing out the ground to bury them beneath. It's always been my way to bury the dead unless they've been consumed by fire. I can't stand the fucking stink of mortal remains.

"Fuck. It seems we can go nowhere without leaving lumps and holes in the ground." I speak softly, but Pybba hears me well enough.

"Try riding fucking unarmed. See how far that gets you," Pybba states, stalking off to find Rudolf, not bothering to wait for an answer. He makes a good point.

Gyrth and Sæbald labour together to lay the dead in the darkness of the earth, close to the woodlands. I make my way to them, peering at the blue-tinged flesh, and then eyeing the pile of spoils.

"More fucking horses," I declare loudly, not speaking to anyone, as Wulfhere and Hiltiberht bring the animals together in one spot.

"I don't need spare mounts, not here." I don't want to leave the horses, but neither can I take them with me, not if I want to approach unseen.

"Leave them in the woodlands," Wulfhere offers, and I could follow his suggestion, but the animals will get lost. I know they would. And they're valuable to me, even if I can do without them, here and now.

"No, we'll have to send someone back with them. Does anyone want to volunteer?"

I've made my way to Wulfsige's men, and I can see that although they've fought well, a handful of them carry small injuries.

"You two, can you ride?" I call to the two most severely

wounded. The one man sweats profusely, the pain hazing his eyes, as another tightly binds a leaking cut on his upper thigh. It's not close enough to the main artery to kill him, but all the same, it will be painful and needs careful stitching.

"You don't need to go fast, just lead the horses to Warwick." It's not a long journey. "And then seek aid there. They need to sew you up."

The other hurt man has his hand on his head, and whenever he takes the piece of tunic away from it that he's holding there with a white hand, blood slithers down his left cheek. His eyes are unfocused—a head wound.

"Yes, we can do that," the first man states through gritted teeth. I should know their names, but I don't.

"Good, and you have my thanks. String the horses together," I bellow to Wulfhere and Hiltiberht. "They're going to Warwick."

The two work quickly, bringing together the collection of fourteen horses. I thought there were twenty men, so for a moment, I'm confused as I count only fourteen.

"One of the daft buggers has disappeared into the woodlands, Lord Coelwulf," Wulfhere admits, correctly interpreting my wrinkled forehead. "Stupid git. He's black as night, and I can't see him anywhere."

"Someone will get a nice surprise when they come upon him," I chuckle. He was never my horse in the first place, so I can hardly be angry that he's gone.

With the two men helped back onto their mounts, and the stray animals loosely held together, rein to rein, seven to each man, I watch the wounded men set off, back the way we've come only that morning. And then I turn to the south.

"There's five of them," I speak loud enough for everyone to hear me. "But I don't think that's the end of it. I'm sure there's fucking more. Ride even more alert."

I don't set a forward scout, but Gyrth and Sæbald meander their way to the rear, and I let them. The sun is well past its zenith, as we resume our journey. I don't want to arrive when it's dark, but neither can I rush the horses. I don't know what I might be riding into.

Instead, I lead my men, eyes and ears vigilant, along the path the five riders took earlier. I'm sure they'll have reached their destination already, and that accounts for much of my hesitation. If they're going to Northampton, I'm resolved that the numbers of Raiders there will far outnumber my small force.

That concerns me. If the Raiders are encamped in Northampton, and they know I'm coming, then how will I ensure they leave? It's too late in the year to call out the fyrd, and in all honesty, I don't wish to pit farmers and traders against the fucking Raiders. Even the least skilled Raider is too accomplished for men more used to counting coins or pigs.

Neither can my ealdormen get their men to me quickly. And potentially, they won't want to. What do they care of Northampton? All, apart from Ealdorman Ælhun, will just be pleased that the Raiders aren't closer to their landholdings. Ealdorman Wulfstan is dead, and no one has replaced him. I could perhaps seek the aid of the bishop for the area, but Bishop Ceobred is ancient, and he's in Worcester. There's no time to call for reinforcements.

And that only drags my thoughts back to Edmund. Where the fuck has he gone? I've never known him to act so irrationally. Certainly, he's never blatantly lied before, stealing my men away from me. What am I going to do with the unruly bastard?

Haden is placid beneath me, taking the time to recover from our fast pace. I'm keen to hunt down my missing men, and the Raiders. I hope they're in the same fucking place, although I want Edmund to be glorying in their deaths and not vice versa.

I don't know whether it's the sound of running water or the stench of smoke in the air that alerts me first to our arrival close to the settlement of Northampton. It's certainly not the sound of raised voices or clattering hooves over the disintegrating stony surface of the road. All the same, I turn to caution my warriors. Pybba's eye roll tells me all I need about that.

Thick tree cover to the side of Watling Street, allows me to lead Haden beneath the reaching branches, my warriors and those of Ealdorman Ælhun's following.

It's not the easiest path to take, the reaching branches determined to knock me from my saddle, and the thick tree cover making it feel as though sunset is close, but I'm not about to ride into any sort of ambush. Sooner a few knocks than being found.

The rest of my warriors are surprisingly quiet. I've ridden into many unknowns before, and it's never enforced silence on them. Even Rudolf holds his tongue, and that tells me too much.

Wulfred and the man who went with him, haven't yet returned with Wulfsige, and the remainder of Ealdorman Ælhun's men. That's probably for the best, although I spare a thought that they might rush along Watling Street, missing us entirely now that we've veered from the main road. No, I reconsider, it'll take them time yet. I have no idea how far Wulfsige will have progressed to his destination. Before they can come south, he must be found.

Only as the tree cover noticeably thins, do I slide from Haden's back, tossing back the reins to Rudolf, to creep forward through the undergrowth, alone.

The smell of growth and decay is ripe in the air, and I startle as a small creature rushes away from my path. Poor fucker. I'm as terrified as it is.

In front of me, the sound of running water increases to a near-deafening roar, and yet I still wince when I carelessly place my boot, and a loud crack seems to echo all around me, as a dry branch snaps below my foot.

"Shit," I whisper, pausing to ensure I've not been detected. When no cry of outrage greets the sound, I resume my hesitant journey to the banks of yet another river. Mercia is surely cursed by so many of the damn things. Perhaps, I should consider having them all guarded against any Raider incursions. Maybe they should all be blocked, as I instructed the ealdormen to do at Repton. I confess, it feels as though the rivers invite the Raiders into the interior of Mercia. Even I would find it difficult to ignore such an tempting invitation.

Still crouched beneath the spreading trees, I'm suddenly aware of soft footfalls behind me. My hand reaches for my seax, and I turn, blade out, only to face Rudolf, a smirk on his young face.

"I thought you might need some assistance to see as much as possible," he states, an eyebrow raised as though daring me to deny his logic.

"Well keep fucking quiet then," I grumble.

"You keep fucking quiet yourself," he retorts, and I consider that he would have been a better choice, with his lighter steps and slimmer build. But, if I'm going to send my men into another battle, I want to see the sight with my eyes first.

Only ten steps later, and I can see the vast expanse of the river easily, and I can even see the bridge that spans it, further downstream. It glints in the gentle glow of the day, almost enticing people to cross it. I can't see if it's guarded.

It doesn't seem to be a particularly large bridge, but it isn't the bridge that calls for my attention, but rather the lack of ships along this stretch of the river.

"I thought they'd have come with their fucking ships?" I complain, perplexed.

"They've brought horses," Rudolf points, and I follow his outstretched hand. Only now do I see the defences that surround the site they've chosen as their camp, complete with ditch and rampart.

Men and women, labour inside the growing ditch, calling one to another as they do so. But I can't see how Rudolf knows they've brought horses with them, not ships.

"Look," he states once more, understanding my confusion, and this time my eyes settle on a series of carts, piled high with hay for the animals, rumbling their way over the wooden bridge and into the settlement itself. How I've not heard them before, I don't know.

"But no fucking ships?" I state, just because I can't quite reconcile what I see with what I know about the Raiders.

When Rudolf fails to answer, my eyes flick toward him in surprise. He's never been one to be silent. But he is. And more. He's completely and utterly still, other than where his right-hand reaches to the weapons belt I gave him only a few weeks ago.

He bites his top lip, the skin there showing pale beneath the summer colour he's acquired on our many excursions.

His eyes are trained, not on the Raiders on the other side of the river, but on something in the deeper gloom of the woodlands to our left.

I turn to follow his gaze, hardly daring to breathe, and yet reaching for my seax as well, trying to move as silently as Rudolf has managed. But I can't see anything other than the blackness of the tightly packed tree trunks. I want to hiss to him, ask him what he's heard, but instead, I concentrate on my breathing, slowing it enough that I can hear the silence. Or rather, not quite the silence.

"Who the fuck is it?" I barely move my lips as I ask the question.

Rudolf shrugs his shoulders, refusing to look away from whatever's caught his attention.

"How many?" I think to ask then because it's more important. Of course, these must be Raiders, no doubt hunting for easily garnered firewood from the forest floor. They must scamper like pigs through the changing forest landscape. Fuckers.

"Too fucking many," Rudolf breathes, his posture tensing as though the enemy is before us already.

"For us two, or the rest of the men?"

But Rudolf doesn't answer. I can see his mouth moving, but there's no sound. I train my eyes back into the shadows, but I still fail to determine how many Raiders there are. Clever fuckers, hiding amongst the mass of trees, with the river at their back.

I can't believe I've underestimated them again. How will I ever hold Mercia if I keep taking the Raiders for fucking fools?

"Bloody bollocks," Rudolf speaks so loudly, I almost jump in surprise, my seax already moving to stab at whoever is before us, but Rudolf's standing, and moving quickly toward the object of his attention.

"Wait," I hiss at his back. When he ignores me, I sigh.

"Shit," and I'm following him, with only the briefest of

glances to where I know the rest of my men are waiting for me. I'd sooner they were with me, but I can't allow Rudolf to face an opponent alone. I'm unsure what's come over the daft bastard.

Increasing my speed, fearful that I'll lose Rudolf, or get lost myself, trying to follow his twisting path around and below the reaching bows of the trees, I pay no attention to the spongy ground beneath me. I grip my seax and train my eyes on the flash of Rudolf's exposed white elbow.

"Slow the fuck down," I huff with annoyance, reminded yet again of the fleetness of the young. Only I speak to myself, between one blink and the next, Rudolf has disappeared into the encroaching murkiness.

"Bastard." I feel a fool, abruptly still, unsure which way to go, turning as though Rudolf will magically reappear just because I want him to. I can't even remember how I came to be here. I could go back, find Pybba and the others, but the trees seem to have closed in around me, and there's no obvious path that I've been following.

"Where have you fucking gone?" I speak the words aloud, trying not to panic, and, of course, receive no answer in reply from the silent trees.

"Fuck." I can't leave Rudolf. He might be captured, or worse, bleeding his last while I stand and vacillate. Aware that my passage is too loud in the silent woodlands, I strike out after him, hoping that I'm on the right course. Sooner or later I'll either find Rudolf, whatever prey he hunts or the riverbank. It better be bloody Rudolf I see first, or he'll have to answer for his recklessness.

Once more, I appreciate the fury my actions excite amongst my men when I wander alone. It's fucking infuriating.

And then I hear the sound I'm dreading, that of something falling, wetly to the ground. My legs power beneath me, as I dash through the trees, trying to avoid the erratic hanging branches and plants that reach upwards, trying to snag my pounding feet.

A sudden war cry ripples the air, sending birds fleeing skywards, their wings a thwack of noise in the silence. Our presence here can surely no longer be a secret.

I need to find Rudolf, and then we must make our way back to the rest of my force.

But Rudolf is nowhere to be fucking found. Panting, I bend forward, hands on my thighs, trying to find the cause of the continuing sound. Surely, if he's battling for his life, there should be the echo of iron on wood, or flesh on flesh. But there's nothing, other than my breathing. I think there would have to be a shield wall of fifty men banging their shields for me to hear above the roar of my heart and the blood that pulses in my ears.

"Shit, shit, fuck," I gasp. I can't lose yet another of my men. Edmund refuses to follow my orders, and now Rudolf is gone as well.

My breath runs faster. I can't control my warband, let alone all of Mercia. The weight of my new responsibilities threatens to down me. Only then I hear a shriek, and I'm running again, my fears banished.

"Rudolf," I mouth the word, not wanting to draw attention to myself, or drown out the next shriek, and then the next.

I reach out, each foot pounding at the matted ground beneath me.

Only then I'm falling, hands splayed to either side, the grip on my seax tightening, as I see nothing but the brown of trees, and the green of leaves, and the sharp prickle of pine cones digging into my back and legs. And then my head hits something else, a stray stone, and my cries of outrage and pain die on my lips, and the world goes black.

CHAPTER 6

"Fuck off," I wake with a start, reaching out to grab the pale hand that slaps my cheeks.

A squeal greets my actions, and I wince.

"Rudolf?"

"Ah, you're awake?" The voice that answer mine is not Rudolf's.

"What the fuck?" I stagger to a sitting position, the world lurching horribly to one side, wincing at the stab of pain that snakes its way down my neck.

"Pleased to fucking see you too?" Edmund's smirking face leers at me, while Rudolf rushes to hand me a water bottle to slug.

"Why the fuck did you leave Worcester without me?" I demand to know, swallowing thirstily and then handing the bottle to Rudolf so that I can stand. My head pounds, and with my right hand, I reach up and feel the lump that's formed just above my right eye.

"Bastard thing." It feels enormous, but probably isn't, only then I'm bending over and voiding the water into the mulch. The stench is disgusting, as I rear upwards, keen to be away from it.

"Take your fucking time," Rudolf instructs me, hovering close by, his voice filled with disbelief, whereas Edmund has stalked away from me, Hereman close to him. I feel the interested gaze of all of my missing men, even as I sway, and reach for a handy branch to keep me upright.

"Why are you skulking in the woods?" I want answers, now. I'm grateful when Rudolf returns the water bottle to me so that I can swill the taste of vomit from my mouth.

"What are you doing skulking in the fucking woods?" is Edmund's antagonistic response, and I swear, if I could move without wanting to be sick, I'd lay him on the floor, and pummel the truth from him with my fists on his face. I wouldn't think to spare his missing eye, either.

"Looking for the fucking Raiders," Rudolf answers for me, and I flash a look of fury at him. He arches an eyebrow for my pains. I have no idea how long I've been unconscious. In all likelihood, Rudolf has already told Edmund everything and, I'm spitting over nothing.

"So are we," Hereman condescends to answer. I meet his even gaze, his eye only just fully healed from the attack at the river ford on the way to Torksey, considering whether he knows that I know they left Worcester on Edmund's say so and not my own. Damn fucker.

"And have you found them?" I ask, really starting to wish that the view before me was swaying less. I slump to the floor, head as low as I can put it, while still being able to see everyone. The scent of the leaf-strewn floor both seems to help and to aggravate my nausea.

"I think you know the answer to that," Edmund grunts, his remaining green eye full of accusation, as he points toward where I assume Northampton lies. I've no idea where I entered the woodlands anymore.

I want to wipe that look from his face. He has no right to feel aggrieved. He's the liar here, not me. He's the bastard that left Worcester without so much as a word to me, while I was forced to speak to the ealdormen and bishops of Mercia.

I meet his glare, not prepared to back down. Luckily, there's someone with more sense than the pair of us.

"They found the Raiders on the Welland, but tracked them to here." Rudolf amazes me with his statement of facts. When did he become so fucking wise?

"And the Raiders rode?" I direct the question at Rudolf, not Edmund. Rudolf speaks more sense than Edmund.

"Yes, they had horses, not ships. They haven't actually seen any ships. Not yet."

"So, they must be coming here."

"Must they?" Hereman interjects forcefully. I think he's trying to tell me something, with just a look, but I feel too queasy to determine what it is without him speaking plainly.

"We've been watching them since early this morning. We saw those other riders rush into Northampton. I should have known you'd be behind their sudden arrival and obvious haste."

"How many inside Northampton?" I direct the question at Edmund, even though it's Hereman who speaks, and it's Wærwulf who answers, coming into focus in front of me.

"It's impossible to tell. Enough. They're mostly hidden behind the new earthworks being built. All we've seen are the five riders, and the men and women labouring in the ditch. And of course, the lads who bring the feed for the horses."

I breathe slowly, trying to ignore my pounding head, to make sense of this new information.

"So, they're making it habitable?" Fucking bastards. How dare they?

"No, they're making it defensible," Wærwulf speaks clearly. He's had more time to think about the developments.

"They expect more Raiders to join them?" I'm still trying to make sense of what's happening. I wish my head would stop fucking thumping.

"Seems to me they more expect King Coelwulf of Mercia than they do ships filled with Raiders."

Wærwulf's words interest me, but as I try and focus on him, nausea swells once more, and I have to duck my head and void the water I've been swilling around my mouth and had only just swallowed.

"Bloody bollocks," I complain, not liking the weakness in my voice. My leg wound accidentally given to me by Hereman has finally healed, and I can walk without a limp. I don't need another one to take its place.

"Rudolf, go and find the others. Bring them back here, with the horses. Take Osbert with you."

Rudolf scampers eagerly to do as I ask, and I watch him retreat into the darkness. Only then do I turn to Edmund.

"The rest of you, fuck off. Edmund and I need to speak."

My men amble away, swift glances assuring me that they're fully aware of what's about to happen. I consider that they knew they followed Edmund's orders, but quickly dismiss it. They know now because Rudolf has told them as much. Otherwise, they wouldn't have been quite so willing to leave us alone.

"Sit with me," I encourage Edmund when he stands before me, arms crossed, foot tapping angrily on the ground. He emanates fury.

"Suit yourself, you daft shit," I eventually comment when he refuses my invitation.

"I thought we were good," I state when he says nothing further. I sense the tension in his shoulders, and in the way his fingers drum over his exposed forearms.

"Good about what?" Edmund mutters.

"About what happened to Icel." It pains me to say Icel's name aloud, but Edmund's wince and indrawn breath assure me it hurts him more to hear it.

"This isn't about that," Edmund states, his tone belligerent. He's been this way since Torksey. It's as though my words are sharper than blades, honed purely to wound.

"Then explain why you thought it would be acceptable to fuck off with half my men on some wild chase looking for a man who's dead, on no more than the whisper of a chance that he isn't? It's hardly fucking rational."

"We don't know he's dead," the response is whip-sharp. I breathe heavily through tight lips, hoping I won't vomit again.

"You told me Icel was dead. You told me Jarl Halfdan killed him. The rest of the men agreed with you, as did Ealdorman Ælhun's warriors."

"Then where's his fucking body?" The voice rings with vindication as both arms sweep wide, and I genuinely wish I could batter some sense into the grieving bastard.

"It doesn't truly matter, does it? Yes, I would have liked to bring him back to Kingsholm, but he's dead, body or not. Icel is gone. We'll never hear his fucking stupid stories again, of which king he served, and how everyone he ever fought with was just better than we are. I would have thought you'd be pleased to never listen to him again."

"You can't know that?"

"How? How can I not know that when you told me? Should I doubt you, after all these years? Have you suddenly started talking shit to me? Become a traitor? Tell me, Edmund, because I fucking need to know?"

I speak calmly enough, but all the same, my words elicit a veritable storm of emotions on his scarred face. Even with just the one eye, I can see how deeply I wound him. His mouth opens and closes, a solitary tear sliding from his remaining eye, to fall, unheeded into another scar that slices his chin.

He's a broken man. But angry with it. It's not a good combination. I've seen it before. Such grief breaks a man. I won't allow that to happen to Edmund. I owe him better than that. Icel would never forgive me if I permitted Edmund to turn bitter. Well, he probably wouldn't. Maybe.

"You blamed me?" The words are almost a whimper.

"I did. I was angry and wounded, and I'd done nothing but fight for days on end, knowing that half of my damn men were missing. And you blamed yourself as well. You told me it was your fault."

"It was my fault."

"How? Did you make the killing blow? Icel was a warrior. He'd lived a longer life than any of us. I didn't want him murdered by Jarl Halfdan, but equally, he'd have wanted to die protecting the men he called his family."

I can't keep the heat from my voice. My throat burns, and not just from the queasiness of my head wound. It hurts to speak like this, to be so fucking blunt. I didn't think we had to do this. I thought we knew each other fucking well enough.

Edmund finally slumps to the floor, the strength seeming to desert him between one breath and the next, as his legs curl and he sits before me, cross-legged. His head stays low, his shoulders not shaking, but not far from it.

"If Icel lives, I'll find him," the growl that rumbles from him is more akin to a hundred horses on the gallop than the voice of a man.

"If, Edmund, if. And you say he's dead."

"Then where's his body?" I sigh. I'm not in the mood to speak in circles.

"Have you seen him? With the Raiders."

"No. But that doesn't mean he isn't with another group of them. I can't see that these are the only Raiders to try and take Mercia from a different angle." Edmund speaks to convince me. I wish I could allow such thoughts to direct me.

"Icel is dead. I would have it other than that. And if he does live, then we *will* find him. But not like this. Edmund, we lost Icel when we were divided. That was my choice and my decision. We need to stay together now. The target on our backs has suddenly become so much greater."

"I will find him," Edmund persists in repeating.

"Then, I hope you do. But if you're staying a member of my war-band, then you need to direct your efforts elsewhere. The focus is on banishing the Raiders, not on finding Icel."

"Surely, it's the same thing?"

"Not necessarily."

"So, you're saying that I can't hunt for Icel, and ride with the rest of your men?"

"No, I'm saying you need to think of Mercia first, and Icel second."

"You won't hunt for Icel?"

"I'll not follow the dream that a man I've been told is dead, yet lives." Edmund finally meets my gaze. His teeth grind, lower, against the upper, and the set of his jaw assures me that rather than bringing Edmund around to my point of view, I'm only working to drive him away from me.

This wasn't my intention. I need Edmund. I need fucking Icel, but he's dead.

"Then I'll go my own way then," Edmund is already making to stand, but he's no longer alone. Hereman flanks him, and it's Hereman who places his hands on the shoulders of his brother, keeping him low to the ground.

"Fuck off, Hereman," Edmund mutters, but the fight is already leaving him.

"We can't give up our dream of Mercia for Icel. Can you imagine what the old cunt would have said? In the reign of Wiglaf, I knew men who pursued a private vendetta against the Raiders, contrary to their king's wish. They were foolish men, and King Ecgberht of Wessex took advantage of the division to claim Mercia, driving Wiglaf into exile."

I think Hereman will leave it there, but he doesn't.

"In the reign of Beorhtwulf, I knew men who died searching for a man they knew to be dead. Mercia fell to the Raiders because of their stupidity."

I think to caution Hereman against further comment; only he's no longer alone.

Wulfred has appeared, limping beside his horse, his brown hair and beard, black under the dense canopy.

"In the fucking reign of Burgred, warriors fought amongst themselves, rather than against the bastard Raiders."

I tilt my head to one side, showing my appreciation for the beautiful turn of phrase. Wulfred winks at me, and I almost spoil the illusion by laughing out loud.

Beneath Hereman's hands, Edmund seems to be seething, and I think he'll stand, finally floor his brother as he's always wanted to do. His restraint surprises me, but it probably shouldn't.

"In the reign of Coelwulf," Rudolf quickly begins. "I fought with men who could kill the Raiders almost as quickly as think it, only they were divided, blaming one another for the death of a much-loved comrade, and the fucking Raiders and Wessex claimed Mercia as their own." His young voice is so doom-laden, it sends a shiver of unease along my spine, more sobering than the coldest of water.

"And all this would be my fault?" Edmund demands to know, refusing to be swayed by these new voices.

"You're the king's oath-sworn man." Hereman uncompromisingly concludes. "The king's man." He repeats the words, and I notice the startled glance that Wulfred shoots his way. Maybe none of them has realised that their oaths are no longer just to Lord Coelwulf of Kingsholm, but to King Coelwulf, of Mercia.

Maybe I haven't even noticed.

"Fuck," Edmund fixes me with a piercing glare, and I hold his gaze. Just as when our eyes met during my Coronation, only this time I think Edmund truly acknowledges that we're reconciled, even if we disagree about Icel's chances of being alive.

"Fine. I'll support you. As always. You have my oath, as before."

Only then does Hereman release his hands from Edmund's shoulders, and as he does so, I hear the soft tread of more and more men, and look up to see all of my oath-sworn men repledging themselves to me. All of their faces hold respect, and if it weren't so damn heartfelt, I'd laugh at such a scene. Vomit stains my tunic, my forehead carries an egg-shaped swelling, and my clothes, where there's no bile, are rumpled and covered in leaves.

They speak almost as one, refusing to stumble over the words, even though they've only ever spoken them once, or at most, twice before.

"By the Lord, I pledge to be loyal and true to Coelwulf, and love all that he loves, and hate all that he hates, in accordance with God's rights and my noble obligations; and never, willingly and intentionally, in word or deed, do anything that is hateful to him; on condition that he keep me as was our agreement, when I subjected myself to him and took his service."

Fucking bastards. Give me their oaths when I'm concussed, stinking of sick and trying to keep hold of whatever I ate this morning. Not for my warriors, fine clothes and gold and silver ornaments.

I allow the silence to fill the space we occupy until it feels as though it will spill into the sky, just as a flock of sparrows startled by the sound of iron on wood.

"And I pledge myself to you as your king, and oath-sworn leader." My voice fills with resolve, and yet the fuckers are already starting to smile, Rudolf nearly giggling.

"What?" I demand furiously, trying to turn to see if something funny happens behind me.

"Look at the fucking state of you," Rudolf seems to answer for them all, as Hereman strides to my side, and heaves me upright. "You're covered in leaves, and you've got drool running down your chin." I swipe angrily at the wetness.

"You're the daft bastards who decided to get all serious on me." I counter, unprepared to say I'd been thinking the same thing.

Still, they all laugh, and then the moment is gone, as they meander away to tend to horses or to empty their bladders.

Only Edmund and Hereman remain, one of either side of me, as I stagger to where the main body of their camp is.

"So, what do you plan to do now?" Edmund asks the question.

"What we always do. Hunt the Raiders. Kill the bastards. Keep Mercia safe."

What remains unsaid amongst all that is the fact that no matter Edmund's pledge to me, all three of us know he'll be hunting for Icel.

I can only wish him luck with his fruitless endeavour.

CHAPTER 7

"We need to do more than watch them," I'm unsurprised that Wulfsige disapproves of my plan. I watch him from my side of the fire. I've allowed one because we're so deep within the woodlands, and the night is going to be bloody bitter, and the smoke can barely escape through the thick tree canopy overhead. The smell might give us away, but it takes a brave man to hunt down such a scent when the night is dark and cold.

"I would sooner just attack them as well. But we need to know how many there are before we do anything else. They have a ditch and ramparts. They mean to stay, and we can't allow that. Neither can we sacrifice our warriors on those defences needlessly."

"They already know you're close." Of course, he's been told about our earlier altercation. I almost wish he didn't know. It has soured this conversation.

"They know that I'm on Watling Street. By now, they must think we've either gone to London, as they said, or gone about our own business."

"They might be stalking us as we speak," Wulfsige states forcefully, his forehead so wrinkled in thought I can see it even in the flickering shadows of the orange flames.

"They might be, but if they are, we have many warriors watching for them." I indicate the circle we sit within, and further out, where the backs of my warriors face me. They are all alert and ready for whatever the night might bring. I don't anticipate the Raiders will attack. Why would they when space is so confined by the tightly grouped tree trunks, and in all likelihood, they don't even know that we're close?

"Tonight, Hereman, Pybba and Rudolf will get as close as they can to the settlement. We need to understand their intentions. There are no ships." This point is the one that confuses me the most and seemingly infuriates Wulfsige.

"If they have no ships, then they can't escape along the river if we attack them."

I sigh. We've had this argument already.

"If we can't get inside their defences, then we can't attack them."

"But the ditch is still being dug out, and even Edmund admits that there are pieces of the rampart missing. I would not have expected you to shy away from an attack."

I pause, hold my breath, try not to allow what I'm thinking to reflect on my face.

"I lead the men. My decision is final." At my announcement, Wulfsige storms to his feet and I watch him prowl away from the fire, only to disappear into the vast darkness beyond. He better fucking remain quiet while he fumes.

"Fucking bastard arse," I smirk at Wulfred's words, but only as I lower my head and hang it almost below my shoulders. When I straighten up once more, my face shows none of my feelings. I've managed to eat and drink, and although a smiling Rudolf has assured me I have a rounded-egg protruding from my forehead, I no longer feel nauseous. I can stand and fight if I need to. I've checked, swinging my seax from side to side, stabbing a few tree branches just to check my aim. The delay is not because I need time to recover from my stupid fall.

"Not like you to be so damn fucking sensible," Goda settles beside me, his stint on guard duty evidently at an end.

"Why, thank you for fucking noticing," I comment acerbically. I'm growing tired of having my decisions questioned.

"It wasn't a compliment," Goda chuckles, already stretching

out to lie with his head facing toward the fire. I could do with some sleep as well, but I feel restless. I should have gone with Hereman, Pybba and Rudolf to take another look at what's happening over the river.

"All the same, I'm going to take it as one."

"Suit yourself. Now, get some bloody sleep, you look like shit."

With his comment made, Goda quickly settles, and his light snores thrum through the ground. I would love to sleep, but as much as my eyes sting, I know that sleep won't come. My head aches and my heart beats too loudly inside my chest. I've tried to breathe it away, but neither of my symptoms will abate. And they won't. Not until I sleep. Only I can't fucking sleep.

Frustrated, I stretch out on the ground, my cloak tight around my head, my eyes focused on the trail of smoke as it leaves the fire, only to quickly disappear in the canopy of reaching trees above my head. The smoke is rimmed in light, not from the fire, but from what must be an exceptionally bright moon shimmering overhead. I'm pleased we have the thick tree trunks to mask us.

My thoughts tumble from one problem to another, the sounds of others asleep failing to soothe me, although the soft conversations between those on watch duty, does.

I startle awake, a hand shaking my shoulder, my hand already on my seax, before I relax, recognising Edmund.

"Time to wake up," he comments gruffly, and I blink grit from my eyes, as I stagger upright.

"Fuck," my hand touches my egg-shaped swelling, and even I can tell it's huge. The camp is up and about, only myself, and a spattering of others, still sleeping. These must be the men who took the worst watch of all, that in the middle of the night.

"Are they back?" I demand to know, but he shakes his head.

"It's still early."

"So why wake me?" I could have done with more sleep.

"There's another problem," Edmund admits, and I'm groaning as I finally make it to my feet.

"I need a piss. Give me a moment." My bladder aches painfully, but rather than leave me be, Edmund follows me through the twisting path I'm forced to take because of the number of tightly-packed branches.

"Will you fuck off," I eventually round on him, not wishing to empty my bladder while he watches.

"Oh, just fucking get on with it. It's not like I've not seen it before. We need to talk about Wulfsige."

Sighing, I empty my stream into the thick mulch, wrinkling at the sour smell. "What's the matter with Wulfsige?"

"He's gone."

"What do you mean he's gone?"

"What I said. Listen to me. He's gone, along with ten of his men. The others haven't realised yet, but I have."

"How the fuck is that even possible? We've had people on watch duty all night." I turn to face him, running my hands down my trews, wishing I had water to bathe with and something to drive away the feisty taste in my mouth.

"They must have gone with him. But sure as shit's shit, eleven horses are missing, and I've not heard the bastard bitching since I woke."

"Fuck. We don't need him being slaughtered by the Raiders."

"No, and we don't need him being captured and telling them where we are, either."

"We'll have to go after them."

"How, we don't even know where they went?"

"No doubt they went to Northampton or Warwick."

"Sooner Warwick than Northampton. If they've gone to Northampton, then they're probably about to meet an unpleasant end."

"He was fucking determined that we needed to attack and not sit on our arses."

"Well let's hope he's not buggered it all up with his failure to follow instructions."

"We'll know soon enough," I state, frustrated once more that so many interpret my commands as somehow negotiable. "Let's eat. I'm starving." I stomp back toward the fire, hoping someone has thought to prepare food.

"That's it. You're just going to eat? I thought you were going to go after them."

"Well, I've changed my mind. We don't know where he is. If he's gone to Northampton, then he's there by now. Either Hereman and the others will see them, and let us know, or they won't see them, and then we'll know they've gone to Warwick."

"It's hardly a master plan."

"Why thank you for the accolade," I grumble. What he expects me to do, I don't know.

Only then I pause, turn and face Edmund. As with Rudolf, it's probably easier if I answer all of his questions, and not just the one's he's verbalised.

"Wulfsige has gone. That was his decision and against my wishes. The Raiders are here, against my wishes. I'm hardly in control of any of this. I wish I fucking were. We'll see what Hereman, Pybba and Rudolf tell us, and then we'll make a choice. Yes, we're eleven men down, but the odds are so stacked against us, I can't see that it truly matters. Not now. And I'm fucking starving, so I'm going to eat."

I settle before the embers of the fire, pleased when Wulfhere hands me a bowl of pottage. It's just about warm, and I almost swallow my tongue in my haste. I wish there were more to fill my hollow stomach, but then no sooner have I thought that than my stomach rolls.

"Fuck." I remember then why I'm so damn hungry. I reach up, run my fingers gingerly over the rounded lump, and gratefully swill the beaker of water that Wulfhere hands me without being asked. Then I just sit there, concentrating on breathing and not vomiting, while Edmund glares into the fire, his food almost forgotten. I would have asked him for it, but now the smell is almost too much for me. I stand abruptly and stalk away. Better to be away from everyone when I have to bend over and empty my breakfast into the bushes.

Not that I'm left alone for long. When am I ever?

"Lord Coelwulf," I would sigh with frustration, only it's Eoppa.

He's still struggling to come to terms with the loss of Hereberht at Torksey, and so I stay my impatience.

"Eoppa. I feel queasy still, so be prepared to jump aside at a moment's notice."

He nods, and yet no trace of humour touches his cheeks. His sleeves are rolled up against his elbow, and I see a flicker of scar tissue on his left arm. It's a reminder that we've both survived many battles. And notice that one day we simply won't. And then what will all this have accomplished?

"I don't like that Wulfsige," Eoppa offers, his voice low.

"He's gone," I state before I can determine the wisdom of sharing the news with him.

"Fucking cock," Eoppa complains. He walks with me, and together we venture away from the campsite and into the darker areas of the woodland. Not that it's that dark, instead it feels as though a storm is coming. The twilight is disorientating. I've only just woken, and already I stifle a yawn as though it's time to rest once more.

"Yes. That he is," I say each word distinctly, keen to show that I'm just as angered by Wulfsige's desertion as every one of my warriors, and those of Ealdorman Ælhun's men who've been left behind.

"I take it he's run back to Warwick, like a frightened child. He's been unhappy ever since we crossed the Foss Way."

"Warwick or Northampton. I don't rightly know. Time will tell."

Eoppa nods as I glance at him, and I wonder what he wants with me. Only he falls silent, his steps a counterpart to mine over the springy surface of knotted roots and discarded leaves and pine needles. I appreciate that he just wanted the comfort of company with no need to talk or joke, or pretend that what we're doing isn't foolhardy.

I keep half an ear listening for the sounds of the camp, keen not to stray too far. I carry my seax and sword, but not my shield. I don't want to happen upon the Raiders like this, but equally, I'm convinced I could defend myself adequately. A shield is helpful in a pitched battle, but if it were merely a fight to the death, I'm sure my blades would keep me alive.

The same for Eoppa. I note that he carries his weapons belt as well. And both of us wear our leather byrnies. We might, I concede, be too well armed for a simple stroll to settle my stomach.

Eoppa's next words surprise me.

"When this is over, I think I might want to return to Kingsholm."

I startle, swivel my head to meet bright eyes. I can see how much this pains Eoppa. But, it's always a choice that lies open for my warriors. I know not everyone is content to meet his death in bloody combat.

"As you will," I almost choke on the words, but this is part of the trust that exists between us all. My sworn warriors must feel able to say as much to me, to acknowledge and appreciate that they're no longer as skilled as they once were, or that the thirst is simply no longer there.

"My thanks," and he bows his head and makes as though to turn away.

"Stay with me. My stomach still lurches," I ask of him, keen to enjoy Eoppa's comradeship while he remains as one of my riders. I'm not going to ask him about the reasons for his decision. I need not know the deepest thoughts of those who travel with me.

But as I turn, and head back the way we've come, Eoppa speaks.

"It's just not the fucking same," he admits, head down, eyes fixed on his boots. "A man needs someone he trusts implicitly at his back."

"He does, yes," I confirm. I think Eoppa will say more to me, but he doesn't, instead falling silent again, and then, when we reach the campsite, moving away from me. I watch him go with a sudden lump in my throat.

It's not the same when my men die, or when they decide to live out their days at Kingsholm, rather than at my side.

I wonder whether I'll ever feel the same urge to sit quietly by a fire and think of nothing more than what I might have for dinner the following day.

Then I laugh at myself.

Chance would be a fine fucking thing.

CHAPTER 8

"What did you do?" I direct the question at Rudolf, not Hereman and Pybba.

I can tell, just from looking at Rudolf that he's done something he shouldn't. The tell is his shifty looking eyes that won't meet mine. Rudolf has always been able to match me, eye for an eye, no matter what the little shit had done in his younger days. Even when he accidentally threw the shit bucket over my byrnie instead of the fresh water. But not today. The stray piece of hay that sticks up from beneath his tunic, only adds to my suspicion that I'm correct to be suspicious.

Pybba looks to be simmering with rage, and even Hereman is far from his usual uninterested self. His green eyes flash, reflecting the rage of the fire that we've kept burning at the centre of our camp.

The fact that it's dark once more, and the three of them have been missing all day long, only cements my hunch.

"I'll let you fucking tell him," Hereman strides away, toward the smell of roasting pheasant, caught by Ordlaf and Wulfstan earlier, in an enterprise that was about as quiet as a herd of cattle marauding through a church. The smell is delicious, and I could fucking kill Rudolf for pulling me away from it. All the same, I owe him the opportunity to explain. It seems that Hereman is done with him.

"Well?" I demand to know. Pybba has taken two soft steps

behind Rudolf, and now he catches my eye, the faintest hint of a smirk on his face whereas a moment before he was furious. I can see how I need to play this.

"What did you do, Rudolf?" I ask once more, although I follow it up with, "at least it didn't kill you. I'm pleased about that."

Rudolf seems to perk up a little at that. He finally meets my gaze, takes a deep, steadying breath and begins.

"It was an opportunity too good to miss, and so, I took the place of the young lad, and led the oxen into Northampton itself. It's not as if I don't know how to lead a bloody ox, is it?" I still at the words, already wanting to call him a fucking fool, but again, from behind him, Pybba shakes his head. He's cautioning me, and although Edmund has his mouth open to berate the younger man, I speak first, filling the space with just one word, a nudge for Rudolf to resume his story, a warning that Edmund should shut his fucking mouth.

"Continue."

"It meant I got to see all we need to know about what's happening inside Northampton. And the lad was about my age anyway. I wasn't expected to be able to understand their Danish or anything." He glances at me, almost with pleading in his eyes. I pity him for a moment. I can't imagine that Hereman and Pybba have been particularly appreciative of the risks he took. And at that age, it's all about the risk, and there's nothing calculated about it.

I can already see exactly the situation that Rudolf is explaining to me, and in all honesty, he probably did well to think on his feet. No doubt, Hereman and Pybba's unease stems more from the fact that Rudolf had been gone a long time, and if anything had happened to Rudolf, they'd have had to tell me. I doubt I'd have taken the news half as well as I am the success of his half-brained endeavours.

"So, what is happening inside Northampton?"

Rudolf expels a long breath at my question, and I can't look at Pybba anymore because he's laughing softly to himself, his chest shaking although no sound pours forth from his mouth.

"Pybba and Hereman didn't ask me that," Rudolf complains, his voice high with outrage, and once more, I have a far too vivid image of what's been happening between the three of them as they've made their way back to me. I have some sympathy for him.

Hereman and Pybba can be bitter older men, especially when they're recovering from such a fright.

"Well, firstly, there are still many Mercians in Northampton, mostly women, children and the old, well, apart from the blacksmith." This doesn't surprise me. It's similar to what happened at Repton. "And the Raiders are making them work for them, but only in so much as they have to cook and provide ale and stuff. The real work, of digging out the old defences, is being done by the Raiders themselves. There are men and women, all of them seemingly well-armed."

"Who leads them?" It's this that I want to know the answer to, and beside me, I can feel Edmund almost jumping in frustration to ask if Rudolf saw Icel. I credit Rudolf with more acumen than that. I'm sure that if he had, he'd have said that first, despite the condemnation from Pybba and Hereman.

"I didn't see whoever was in charge. Whoever it is stayed inside the hall the whole time I was there. The Mercians spoke of 'jarls' but not which ones."

This failure seems to pain Rudolf.

"How many were there?" In light of not knowing who leads the Raiders, this is the second most important fact I need to establish.

"At least eighty. But not many more. The stables have horses, but not more than thirty, so they don't all ride."

"Or they're not all there?" I ask, but Rudolf shakes his head.

"No, each stable was occupied. Unless they keep the animals elsewhere, then they were all inside."

"And did you see the Raiders who escaped from us?"

"No, but possibly yes. There were a few horses with cuts, who looked as though they'd been run hard. But no, I didn't recognise anyone. The Raiders were all stripped to the waist while they worked, without even seaxs or weapons belt. They feel pretty damn comfortable in there. Only three men were watching the bridge that leads inside Northampton. And they've got nothing to fear from the Mercians. They've never even heard of you." Rudolf juts his chin toward me as he speaks, and I nod slowly. This doesn't surprise me.

"Did you see Wulfsige and his men?" Now confusion knits Rudolf's brow, as it does Pybba's as well.

"He's missing, and so are ten of his men."

"No, they weren't inside Northampton, and no one spoke of mounted Mercians."

"So, he went to Warwick then. Fucking arse," Edmund mumbles beside me. I agree with him, but I don't say as much.

"Wulfhere and I could get inside again, using the same trick," Rudolf's eyes gleam with the knowledge, and I reach forward and cuff him around the head, regardless of the fact he's now classed as a warrior.

"Don't go offering the services of another. But you've done well. Thank you. I'll have more questions when I think of them."

Rudolf grins at me; his normally unperturbed brightness quickly returned to his face.

"I told you," he turns to Pybba, but Pybba has cleared his expression of all amusement, and merely glares at the younger man.

"You were a lucky fucker, and you know it. Don't do it again." And with no more words, Pybba storms from his side, leaving me with Rudolf and Edmund. Rudolf is quick off the mark. His eyes sweep from me to Edmund, and he too follows the other men into the heart of the camp.

I can hear others calling to him, some teasing, others less …. effusive, and I wait for Edmund to start his demands.

"Tell me what you saw," Edmund demands of Hereman. His brother seems surprised by the question, no doubt content that Rudolf has shared all that needed sharing, as he returns to us, pheasant wing in his hand. The earlier fury has left his face, and I consider that he was bloody hungry as well as pissed off.

"Some fucking Raiders, a few Mercians and that damn ox that Rudolf insisted on taking in and out of Northampton. Stupid bloody thing," and as Hereman goes the way of the others once more, I find myself grinning. Bloody Hereman.

"Was he talking about Rudolf or the ox?" Edmund asks, watching his brother. And then I snort, trying to mask it in a cough, only Edmund winks at me and then we're both laughing, and fuck, it feels incredible to do something so bloody normal.

There's hay in my nostrils, and I desperately want to sneeze but I can't. I can't give away this reckless game that we're playing.

Rudolf had it right when he said he and Wulfhere could sneak inside Northampton again, only I'm not allowing Wulfhere to get involved. I'm happy to risk myself, but not him.

The smell of freshly scythed hay is refreshing, and yet at the same time, it threatens to give me away. I lift my arm carefully, hoping that the movement doesn't dislodge the stuff that covers me and breathe deeply of my armpit. It's not the most appetising of smells, but it filters the hay.

Not that I'm alone inside the wooden cart. Of course, I'm not. I've brought Wærwulf with me, for his language skills, and if we happen to have snuck away from the main camp, without anyone knowing where we are, then I'll take the criticism when we return.

Rudolf is jaunty at the front of the cart, the lad who normally makes the journey, more than pleased to be spared the fear and worry. He's returned to his bed. I don't blame him. It's early enough that grey still rims the sky, the threat of the day's brightness still some time away.

The rumble of the cart as it crosses the wooden bridge leading into the settlement jars me from my thoughts. I can't think too carefully about what I'm doing. It's madness, but these times seem to call for reckless acts that I'd never normally consider let alone enact.

I can hear the sleepy voices of the Raiders on guard duty, and I tense, but they don't even speak to Rudolf, head held low, crouched beneath his cloak. It seems they really don't expect the Mercians to rise against them. Cocky fuckers.

With the River Nene crossed, Rudolf directs the slow, plodding ox along the hard-packed road, and the wheels rumble back to the more usual sound. I can hear almost no voices, but I'm sure that someone, somewhere, must be awake inside Northampton, other than the watch guards.

The first thing that greets me is the smell. It's not the ripe one of too many people living in too small a space, but rather a fresh fragrance, as though whoever is here actually cares enough to ensure that the latrines are kept free-flowing, and the horses' shit isn't piled all together in one corner and left to turn rank.

A tuneless whistle greets my ears, and if I could, I'd give Rudolf a short hiss and tell him to shut the fuck up. He can't carry a tune, even when it's being banged out on a drum next to him.

It's a relief when we come to a stop, and another sleepy voice calls out in surprise.

"I'll do it," Rudolf offers an answer, and the silence of thirty animals awaiting their first meal of the day roars into my ears.

"Come on then," he whispers, and I push myself upright, dislodging hay all over Wærwulf, who follows my actions. I leap lightly from the cart and brush the stray pieces of hay from my tunic.

I wear my weapons belt, but it has only a seax fastened to it. I can't come too well-armed. No one would miss my sword and war-axe glistening from my waist if I were discovered. A seax might not arouse too much suspicion. Almost everyone carries some sort of blade.

Quickly, I take in the state of the settlement before me. Rudolf has brought the ox-cart inside the wooden building which houses the horses. From inside the door, while Rudolf slowly begins to move the hay from the back of the cart, a nod of his head indicating where the stable boys yet sleep, I can see that indeed Northampton is a tidy place.

There's a large hall, visible above another row of low-roofed buildings, and the sides of the ancient rampart can be glimpsed behind the buildings, but not so close that I feel confined.

It seems the Raiders, when they came here twenty-five years ago, planned on keeping a vast area safe behind the rampart. The space is at least double that at Repton, if not treble, and a feeling of unease flickers down my back.

The Raiders mean to make this a permanent base, of that I'm sure. Only the continual lack of ships in the river gives me any sort of solace. This is something that they're creating, and it's not complete. Not yet.

Wærwulf stands close to me, as we both try and orientate ourselves. Rudolf slowly works away. His job is simple; take as long as he can to finish his task. But to somehow make sure the work is complete for when Wærwulf and I return, even though we have no idea when that will be. Once more, I give the lad an impossible task and know that he'll succeed, as he always does. Our roles are more precarious.

On stealthy feet, I make my way across the open courtyard in front of the stables, taking advantage of any shadows to obscure my movements. If I can, I want to assess how well provisioned the Raiders are. Wærwulf, if he can, is to try and gain admittance to the hall, and find out who leads here. Once more, he must pretend to be a Raider.

The ground beneath my feet is dry, the risk of slipping small, as I round the corner. There are more dwellings here, and as I stride beyond them, as though I belong, I hear little above the rumble and moaning of people snoring, or being a little more amorous.

I pause, trying to decide whether to risk stepping inside, but instead focus on what I can see of the rampart.

It's not exactly intact, but neither is it beyond repair. I imagine that while Rudolf saw men and women labouring in the ditch, their job is two-fold, to both clear it, and to ensure the mud bank rises higher and higher. The smell of fresh wood coming from one of the sheds assures me that the men and women plan on hammering the pieces into place, and perhaps even building a walkway to crown the rampart.

It's evident that they mean to stay. That fucking frustrates me.

I haven't ridden them down from Repton to Torksey just to have them fucking appear somewhere else. Damn the bastards.

I continue to explore, finding the grain stores, as well as the raised meat store, where casks surely hold meat cured for the long winter months. There's a good amount, but certainly not enough to feed the number of warriors that sheltered at Repton.

And then I follow the line of the old banked wall, seeing how it curves and checking it for any signs of weakness above the fact that it's not been used for two decades. It encloses the settlement where there is no river to fulfil that task. The Mercians who make Northampton their home, have been savvy enough to build behind the mud wall, on the assumption that the Raiders won't breach the river that forms the other two sides.

But the rampart does have a weakness, and I eye the hole where a gate must have once hung with interest. The pile of wooden planks waiting beside the empty gateway, assures me that the Raiders mean to fill the void. I think they should have done it sooner—just another sign of their overconfidence.

The inhabitants of Northampton have not expanded beyond the bounds of the wall, other than to plant the fields. Not even the animals are allowed to graze there. And that again makes me consider the lack of ships. Other than for two ships close to the woodlands I emerged from earlier, I've not seen any, apart from a small craft that must be used for fishing in the river.

I keep one ear strained, hopeful that such alertness will be repaid with no outcry as Rudolf or Wærwulf are discovered. But all remains quiet, and with little more to see, I make my way back to the stables.

Rudolf still whistles tunelessly, although he acknowledges my arrival with a raised eyebrow. There's no sign of Wærwulf, but it's so early in the day, it seems that no one is awake. With a growl of frustration, I move to the stack of cleared horse manure and begin to hoist it onto the wooden cart.

This is the part of the plan that I don't much want to endure, but it's not as if Rudolf can ride in alone, and then ride out with two other men. Not that I need to hide, not yet. In fact, in a fit of pique, I leave a small space in the middle of the cart, piling up the manure all around it. If I'm lucky, maybe I won't need to hide beneath the stinking shit after all.

Only when Rudolf joins me, and the sweat begins to bead down my face, do I appreciate just how much time has elapsed. Well, that and Rudolf's hissed question. "Where the fuck is he?"

I shake my head, keen to ensure we're ready to leave when he does reappear.

"We can hardly go looking for fucking Wærwulf," I retort. So far, I've learned a great deal, and I don't want the Raiders to know that they've been infiltrated quite as thoroughly as they have.

"But, we do need to leave before the guards are replaced by someone a little more alert." I try not to show my concern, pausing only to peer to where I last caught sight of Wærwulf. I'm hoping that he'll just appear in front of me, but of course, he doesn't. With the horse manure in place, time seems to pass even more slowly, while the members of the garrison, seem to appear more and more often.

"Fuck," I'm forced to hunker down beside the cart when the passage of footsteps aims towards the stables. Rudolf has adopted a slightly forlorn expression as he pushes a broom around the space, pretending to tidy up the mess of his passage.

I'm ready to leap to action if I have to, my fingers hovering over my seax. But abruptly, the footsteps retrace their path and silence resounds once more.

"Where the fuck is he?" even I'm growing impatient and beginning to wish I hadn't been such a stupid bastard as to think I could sneak into the enemy stronghold and not be seen.

Rudolf doesn't reply but instead works to replace his broom next to the other tools before making his way to the cart. As much as I don't want to be any closer to the fragrant stench than possible, I know I need to be on the cart, ready for when we can make our escape.

Only all is tranquil, apart from the horses enjoying their hay and then drinking noisily from the troughs they have. Outside, the gloom is giving way to daybreak, and I know we should be going, but I'm not fucking leaving Wærwulf behind. I simply won't.

My eyes dare the darkness to turn ever brighter, but of course, it fucking does all the same.

"Bastard," I whisper so softly, even I don't hear the words. And then I hear clipped footsteps, and Rudolf's horrified eyes flicker to mine.

I nod my head at him, finally climbing into the green slime of horse manure, and seeking the clearer spot, in the centre, a hemp sack around my shoulders. It won't keep the stench away, but it might save my clothes. With swift movements, Rudolf follows me, laying the sack over my back, and shovelling a thin layer of the manure onto me.

It lands with a warmth that almost makes me vomit, as I cushion my head on my raised arms, face to the floor, forgetting my egg-shaped bump in the process. It thrums with renewed pain as I smack it against my arm.

The footsteps grow ever louder, and then I sense, rather than see, Rudolf relax, as another body joins mine. There's no time for conversation, as Rudolf makes his way to the front of the cart and encourages the slow ox to make its way out of the stables.

The rumble of the cart's wheels fills my hearing, but above it all, I can hear Rudolf's tuneless whistle as he calls once more to the sleepy guards and the rush of water assures me that we've escaped from inside Northampton, with the rumble of wooden wheels over the wooden boards of the bridge.

I would laugh at the simple-ness of it all. Only it fucking stinks, and I barely dare breathe, let alone laugh.

"Where the fuck, have you been?" It's Edmund who demands an answer, while I grin half-heartedly at him. "What the fuck is that smell?" he continues, his hand in front of his face, as though he can swish it aside. I grin ever wider.

"Just a bit of horse shit," I offer, already loosening my weapon's belt and hauling my tunic over my head. The stench almost makes me gag inside my tunic, but I hold myself together, pleased to breathe fresh air for the first time since my exit from Northampton.

Edmund glares at me, as I stride beyond him, through and then out of the camp, my target a small beck that flows close. I need to bathe. There's no fucking denying it.

Wærwulf follows me, as does Rudolf, and of course, Edmund, trailing us as though he's the fly come to feed on the shit.

Edmund's going to be pissed, that much I know, but Wærwulf has uncovered a great deal of information, and I'm happy that the risk was worth it. The balls of the Raiders annoys the shit out of me. Even now, after all the warriors that the Mercians and I have killed, they still think that we're no risk to them. They don't yet fear me, as they should. And they fucking should.

The fact that Hereman also follows in Edmund's wake amuses me. Since we all thought Edmund dead, they've rarely allowed five steps to separate them. I almost wish it would return to the bickering of all the years I've known them. This closeness is more menacing than anything else. I harbour no illusion that Hereman will support Edmund, no matter what he does, and equally, that Edmund will support Hereman.

Not that they didn't in the past. But now it will be without the snide remarks and rolled eyes. They could prove to be a deadly combination.

I jump down the steep incline so that I'm level with the beck, and then I kick my boots off and remove my trews as well. Everything I own needs cleaning. All of it.

"Bastard," I complain, the cold water making me shiver with just a toe in it.

"Well it's that or stink of shit," Hereman unhelpfully calls, his eyes raking in my nakedness without embarrassment. I can feel myself shrivel before his inspection.

"Fucking bastard," I mutter, quickly moving to fully submerge myself, including my head, in the cold water that I swear flows from the frozen north and not from the damn river close to

Northampton.

Pushing free from the surface of the water, I sniff, and Edmund chuckles.

"Keep going. You still reek." He throws a piece of thick moss at me, and I grip it in my white knuckles, jaw clamped tightly shut, determined to show no weakness before him.

I spare a thought for Wærwulf, as he shrieks with the shock of the cold. He has no choice but to follow me.

"Now, where the fuck have you been?" Edmund demands to know, resting a foot on the stone closest to me, and effectively baring the way I entered the water. His intent is clear.

"I think you probably know," I taunt, and he growls, his green eye flashing with fury.

"You damn fucker. You could have sent anyone. Why fucking risk yourself?"

I shrug, using the moss to scrub at the manure that stains my fingers and shoulders, crouching low in the water. It might be bloody cold, but it's also pleasant.

"I needed to see."

"And what did you see?" Hereman provokes me, sitting on the riverbank, and picking at his nails with his eating knife.

I turn to Wærwulf then, expecting him to explain what he knows, but he shakes his head, making it clear that he has no intention of infuriating Edmund. His skin is pale from the cold water. I imagine I look no better.

"I saw enough to know what needs to be done." Edmund's eye still glints, but his tense posture almost relaxes.

"And what, oh mighty king of Mercia, is that?" Edmund's voice drips with condescension. I grin, my powerful legs bunched beneath me so that I can use them to erupt from the water, dislodging more than a lapful of water all over Edmund, before bending to thrust my arse into his face as I pick up my weapons belt and seax with only a slight grimace for the smell that still lingers.

"Cock," Edmund growls, while Hereman stumbles as he tries to jump out of my way. I streak passed the pair of them, delighted by the sound of Rudolf's laughter as I make my way,

naked, back to where I've left my spare clothes.
"I know what we need to do," I call over my shoulder.

CHAPTER 9

Rudolf's eyes are enormous in the darkness before dawn.

"You've already done it twice, now get your arse in gear," I hiss at him, making him jump, even though he watches my mouth form the words rather than hearing them.

"But," only his complaint dies on his lips. He squares his shoulders, allows a final glare for Edmund, who's the real reason Rudolf is so unhappy and strikes out from the shadows of the trees.

Overhead a bright moon is entirely obscured by thick clouds, and I shiver just thinking of the intent behind them all. Quickly, I remember our damp ride along the Trent. I hope I won't be doing the same here.

Behind us, the rest of my warriors, including those of Ealdorman Ælhun's, wait, the horses further back, but saddled and ready to go, when we need them. Which might be sooner or later, I really don't know.

I watch Rudolf and Wulfhere walk clear of the woodlands. The smell of a newly kindled fire reaches my nostrils, and I know the family who provides the hay for the horses stabled inside Northampton are awake and preparing for another day of heavy toil under the Raiders.

I try not to watch Rudolf and Wulfhere, my heartbeat loud in my ears, but I do, all the same, every muscle tense. I don't want to be responsible for their deaths should this all go wrong. Only it fucking won't. I know it. Only I worry it will.

I lick my suddenly dry lips, wishing I had a more significant part to play in this part of our plan. But I don't. Everything I have planned comes down to whether Rudolf and Wulfhere can bring the carts close enough to the woods that we can slither under the supplies without being seen.

Wærwulf has spent much of the night, alongside Edmund, just watching Northampton, alert to anything that might reveal we've been discovered. The fact they haven't seen anything is surprisingly not reassuring. It all feels a little too easy but also smacks of complacency. I don't like either of those occurrences.

I'd sooner the men under the command of the jarls knew we were here than that they were too damn confident of success to worry that they might be being stalked.

The jangle of harness reaches my ears, and if possible, I strain even more. I've lost sight of Wulfhere and Rudolf in the darkness, and I have to rely only on sound. I hope it's enough.

"Fucking ridiculous plan," Edmund grumbles beside me. His face is more than half-hidden in shadow, and I can't see well enough to know whether the protest is genuine or if he just says it because he needs to hear a voice. I ignore him. I could say any number of things in response, most pointedly I could raise our attack on Repton. But I know better than to believe success must follow success. At some point, one of my ideas will go to shit. I know it. It's happened before.

"They're coming," the hiss comes from Wærwulf, muttered along the thin line of men until I hear it.

"Clever little fuckers," Hereman complains, and it is a complaint. This time I can't prevent my jaw from opening wide in outrage. Hereman, with all his half-cocked schemes and ideas is hardly fit to moan when someone else's half-baked idea seems to go according to plan. But then, Hereman relies on blind luck and not a little skill. Rudolf and Wulfhere are merely relying on a lazy youth who doesn't want to leave his bed to enter Northampton.

"Be ready," I whisper the instruction back toward Wærwulf. It's not the cleverest of schemes, but we need to get inside Northampton, and it's either on the back of one of the hay carts or across the river. And I don't fancy a dip in the cold water. I'm still more than half convinced that the Raiders have their ships stashed somewhere out of sight. Although Wærwulf assures me that the Raiders rode to Northampton, I still don't understand why they wouldn't have made use of a perfectly good river, or why there would be too few horses to accommodate them all.

The sound of the slow-moving carts comes ever closer, and I turn to Edmund. He's shaking, his face white with strain, almost brighter than the hidden moon overhead.

"You and the men wait here until the rest of us are inside and give the sign." Edmund nods, although he looks as though going to war is the last thing he wants to do.

The men I've chosen to hide under the hay are those I believe will cope the best with the deception. Edmund is too noticeable to be included. If he were discovered, I'm sure half the Raiders would know who he was without even having to think about it. That is the problem with carrying such a wound. The same applies to Pybba.

I've chosen those nimble enough to make the transition from the dark woods onto the back of the carts quickly. In fact, of them all, I know I'm the one that will take the longest, but I'm not sending my men in alone. I need to be with them, as always.

For the same reason, Pybba glowers at me from along the line of waiting men. He thinks his missing hand is no impediment, and it wouldn't be, in a straight fight, but this isn't a straight fight.

"Go," I instruct, and Wærwulf and Goda all but roll from the trees, coming to rest beneath the wheel of the cart that Wulfhere has not quite brought to a halt, as he pretends to fiddle with the harness. I watch the two men almost pour over the side of the cart, quickly covering themselves with the hay and lying flat. Their actions are more fluid than I can ever hope to achieve. I daren't even meet Edmund's gaze.

And then Wulfhere is gone, and Rudolf determines to bring his cart to a stop, not quite in the same place as Wulfhere, but close enough that Gyrth can roll his way to it.

"Don't fuck this up," Edmund's words are far from reassuring as I follow Gyrth. I almost consider going back, to tell him exactly what I think of his support, but that would indeed 'fuck it up', and so I stay focused, scrambling to lever my body onto the cart before Rudolf resumes his journey.

The smell of the hay assaults my nose, and for a long and worrying moment, I think I'm going to sneeze. Only I doubt. I reach out and grip Gyrth on the shoulder, assuring both of us that we're not alone.

"Fuck," Rudolf, perhaps belatedly realising he should have gone first, encourages the ox to move more quickly, and I'm rocked against the wooden floor of the cart, my seax threatening to slide free from my weapons belt.

I grip it more tightly and also quest for the other weapons that I'm hoping Rudolf has hidden well beneath the pile of hay.

Heavy hooves falling on the wooden bridge alerts me that we're close to Northampton. Any moment now, I expect the guards to call a greeting to Rudolf, only they don't.

Instead, I sense that we're inside Northampton itself as the cart's wheels stabilise, only to run over a smaller extent of wood, before pulling away once more onto the hard-packed surface of the road. I again worry that it's all too simple. No one has even questioned why there are two carts and not just one this morning. I would close my eyes, but I want to see everything, even from underneath the hay.

And then the cart rumbles to a halt. I feel Rudolf leap aside from his place at the front of the cart. Only, I can't feel the shadow of the stable building over my head.

"Shit," Rudolf's whisper is far from reassuring. "There are sacks of oats blocking the way." This isn't the news I want to hear. "No wonder the lazy shit was so pleased not to have to bring the cart today. He's left half of yesterday's job undone." Rudolf's voice thrums with annoyance, and then he squeals softly and leaps out of the way.

"Sorry," Wulfhere's voice is low and filled with regret, and I stifle laughter. The boy can't even control the slowest ox I've ever known. Rudolf is probably lucky he still stands and hasn't been crushed by the least likely of killer animals.

"Help me," Rudolf encourages Wulfhere, and it's so fucking painful listening to the two slender youths try and haul the heavy oats aside. I would help them, in fact, every moment longer than it takes, threatens the success of our scheme, but I can't risk being seen. I need to get off the cart inside the stables.

The remainder of my warriors won't yet be in position. It feels as though half the night has elapsed, but there's still no hint of dawn breaking. It's too soon.

I reach out once more, grip Gyrth's shoulder in reassurance, as we lie, afraid to even breathe too deeply, as Wulfhere and Rudolf bicker almost silently.

Only then Rudolf is back on the cart, and we're finally moving inside the stables.

The stench of horse manure makes me shiver, and almost gag, hoping that I won't have to use the same means of exit to escape from Northampton.

"All clear," Rudolf speaks to the pile of hay, and I gratefully push upwards, pulling stray pieces of hay loose from my hair and byrnie.

"Bloody bastard," Rudolf is sweating, his young face, red and gleaming with water, as he watches Wulfhere bring his cart inside the stables as well. He's visible as a shadow against the gloom of night, and then the ox seems to lumber to a stop just in front of me. The younger lad looks terrified for a moment, as I'm almost face to face with the ox's damp-breath, but then I grin broadly.

"Well done," I congratulate him, as Goda and Wærwulf leap from the back of the cart, and we all gather together. Rudolf reaches for and finds the rest of our equipment that he's hidden in the cart.

I grip my double-headed eagle sword gratefully, wishing I had my shield, but knowing the risk we took with the weapons we have was already too high.

"Right, to the guard post." The plan is simple enough. Provided it works. Wærwulf confirmed that there were more than eighty men and women inside Northampton. It's too many for the six of us to kill, but with the rest of my warriors inside Northampton as well, it'll be a much fairer battle.

"You know how to escape if you need to?" I direct this at both Rudolf and Wulfhere, although I already know that Rudolf will not take the other exit that I discovered. Wulfhere nods eagerly, tying his weapons belt around his slim waist, and reaching for his seax to reassure himself that it's there. I gifted him the blade. He's proud of it, and I can only hope that he gets to live long enough to dent the sharp blade.

"Right, let's do this," and Gyrth, Goda, Wærwulf and I slink from inside the stables, using the shadows to mask our steps back to where the guards attend to the bridge. Unseen by most, there's a shallow ditch running around this part of the settlement, a second deterrent that wouldn't be comprehended by anyone attacking. Such a small thing would confuse a war host that didn't expect such a tactic. But I don't think it's a significant enough impediment, not really.

On stealthy feet, little but the whites of our eyes showing, I lead the way back to where we gained our entrance into Northampton. Rudolf and Wulfhere are to remain behind, but I anticipate them disobeying my instructions. After all, every other fucker does. It means I'm unsurprised when I hear more than three different pairs of footsteps following me.

"Damn fuckers," I mumble incoherently, eyes focused on where I'm going, not on what follows me.

Within sight of the guards, a small fire burning beside them to light the path, I pull my men to one side. My chest heaves, although I feel as though I'm doing nothing. I take the time to calm myself. Stealth remains vitally important. At the moment, I swear the four sleepy men might think there was a bloody bear about to descend on them for all the noise I'm making.

Only when I hear nothing but the soft swish of air in and out of my body, do I wave my hand, indicating who should kill which of the guards, and then we move out. This is the vital part of the operation. Well, one of them. In fact, fuck, no, every part of this terrible plan is critical. If one part fails, the whole thing will.

"Shit," I whisper, the word little more than added to my breath. This war business was far easier when I had only the ancient kingdom of the Hwicce and my men to consider.

I move stealthily, keen to stay in the shadows and out of the dancing shapes of the flames that might just catch some part of my dark clothes, alerting the Raiders to the fact that they're not alone.

If these warriors were mine, I'd kill them rather than let them take the night watch. For all that, they seem alert enough, only in the wrong direction. They don't know the enemy is already inside Northampton.

With a final soft scurry, hoping I don't kick a stone or dislodge a discarded piece of horse manure to send silently tumbling against their foot, I'm behind my target.

In the darkness, all I can tell is that the warrior is shorter than I am, with shoulders that are much narrower than mine.

I slither up behind him, quieter than the gentle breeze, and with sharp movements, his chin is in my left hand, and my seax is tearing across his throat with more force than I'd normally use. Without so much as a garbled oath, the man trembles and then falls, and I move quickly to catch him, knowing he might be slick with shed blood. I don't know if my warriors have been as quick. I can't risk alerting the three remaining men to what's happening by allowing my kill to tumble to the floor.

As I support the dead man's weight, I risk a glance to my left, pleased to see that all of the guards are now dead and without so much as a gasp of shrieked air expelled, never to be reclaimed.

I also turn to gaze into the darkness of the compound. Nothing stirs. Nothing.

"Help me," I demand of Rudolf, and he darts to grab the dead man's legs, and between us, we move beyond the gate to lie the body in the shallow ditch, Wulfhere quickly taking the place of the dead man, to stand alert, Gyrth, Goda and Wulfhere doing the same. To anyone who happens to look toward the fire, they'll still see four men, as there should be. They won't know that four are dead, or even that the four who stand are their enemy.

"I'll help the others," I whisper to Rudolf, and he follows me back to Gyrth, taking his place as I take the legs of the men Gyrth killed.

"Fuck, he's heavy," I complain, sweat beading my face, despite the cold wind. Gyrth merely grunts and I know he thinks the same. Our steps are slow and laboured as we follow the same short path to where I dumped the last body. Only then I have to take a moment, bend double, catch my laboured breath.

"Fat bastard," Gyrth heaves the words beside me. It feels as though we're too loud, but I can hear nothing over our panting, and so I don't really know.

As soon as we can, we both return to the others, and now Gyrth assists Goda in moving the dead man, while I stand in Goda's place.

This man is clearly far lighter, and quickly both men return, to allow Goda to assist Wærwulf, while Gyrth takes the place of the watchman. The two men wait, not wanting to return and add too many to the number that should be standing to attention, close to the fire.

Instead, I give a piercing whistle, hoping it's loud enough. My chest has stopped heaving, and I'm ready for what comes next. For long moments, nothing happens, but then the unmistaken sound of men coming at speed reaches my ears, although they step more softly over the wooden bridge, and I grin.

Edmund and Hereman have led the rest of them to me. Now begins the real slaughter. My men pool around me, hidden once more in the shadows, as the fire is all but obscured.

"Wulfhere and Rudolf, you remain here, with Pybba and Sæbald." I purposefully refuse to hear the groans of complaint from all the men. The six owing their oaths to Ealdorman Ælhun already know they won't be taking part in the coming slaughter. They're less outraged than my men to be given such a task.

"Wærwulf, lead the way." It's Wærwulf who gave me the information that I needed. To him went the highest risk, and now I'll give him the honour of beginning this battle.

A flash of blond before me and Wærwulf doesn't need telling twice. He uses the same shadows that we did to mask our path from the stables to the guards, and then, at the stables, he strikes out to the right, toward the great hall where the jarl's warriors sleep, thinking they're protected from the horrors of the Mercians by their four comrades, dead now, and forever sleeping.

How wrong they are.

The wooden hall appears before me, just as the gloom begins to ease. We started this battle in full dark, but we'll end it with more than just the sun leaching across the sky, setting it aflame.

The fuckers should have stayed far from Mercian land. I intend to make it very clear, once more, what happens to those who try to claim that which doesn't belong to them. And more importantly, to those who underestimate Mercia's new king.

CHAPTER 10

Wærwulf strides from the shadows, his arm slung around Osbert's shoulders, as though Osbert holds him upright because he's pissed as a fart, steps wavering. The two door wardens shift from the shadows, as though they stand erect whereas before they were merely leaning against the sturdy wooden posts to either side of the main door.

I don't understand the drawled words the one speaks, but I appreciate the intent behind them and grip my seax loosely as Wærwulf replies in his equally drawled Danish. A grunt and the door is opened wide by the second man, only Osbert and Wærwulf are no longer where they were a moment ago.

While the door warden turns in surprise, he loses his life, Osbert slicing cleanly across his neck, the complaint dying before the words can pour forth.

Wærwulf dispatches the first man just as quickly, and then I rush from the darkness, keen to be the first inside the hall.

Wærwulf has explained what I'll find inside, and he's not wrong.

The hall, not as huge as I expected it to be, is somnolent before me. Men and women sleep, wrapped in cloaks, the fire little more than a mat of angry embers at the centre. I grin.

I don't like to kill men and women like this. But they should have been more fucking alert.

On silent feet, I make my way to the furthest reaches of the hall, being careful where I step. Edmund follows me, Hereman close by as well. We've designated our task as being the hardest of all. We must start from the far end, our seaxs busy as others start the slaughter from closer to the door.

The sound of snoring fills the room, only to falter as I swivel my head, peering into the gloom, desperate to know that we're not discovered. I'm far from alone. White eyes peer into the murkiness, and then the sound rumbles through the hall once more.

"How the fuck you can sleep through that, I'll never know," Wulfred's comment, not loud, but audible for those awake to hear, brings a grin to my tight face.

And then the grisly work begins close to the door, as my warriors spread out in the shape of a cartwheel, each knowing where they're going, keen to kill. Wærwulf's scratched diagram on the floor of the forest has proven to be unfailingly accurate.

A foot falls too loudly behind me, and I hear Hereman grumble as he seems to prevent his brother from falling. Fuck, I thought it too much for Edmund, but he would not hear my reasoning, saying he can see better than I can. And he can, in daylight, but it's far from daylight in here.

Before Edmund can wake the sleeping, I bend, feeling the creak in my back that never used to be there. Peeling back the arm of the sleeping warrior, I slice deeply and quickly. A gurgle of expelled air and I scent nothing but piss and blood. And then I'm onto the next torpid warrior.

There are eighty of them, or at least there should be. How fucking stupid of them all to sleep in such a way, to trust only six to guard them in enemy land. The fucking arrogance astounds me.

Yet, I can't help but think this is easier than the battles I've fought from Repton to Torksey. I don't like such effortless kills, but fuck, it makes the work easier when everyone sleeps.

Only, of course, they don't sleep forever.

"Ah," the cry from the farthest corner rouses those close enough to hear, heads coming upwards as they seek out the cause of the noise.

"*Angreb*," quickly follows, and the warrior's roar only increases in volume, as his eyes seem to bulge from his face, casting him into a stranger green haze, his hand reaching for his weapons as he leaps to his feet. No one is close enough to silence him quickly.

"Shit." I'm already rushing through those who still sleep, trying not to stamp on an outstretched hand or foot. It's not fucking easy, or fast enough.

"*Angreb. Angreb.*" The voice is loud enough to wake the fucking dead, and indeed, before I can cover even half of the distance, more and more bodies are erupting from the snoring floor, as though bats descending from their sleeping heights, only in reverse.

I lash out with my seax, taking the first shocked warrior through his open mouth, and then being forced to wrench back my weapon from where it grates over white teeth. And then there are hands seeking my neck, growing tighter and tighter. I flick my head toward where I hope the face that belongs to those hands will be.

The shattering of bone reaches my ears, and a flicker of hot blood lands on my chin. With my seax finally free from the teeth, I stab down, into the man's belly, and his hands release from my neck, just before the weakness of not being able to breathe takes me. The bastard must have had hands the size of Icel's to make their way all around my thick neck.

In the darkness, I can sense him, more than see him, and my seax is busy. Stabbing anywhere I can reach on his body. The aroma of piss pushes beyond the stench of iron, but the man still lives. Slowly, so slowly I almost think the edge of his seax will never come close to me, he takes aim.

Only then blood erupts over my face, the point of a blade almost touching my nose, from inside the man's mouth

"What the fuck?" I exclaim, ducking for good measure. From behind the dying man, Hereman appears, his hot breath rank in my face.

"Bastard," Hereman exclaims, and whether he means me or the enemy, I'm not sure. Without pausing, he's moving toward the man who still shouts, not entirely pushing me out of the way, but not far from it.

"Bastard," I mirror Hereman's protest, but it's aimed at him and not the enemy.

And then I slip. The sound following me downwards, ending with a resounding thunk, the final letter of the word bitten off, as I hit the wooden floor, the slippery substance undoing me.

"Fuck," I spit the taste of another's blood and piss from my mouth, as I struggle to my feet. Only it's all but impossible. My boots keep jutting out beneath me, my hands as slick as my boots, and I fall. This time my breath escapes my body as a loud rattle, and I try once more, and then again and again. More and more of the sleeping are waking as the hall descends into chaos, and I'm stuck on my fucking arse.

This was not what I wanted, not at all. But if I can just make it to my fucking feet, it will make what must happen so much bloody easier.

And then I realise what I must do because what I'm doing isn't working.

Carefully, I place one foot on the dead man to the side of me, ensuring it nestles in the ruffled fabric of his cloak. I do the same to the other side and then push upwards with my hands bunched in the tunic of both bodies, leaving red welters beneath my hands.

I'm upright, but my legs are so far apart, my balance is haphazard. When I lift my head, one of the Raiders is watching me, a perplexed expression on his sleep-rumbled face, his blades in his hands.

And then the fucker grins, and I know what his next move will be, even before he does.

Only the slippery floor that's kept me pinned down is not just my enemy; it's also my ally. As the man lifts his right foot, his left slips beneath him and he tumbles, arms flailing madly to recover his balance. But it's no good. With a satisfying thud, he lands on the floor, beneath me. It's nothing for me to snap my legs together and stamp on his stomach with all of my weight. His body bucks, his head coming up to meet my waiting seax.

"Who's the fucking idiot now?" I grumble.

The kill gives me much less pleasure than just being on my feet once more. With purposeful steps, I stride over the dead man, my eyes fixed on the tight knot of fighting to the corner of the hall.

Hereman is busy at his work, but six Raiders attempt to overpower him. At the same time, the rest of my men move around the hall, their actions calm and assured despite the cries of those woken from sleep, and those sobbing over their wounds before they settle into the sleep from which they'll be no waking.

"Bastard." Edmund stumbles to join me, and I'd push him aside, but there's something about the expression on his face that tells me it would be more trouble to try and protect him than it will be just to let him assist his brother.

"Fuckers," Edmund roars, his seax bloodied and ready to drink deeper yet. Four heads turn to watch his approach, and the first dies with a blade through his throat before he can even voice the smug retort seeing a one-eyed warrior always seems to warrant.

My eyebrows lift at the deadly move. Edmund has lost none of his skills.

As he moves onto the second man, I take the third, seeing an older warrior watching me. The scars on his arms tell their tale, as does the angle of his nose, and the notches on his seax.

A warrior then. An old and very much tried one.

I almost bow to the man, too clearly reminded of Icel when I gaze at him, but he interprets my hesitation and quickly dashes toward me, surprising me with his turn of speed.

"Shit," I rear backwards to avoid his reaching blade, almost colliding with Edmund's opponent as I do so.

"Shit," I mutter once more, but my arm moves of its own volition, countering the heavy blow easily. The man bites his lip, reappraising me, perhaps seeing something he didn't expect to. I thrust his seax aside, hoping to knock him off balance, as I try to land a slice on his left arm. I would like to add another wound to the many that sprout there already. Perhaps it's his weaker side. I don't know.

But the man moves just as quickly as I do to counter the action. Behind me, I feel Edmund's man drop to the floor, dead already, and in front of me, Hereman has moved to take the life of his third opponent. Perhaps I should have left the two to it, after all. I'm not exactly fucking helping.

I try another blow, on the right side of the man's body this time, and although he tries to swerve from the path of my blade, he fails, and I make my first cut. I expect it to make him wary, but it does precisely the opposite.

With compressed lips, defiance in his pain-hazed eyes, he surges forward, his seax seeming to merge into two weapons before me with the speed he uses.

I grin. This is a truly skilled warrior. I would sooner have met him on the slaughter field than here. I would sooner he had been the last man standing from the Raiders who came against us, and then we could have extolled his skills. But no, he must die, here, in this hall, as so many others have already done so. It's not the sort of death he fucking deserves.

Languidly, I counter his blows, everything seeming to slow down around me, as not only do I interpret where his blade truly is, but move to prevent its impact even before he's decided where to attack

His actions are faster than blue lightning illuminating the sky with its many fractured branches, but I'm quicker. The rest of the bloodied hall seems to fade away, and there's just him and me fighting in a tight knot together, mindful of where we place our feet because so many lie dead beneath us. Once more, the floor is slick, but not as slippery as when I fell.

I watch my opponent grow winded, his chest heaving as his right arm moves to weave his seax dance around me. But no matter what he does, he can't get so much as a glancing blow on my body. Slowly, realisation dawns on his face, but once more, it only redoubles his efforts to end my life.

I almost wish I could get to know this man, to discover the tales that his scars and wonky nose could tell me. But no, he's my enemy, and finally, my seax snakes beyond his guard, the blade hungry to drink once more after so much work. I sink it, not without care, into where I know his heart beats too fast.

With his free hand, he grips my seax handle, his hand so strong around mine, and with a final contemptuous gaze, he thrusts the seax deeper and deeper, his breath rattling in his throat, the light dimming from his eyes as I watch.

I incline my head to him, a mark of respect for a man who's clearly lived through so much.

And then his grip falters, his hand falls away, and he follows. Just another to add to the slaughter.

Only then do I appreciate the near silence in the hall, feel the gaze of my warriors and those of Ealdorman Ælhun. I would take their acclaim, but of course, I don't.

"What?" I almost shout. "You've never seen me kill a fucking man before?"

Grins greet my words, but it's to Edmund that I turn, the slow clap of his hands ringing loudly.

"No, we've never seen you kill someone fucking old enough to be your grandfather before," he cackles, "and take so bloody long to do so." My mouth drops open in shock at such a statement, but then Edmund is laughing, the battle joy pouring from him, and I realise the daft fuck has enjoyed this far more than he really should.

CHAPTER 11

"Is everybody dead?" It seems a strange question to ask, and yet I must all the same. In the gloom, it's difficult to see a great deal, and then a shower of sparks rises from the hearth as someone throws a log onto it, and simultaneously, the wooden door is flung open.

In the sudden brightness, I blink, trying to peer through the shimmering haze laden with falling rubies, the delicate pattering of drops falling onto my cheeks.

"The fuckers are all dead," Wulfred bellows, and my eyes swivel to where he stands, running his seax over a piece of linen in his hand, close to the door.

"All dead here," Ælfgar's voice hails me from one of the darker corners, and it elicits a flurry of agreement from others.

"Do we all still live?" This should have been my first fucking question. It speaks of trusting my men to do their job well.

A further chorus of 'aye' and 'yes' and 'shit, yeah,' resound and I nod, pleased to hear that.

"Is anyone injured?" I don't honestly expect anyone to admit to a wound, and I'm unsurprised when silence greets me.

"Right, get these fuckers out of here," I command, sheathing my seax, and striding confidently to the doorway. I just need a mouthful of clean air, not soiled with the stench of the dying.

Wulfred watches my approach, and only the droop of his face alerts me to the fact that anything's wrong.

"What the fuck?" the words burst from his mouth, and I imagine I know the problem.

"It's not bloody mine," I complain, already moving to remove my belt, thrust it into his hand, and then pull the tunic clear from my head. It doesn't come away easily, seeming to stick in some places, and for a moment I gasp, not wanting to breathe in the horrible smell but having no choice.

When I erupt from my tunic, Wulfred is watching me with appraising eyes.

"Aye, you daft bastard. It's not yours," he agrees, thrusting my weapons belt at me, even though I want to try and scrape the blood away. But Wulfred has his eyes on something else, something outside, his tongue poking through his lips, as he abruptly sprints from beside me.

"What?" I call after him, but I get no response as he darts behind a building, and disappears.

"Shit," and then, "Beornstan, get your arse here," he comes to do my bidding, dropping the arms of the man he'd been about to cart to the doorway, a question on his face for my naked torso that would make me smile if I weren't in a hurry.

"Wulfred went that way. I'm going after him," I shout when I'm sure he's close enough to see where I point.

Beornstan grunts in agreement, and then I'm running after Wulfred, Beornstan bellowing for Osbert and Edmund. It seems he's not going to own the responsibility for my potentially rash actions alone.

The ground beneath my feet is hard from the passage of many feet, and I think I know where Wulfred is heading. I can only imagine that someone lives and is trying to escape. I can't decide, as my chest heaves, and I try not to shiver in the chill morning air, if that's a good thing or not.

In the past, I've made a habit of keeping a man alive to tell of my victories. It's only recently that I've not done so. Do I want the Raiders who sent these men and women to Northampton to know that those plans have failed? All that Wærwulf managed to find out was that these warriors owed their oath to Jarl Guthrum. More than that, Wærwulf couldn't determine, not as men and women woke from their slumbers. But, he did find out how many door wardens there were, and where everybody slept. That was more than enough to launch this attack.

I turn at the same building that Wulfred did, the remains of the rampart to my left. But I can't see Wulfred in front of me. This part of the settlement is shrouded in darkness even now, long shadows making the area appear blacker than night, and I grimace as my foot impacts a muddy puddle. Fuck knows whether it's water or something less pleasant. Not that I'm not covered in enough crap as it is.

I catch my balance, and continue to run, hoping I follow the correct path, and then I see it, opening up before me.

The rampart around the settlement is almost whole, but not here. Here, there was once a gateway, long since crumbled away, and it's here that I expect to find Wulfred.

And I do. He's standing, heaving great gouts of air into his rapidly moving chest, his finger pointing outside the rampart. I follow it and can see a figure dashing along what must have once been a roadway, and one that's fallen to ruin, the lushness of creeping weeds threatening to split the surface.

"Sorry, fucking bastard," Wulfred gasps, but I shake my head to deny the words.

"No, this is as it should be. A survivor to tell of what we did here. I'm keen to know what fucking Jarl Guthrum plans next. Whether we like it or not, our situation at Repton is reversed, and I'm not going to shy away from whatever reprisals he has planned. And, I'm going to ensure this fucking gateway is boarded up."

"My Lord Coelwulf," Rudolf's despondent cry greets me from close to the bridge as I trudge back toward the great hall.

"What?"

"Is it done?" he demands to know, and I cock my head to one side, arms out to either side of my naked torso.

"Does it look as though it's done?" I retort. I'm assuming he can see me in the growing light.

My voice is loud and echoes in the silence of a settlement where everyone except us, and the horses, is dead, or a Mercian.

Rudolf wrinkles his young forehead, as I walk closer to him, and then grins.

"Fucking hope so," he offers. "What the fuck happened to you?"

"I slipped," is the only explanation I offer, peering to make sure the three other men are well, and trying not to notice the horror on young Wulfhere's face. Surely, he's seen me looking like this before? Or maybe not. I'm not one to wander around naked, no matter that I have in recent days.

"Is everything quiet here?" I ask, just to be assured.

Pybba is shaking his head at me, almost as horrified as Wulfhere, and for him, I feel an explanation might be needed.

"It was slippery, and there was a lot of blood on the floor, and I fell."

His face settles in a frown of unease. I'm not entirely sure what he wants from me.

"So, they're all fucking dead then?" Pybba seeks confirmation, and I nod, wishing I had something to drink.

"All dead, and now we need to get the fuckers out of there, and shore up the hole in the defences at the back. And probably here as well."

"Can I go and see?" Rudolf asks hopefully, Wulfhere looking as though he probably wants to go, but isn't sure yet. His face is bleached of colour, his lips thin and tight.

"Yes, but bring me back some water," I instruct him, "and don't take all the good gold and silver. Some of the others might fucking want some as well," I caution him, but his impetuous grin is all I need to see to know that he won't heed my words.

Wulfhere follows him hesitantly until Sæbald calls to him.

"Bring me back something good," he commands, and the two lads are gone, their pace doubling, and I slump to the floor. Ideally, I'd like nothing more than to jump in the river and clean myself, but I don't have my spare clothes, and the morning air is more refreshing than I might like.

"And a cloak," I send after Rudolf, not sure whether he hears me or not because he's so busy speaking to Wulfhere, imparting his years of battlefield plundering knowledge to the other boy. It seems they've become firm friends, and that Rudolf is the expert to teach the younger lad.

The three of us settle to silence. My mind busy considering what needs to be done, and more importantly, what can actually be done to keep Northampton safe.

"The defences are a good idea, aren't they?" I ask this of both Pybba and Sæbald, but only Pybba seems to be listening to me because I only get one reply.

"Aye, not bad. They did the same at Repton and Torksey as well. Maybe we could do the same throughout Mercia. I believe the Wessex king builds such things." I'm surprised that Pybba knows anything about events in Wessex, but I don't question him.

"There's a gap, at the rear, an abandoned gate. We need to enclose it. But there's a lot of wood. They meant to do it but hadn't yet."

"And build a deeper ditch along the riverfront," Pybba interjects. It seems his thoughts have been similar to mine. That pleases me more than it should. It's reassuring to know that another shares my vision.

"Maybe you could have waited for them to finish before you fucking killed them all," Pybba speaks with a wry smirk on his face, lifting his stump to show why he speaks as he does.

"We'll have to get reinforcements from Ealdorman Ælhun," I confirm, sucking my lips, and wishing I could taste more than salt when I do so. I really need something to drink. And to eat, as my stomach emits a loud rumble that rouses even Sæbald from his deep thoughts.

"You'd need a lot of fucking warriors to keep the walls and ditches guarded," Sæbald mumbles. I hadn't considered that. I hadn't realised he was actually listening.

"If it came to a siege," Sæbald helpfully offers when I look confused. I'm not used to being the one inside the siege. The thought intrigues me.

"How many warriors?"

Sæbald looks thoughtful.

"Enough. Enough to guard it, and of course, enough to keep it well maintained. This place is what, two decades old, and look at it. The ditch needs dredging, and the gateway has fallen away to ruin. Hardly built to last."

I arch an eyebrow, impressed by Sæbald's clarity of thought.

"So, so many warriors to a certain length of the palisade, and probably double the amount to keep the ditches clear. Is this place even big enough to house so many?"

"They needn't live here all the time," Sæbald mumbles, but his ears have pricked, and I can almost see him sensing the wind. I wonder what he's heard, only then I hear it as well, and my hand reaches for my blood-smeared blade as well. I should have cleaned it. I wouldn't tolerate the same from Rudolf.

"Fuck," I complain. "We don't need to be tested just yet." Sæbald's gaze is fixed on the open land before us, to the far side of the river, before the woodlands begin, whereas I'm looking hopefully back toward the interior of the settlement. I need Rudolf or one of the men to notice what's happening. Of course, none of the fuckers has left the hall, not yet. Maybe I shouldn't encourage them to pilfer as much as they do.

Three men can't stand against whatever is heading this way, because it now sounds like a whole host of mounted warriors. Have I fucking made the same mistake I did at Repton when I thought the Raiders were all inside only to discover that they weren't?

The Gwent Welshman, Lord Cadell and Bishop Eadberht's men, led by Heahstan, found three such infestations in Mercia. Cadell assured me the men were dead, with just the right hint of defiance in his tone, for me to believe that he'd done as he said. Certainly, Heahstan didn't deny the boast, and I'm convinced he would have done. There was healthy respect between the two men that can only come from being enemies so long that there's a strange honour between them. I know it well.

"Quick, we'll guard the bridge," and I rush forward, keen to prevent entry by utilising the narrowness of the wooden bridge, just as the men and women did at Swarkeston. There might only be three of us, but the bridge can only just support the width of the cart. I'm sure no more than three warriors abreast could make any headway.

And anyway, there are only three of us. I can't spare either Pybba or Sæbald to summon the others. Three men is a ridiculous number to keep Northampton safe from attack; two would be ludicrous.

I consider the men and horses waiting for us in our hidden camp, deep inside the woodlands. They were explicitly told to stay put until all was safe. I both hope that they've not broken their cover and that a group of Raiders has not discovered them. My thoughts turn to young Hiltiberht. I hope he hasn't decided to risk everything, as Rudolf would.

No one knew where we were. No one.

And then there's no need for more questions because a host of mounted warriors appears on the far side of the river, the early morning sunlight glinting from helms and byrnies, from bridles and shields.

"Ealdorman Ælhun," I recognise him immediately, Wulfsige at his side, the other man trying not to look quite as proud of himself as he does.

"My Lord King," Ealdorman Ælhun's voice drums with respect but also uncertainty. I tilt my head to the left, sucking my dried lips again, and consider how this will play out.

Ealdorman Ælhun has made his way to Northampton incredibly quickly. He was supposed to remain in Worcester, with my Aunt and Bishop Wærferth. What exactly has Wulfsige said to him?

Behind me, I feel a handful of my warriors appear, as though from the very river mist itself, hands on weapons. I would grin with delight. I should have known fucking better than to fear that they wouldn't recognise my peril.

A strained silence fills the air, and I consider whether I should speak first or allow Ealdorman Ælhun to do so. I'd grown to respect the man. Was I wrong to do so?

Beside me, Pybba coughs softly, and I wrench my eyes from the sight before me, to the older man. His eyes are trying to tell me something, but fuck knows what it is.

"All is well in Worcester?" I call, deciding these are the correct words to say.

"Yes, yes, My Lord King," Ealdorman Ælhun seems keen to reassure me, and I grunt, pleased to hear as such.

"And you?" Ealdorman Ælhun asks. "You are well?"

"Yes, quite." This conversation is growing tedious quickly. "We've just reclaimed Northampton from the Raiders. Your men can be put to good use rebuilding the gate and burying the dead. It's a fucking mess in the main hall."

Ealdorman Ælhun winces at my words. I'd not thought him one to shy away from the realities of battle.

"Come, be welcome to Northampton," I only just don't bow to him, so used to having to give up my battle sites to those who think they commanded me to act. King Burgred was not the sort of prickly bastard to risk offending.

All credit to the ealdorman, only a tiny flicker of unease covers his face before he encourages his horse forward, while Sæbald, Pybba and I move aside from our less than friendly position on the bridge. I slide my blade back into the scabbard, wincing at the soft sound. It should be the sharp smack of metal on metal. I really need to clean my fucking blade.

The sound of hooves is loud over the bridge, and while the ealdorman makes the short journey, I keep my eye on those who escorted him.

The number seems far more substantial than that he advised owed their oath to him. I wish I could remember the exact number, and look at Pybba as though he might know. But of course, it's Edmund and then Rudolf who keep track of such things.

All I can say with certainty is that there are more men than I currently command. It seems that the ealdorman was either dishonest with me, which surprises me, or he's recruited extra to the cause. Just what the fuck did Wulfsige say to his oath-lord and why has he come hurtling all the way to bloody Northampton? I almost can't believe it's possible in such a short space of time, trying to replay the journey I've undertaken to get here.

I feel a prickle of unease but dismiss it. I've only just been through that tedious ceremony to proclaim me king. They won't be about to take that from me. Bishop Wærferth assured me that they couldn't. I'm the king, until my death, or I mutter the words that renounce my position. Hopefully, neither of those things is about to happen anytime soon.

Wulfhere is suddenly at my side, a triumphant grin on his face and I take the jug he offers and swig it almost in one go. The water is cold, even if it's been standing all night. I do Wulfhere the honour of not noticing the gore on his fingers or the flashing golden cross at his neck. It's far too rich for someone of his status to own. It seems that he's stolen it back from the Raiders. Fair fucks to the lad.

Ealdorman Ælhun is quick to swing down from the back of his high-stepping chestnut mare, and equally quickly, Wulfhere is there to take charge of the animal. Ealdorman Ælhun peers into Northampton itself, but only now are the men beginning to emerge from the hall, bodies dragging behind them, or swinging between them. They're not exactly quiet, and I wince to hear their conversation.

"I see we may have arrived too late to be of assistance," the unease is still evident to hear.

"Walk with me," I offer him, surprised by the firmness in my voice, and my decision.

Pybba's grunt could be taken as either relief or amusement, and so I ignore it and instead move to walk along the riverbank.

There's a beaten down path here, the undergrowth lying flat from the passage of many feet. It's not quite wide enough for us to walk side by side, but I willingly step onto the grass, aware of my naked torso, and wishing I'd not been quite so impetuous to be done with the stink of blood.

"Why are you here?" I ask when I'm convinced we're far

enough away that others won't hear our words, even if they can try and interpret what we're saying by the stances we take.

Ealdorman Ælhun pauses, as though taking the time to consider his response

"Wulfsige sent a messenger to me, an urgent one. He said the Raiders outnumbered your force and you were likely to charge to your death." I narrow my eyes at that, unsure whether to believe it or not.

"Bishop Wærferth and Lady Cyneswith overheard the message, had me rush here, to find you."

For a moment, I pause, considering who the fuck Lady Cyneswith is, and what she's got to do with this, and then I remember. I really must get used to hearing my Aunt's name spoken aloud by others.

It might be the truth, but I doubt it. Equally, I can't determine why the ealdorman might lie to me. After all, I can ask my Aunt and the bishop. They'll tell me the truth.

"What exactly did Wulfsige say to you?"

"He said there were Raiders in Northampton, and that you were outnumbered."

None of this is ringing true. We didn't know how many were inside Northampton, not when Wulfsige left me, taking his ten men with him.

"It's fortuitous that you arrived when you did." For now, I'm going to have to believe his words. Or rather, I'm going to have to let him think that I believe them. I'm not sure that I do. Not at all. But I do need his warriors to hold Northampton for me. It would be ridiculous to send them away under a cloud of suspicion. I turn now, face the ealdorman, keen to see how he absorbs the rest of my words.

"The Raiders meant to make Northampton their own, just as at Repton and Torksey. They're all dead, apart from one, although the fucker's escaped. My plan now is to complete the defensive works they've begun. You and your men can assist in that. At the same time, we need to keep scouting. There are no ships here, although there's a river. There were eighty or so of the fuckers, but only thirty horses. I believe the main body of Raiders is elsewhere. I need to find them."

Ealdorman Ælhun nods, and I'm sure there's a flash of relief on his face bearded face that I'm not about to question him further.

"Are these all your men?" I ask, indicating the remaining men and horses making their way across the bridge. There are a lot of them. I would almost think the ealdorman had cobbled together a band of warriors to assist him in taking Northampton for himself.

"No, no. Not all of them. Bishop Wærferth sent a contingent of fifteen of his warriors, and your Aunt also sent five fresh men."

I wish Edmund were here to remind me of how many men Ealdorman Ælhun could command to assist me at Repton. But, there are too many ealdormen, and the number refuses to come clear to my mind. Was it fifty-something, or eighty-something. I'm fucked if I know.

"She's a quick-thinking woman," I offer. Ealdorman Ælhun mumbles something, perhaps an agreement, but maybe not. My Aunt tends to have that effect on men who think they're intelligent but perhaps aren't quite as quick-witted as they might think. I've seen it happen before. I've had it happen to me before. It's far more enjoyable to witness another under her spell.

"Have your men set a watch at the exposed gate to the rear, and here, over the bridge. And send a further twenty to help with the dead. As soon as they're gone from the hall, we can find some food and eat. I'll send for the remainder of my men." With my decision made, I stride back toward the bridge, aware that Pybba and Sæbald watch me just as keenly as Wulfsige.

I'm still unsure what to make of Wulfsige.

"Someone find me a fucking tunic," I command, only for Wulfhere to appear, a bucket of water in one hand, a piece of material in the other. Eagerly, I dunk the water over my head, using my ruined tunic to scrub at the dried blood. And then sniff the bundle of fabric that it transpires is a tunic. I'm surprised to find it fresh, and Wulfhere grins once more. The little fucker is spending too much time with Rudolf and learning to use his initiative. It won't end well.

"Found it hanging out to dry," Wulfhere confirms smartly, and I pull it over my head, pleased that not only does it fit, but fits well, as I flex my arms into it, pulling it over my tightly-corded stomach.

"Well done," I offer him when my head is through the material, and I'm settling it over my stomach. I reach out to ruffle his hair, but he dodges me and rushes away once more.

"Shit," I mutter, but Pybba chuckles beside me.

"You bring out the best in everyone," he confides, but his eyes hold many more questions, all of them I decide to ignore. For now.

"Hereman," he lounges against the wall, watching the new arrivals with narrow eyes.

"Coelwulf," he uses my name, rather than 'My Lord', and although I've told them to do so, his use of it now is a calculated gesture. Hereman is an excellent example of someone others might think lacking wit. How wrong they would be.

"Take three men, bring the rest here." He nods, already striding to summon Ælfgar, Osbert and Eoppa to his side. I would watch them, but I've finally found the five men my Aunt has sent to me. They've trailed at the back of Ealdorman Ælhun's men, no doubt far from keen to be caught up in whatever's happening in front.

But I know the five of them well. And a smirk splits my face on seeing them.

"I might get some fucking answers now," I allow, but Pybba is watching the new arrivals with shock on his face, and it's all I can do not to laugh out loud.

Fuck, my Aunt has really decided to stir the pot this time.

CHAPTER 12

"Tatberht, Siric, Leonath, Gardulf, Penda," I hail them all by name, beckoning them to join me, with a grin on my face as their mounts crest the bridge one at a time.

At my side, Pybba has stiffened, and he won't be the only one to view this development with unease bordering on anger.

My Aunt. She does things even I wouldn't even fucking consider, and then she just expects me to pick up the pieces. If I weren't so in awe of her, I might well be angry myself, but there's no point. What's done is done.

"My Lord King," Tatberht reaches me first, a stiff bow and then he slides from the back of his horse with only the most audible groan of tired muscles I've ever heard.

Behind him, the others diplomatically take their time to join him, and I envelop him in a huge embrace.

"What the fuck are you doing here, you daft bastard?" Tatberht is older even than Icel was, the knowledge threatening to remove my good cheer at seeing him. But a reminder, if I needed one, that he's put away his sword and seax, and has spent the best part of the last two years warming his feet, or his arse, before the fire in my Aunt's hall. It's really my hall, but I'll never dare lay claim to it while she lives.

I don't think the two like each other, but I might be wrong. Still, I can't believe my Aunt cruel enough to send an older man to his probable death.

"I insisted, I insisted," he counters my complaint, the force of his hand smacking my back almost knocking the wind from me. "She said no, and I said yes, and it all would have become quite nasty, but I rode out early and then she couldn't fucking stop me."

Tatberht pulls back from me, a wink in his milky left eye.

"I was missing all the damn fun." Only then his eye rests on the men bringing the bodies clear from the massacre in the hall, and he falters a little. "It seems I still am," he laughs, and I grin at him.

"You know me, always finding someone new to kill."

"Aye, well, I've come to try my luck as well. Maybe for the last time, but someone needed to show these four clart-headed bastards how to behave with the bloody ealdorman." This he speaks more softly, but not quietly enough that Ealdorman Ælhun doesn't overhear, and stiffen at the words. I would laugh again, but I'm trying to learn some tact. My Aunt would say it was too late in life, but I labour all the same. I like to surprise her sometimes.

"Hereman will be pleased to see you," I confirm. "Rudolf as well." I don't mention Wulfhere. I want Tatberht to be surprised when he sees his grandson. Rudolf is not his grandson, but he may as well have been. Tatberht certainly lavished his time equally on the two boys when they were young.

Tatberht's hair has long ago turned entirely white. I've never seen so much hair on a man of his age, and never one haloed as he is. His left eye turned milky just before he asked to be excused from riding with me, and now only a single blue eye peers at me, from behind heavily furrowed eyebrows, and cheeks that threaten to spill down his neck. He's an older man, but a well-trusted one, and fuck, it's good to see him.

"And where's that foul-mouthed old git, Wulfred?"

"Here, you daft old bastard," and then Wulfred and Tatberht embrace as well, and before I can ask Tatberht for more information, the two are walking away, the mount trailing behind them with all the good grace of long years of experience. The two are well-suited.

"My Lord King," I've not seen Siric since before I was declared a king. I listen to the surprise in his voice at addressing me in such a way.

"No one calls him that," Pybba says, his lips downcast. I doubt he's been able to look away from Penda throughout my greeting to Tatberht.

"My Lord," but the final word dies on Siric's full lips, the hint of amusement in his eyes as I shake my head.

"My men call me Coelwulf, as always. Unless there's someone around who needs impressing."

"Ah, well then, My Lord King. I need to impress a few of these young bucks," and he chuckles, his long neck thrown back, exposing the slithering white of an old wound. He shouldn't have survived such a cut. But he did, and Siric has been living on borrowed time ever since. And he knows it.

"I'll leave you to it," he offers, riding on to where Wulfred and Tatberht still make their slow way inside the settlement itself. My eyes are caught by movement across the bridge. I raise my hand to hail the family who owns the carts and has been feeding the horses inside Northampton. I want them to know there's nothing to fear, even as mounted, well-armed men, make the crossing.

"Coelwulf," Leonath took a wound at the beginning of the year that left him fighting the wound-rot, so pale with the fever that I could have taken him for a northman. My Aunt has clearly declared him fit enough to re-join my ranks of men. That pleases me. I could do with a man of his quick-thinking and reasoning.

"Leonath. It's good to see you. Has she finally released you?"

He rolls his brown eyes at my words.

"I thank her for saving my life. But all the same. I've been hale for many weeks now." He sounds disgusted to have missed the fighting at Repton and Torksey.

"I wouldn't worry. There are Raiders here too. I'm sure you'll get the opportunity to slay a few of them, and probably sooner than you might think." Leonath nods, his missing front tooth just visible as he surveys Northampton through narrowed eyes. Behind him Penda and Gardulf wait, their mounts growing restless.

"Right, let's see what needs doing," Leonath moves away, and I turn to Gardulf.

He looks so like his father; it's a shock to find two eyes looking at me, rather than just the one.

The youth is not my greatest supporter. I can tell from the upturn of his chin that he thinks this all somehow beneath him. I don't hold it against Gardulf. He's old enough to remember my brother and my brother adored his friend's only son. In Gardulf's eyes, I see criticisms of every choice I've ever made. That I agree with him on many counts is the reason I tolerate the arrogant sod.

"Gardulf, well met," I stand clear, make my voice clipped. This is what he expects from me. With no one else, other than my Aunt, do I feel the need to be so formal and careful of my position.

"My Lord King," his voice is lighter than it should be. I knew, even before he spoke that he'd insist on calling me king. There's no chance that he'll even call me Coelwulf. In the past, I have always been 'lord' to him. His lord but not, in his eyes, a very fucking good one.

He says nothing further but moves into Northampton. I'm pleased that I won't have to witness his reunion with Edmund. It will not be pleasant. The two have a strained relationship. It's always been the same, or so Pybba has told me. Ever since Edmund appeared with the small child seated before him on his saddle one day well over a decade ago. Edmund acknowledges Gardulf as his child. I'm not sure Gardulf is as keen to return the acceptance.

But I will not meddle. Just like Edmund and Hereman, provided the bickering and unease don't get in the way of what needs doing, I'll tolerate them within my warband.

I open my mouth to welcome Penda, but Pybba is there before me, stepping close to the slight lad. Whatever passes between them, I don't hear, and indeed, would walk away from, only I can't. First, I watch Pybba stiffen on his horse and then whisper something furiously to his grandfather, and then I watch Penda's stance turn tight in response. Fuck. My Aunt has decided that my life isn't complicated enough as it is.

When Pybba strides beyond me, and back into Northampton, he's holding his right arm tightly in his left, and I know better than to speak to him.

I dredge a smile from somewhere for Penda. It's not his fault. He could hardly deny my Aunt. I can't deny my Aunt, and I'm the fucking king.

"Welcome to Northampton," I offer, swinging my hand behind me to indicate the settlement. For a moment, I think Penda is too caught up in the argument with Pybba to respond, only he shakes himself, almost jumps clear from his small horse, only to bow formally before me.

"My Lord King," Penda's voice thrums with the words, almost as powerful as Bishop Wærferth's and I consider again, as I so often do, why he wants to be a warrior and not a holy man, as my Aunt desires, and as his grandfather does.

"Call me Coelwulf," I retort, and his bright eyes meet mine, and he nods.

"As you will, Lord Coelwulf." And then he pauses. In the absence of words, I scrutinise him. Penda has the look of Pybba about him. It's not so much that he resembles the older man, but that he holds himself in the same way. There's no denying the family relationship.

"Your Aunt asked me to accompany the other warriors. She wanted you to know that events in Worcester are calm. The ealdormen are happy to comply with your leadership. Well, they appear to be. She's not sure what's happening with this Ealdorman Ælhun and his warrior. She bid me to tell you to be wary because they are secretive."

I laugh then, and grip his forearm and tug him into an embrace. Penda looks as though he's going to refuse but then allows the familiarity. I could crush him if I wanted to.

"We need to work on feeding you," I tease, stepping back to examine him more carefully.

"How old are you now?"

"Fifteen," he says the words with pride.

"Fuck, I remember being fifteen. It's a shit age," I laugh and he nods glumly.

"Yes, it is," and his eyes move behind me, no doubt watching Pybba, ruefully.

"And that's why my Aunt sent you?"

"Of course. She said no one would think I was the one entrusted with all the secrets. She said men only look for what they think will happen, not what's really happening. Then she said something about eyes, fools and noses. I'd stopped listening by then." Penda shrugs again, but his lips are turned upward, showing his amusement at my Aunt involving him in this. She certainly found herself a willing accomplice.

"Now that you're here, you must give me your oath that you won't get yourself killed. Your grandfather would never forgive me."

"I'll give you my oath, but not for him. For you, and Lady Cyneswith. She already made me give my oath on some holy relics that I wouldn't do anything, 'I might live to regret,' as she put it."

"It seems Lady Cyneswith is even wiser than I realised." I attempt to look severe but fail.

"Are the Welsh behaving?" I ask, instead. Inside the settlement, it's a hubbub of activity. The dead are still being dragged outside. We'll have to burn them or bury them. There's a lot of bodies. Not as many as Repton, or Torksey, but still a huge amount. I'm not prepared to tolerate that sort of stink from leaving them above ground.

"Seem to be. That Lord Cadell is quite keen on you. But who knows what his brother thinks. For now, yes, the Welsh are behaving, and the bridge is complete at Gloucester. Trade has resumed, and people are not quite prepared to kill the fuckers every time they encounter one of them."

"Fair enough." I can admit that it's better if there's trade and not war with the Welsh. I can only fight so many people at once. Damn the bastards. I wish they didn't share such a long border with us.

"And how did you get here so quickly?" I think to ask.

And now Penda grins again.

"She said you'd need us."

"Did she now?" I consider again what she suspects is about to happen. She's always been perceptive for all Kingsholm has been her home for so long, and she doesn't much like to leave it.

I would say more, but suddenly the air reverberates with violence, my hand reaching for my soiled seax as though Raiders are close.

"Took longer than I thought it would," Penda grins at me again, and I'd laugh along with him, but I've put it off for too long already. Or so it seems.

"Take my watch," Penda nods, turning to face across the bridge, but I'm already striding away.

There is no one, not a single person, who hasn't stopped what they're doing to gaze in shock at what's happening inside Northampton. Bloody Edmund. My bloody Aunt. Sometimes I think she doesn't actually fucking like me very much at all. I'm merely the rough clay she has to work with, and sometimes, she likes to check I won't fracture under too much heat.

A body unceremoniously flops on the floor, the two men who were carrying it, turning with eager eyes to find the source of the commotion.

Ingwald has the decency to try and wipe the smirk from his blood-smeared face when he sees me, but Oda has no such compunction.

"What's boiled his fucking piss?" Ingwald asks, but I decline to answer. It's not as though it's going to be hard to find out why Edmund is so incensed.

The words are on my lips to tell Ingwald and Oda to get back to it, only Edmund rears up before me, and it's all I can do to stop careering into him and knocking him to the ground.

"Was this your fucked-up plan all along?" As he speaks, Edmund jabs his finger against my chest, and I'm just surprised that it's not a blade there. It seems he's learnt some restraint after all.

I don't have the opportunity to reply before Edmund resumes his rant.

"Why, why would you even consider letting him come here? Why?"

His face is white, his remaining eye jittery in its socket, and when he spits his words at me, it's not only words that land, super-heated, onto my face.

Hereman ambles over to Edmund, and Gardulf is behind them all, watching his father's antics with a slight shrug of his shoulders. If he holds me in contempt, I daren't consider what his current thoughts are about his father.

Pybba is there as well, but it seems his attempts to prevent this from happening have failed.

"Is this to punish me? Is that what this cracked-pot idea is all about?" Still, Edmund seethes, only now he paces before me, three quick steps one way, and then three back again. His entire body quivers with fury, and again I consider the game my Aunt was playing when she sent the young lads this way. Siric and Leonath I can understand. Tatberht has made the decision himself. But Penda and Gardulf would have been safer at Kingsholm. She knows that. I know that.

Safer, but pent up and caged. Both lads should be riding with me. Gardulf is older than Rudolf, and Edmund has no problem with him being classed as one of my warriors. Likewise, Wulfhere is younger than Penda, and Pybba has no problem with that either. These older men and their relatives! To date, I've been sensitive to their needs. It seems my Aunt has decided that as king, I need to be less kind to my most loyal warriors.

"Have you fucking finished?" I demand, and before Edmund can pause to suck in another furious breath.

"No, no, I fucking haven't. I'm never going to be finished with this. Gardulf, get your arse back here, with that damn horse, and make your way back to fucking Kingsholm. I command it."

Gardulf's face pales at the words, and I give just the smallest shake of my head. He doesn't need to do that. It could well be more dangerous out on the roads than it is at Northampton. Edmund isn't thinking clearly.

By now, Ealdorman Ælhun has been summoned to the commotion, and he stands, hands resting on his weapons belt, as though he'll step in to kill my friend if needed. Wulfsige is there as well, and I could do without his self-assured smirk of amusement at such a show from Edmund.

"Gardulf," when I don't reply, Edmund hollers for his son again, but Pybba has wisely gone to him, and speaks quietly to the lad, managing to pull him away from the fracas. Why Pybba can see the error of Edmund's ways so clearly in regard to Gardulf, but not to his own grandson, I have no fucking idea.

I speak softly, hoping my tone will do more than the words I'm about to mutter. "It's beyond the time he rode with us. He's a fine warrior. Skilled and clever, quick on his feet."

Edmund's face somehow drains even further as I speak, and I can see him preparing to scream at me once more.

"Edmund, come, we'll talk about this away from the others." Only then does Edmund even seem to understand that he's the object of everyone's attention.

His eye settles on Ingwald and Oda.

"Get that bloody body out of here, you daft shits," he bellows at them, and both men jump, as though bollocked by their king. I've never seen them look quite so sheepish before.

"And the fucking rest of you," and Edmund includes Ealdorman Ælhun in that, and again, I think I'm not the right man to have been declared king.

Only then does Edmund meet my eyes once more.

"What's all this shit about?" he asks, the calmest he's been, which isn't that calm. Hereman still waits behind him, but others are slowly turning away to resume whatever it is they're supposed to be doing.

"Walk with me," I ask, and he nods, a glance over his shoulder assuring him that Gardulf is gone.

"He shouldn't be fucking here," Edmund flatly states when we're beyond the settlement, and walking alongside the riverbank. Behind me, the work of ensuring we truly hold Northampton is continuing apace. I'm the one who does the killing and the taking. What happens when a place once more belongs to Mercia is, I confess, only of so much interest to me.

"I didn't summon these men to come here." Edmund startles, and then looks at me, and barks a harsh croak of laughter.

"He's not a bloody man!"

"He is. And you know it. At his age, you were deemed a man."

"At his age, I was a fucking man," Edmund rumbles. I can see that he's desperately trying to keep hold of his temper. I'm not entirely convinced he's doing a good job of it.

"And so is he," I try, but Edmund shakes his head so violently, I almost think he'll trip over his feet.

"No. He's never stood in a shield wall. He's killed nothing other than a damn pig. He's not a man."

"And whose fucking fault is that?" I get the jibe in when Edmund pauses to consider another way of insulting his son.

"Whose fault! Whose fault? Well, it's not fucking mine."

I let that statement hang in the air. I'm not about to refute it. Not again. Edmund knows the truth too well, or he's not the man I think he is.

"He's a child," the strain is real, and I consider if I might feel the same if I had a son.

"He's a man," I reiterate the fact firmly, and without rancour. I owe this to Edmund.

"He's. He's." Amazingly words fail Edmund.

"A man, and he wants to make you proud and fight for Mercia. Would you deny him that chance?"

The accusation wounds Edmund. I can tell.

"Would you really want him to endure the humiliation of being shunned by the other men because his father won't let him earn battle-glory?"

Nothing but silence greets my question, although Edmund is opening and closing his mouth as though he wants to say something, but can't decide on the correct words.

Hereman finally catches us, while I pause and look out at the river, surveying it, and wondering once more why the fuck the Raiders didn't bring their damn ships here.

Edmund's gaze settles on him.

"Would you allow Gardulf to fucking fight, if he was yours?"

"Yes," Hereman pronounces quickly, as though surprised that Edmund needs even ask. "A man must fight for his kingdom. It's the way it is."

Once more, Edmund is stunned by the fresh betrayal, and I think he'll lash out at his brother. If he does, I decide, I'll tumble Edmund into the cold water beneath us. There's nothing like a cold dunking to make a man see sense.

I turn, offer Hereman my thanks with a twist of my lips, and then just wait, watching a duck and a fish annoy each other, the fish nibbling at the duck's feet. It hardly seems possible that it's still the same day as when we began our attack on Northampton.

Hereman agrees with my words to Edmund. I didn't think that he wouldn't. My Aunt has forced the situation. I hardly dare think what that might make him do when he next sees her. The two have shared some sort of relationship for many years. I've never pried to discover what that is. If they take pleasure in each other, then I have no problem with that. Equally, I know that Edmund has a wandering eye. I've kept that from my Aunt. I do have a problem with that.

These twisted paths of loyalty and honour we weave for those we care for never fails to amaze me.

I think Edmund will argue with me some more, but instead, he sighs and then begins to make his way back toward the interior of Northampton, his steps quick, almost a run. Whether he apologises to his son or not, there'll be words spoken between them.

"Crazy fucking bastard," Hereman complains. But he makes no move to follow his brother.

"Why is Gardulf here?" Hereman eventually asks, and I'm surprised that Edmund hasn't asked this.

"My Aunt sent him. It wasn't my decision," I admit. I know that Edmund will find this out eventually. He's going to be even angrier than he is now.

But Hereman surprises me by laughing.

"She warned him," he confesses, his large hands pressed against his torso as he chuckles. "She said she'd find a way to ensure Gardulf became a warrior when he refused to let him ride out last time. He'll be pissed when he realises that she's behind this."

"Well, if she warned him, then he only has himself to blame. Who is Gardulf's mother? Do you know?"

Hereman nods, although he doesn't meet my eyes.

"Oh, yes. I know who Gardulf's mother was. Pair of fucking fools that they were." But Hereman walks away from me, offering nothing further. I shrug my shoulders, peer at the water once more, and decide.

The chill of the water covering my body drives the air from my lungs, but when I surface, unsurprised to find Hereman has rushed to the side to make sure I'm well, I feel both cleaner and more alert than I have been for a few days.

"Take my things," I holler, and Hereman dutifully bends to collect my bundle of possessions that I've discarded, as I swim back to the bridge.

My strokes through the water are firm, my left foot every so often, breaking the surface.

It seems I've almost dealt with one of the awkward situations that my Aunt has sent me. Now, I just need to ensure Pybba, and Penda's disagreement is resolved as quickly, and then? Well then, I need only work out what Wulfsige is up to, and find the Raiders. Of course, amongst all this, I mustn't forget who the fucking real enemy is.

Northampton belongs to Mercia once more, but what Raider plans I've scuppered are as yet a mystery to me.

CHAPTER 13

"**B**loody hell, it always makes my fucking stomach rumble." I grin on hearing Rudolf's comment. He says it quietly, as though speaking to the leaping flames, but I hear it all the same.

"A good bit of crackling," I comment, bending low to speak into his ear. He startles, and I arch an eyebrow at him.

It's dark out; only it's not. The flames from the funeral pyre leap high enough to illuminate the entirety of the bridge, and also the shadowed recesses of the woodlands beyond.

The men left behind, when the attack on Northampton took place, made their appearance as the last flickers of the very late summer day winked out, one moment light enough to see, the next too dark. The funeral pyre has come in handy. But yes, it does fucking stink.

"We should have burned them at the breach in the defences," I agree with Hereman's dire words, but the decision had already been made, and it was bad enough lugging the dead here, without moving them somewhere else afterwards.

"The four dead men we've staked out there will have to be enough of a warning."

While the majority of the dead are here, slowly browning and blackening under the advance of the flames, I did demand a small show of strength. It's not pleasant, and I insisted on helping with the task, but it is effective. And anyway, the fuckers are dead. It's not as though I left them there to die.

The work to reinforce the open gateway is already well underway. Wooden stakes are sticking up from the ground now, the points angled toward the east, and while the ditch is smaller than the one that runs everywhere else, there is at least a ditch. I'm going to close off any access to the east of Northampton. For the foreseeable future, everyone will have to arrive and leave via the small wooden bridge that spans the Nene and then move around Northampton to where the water level drops. It's not a ford. Everyone is going to get bloody wet in the process.

In time, I'm going to have the waterway blocked. I just need a few ships to complete the task, and they're still missing from Northampton, just the two remaining, alongside the small fishing boat.

Rudolf almost moans with anticipation at my words, and I chuckle again.

"You only just bloody ate," I roll my eyes at Rudolf.

"You always say that we should eat when we get the opportunity. Who knows when I might get that fucking chance again? We could be attacked in the night. Who knows?"

While Rudolf jokes, his words have the opposite effect on me, and I feel a slither of trepidation. Maybe we will be attacked tonight? Certainly, the funeral pyre advertises our presence far and wide.

"Then help yourself to some more," but I'm walking away, suddenly keen not to witness this mass burning, but rather to check the provisions that have been put in place.

First, I walk to the wooden bridge. The river is sluggish beneath it. I can hear it oozing and sucking, and my mind immediately equates the sound to that of a man extracting the marrow from a bone. The thought is far from pleasant.

I have my men on guard at the bridge. And there are six of them. Such a number looks ludicrous. Not that any of them are complaining. And amongst their number is Gardulf. He eyes me squarely as I examine the lot of them.

"You have everything you need?" this I direct at Wærwulf, who, for the time being, seems to be the most senior of my men on guard duty. Gardulf is something of a spare. I've given him such a post in the hope that Edmund won't rail at such a responsibility and yet Gardulf will feel as though he's been tasked with something meaningful. I really don't think I should be stretching my rule over them in such a way, but while I can, I'll be as sensitive as I can about everyone's bruised pride.

"Aye. We're set. Tell Tatberht he and the rest will need thick cloaks. It's getting cool out here." I nod and meet the eyes of the others, Gyrth, Osbert, Beornstan and Penda. I'm not sure what's been said between Penda and his grandfather. The lad looks happy enough, though, and I'm pleased not to have to interfere in another family argument.

"Be wary and be alert. Anything strange happens, rouse everyone. Anything. Even if it's just a cow farting in the meadow." I nod toward the homestead of the farmer who provides the hay for the horses. He also has several livestock, and the sound of them can be heard, even across the river. No wonder the animals stink so much. I'm surprised he's not slaughtered them yet to tide his family over the coming long winter.

Wærwulf cracks a smile but grunts his agreement.

"It'll be a quiet night," he assures me, as I slap him on the back and make my way inside the settlement itself. I want to visit the empty gateway at the rear, but Ealdorman Ælhun intercepts me. Tiredness rims his eyes, and I'm not surprised. He and his men made the journey quickly. While the youngsters have had no problem sitting in a saddle all day long, the older men are aching and exhausted.

"We found someone," this surprises me, I'm sure that Northampton has been searched, even under floorboards and beneath the raised grain stores, the Mercians who survived the attack, keen to reveal all of Northampton's secrets.

"Fuck, how did we miss them?"

"It's not really surprising when you see where she was trapped."

Perplexed, I follow the ealdorman into the great hall. The stench of blood, piss and death has been largely removed, although there are some stains that might never be scrubbed away. The fire has been burning all day, herbs routinely thrown on it to sweeten the smell of both the dead and the living.

Beside the fire, a small group seems to sit in a loose circle, and I step toward them.

"No, this way first," and Ealdorman Ælhun nods his head toward a doorway, no doubt a bed-chamber behind it.

"We've been in there."

"Yes, we all have. But there was something we didn't see."

"Show me."

"Watch your step."

Stepping into the room, I'm amazed to find the floorboards missing almost directly inside the doorway. Ealdorman Ælhun has a candle in his hand, and he bends, holding it low.

"Fucking bastards." There's a hole, it can't be called anything but that, and it stinks, of misery and bodily waste, the scent beyond unpleasant.

"What's that?" I ask, pointing to a bundle of what seems to be rags.

"A dead baby."

"Bastards."

"Indeed. But go carefully with her."

I nod, already realising that I can't direct my fury at her.

"How long has she been in there?" I ask, but Ealdorman Ælhun shrugs his shoulders as he follows me back into the hall itself.

The circle of men has fallen back, and I'm unsurprised to find both Rudolf and Pybba guarding the woman, Rudolf with a fierce glow in his eyes that tells me, even if I didn't already know, that he's never encountered such before. It might break him. I hope it doesn't.

The light is weak, but the woman's paleness gleams as though she's risen from the dead. It speaks of her confinement, and I'm forced to reconsider what I think I know about Northampton. It seems the Raiders have been here for longer than I thought. It seems they aren't survivors from Torksey or Repton.

"My Lady," I speak softly, and still she jumps, her hands

are tight claws bound into the tatters of dress that cover her scratched, filthy legs. She has a thick cloak around her shoulders, and still, she trembles. Her eyes aren't the wide, terrified ones I might expect to encounter. Instead, the haze of chestnut in them is dull. This woman has endured much.

Her chin wobbles, and when she speaks her voice is rough from disuse.

"My Lord King." Just saying that seems to exhaust her, and I can feel Rudolf's glare. He wants me to shut up and leave the woman alone. I would if I could. But the Raiders are all dead, and she might know more than even Wærwulf was able to discover.

"Have you eaten?" I ask, as kindly as I can. I don't know where to put myself. If I stand, I tower over her. If I sit, I'll be too close.

In the end, I hook a bench and bring it close enough that I can see her well, but not that I can reach out and touch her. It scraped over the floor, and her shaking intensified. I curse my foolishness.

"Yes, I have."

"Good." I pause then, peering into the fire, wishing for some sort of inspiration. I have hard questions to ask, but I don't want to ask them.

"They took me prisoner at Torksey," the woman offers. "They've kept me ever since. Hidden away, out of sight, and since our arrival here, beneath the wooden floorboards. He wanted the child, but it was born too soon, and died." The hesitation in the words makes me thinks that might not be quite the correct sequence of events, but my Aunt would warn me about interrogating her further.

"What's your name?" It seems I should know this.

"Werburg," she offers, and suddenly I know who she is. I cast a wide-eyed glance at Ealdorman Ælhun, and he nods in agreement.

"Fuck, you're Ealdorman Wulfstan's daughter."

Now, and despite all the muck, she appears regal. Her head is high, her neck arched, and I'm going to have to tell her that I killed her father. The treasonous fuck. Although maybe not.

Maybe he had no choice. And that's not all; her brother is dead as well. Fuck. Ealdorman Ælhun could have warned me.

"I am yes. Werburg, daughter of Ealdorman Wulfstan, although they told me he was dead. Is that true?" I can't tell whether she hopes he is or not because her tone is flat.

"Yes, he's dead." I hesitate but realise there's no point in denying the truth. "I killed him."

Those eyes are suddenly sharp, and I realise how she's survived her ordeal. She's brave, far braver than I am.

"Then, he is dead. And Jarl Sigurd will have gained nothing from his union with my father, or with me." That seems to satisfy her, and her hands unclench as Rudolf hands her a beaker of water. He fairly glows with his desire to protect her. I doubt she'd welcome knowing she elicits such concern from one of my warriors.

"But Jarl Sigurd is dead. So, who kept you here?"

"His brother. He thought to use the child to claim the Mercian lands of my father."

"And he's dead?"

"I thought all the men were dead."

"They were if they were in Northampton this morning."

"Then he's fucking dead," there's a slither of satisfaction in the announcement.

"They burn. Outside, if you wish to see."

Again, I feel the appraisal in those eyes. It seems that Werburg is a woman made of the same iron and ice that thrums through my Aunt. Without such women, where would we men be?

"I will watch."

"Shall I escort you?"

"No, I'll have Rudolf and Pybba. They'll ensure I'm well protected."

"One more thing," but I think Werburg already knows.

"Ealdorman Ælhun told me of my brother's death. He wasn't always a good brother, but he was a loyal Mercian." I incline my head to hear the pride in her voice. I'm pleased she has a relative she doesn't detest.

I stand to move aside. I've not asked why she didn't call out for help. I think I know the answer.

Werburg surprises me by speaking again, her words soft, a little urgent, but really just relieved to share her secret. "They plan to take Mercia from the east now, not from the north. The three jarls, Guthrum, Oscetel and Anwend have designs on building and reinforcing such places as this. This is only the beginning for them. But, most of the Raiders are at Grantabridge, or still at Lena in East Anglia. They're more cautious than Jarl Halfdan."

"Then Halfdan is not amongst their number."

"No. No, Halfdan is not." And I nod and move aside so that she can stand, on only slightly wobbly legs, and walk outside. Only, as I watch her go, she veers back toward the room where she's been kept as a captive. I swallow heavily. I know her intentions.

I turn to Pybba, and he grimly meets my gaze, his remaining hand grabbing hold of Rudolf so that he doesn't follow the woman inside. His touch lingers, despite Rudolf's attempt to shake him loose, and then Werburg appears, the bundle in her arms.

I see the shudder run over Rudolf's body, but I can't turn my eyes away from Werburg. I imagine I know what she wants to do. I imagine it will give her the sort of end to this matter that she needs, but it will not be easy for Rudolf to witness. I almost move to intercept her, but she stalks from the room, chin high, no longer the frightened creature I spoke to only moments ago.

I have to allow her to do what she must, even as I taste ash in my mouth, and witness Rudolf's horrified glance.

Such cruelty on the part of the Raiders will spark fury amongst my warriors. They're fucking brutal and bloody men, but they owe their oath just as much to my Aunt as they do to me. They're not for allowing such pitiless suffering to happen to any woman of Mercia. And Werburg has been treated viciously, kept merely for the baby growing in her belly, the bastard child that she now means to consign to the flames along with its dead Uncle.

Ealdorman Ælhun joins me. His face was worried before Werburg spoke. Now it seems horrified. I've already decided hers might be the voice that the messenger who rushed to Worcester, heard. It makes perfect sense. Icel was never here. Icel is as dead as the child Werburg has murdered.

"They don't plan on leaving then?" Ealdorman Ælhun asks once Werburg has departed the room and the heavy silence has started to lift. Although the question seems superfluous, I accept that he needs to hear me say it.

"No, they're not fucking leaving. They mean to change tactics."

"So, what will you do?" Ealdorman Ælhun demands to know, and across the fire, I see Edmund watching me closely, his one eye daring me.

"We change tactics as well. There's always more than one way to kill a man. We just need to think a little differently."

Although I feel unease deep inside me at the daunting task given to me, I also understand that the current ealdormen and bishops would have no response for the Raiders. It seems as though I must be the one to banish the infestation.

I'll just have to fucking get on with it then.

Ealdorman Ælhun is far from pleased with the task I give him.

"You can ride further east, if you'd prefer," I don't mock him with the words. It's just a simple statement. He can reinforce Northampton, or he can head toward Grantabridge, and maybe even Lena, although even I would find it challenging to call Lena Mercian. Not that it's necessarily East Anglian either. I won't admit it's entirely fallen to the Raiders, though. It's far too close to Mercia for comfort. And one thing is perfectly clear to me, the fucking Raiders are not the Welsh, to ebb and flow, to be allies or enemies depending on little more than the way the wind blows. There's honour amongst the Welsh and the Mercians. It's missing between the Raiders and the Mercians.

Ealdorman Ælhun looks pained. The task is not a small one. But neither will it necessarily risk his life.

"But you're the king; you should not be riding to war." I can understand why he speaks as he does.

"King Burgred didn't ride to war but relied on his warriors. And look what it gave him? The Raiders don't respect kings who are unprepared to kill. They think them weak."

Ealdorman Ælhun's mouth opens and then snaps closed again, resolve replacing the indecision.

"I'll do as you command." It was never really an option to decline, but I dip my head all the same in acknowledgement.

"Excellent. Do everything that I told you to do." I don't like having to rely on another to ensure all is done as I demand. But I can't be in two places at once, let alone the three or four that I would need to in order to fulfil my intentions.

As I ride through the almost complete rebuild of the open gateway, beyond the bodies that still hang from their makeshift crosses, flesh all blackened and eyes picked away by the birds, I hazard a glance behind me.

The ditch is now whole, as deep as the other parts, and the entire thing has been dredged clear of the filth of two decades. In the place of dead animals, discarded pots and any other shit people have thought to fling into it, tapered spikes lie hidden, just waiting for the Raiders to spear themselves on.

Above the rampart, a wooden platform is starting to take shape. It will allow men to watch the east, to ensure no one attempts to attack by stealth.

To the front of Northampton, out of sight, the rampart now runs to the water's edge, and again, a ditch is once more deep enough to prevent easy access. If people want to take a ship along the Nene to reach Northampton, they'll find no easy places to climb ashore. Even the wooden bridge has been reinforced. Ealdorman Ælhun's men will guard it from the side of Northampton, a thick gateway nestling there now, only to be opened when sure of the person asking for admittance. Along the length of the bridge, a few surprises have been placed that few know.

I'm not convinced that Northampton is invincible to attack, but it's much better defended than it was before. And to think, if the Raiders hadn't begun the work, I might not have considered continuing it. Damn fuckers have only themselves to blame.

Werburg has been taken to my Aunt, by a contingent of eight of my men, Rudolf and Pybba amongst them. They returned only yesterday with reassuring news of the peace in the rest of Mercia, and with their other task completed.

Now, Rudolf and Pybba ride with me, as do Penda and Gardulf, and the majority of my loyal warriors. We've been in Northampton for over ten days, and winter advances apace. Each night is colder than the one before, and the ground is growing hard and unforgiving. The sound of hooves rings loudly.

Tatberht took little persuasion to remain behind in Northampton, alongside Ælfgar. The two men are to ensure Ealdorman Ælhun performs as I expect him to. They know what to do if there are problems. I think the task I give them requires more bravery than hunting down Raiders.

Edmund is far from reconciled to allowing Gardulf to join us. It's not by chance that Gardulf rides to the rear, with Pybba and Hereman, whereas I keep Edmund close to me.

Beneath me, Haden is pleased to be free from the cluttered stables. I can tell in the jaunty steps along the hard trackway. We're going to find the Raiders. Again. It seems he's as delighted as I am.

"I don't know why we don't just fucking wait for them," Edmund is slacking his frustration about Gardulf by plaguing me about the decisions I've made. No one else, apart from Rudolf, would be as comfortable questioning me.

He's only just stopped complaining that I didn't send Gardulf back to Kingsholm when I had the chance. Now, he wants to moan about something else.

"I don't want to fucking sit and wait for them. They probably don't even know that Northampton is lost to them."

Edmund sucks his lower lip, his eyebrow arched.

"What, you don't think the fucking great big banner is giving it away?"

Edmund has a fair point, but I'm not about to concede.

My Aunt has somehow constructed a banner that's longer

than three horses and taller than two, proudly depicting the two-headed eagle of Mercia in bright golden and red stitching. The linen has been bleached the starkest white I've ever seen, and I think it must be visible from Repton. Rudolf presented it to me on his return, almost reverentially, even including a bow. I think he'd have gone down on one knee if he could. I imagine my Aunt was severe with him about the responsibility she entrusted to him.

"Only if someone comes this way to see it," I complain back at him. Haden's ear twitches at being in such proximity to Edmund's mount. Edmund might have been pleased to ride his horse once more, giving up Icel's in the process, but Haden certainly preferred Samson. I think I agree with him. Jethson is as unsettled as his rider, more likely to go fucking backwards than forwards.

"The survivor must have made it to them by now, surely?"

"Maybe, if he lived. He might have fucking died along the way."

Edmund's silence tells me that he can't argue with my logic on this occasion. I decide to enjoy the brief triumph.

PART 2

CHAPTER 14

My seax slices through the neck without so much as a whimper from the dying man. I lay him back down with more reverence than I treated him when he lived. Silence is key. And my men and I are not ones for being fucking quiet.

The whisper of feet over the crisp leaf litter carpeting the floor seems too loud, and yet not one stirs from their slumbers. Cocky fuckers.

The guard was easy to kill. A tossed stone saw him stumble from his poorly concealed hiding place beneath a huge rock to the side of the trackway. It was easy to sneak my hand around his mouth and over his nose, cutting off his air, even though he buckled and gasped beneath me, realising in those final moments that he wasn't quite as fucking clever as he thought.

Now he lies in that hiding place, the one he was so proud of finding. Damn fool. I could see him even with my eyesight. Edmund had spied him from a much greater distance, his single eye just as keen as when he still owned two.

There are eleven of them, surrounding a slowly dissipating fire. The nights have been cold of late. Even I'm pleased to pull my cloak tightly around me, and I usually toss it aside. The scent of winter is ripe in the morning, and the evening, with the promise of the dark times to come, and with each new day, there's a dragging realisation that the Raiders will not be banished before winter.

And yet. I won't give up, not yet.

We've been watching the settlement at Grantabridge for the last few days. I've observed warriors come and go with almost no regard for their safety. This must have been what it was like at Repton, before I arrived, with the might of Mercia behind me.

Despite being chased from Repton, and then from Torksey, the Raiders remain confident of success. That knowledge has seared itself into my very being.

It's evident that the lone survivor from Northampton didn't live to return to Grantabridge. If he had, these desultory scouting parties would be more alert. I'm surprised they even bothered to leave someone on watch, many of the other parties haven't. But if my scheme is to work, I need the Raiders to know they've been discovered.

"Is everybody dead?" I call softly.

A chorus of 'yes's' greets my question. There are fourteen of us, including Edmund and I. Hereman, Lyfing, Gyrth, Sæbald, Ordheah, Ingwald, Goda, Wærwulf, Eahric, Osbert, Wulfred, and Eoppa, have made quick kills. I've chosen them because I'm keen to have all of my men used to warring with each other again. We've been divided too many times of late.

"Good."

I move to the guttering fire and throw some of the browned leaves onto the glowing embers. Immediately, flames spring skyward, and Edmund drags one of the still-warm bodies close. We need our attack to be noticed. We need the Raiders to grow concerned enough that they seek us out in the vast landscape.

I'm not going to take my warriors across the wide river to the settlement at Grantabridge itself. As much as I want the Raiders gone, I know that would only be inviting our deaths, and none of us is ready for that. Far from it.

As Edmund unceremoniously dumps the head of the dead man in the resurgent fire, flames lick along hair that gleams darkly in the night. An inferno of sparks erupts.

"Fuck," Edmund prances backwards, caught by surprise. I'm always amazed by just how quickly hair disappears with the application of flame.

"Bring the others closer." We position them, like spokes on a wheel, around the flaming body, and only then do we slither back into the trees, the destruction in our wake the only thing to show that we've ever been there.

Grantabridge would just be visible from our position if it weren't night. It should take little time for the scouting party to be missed, and not much longer until someone with half a brain begins to make some connection between the missing men and the brightly burning flames, glimpsed during the night.

I need to entice the bastards across the river. I need them to give up their position of strength. If this isn't enough to do so, then I'll continue, until the jarls inside Grantabridge appreciate that every war band they send over the river is never going to come home.

I'm not used to such a slow means of bringing about an altercation between the Mercians and the Raiders.

"Right, let's get back to the rest of the men. Gather most of the mounts," I instruct. I'd like to linger to see if our provocative attack brings an immediate response, but we need to stay hidden. Reluctantly, I follow my order.

We find Siric and Leonath where we left them, hands on weapons belts, ready to defend the rest of the warriors if needed.

"Eagle," I whisper when I deem I'm close enough for the pair to hear. Although it's dark, I see Siric startle and then relax, the dim moon just catching the iron rivets on his byrnie.

"You've been longer than I thought," Leonath complains as I pass him.

"It took as long as it fucking took. The bastards are dead, that's what matters. Have you seen anyone?" I demand to know.

"No, all quiet, apart from the fucking snoring." I pause, and I can hear the grunts of those we left sleeping.

"Well done. I'll relieve you," I offer. "Get some sleep," I instruct them both. I'm too alert to sleep. I know I'll regret it tomorrow, but for now, I want to be the one guarding my warriors.

Hereman settles beside me, and I allow it, as the rest of the men troop inside our shelter. It's far better hidden than the one the Raiders we just killed used, for all it's in the open. We have no fire to draw watching eyes to us, but I don't need one, not with my blood running hot.

"It won't be enough," Hereman offers. His tone is bland. I don't know whether he approves of our skulking around or not.

I sigh heavily.

"No, it won't, but we have to force the bastards out. Tomorrow we'll probably have to do the same again; only the next scouting party will be a little more alert."

"And the next one after that."

"I agree, but we can't go into Grantabridge ourselves. It's not like Torksey or Repton. It's much bigger, and it appears as though they've learned some valuable lessons from events in those two places."

"They're still on a fucking river," Hereman mutters sullenly, not quite prepared to agree with me. Not yet.

"And we're on the other side of it, and we don't have a damn ship. And they have many ships." It brings me some relief to know that I've found the damn missing ships. Finally.

Silence falls between us, broken only by the farting and snorting of the sleeping warriors. I find myself smiling at the night time noises, just waiting for some sort of dispute to break out. It normally does.

"We'll just have to make it fucking work," Hereman eventually offers, and I grin even wider. If Hereman agrees with me, then my plans might just be fucking crazy enough to actually work.

I don't hear the fury of the Raiders who find the dead bodies, but I witness it all the same. I'm hidden from sight; once more, my eyes trained on Grantabridge. All morning, I've been tracking the comings and goings across the heavily guarded bridge.

In return, I've been sending off groups of men to follow the Raiders who leave and return at random intervals. The first group of Raiders to return, seem to flee across the vast expanse of land before us, the ancient woodlands cleared, and now littered with saplings. I find myself shaking my head at the poor riding skills of the Raiders. I never fail to be surprised by the lack of expertise. How they don't all fall to their deaths, owes more to blind luck than anything else.

There's a small bridge spanning the river, not much wider than a horse's backside. I'm sure it's built from redeployed pieces of ship timber, but I can't get close enough to be sure. I'm not about to ask Edmund to confirm my suspicions. He still seethes about Gardulf, and I refuse to give him an opening to start all over again.

The lead rider almost ploughs into the five people guarding the end of the bridge in his rush to reach Grantabridge. Others come more slowly, leading back the few horses that we left with the dead. I didn't want to leave too many. There are slumped shapes over the backs of the horses, and I appreciate that they've brought back the dead from the macabre circle we created. I hope they were disturbed by the careful placement of the bodies.

Yet, no matter the entreaties of the lead warrior, the five guards won't allow him and his men to cross the bridge. I wait, hand resting on my seax, to see what will happen next. Weapons are raised to prevent the lead horseman, and the animal shies away from the threat there, almost toppling the man. The ire pours from the rider.

I want the Raiders to be more than pissed off. I want them to be furious, but as Hereman said, it's going to take more than just one attack.

"What the fuck are they doing?" Edmund asks the question, and I shrug my shoulders, although he doesn't turn away from watching our enemy. If he can't see, then how he expects me to know, I've got no fucking idea.

I bite my lip. I'm willing one of the jarls to make an appearance. I hope that something about their stance will make it evident that they're in overall command of the Raiders. I doubt we're close enough for Edmund to make out individual features, but to know that the jarls are there will reassure me that I'm in the right place.

"Someone's coming," Edmund informs, and even though I'm watching the bridge before me, I blink, realising that I've been looking without seeing.

"It must be one of the jarls."

"Which one?" I'm impatient to know.

Edmund falls silent, concentrating, as I watch a handful of warriors from the far side of the river make their way to the bridge across an expanse of withering green grasses. The guards still won't allow the man and the dead to step foot on the bridge. I take this to mean that, despite all appearances to the contrary, they are wary in their endeavours. It brings me only a small amount of satisfaction.

"It's a snake, I'm sure of it," Edmund announces, and then he turns to look at me, when I make no remark, meeting my blank stare.

"The sigil is a snake," he sighs. "Jarl Oscetel."

"Oscetel?" This surprises me, although I'm unsure why. Werburg said the three jarls were together.

"The one with the fucking serpent on his face." Edmund's words immediately remove me to that day when my life was in the hands of my warriors, and the Raiders. I shudder, and Edmund turns aside, as though he can't stand to see my weakness. Damn the fucker. He always expects too much from me.

Not that I don't from him.

"What are they saying?" I realise the stupidity of the question as soon as I speak it.

"What does it look like's happening?" I quickly ask before Edmund can round on me.

"It looks like some stupid bastards are talking. A bit like here," Edmund offers in a quieter voice, easy enough to hear all the same.

"They're letting them cross the bridge." This I can see, but Edmund has turned his head slightly, blocking my view, and I wish I could see beyond him, but I don't possess the skill to look through people. Neither can I risk moving and having our hiding place discovered just because I'm impatient. Men and women who are overly alert are likely to spot even the smallest of movements.

"They're getting ready to ride out."

"Good," this is what I want to happen. I want as many of the fuckers out looking for the people who murdered their comrades as possible. The more of them who leave Grantabridge, the more we can fucking kill when they don't have a ditch and embankment to keep them safe.

"I would say another forty, maybe fifty."

"So many?"

"Yes," and Edmund hastily crouches down, his back to the stone we've found to hunker beside. We're to the far right of the bridge, hidden in the thick woodlands that carpet the landscape. Beneath the trees, there are a hundred or more beaten trackways. It's easy to get lost.

"What?" I follow him in hiding, just in case Edmund thinks he's been seen.

But Edmund's face has grown pale, and his breathing too fast.

"What is it?" I demand to know, although I have my suspicions. I've not shared with him my belief that the messenger at Worcester spoke of Werburg and he carries his hope that Icel still lives, heavily.

"Nothing, nothing," Edmund coughs, and presses his back against the stone, lifting his body higher, before he turns to look toward Grantabridge once more.

"Don't look for things that aren't fucking there," I caution him, a hand on his shoulder, but he shakes me loose.

"Forty men are forming up on this side of the river. It looks as though Jarl Oscetel is going to lead them out."

This is more than I'd hoped.

"Really?" I demand to know.

"No, I just said it for the fucking sake of it. Yes, forty of them. I've counted them. They're going to head west, probably to scout last night's camp."

"Good." This is what I want to happen. I ignore Edmund's aggrieved tone. I spare a thought for those of my warriors who've been hidden away for much of the morning, just on the possibility that this might happen. I hope Hereman has found some patience.

"No. Wait." Edmund's voice is suddenly urgent.

"What now?" I turn to glare at the collection of men and horses.

"Jarl Oscetel is riding back across the bridge."

"Ah well, we'll just have to kill whoever he sends," I shrug. Ideally, I wanted to snare one of the jarls early on. But if we can't, then we can't. There'll be time.

"Yes, definitely, Jarl Oscetel has gone back across the bridge."

"Then we'll kill the fucking rest of them," I announce, pleased that some of my hopes are going to be realised.

I want to be with my warriors, not here, hiding behind a rock.

"Come on," I urge Edmund, edging back to where Haden and Jethson have been waiting for us, with Wulfhere to ensure they don't fight each other without us there to keep them in order.

"Wait, wait," Edmund still advocates caution, and I grow impatient. It wasn't my intention that my warriors should face the Raiders alone.

"What is it now?" I try to keep my voice low, but the frustration thrums through it, making it louder than it should be.

"I was just...." But his voice trails off.

"Edmund, come the fuck on. We need to be with the others."

I place my hand on his shoulder, prepared to pull him away if I need to, but abruptly he peels himself away from our place of concealment. And then we're scampering through the woodlands, desperate to get back to the horses, and Wulfhere.

A determined Wulfhere greets me as we crash through the undergrowth, all thoughts of silence forgotten about in the rush to be back. He stands before the three horses, his hands on a seax, although Haden chews contentedly on grass roots. The relief on Wulfhere's face when he recognises us undoes all his honourable intentions.

"Come on. We need to be gone from here."

Wulfhere has slowly watched the collection of horses and

THE LAST HORSE

warriors drain away. We began this morning with twelve men and thirteen horses. Now there's only him.

"Is it happening?" Wulfhere asks slightly breathlessly.

"Yes, come on. Fewer questions, more fucking haste."

I mount Haden easily and then turn to aim him along the trackway we forged. I feel as though all I've done for days is shove a path through unyielding tree branches. On this occasion, I'm grateful that the majority of branches have been broken already and that there's a reasonably straightforward path to see. Not that I can force Haden to high speed over the rugged ground, but as we know where we're going, having beaten the path between our two hiding places, and the Raiders don't, I believe we can still arrive before they do.

At least, I fucking hope we can.

A slither of worry, compels me to encourage Haden too eagerly, and he repays me with a stubborn refusal to hurry.

"You damn brut," I complain to him, only Wulfhere has realised my problem, and pushes his horse in front of Haden. And of course, the huge piebald cob doesn't appreciate that at all. We quickly catch Wulfhere and then thunder beyond him. Wulfhere's smirk of happiness amuses me, even as I worry for my other warriors.

It's not been easy to divide my men. Not when every task is likely to bring about bloodshed and peril. But, I've cast my concerns aside. This is what drives them. They live for this. This is why they're my warriors and not some bloody ealdorman's. And, it's only been for the length of today.

Quickly, I retrace my earlier path, keen to seek out the markers that assure me I'm going the correct way. The broken and twisted fallen tree with moss growing along its length reassures me that I am, as we ride higher and higher into the surrounding hills. When we come upon the pile of stones, whether natural or there by design I don't know, Haden's ear pricks and only a moment later, I hear it as well.

"Stay here," I leap from Haden's saddle, Edmund doing the same, and try not to notice the disappointment on Wulfhere's

155

face. He knew he wasn't going to get to fight. But it seems there was hope all the same.

The Raiders are far from quiet. I can tell exactly where they are, and I quickly realise that thanks to Haden's delaying tactics, I'm not going to reach the disturbed campsite before the Raiders do.

"Shit," I turn to Edmund, but he makes no move to stop.

"We'll do what we can from the back," he puffs, and I appreciate his keenness.

"Wouldn't be the first time," I grunt, crouching low once more to avoid the low hanging branch, heavy with pine cones. Below, I can see the campsite we infiltrated last night. The bodies have all been removed, well, apart from those that burned almost enough to crumble away to nothing more than ash. They're visible as pale outlines amongst the brown leaves.

A thunder of hooves, and a man I don't recognise, reins in his mount. It seems he has more skill than some of the others, who jostle around, some horses almost riding into others. Damn fools. It boils my piss that the riders have such fine horses, and yet possess such little skill.

My warriors are hiding amongst the deep undergrowth and low-hanging branches to the far side of the camp, and even I can't see them, and I know where they are. They've been forced to wait, while the dead were found and taken away. I can only imagine how impatient they are, especially Hereman.

The man, who seems to lead, jumps from his horse's back and bends to run his hands through the ashes of the fire, dropping it quickly as though singed by flames.

"It's still hot," he exclaims. I know then that he's not the most intelligent of men. Of course, it's still hot. The fire would have barely burned itself out from the bright flames that devoured the bodies the previous night.

"Spread out, look for any sign of who did this."

He snaps the instruction to the horsemen, but only a handful of them lower themselves to follow the command. The rest look around, uneasy, staying where they are, crowded as close as they can to the bloodied campsite, while also staying far from it. There's a beaten track here, leading through the thick trees both to the east and to the west.

"Sigtryggr, Avarr, ride on. Gofrith, Bar∂r, watch our backs."

They're right to be wary, but they're not looking in the right places.

By then, I've managed to catch sight of Hereman. He nods, little more than his eyes visible from the treeline, as I try and caution him to bide his time with only my stance.

The Raiders are already jumpy. The mounts shuffle backwards and forward beneath them, and when we finally attack, we'll have the advantage of speed and not the encumbrance of a horse. Wulfhere watches Haden and Jethson, and the others have hidden their mounts as well.

"Who did this?" the Raider mutters, and again, I think him far from clever. Who does he think did it? They're in a fucking enemy land. They've been beaten back more times than I can count.

He turns, to peer along the beaten trackway that they've been using since they came to Grantabridge. It leads to Ermine Street, and I consider whether the men we killed were planning to head to London, or back towards Torksey. Either option would be achievable from here.

Where does he think his enemy has come from?

I want to see what he does next, and I hope Hereman realises that. I want to kill them, but I also need to know what they fear. Maybe the Raiders at Grantabridge have more than one enemy. Perhaps I could find that other enemy, unite with them, and make the Mercians stronger.

Probably I won't.

The Mercians have forged alliances in the past with Wessex. They've not ended well.

Abruptly, the man decides, I can see it forming on his lips, and I want to hear what it is, but suddenly, a sharp snap fills the air.

"Shit."

And then Hereman and Ingwald surge from the undergrowth.

It's both the quietest attack I've ever seen, and also, the loudest.

The broken branch has enemy hands reaching for weapons, but too slowly, as though the Raiders expect the perpetrator to be one of their own. As though this had happened before and was little more than a false alarm,

"Fuck," but I'm surging upwards as well, my seax in hand, my other weapons where they need to be, should I need them. There's no need to check that they're still in place.

"*Angreb*," the leader bellows, using Danish for once, no doubt to ensure that everyone understands what he says.

And then I reach my first enemy. I appear from the opposite side to the rest of my men, Hereman and Ingwald joined by Eahric and Wulfstan, and the rest, who I can't yet see but that I know must be there. The horse realises I'm there before the rider, and it's almost too easy to reach up and yank the man down from the saddle.

He flails as he falls, eyes wide and his mouth open shock. As he hits the floor, the hand that had been reaching for his weapon is crushed beneath him. I stab downwards with my seax, making an effortless thrust through the join on his shoulder, down into his armpit.

Blood gushes, red and hot over my gloved hand, and he punches upwards, trying to break my nose. The attack is surprisingly forceful, although it hits my chin, and not my nose. And I punch as well, but my aim reaches its target with more force and far more easily.

He crumbles to the floor, and I step around him, to find my next target, sure that he's dead, all he needs to do is take his last breath.

Hereman, Ingwald and the rest of the men have caused a huge commotion to the side of me. But the Raiders further back, those still mounted, are only slowly realising what's happening. And they're my targets.

"Go backwards," I instruct Edmund, as his kill stills in death, the light in the man's eyes being extinguished as I watch.

The horse in front of the rider-less mount is uneasy, shuffling, trying to upend its rider, the smell of blood unsettling.

With the rider focused on his mount and the attack in front, it's almost too easy to pull him to the floor as well, my ruby blade stabbing downwards. He dies without even the promise of his hand reaching the blade that hangs uselessly on his weapons belt.

But the next horse is again rider-less, and I peer over its shoulders, eyes narrowed, seeking out my warriors. I can't be sure, but it appears as though seven of my men face eight or nine of the Raiders. The enemy must think they outnumber them as they attempt to counter the attack. And they do. Or rather, they would, if only the offence were better coordinated.

The sound of iron on iron, and iron on wood, as my warriors carry shields, chimes loudly in the tight clearing. I glance back to see Edmund busy about another kill. The riders at the back of the queue are becoming increasingly aware of what's happening on the thin track in front of them. The swish of a retreating horse's tail assures me that there'll be at least one survivor to tell of this slaughter.

Rushing between the two rider-less horses, I seek out the back of the first of the Raiders about to attack my men.

He's a broad man, equipped with leather byrnie but no helm. He's hammering his war axe against the shield of one of my men.

I grin, and raise my seax.

Only somehow, my intended opponent is aware of my movement. He turns, ignoring the offered shield, and his war axe is arcing through the air before I can even think of defending myself.

"Fuck," I try to move back, but one of the rider-less horses is right behind me, blocking my path.

"Fuck," and I reach for my sword, all the time knowing that it'll be in my hand too late to do any good.

The war axe my opponent hefts is massive, no doubt accounting for his broad shoulders. Even its haft is almost as thick as my wrist. If it hits me, it'll hurt. But that's not my immediate concern.

"Move, you daft fucker," I try and encourage the horse with my backside, but there's really nowhere for it to go. The space that the Raiders used as their camp the previous night was only large enough for the small numbers and their horses. With so many more spread along the track, but unmoving, it's almost impossible to find the room to swing my blade.

But the larger man is much slower than I think he'll be, and my sword is in front of my body, just as the war axe ends its slow arc.

I take the strain with my sword held in my left hand, my right hand keen to make a strike with the seax. Only the man's reach is too long. The handle on his war-axe must be double the standard length, and my attempts with the seax look feeble as they slice nothing but air.

"Bastard," I growl, the weight of the war axe threatening to buckle my left arm. Then I reconsider. My seax snatches out to drink from the man's straining forearm and blood wells along the sun-browned skin.

The wound cuts much deeper than I anticipated, as though through the parchment-thin skin of a silver birch, and the man gasps in surprise.

Only then, I realise why. My blade cut deep, too deep, and too close to his wrist, and already the flow of blood has become a torrent.

"Shit," I would have preferred to kill the man a better way, but all the same, I craved his death.

Panic-stricken blue eyes look my way as the weight of the war-axe grows more and more against my left arm, and the man quickly loses control over it. The irony isn't lost on me, that now I'm the only reason the weapon remains to threaten me.

Hastily, I kick out, keen to over-balance the figure. His blood pools to the ground as though a torrential downpour flows only over him. But my enemy doesn't move. While his face seems to drain of all life before me, his lips tinting with the ice of deepest winter, his right hand reaches for me, grabbing hold of my wrist with surprising force.

"Fuck." If I'm not careful, the man will still be able to claim the kill, even as I'm responsible for his death. We both might lay here together, weapons entangled, strangers and allies alike unsure of which made the fatal strike first.

I kick once more, my foot raised high, keen to drive the war axe from me. I feel the balance in that arm change, and I swing myself quickly away from the weapon, my imprisoned arm threatening to painfully twist as I go. Rather a twisted wrist than dead.

I just manage to veer away from the axe, as my opponent's hand slips from the handle, and it lands with a heavy thud, rooted in the blood-drenched ground. And then I'm thrusting with my head, the crunch as my forehead hits my opponent's nose, a sickening sound, but one that forces the man to release his grip on me finally, even if only in pain.

Quickly, I make the same cut on the other arm with my seax, desperate to ensure the man is dead.

By the time I step back, I'm panting, but the man's eyes are closing, his body swaying, as he stumbles backwards, leans against another of the trapped horses and slowly collapses to the floor.

"Thank fuck for that." I heave air into my body, wishing it wasn't stained with the iron and salt from the dead man.

Not that I have time to savour the moment.

"*Skiderik*," grief-stained eyes flicker from me to the dead man, and I find a smirk to laud over the new threat.

The warrior already carries a weeping wound to his cheek. Another, on his slit trews, slowly darkens the fabric. In his right hand, he holds a small war-axe. But between one blink and the next, he's managed to heft the discarded war-axe, using both of his hands. He must be stronger than he looks.

Leering at me, mouth gaping open, black blood on his teeth and in the thick black beard and moustache that covers much of his face. Only the slither of broken flesh from the bleeding cut shows that the man isn't furred all over.

"Bastard," I repay the kindness, and quickly dance into him, both weapons held loosely in my hands so that I can react to whatever he does next.

He's nowhere near tall enough, or broad enough to be able to make any headway with the stolen weapon. He would have done better sticking with his original blade, but he's thrust that into his weapons belt.

A string of curses flies from his mouth, gobs of blood following, and I understand none of them, although the intent is easy enough to decipher.

I step in close, keen to finish this fight once and for all, but my opponent has other ideas. The war axe scythes through the air, there's no other word for it, aiming for my arms and my stomach, as though meaning to slice me in two.

Hastily, I step back, eager to put more distance between us, only to encounter the unyielding body of another of the trapped horses. It grazes easily, pulling at stray tufty pieces of grass, as the war axe comes ever closer, ever nearer.

There's nothing for it. With a strength I thought beyond me, I bend my knees, arch my neck backwards, and then I'm flying through the air. I land, the breath knocked from me, on the back of the abandoned horse, my opponent finally overbalancing below me because I'm no longer there to keep him upright.

"Thanks," I slap the horse softly on his brown shoulder, but quickly slide free, landing on the sprawled back of my enemy, fighting for balance. His hands outstretched in front of him, the war axe only just not hitting the chestnut horse's rear left leg, and it's nothing for me to stab down with my seax and through his elongated neck. I push and push, his body resisting beneath me, and only when he's still, do I heave on the blade to reclaim it.

It doesn't want to give, not when it's so deeply buried, and I'm forced to kneel, place my weight on the man's neck and tug with all of my strength.

My seax refuses to move, and then it does, all at once, and crimson rain once more shivers through the air. I turn my head away, keen not to imbibe any more of the stuff.

Only there's a blackened blade where I want to put my head,

and once more, I find myself moving without truly thinking, my desire to survive employing all the skills I've learned over the years.

The blackened weapon is pitted and lethal-looking, the marks not there by chance. Whoever my new opponent is, they take pleasure in deriving pain from their opponent. The thought disgusts me. A death should be clean and as quick as possible. A death should be hard-fought and honourably given unless they're asleep. Then it's their own fucking fault.

My sword flashes quickly in my left hand, rearing upwards to knock the new blade aside, but the man who wields it is braced for the movement. Nothing happens other than a painful throbbing exploding up my arm as the two clash.

I duck down then, moving my head to the right, keen to have my neck as far from this new threat as possible in the constricted space. I allow my eyes to travel the length of the sword, and then upwards until I meet the furrowed brows of the man who means to kill me.

There's no emotion on his un-helmed face, but his eyes are colder than ice. In this man, the desire to kill isn't even a desire. It's much baser than that.

I swallow, enjoying the sensation of being able to do so now that the black edge is further away from me. But it won't be for long.

The melee of battle is loud. It seems that the Raiders are decent enough warriors. Or maybe it's just that desperate men will try that little bit harder to stay alive. They might react in ways that their opponents could never have considered.

With the thought, a deluge of ideas floods through my mind. I've already used the horse to assist me, so what else might there be?

I find a cocky grin for my adversary and then glance at the floor. And then my smile becomes wider and far more genuine.

Help can genuinely come from unexpected places. But to take advantage of it, I need to drop my weapons, probably both of them. Not that they're doing me any good at the moment.

Hastily, I slide my seax and sword beneath me, hoping the movements are somehow masked, and then I wrap my hands around the somewhat handily placed branch, just wide enough that it takes both hands to circle it fully.

It's but a moment then to thrust upwards, bringing the branch between the man's widely placed feet. And then higher, the branch broad enough, but not so long, as to make it unwieldy, or the action so slow that it's detected before I can complete it.

With a final thrust, the branch impacts my opponent between the legs and he groans, his bladed hand jumping with the pain. It's all I can do to roll clear of the black weapon, palm my own as the discarded branch crashes to the ground, and then stab upwards. If he thought a piece of wood was painful, the slice of my seax is but a whimper, but deadlier for all that.

I allow my advance to come to an end, just to the rear of the man, and standing, I notice the pool of crimson wine, and it's easy to push the man over. He stumbles and falls, the strength in his long legs abandoning him all at once.

Another to add to the number of Raiders I've killed.

Finally, able to stand, my breath rasps, and I lift my hand to my neck, and it comes away with just the hint of wetness. Fuck, I've not escaped entirely unscathed.

The sound of the battle is starting to die away, the roars of outrage replaced by the whimpers of the wounded and dying. I kick the body, move it aside and grab my sword. Only it seems the man isn't quite dead. For one final time, the blackened edge comes toward my hand. I'm ready for it this time. I stamp on it, and then, because the fucker really needs to know that dead is dead, I kick the weapon aside. His fingers scrabble on the dry ground for just a moment, and then he falls still.

"Thank fuck for that," Edmund's voice is high with the success of the battle.

"Cock," I exclaim, keen to see how the rest of the men are performing.

Edmund's chuckle brings a tight smirk to my face. Damn, it

feels good to be alive.

I force my way through some of the stubborn horses, backsides aimed at me, one of them exploding in a sea of foul wind that almost makes me gag.

"Filthy animal," but I stroke its long sandy neck as it lets me through, and I consider that I've gained yet another decent animal. Maybe I'll keep him. But no. I'll gift him to my Aunt. She requires a better mount. For a woman so proud of her family lineage, she will insist on tramping around the countryside on her old and bow-backed mare.

The scene that greets me beyond the press of bodies both pleases and frustrates me.

Most of the enemy is dead, and the majority of my warriors are unscathed, bending to grab long grasses to sluice the wardew from their weapons. But five of our opponents still stand, in a loose circle, facing outwards, as they protect one another's backs.

Hereman stands watching, weapon raised, ready to get involved if he needs to, but prepared to allow the others to take kills, provided that they can. Siric and Leonath are amongst the men still fighting, as are Eahric and Ingwald. Wulfstan has finally made his killing blow and stands puffing, his cheeks bright pink both with the exertion and the relief.

"About bloody time," Hereman complains to him, only he's smiling, a rare sight and Wulfstan's grin assures me that he's far from offended.

"Daft bastard," Wulfstan complains, moving aside to allow Siric and Leonath more room.

The four remaining men make a sorry sight. One has a deep gash on his left cheek; another is limping, although I can see no obvious leg wound. Siric and Leonath trade blows with two men who must be brothers, or half-brothers, or maybe even father and son. The resemblance is easy to see, but their respective ages are more difficult to guess.

I note that Siric's opponent fights left-handed, Leonath's seemingly skilled with both hands, and it's this which is making the altercation last so long. Eahric and Ingwald's foes both fall below their blades, and now the two remaining men grow ever more frantic. I would let them live, learn all their secrets, but that's not my decision to make. Not when I'm not the one who battles.

"Fucking hurry up," Edmund is far from as understanding as his brother, and I shoot him a pointed look when he speaks too loudly, drawing the gaze of the two men who share such similarities.

Leonath jumps at the opportunity to finally land a blow beyond the multi-skilled warrior, although Siric is less fortunate.

"For fuck's sake," Edmund mutters, as Siric is forced to make five hasty backwards steps, almost tripping over Hereman's extended foot in the process.

"Leave him," I urge. Siric might be out of practice, and there's no real danger for him here. He can take all the time that he needs. If it even looks as though his opponent is going to win, one of us can intervene. I rarely see my men fight when the danger is real. It can reveal far more about their character than just training skirmishes can.

Leonath's opponent grunts as his flesh opens up along his left arm. Rather than counter the blow, he seems to make a quick decision, and bolts from the tight circle, through the only available gap between the trees and the rest of my men and the milling horses.

Where he means to go, I don't fucking know, and in fact, we're all momentarily stunned by the decision, so much so that the man almost disappears before Wulfhere rears upwards, a grin on his young face, his blade extended so that the enemy runs onto it himself. The Raiders legs still move, and Wulfhere stands his ground, the grin slipping from his face quickly, and I'm about to intervene. Only Wulfhere, with more wits than I thought he had, leans forward, nuts the dying man on the forehead, and stunned, his body stops moving, and he slips to the ground.

Wulfhere's blade shimmers maroon in the dappled light through the overhanging trees, a triumphant expression back on his young face.

"Stupid fucking boy," I roar at the youngster, but none of the others takes up my complaint, and even I have to admit that he did bloody well. Lucky for him that the Raider thought only of those behind him, and not what might lurk in the undergrowth.

"Shit," Siric is far from happy. In the process of speeding after his enemy, he's lost his kill, and perhaps worse, we've all witnessed it. Wulfhere is almost crowing with delight, and I imagine there might be an argument about who gets to claim the spoils.

I leave them to it.

"Ingwald, Eahric, check the way is clear to the front, and kill the scouts. Leonath and Hereman, check to the rear, and do the same," I point, to show which way I mean, not wanting them to do the opposite of my intentions. Leonath stands from investigating his kill, a perplexed expression on his face that only serves to highlight his missing tooth.

In his hand he holds a parchment, tightly rolled.

"What does it say?" I demand to know, only for him to shrug his shoulders, walking to pass it to me.

"Can't fucking read," Leonath advises, no trace of rancour in his voice, as he and Hereman walk together, away from the mass of dead warriors, and confused horses. The smell of horse shit and blood is enough to drive even the flies away, and I wrinkle my nose, turning the parchment from side to side in my hand.

It's a small piece of vellum, no wider than my thumb, and it's tightly sealed, the wax glistening in the bright sunlight. I'm tempted to open it immediately, but there's much to do, and really, I can't see what could be so important as to make me change my intentions for the day.

Half of my men are with me, here, rifling through the belongings of the dead, the other half are on patrol, trying to determine the intentions of those who yet live.

"What we doing with them?" Edmund's question breaks my reverie as he kicks one of the cooling bodies. I place the rolled parchment inside the pocket on my weapons belt that usually holds my seax because I've nowhere else to put it. Haden, and his saddlebags, are still hidden away, and Wulfhere is too busy divvying up the spoils with Siric to have remembered he should mind the three horses.

"We don't need the damn horses," I complain. Once more, I've got more horses than I know what to do with them. There's an overflowing stable at Northampton. Now there are near enough another forty of the things, on top of the ones from last night. Not that I want to send them back to Grantabridge. Well, not all of them.

"We'll send the leader back, trussed up on his mount. The rest we'll inter in the hiding place from last night." I turn to point to the spot where I killed another man less than a day before. It's in the under hang of a large piece of whitened stone, with smaller boulders around it, no doubt sheered away from the larger boulder above.

"We can seal them in." I don't have the time to dig graves for them, and neither can I set a fire to burn so many. And, I need the Raiders to be able to find their dead. They need to know that they're being hunted.

"It's always the fucking worst part of winning a bloody battle," Edmund complains, and I'm considering agreeing with him, only a loud cry thrums through the air.

"What the fuck?" my seax is in my hand, as Edmund seems to scent the air and turns his gaze the way Ingwald and Eahric have gone.

The beat of horses' hooves is not far behind.

"Weapons," I bellow to my men because some have clearly not heard the worrying noise.

I don't wait to see if they abide by my command because I'm rushing along the track, keen to see what's happening from a higher vantage point. I thought that this was the only warband to take this route, but I realise I've not spoken to my men who've been hiding all morning. Maybe others have travelled this path or one close to it. It would have been good if they'd fucking mentioned that.

I hasten beyond the rocky formation, keen to find a viewpoint. The sight that greets me brings a determined grin to my face.

"To me," I instruct my remaining warriors. All of them are standing ready, the bodies discarded on the floor just like detritus after a high tide along the River Severn, and they rush to me.

I eye them carefully. Hereman and Leonath are absent. That means that with Edmund and I, we number twelve once more. I'm not prepared to include Wulfhere in my calculations, and indeed, the youth seems to eschew my scrutiny as he merges back into the darkened woodlands, no doubt remembering what his task was supposed to be.

"Shield wall," I order my warriors, Edmund quick to stand beside me.

I can't see enough to know how many Raiders are riding toward me. The track is single-file. I'm pleased that Ingwald and Eahric speed toward me, faces almost purple with exertion. They could have hidden away, but no, they lead the enemy toward me, and that can only mean that more of their number will die today.

I imagine that the two Raiders encountered the scouting party and that their leader, a proud-looking warrior who rides a high-stepping white mare, is keen to determine what's been happening.

"How many?" I ask Edmund, as Gyrth falls into position next to me, and our shields seem to snap together, the movement well practised to make it look effortless, even though it bloody isn't.

"No more than ten," Edmund comments, his forehead furrowed as he peers against the brightness of the day.

"We fucking kill them," I raise my voice to issue my instructions.

"When do we ever leave any of the fuckers alive?" Wulfred demands to know, and I grin, as do the majority of the men. Edmund has fallen silent. Normally he would be quiet and shaking, but the battle-rage hasn't yet dissipated entirely, and I can tell, from the determination on his face, that he has no fear of another encounter.

"They're mounted," I call the caution. I'm considering all the times I've used Haden against the Raiders. Will they do the same? I'm not convinced that they will, but they might surprise me. For once.

I don't spare a thought for where the new threat has been. Maybe they came from Northampton, but it's more likely they've been using Ermine Street for some purpose. Perhaps it's connected to the parchment I still possess. Maybe, perhaps. Who the fuck knows. And I'm probably never going to if I get my wish and we add a few more to the growing list of men I've killed that day.

Abruptly, the lead rider must realise that there's more than just two unmounted men to tackle. Between one heartbeat and the next, his body undergoes a strange transformation, eyes scouring the small shield wall that entirely blocks the track. He has but a moment to decide whether to press on or to retreat, but I know what's going to happen even before he does.

"*Skjolde*," the cry is familiar to me, and in a flurry of motion, the riders all grab their shields and weapons.

"Another fucking fight," I mutter, ensuring the grip on my shield is both loose enough and tight enough to counter any blow.

"Another excuse to kill the fuckers," Wulfred's voice echoes with satisfaction, and I find myself grinning, despite everything that's happened to us in the last few months.

Yes, the fighting has become more frequent, but has much else truly fucking changed?

Eahric and Ingwald race to slide between the wall of shields facing the foe.

"Fuckers," is all Eahric manages to pant before running to grab his shield or a shield from one of the waiting horses. Ingwald is more forthcoming as he hovers close to me.

"They came upon us just as we were killing the two scouts. We killed them all the same and have been running ever since." He pauses then to suck much-needed air into his starved body.

"Eleven of them, although I think one of them fell from their horse. Daft shit didn't notice the low hanging branch." Ingwald drags a bark of laughter from his heaving chest.

"Get a fucking shield," I remind him, and he grins, proving he hadn't forgotten after all.

And then the pounding of hooves is much, much closer, and I brace myself for whatever might come.

The rumble of Danish voices is easy enough to hear but what surprises me is that the lead rider forms his warriors up to either side of him. It seems they mean to attack from the back of their horses, seeming to forget that trees block much of the track.

This worries me, not because I fear to face mounted warriors, but because the daft bastards can't even rein the animals in when there aren't blood-thirsty men attacking them. This might all go very wrong for my men and me, but only if the bastards are lucky.

I almost wish I'd called for our horses.

"Stand firm," I bellow, the tension in shoulders pulling the shields even tighter together. I've used horses against the Raiders before, always successfully. I can't allow the reverse to happen here.

I turn to wink at Edmund, and he swallows heavily and then turns to the warriors to his side. We once spent a long, and ultimately frustrating night discussing what we would do if the Raiders attacked us from horseback. Little was decided upon, apart from one key fact. I just hope that my warriors remember.

I can't, if I'm honest, recall who remained awake throughout the long debate, other than Edmund, Icel and Hereman. The rest, for all I know, might have preferred sleeping to arguing, although I doubt it. My warriors are outspoken bastards, the lot of them.

There's no time to worry about it now. I can see just from the brief peek I risk over the top of my shield, that the lead rider has his men where he wants them

I glance to the left and then to the right.

Ingwald and Eahric have muscled their way amongst us all.

We stand fourteen men together, while the Raiders are ten, or eleven men long, with their mounts. If I thought one of the daft sods could genuinely encourage their horse to rear against the shields, I might be worried, but they won't be able to. Not many men can. Horses are never known for doing what they're instructed unless they bloody feel like it, and these riders and horses won't have the required rapport.

"Brace," I yell, just on the off-chance that the Raiders can understand me.

The thunder of hooves assures me that the Raiders are about to attack, not that I can risk looking, not now. This has to happen precisely, or it will fail miserably and leave us all exposed.

"Now," my word snaps through the air, and as one, we all take to our knees, shields covering our heads, but not our bodies.

I see little but white horses' legs, and black horses' legs, and a few chestnut ones, and even another sandy coloured mount.

The riders expected to face a shield wall. The horses as well, and it's the horses that I want to confuse.

One of the animals does rear upwards, hooves fleeing, but Ingwald easily deflects the heavy blows, while the rest of the horses are left with little choice but to attempt to jump us. They expected to come against us, not over us, and now they have too much speed and no room to stop.

The feeling of displaced air over my head brings a smirk to my face that only disappears when I hear a cry of pain from Leonath and realise that he probably had no idea what was about to happen.

I spare a thought for him, but I'm already standing, moving my shield back to protect my body, and running toward the confused horses and riders.

They're now as trapped as I was earlier. The mounts of the men we've already killed block the only way to escape. The horses have injured only Leonath, and that means the Raiders are both outnumbered and trapped.

The lead rider seems to realise only moments after I do.

"*Skjolde*," the voice is lighter than I would have expected, and the warrior moves with far more speed and skill than I anticipate from the Raiders. Perhaps another fabled warrior woman heads this group of Raiders.

"Attack," I order, and I'm already striking out with my seax, eager to attempt to land a blow before our opponents can gather themselves together.

We've already killed nearly forty of the fuckers. Another ten would make it a more rounded fifty. Not a bad count, for a day of hiding and skulking.

The other riders are much slower in dismounting from their startled beasts, and I land a well-aimed blow on the female warrior just before she can swing her shield in front of her face.

I feel my blade scrape across the thick leather at her shoulder, only drawing blood just before I reach the neck. And then my seax is battered aside.

Edmund has joined me, and he lashes out to the left side of my adversary, just managing to miss the white horse, to open a wider gash down the woman's face.

Now that I face her, I can tell that the warrior is definitely a woman. Her face is softer than a man's might be, although riddled with the puckering of scars that show this isn't her first battle. But, of course, it's the lack of beard or stubble beneath the cheekpieces of the elaborate helm that truly shows this Raider isn't a man.

More and more of the enemy are forming up, but my men weave a path through them, and I appreciate that the shield wall will not reform, not this time.

Abruptly, the white horse rears once more, green eyes wild with the scent of blood and then it's fleeing beyond me, and disappearing back along the path it just came. I hope Wulfhere might be able to control the animal if he can catch her.

Another horse quickly follows suit, this one smaller and piebald, and then the Raiders have more room to move. For a heartbeat.

My seax is busy, the blows aiming for the woman rather than her shield, although her skill can't be denied, as she time and time again moves quickly enough to deflect the blow and stop it landing on her body.

Edmund joins me, but only until another opponent emerges beside her, and then it descends into one on one fighting. Leonath has recovered enough from whatever happened to him when the horses jumped over us, to fight beside me. I can't see his face, but I can hear his panting with each blow he rains down on the shield he faces. I'm forced to close my eyes as slithers of wood flee through the air.

My opponent takes advantage of my slight distraction to land a blow on my shield arm with the massive edge of a sword. For all it throbs, the blade doesn't cut my flesh thanks to the thick leather gloves I wear and which snake their way upwards to almost my elbow. There'll be a bruise there come the morning, but nothing worse.

I lash out with my seax, the move seeming to be wild and reckless, but while the Raider tracks my seax, I jab upwards with my shield, seeking and finding her chin.

"*Skiderik*," the word is muffled, no doubt because of a bitten tongue, although I'm impressed that she doesn't turn away, try and hide her face from another such attack. All the same, it leaves my opponent exposed, the shield in her arm almost lifeless, so that I can pull it downward with my seax hand.

It lands with a heavy thud on the ground, and then the Raider has nothing but skill and a long, reaching sword to keep herself free from my thirsty blade.

First, I take a slice from her upper arm, and as the warrior's face curls in defiance, blood oozing onto pink lips, I reverse my hold and stab upwards once more, using the handle of my seax, not my shield, to batter her chin.

I see her eyes lose focus from the force, and then I move to slice across her neck because it's exposed now. A quick death, for one of my enemy,

"Don't," the words that thunder through the air, stay my hand, even though a pin-prick of blood is already forming on the exposed white expanse.

I'm unsure who spoke, although I realise it's not the warrior. Instead, it's Pybba, and he stands beside me, a hand on my arm, cautioning me not to complete the movement.

I look around, realise I'm the only one still fighting, and that Rudolf is beside the woman, his seax steady against her side. The threat is easy to read from my slight warrior.

"Where the fuck did you come from?" I roar, the urge to make the kill making my arm shake beneath Pybba's firm hold.

"Don't," Pybba states, rather than answer my question, and slowly I lower my seax arm, wondering what the fuck this is about, but knowing that Pybba wouldn't have intervened unless it was imperative.

"We've been following them. Since early morning," Pybba explains, his head nodding to where most of the Raiders are now dead, although he says nothing else. Vaguely, I do remember this warband leaving Grantabridge. But only vaguely.

"And why," I find myself asking, "Is this fucking Raider different to any other?"

"Ah," and Rudolf joins Pybba with his knowing look and cheeky grin. It seems that I might have caught myself a prize.

But the woman is having none of it. Still holding her sword, she swipes at me, and Pybba slowly moves out of the way of the sword, a sour expression on his face. Rudolf hastily grabs the woman's other arm and holds it behind her back.

The wince on her face assures me that Rudolf is stronger than he looks, as I drop my seax onto the floor, and reach out to grab her sword hand. Only slowly does she relinquish her grip on the sword under the force of my pinching grip, and as it too falls to the ground, I truly look at her.

"*Skiderik*," she spits at me, and I allow the gob to fall on my face, taking my time in dragging her arm behind her back to join the other. Once there, Rudolf hastily ties her hands with a strip of leather pulled from his weapons belt. Forced to her knees, the woman bucks against her captivity and I look at Pybba, eyebrows high, keen for an explanation.

Pybba gazes at the woman, as Rudolf removes her helm, and

I'm not alone in gasping.

No hair spills from beneath the shimmering helm, but rather a shaven head, coarse bristles showing the true colour would be deepest black.

"Who the fuck is she?" I ask, one more time.

Pybba takes his time in answering, as though reassuring himself that he's making the correct identification.

"This woman is Jarl Guthrum's sister. We heard her speaking of it."

"Ah," now I begin to understand why Pybba stayed my hand. I've killed many a son of a Raider, but never a sister. Having her as our captive, or even as a bargaining counter, might well do me far more good than just leaving her here with her throat slit.

CHAPTER 15

I have her trussed up and tied to the horse as soon as Wulfhere lumbers into view encouraging the distressed animal, once he's realised it's safe to do so. The dead body of the lead warrior from our first encounter is flung across the animal. I spare a moment of remorse for the terrified beast, but Wulfhere has been treating her to choice morsels he pulls from his pockets. I only just stop myself from asking where he's found such a sorry looking apple. I'm sure he can't have been hoarding it since Northampton.

The woman is defiant. She's said nothing since Pybba stopped me from killing her, but she doesn't really need to. Rage seeps from her, almost more tangible than the light mist of rain that's begun to fall.

Hereman and Leonath have returned, Hereman glowering for missing the opportunity to kill more of the enemy. He's far from happy with Pybba's demand that we not kill the woman.

"Why keep the fucking bitch alive?" he growls, before stalking away to help with moving the dead. It seems he doesn't want an answer after all. But, I find myself asking Pybba the same question.

"She's spent the entire morning bragging of the fact she's Jarl Guthrum's sister," is the only answer Pybba gives me, before striding away as well. He leaves me to work out what sort of advantage this gives us.

I call Edmund to me, Rudolf as well, as I bend to find some

browned leaves to clean the muck from my seax and sword.

"Tell me," I command Rudolf, and for a moment I think he'll be as stubborn as Pybba, but then he relents.

"She speaks our language. All her warriors seemed to, and that meant we could hear what they were saying. She is Jarl Guthrum's sister. She was boasting about knowing all of his plans, and now we know them. If we send her back to him, then he'll know that he's been discovered."

"So, all these dead bodies aren't enough?" Edmund asks, his hands sweeping through the air to take in the view before us where the majority of my men drag the dead to the improvised grave.

"Well, this'll be fucking quicker," Rudolf attempts, and I find a tight smile tugging on my lips because once more Rudolf and Pybba have been thinking more clearly than I have.

"So, what does Jarl Guthrum have planned?" Rudolf's eyes brighten at my question, and he leans closer to me, as though about to impart a huge secret.

"He intends to claim all of Mercia and East Anglia as far as Watling Street."

"What, fucking all of it?" Edmund is more alert now, sitting upright and swigging from a water bottle that doesn't contain water.

"All of it. He reckons he can claim Ealdorman Wulfstan's land holdings because he's bloody dead now, and his daughter is a captive at Northampton, with a baby in her belly."

"Ah." Even I'm beginning to understand Pybba's caution now.

"He says that Wessex is weak under King Alfred. He plans to hold East Anglia and Mercia, and maybe even Wessex as well. He says that King Alfred has been as busy fighting the Raiders this year as Mercia has."

"And what did she," and I indicate the captive with my chin. "Say about King Coelwulf."

A sudden shifty look sweeps over Rudolf's face, and I realise it's not going to be pleasant hearing.

"Tell me. I need to know what they fucking say about me."

"They say you're just as weak as King Burgred, and that you'll be dead pretty soon if you keep on fighting as you do."

"That doesn't sound so bad," I taunt, and Rudolf's nose scrunches up, and he takes a deep breath before expelling it in a rush of words.

"She says you're a fucking hero just waiting to meet your death on the edge of her blade, and Guthrum thinks the same, as does Jarl Oscetel."

"Did she mention Jarl Halfdan?"

"Only to say he's a bit of a fucking tosser as well."

"Well, at least we can agree about some things," I retort, determined not to meet the eyes of the woman, even though I can feel the heat of her glare on my neck.

"She didn't know about Northampton," Rudolf admits.

"What of it?"

"That it's Mercian once more."

"Well, she's going to know soon enough," I stand, the decision made. I like to send one survivor to tell of my triumphs. I'd sooner not give Jarl Guthrum his sister back, but Rudolf is right.

We've been trying to entice the fuckers from Grantabridge. It was a ploy that was going to take some time. Maybe we'll kill enough of them to be able to spend the winter at Kingsholm after all.

Not that our prisoner likes our decision. Far from it.

It's a good thing that Wulfhere has made the horse she rides such an ally. If not, she'd have been off it, and probably impaled on some handy piece of branch sticking up from the haphazard path through the thick woods that surrounds the route we take.

Instead, Wulfhere keeps the horse trailing his mount, and our prisoner is powerless to do more than twist and moan from beneath the gag that seals her mouth closed.

I might have liked to learn more from her, but I won't allow her to make up lies now that she's our prisoner. The information that Pybba, Rudolf, young Gardulf and Osbert managed to overhear is far more likely to be true. I won't pollute it with whatever she makes up now that she's our captive.

I lead the way, keen to be the first to warn of any danger, whereas Hereman sulks at the back of our line of horses. We're reunited, the men who spent the morning hiding, mounted once more, and I only hope that the other eight men, one group of four under Gyrth's command, and the other under Goda's and including Penda, are waiting for me at the meeting place. I don't want to be confronted by Pybba if anything has happened to his grandson. I just have to hope that Goda has kept him safe, as I instructed him when I divided the men this morning, a sly word in his ear, and an appreciation for his skill and tact.

From our meeting place, we'll release Jarl Guthrum's sister, but only after I've sent the majority of my warriors back to Northampton. I want to be provocative, but I also don't want, however many Raiders are inside Grantabridge, chasing us down as soon as they see our bound captive.

I'm hoping for rage. But equally, I want to be in control of what happens next.

Edmund is remarkably silent beside me. I'm not blind to his constant glances toward our captive. I know what he wants to ask. Equally, I can't allow him to voice his question. We can show no fucking weakness. What is one man when so much else is at stake? Yet even I feel my heart grow heavy with the thought. I miss Icel as much as everyone else, only I'm confident that he is dead. Edmund will only find peace when he accepts that. If he ever does.

The afternoon wears on, the sounds of the woodland muted, rain falling steadily. I huddle deep inside my cloak, the sweat of battle drying only slowly on my skin. My arm, where the blade impacted it, aches, and I know that it'll be badly bruised, but a little bruise never killed anyone.

"Cover her fucking eyes," I shout the instruction to Wulfhere, and for a moment he looks startled, and I sense the woman stiffening in the saddle. How, I'm unsure. I've never seen anyone ride as upright as she does.

"I'll do it," Rudolf confirms, his voice animated, as though this is little more than a nice ride in the chill air. That boy's good spirits never seem to dim.

True to his word, Rudolf binds our captive's eyes, and only then do I turn the horses and begin the trek away from the main trackway. Not that our hiding place needs to remain a secret forever, but I still think it better to show caution. When her brother finally releases her, I imagine that she'll think only of revenge. A pity she can't just be grateful to be alive.

A deeper silence falls then. My warriors know to be quiet and not give away our destination. I feel my body tense as I struggle to hear anything, but it appears that we're entirely alone beneath the trees. Haden's steps are sure, the ground still mostly hard-packed and with only the occasional muddy puddles. The summer has been too hot, I hope the winter will not be severe, but I know that the one can often presage the other.

"Coelwulf," I sigh with relief when I hear Gyrth's voice calling to me. As instructed, he, Ordlaf, Beornstan and Oda are waiting for me, with young Hiltiberht, left behind to ensure everyone knew the correct spot. His eyes are wild, but he keeps his silence well enough. In the distance, the sound of the river Granta doesn't reach our ears, and it's impossible to see the settlement itself. A perfect meeting place.

I caution the men to silence, inclining my head to indicate the captive Raider. Gyrth nods, while Beornstan eyes her with surprise, and somehow manages to bite his reply down.

"Come with me," I tell Gyrth, sliding from Haden's back, unsurprised when Edmund follows me beneath the overhanging trees. I don't want Guthrum's sister to know what information we've discovered.

"Tell me," I keep my voice low, a tight smile when I hear Pybba and Rudolf talking about the size of a horse's cock to mask our conversation.

"I never saw the fucking like," Rudolf jokes.

"Well, you never saw a great deal," Pybba offers, and I imagine that Hiltiberht and Wulfhere have no idea what to make of the pair of them.

"The group we followed headed to the south, toward Icknield Way. They scouted, seemed content with what they saw, and then came back to Grantabridge. We stayed hidden but tracked them. They used a ford to cross the river. It wasn't really very revealing." Gyrth sounds unhappy with his task, but I nod, absorbing all the information he has discovered while we've been fighting the Raiders.

"Fuck, why are there so many damn roads around here?" I don't expect an answer. I'm beginning to appreciate just what a clever position the Raiders have chosen. They're in Mercia, but close to East Anglia, over which they have greater control. They have a river to escape along, roads close to them, heading both deeper into Mercia to the north and south, and of course, toward London.

I know the Raiders would like to hold London. They hunger for its wealth and trade. They've tried to take it before.

"Who's that?" Gyrth breaks through my musings.

"Jarl Guthrum's sister. We killed all her riders, and those that went to investigate what happened to the scouting party we attacked in the night."

Gyrth nods, his lips downcast but his eyes alight with the knowledge.

"What's she fucking told you? Nothing, I imagine."

And now, I grin.

"She bragged a great deal to her fellow riders, and Rudolf and Pybba overheard it all."

"Truly? And what are you going to do with her?"

"I'm sending her back, with a dead warrior across her knee. But first, we need to wait for Goda and the rest of the men. And then Hereman and you will be responsible for getting everyone back to Northampton."

Gyrth is about to complain, but Edmund gets there first.

"And what are you going to fucking do?"

"We," and I indicate him with my hand. "Are going to watch the fuckers and make sure they do what we want."

"And if they don't?"

"We'll think of something," I mutter, but Edmund is already storming away from me and back to his horse, his unhappiness far too evident to see.

"What will you do?" Gyrth asks, and I'm honest enough to shake my head.

"I've no fucking idea. But I'm not risking a thousand warriors racing after just twenty-odd of us. Safer to have you all in Northampton, with the rest of Ealdorman Ælhun's men."

"But not safer for you?" Gyrth goads me, but I appreciate his words.

"I'm the fucking king. I'm the biggest prize. There's no safety for me, not anymore." Gyrth doesn't reply, and somehow, I don't hear his steps away from me, until I startle at the noise of more horses arriving, and I know it's time to tell everyone what's about to happen. I can't imagine it's going to go down well. Not at all.

CHAPTER 16

"Well, this is even more fucked up than your usual half-cocked ideas," Edmund's words don't quite match with his almost jovial tone, as he hunkers down beside me.

"You're fucking enjoying this?" I level the accusation, and he doesn't deny it.

"What's not to enjoy?" Edmund continues. "Two men against however the many fuckers there are inside Grantabridge."

We're back at the hiding place from earlier in the day. Before us, I can once more count five men on guard duty beside the bridge. They look to be paying far more attention than the men earlier, and they were already suspicious bastards. I'd like to think it's because they sense something isn't right, but appreciate that it has more to do with the three men watching, from the other side of the river, their eyes scouring the open ground before us, their stance uneasy.

"The three jarls," Edmund spoke with satisfaction when he identified Anwend, Oscetel and Guthrum. At least I know where they are now. It seems that, just as at Repton, they're not the ones out risking their lives. No, they're locked up tight on the far side of the river, with solid ramparts at their back. They must feel secure there, although they have no right to such a belief.

It took much longer than I might have liked, and all of our conversations were conducted in hushed voices, that only occasionally reached the ears of our captive. Hereman, of them all, was the first to agree, although the gleam in his eye made me think he was plotting something. Provided that plotting involves him making it back to Northampton before the Raiders erupt from Grantabridge, I don't much mind what he has in mind. The daft bastard.

Courtesy of an over-talkative sister, Pybba and Rudolf know how many Raiders are stationed inside Grantabridge. The number is similar to Repton. They've had reinforcements from somewhere. They are just like ants, just as Sæbald said. Damn the fucking bastards.

We also know with surety that Jarl Halfdan isn't with them. It seems he's decided on a different path. His goal is the northern kingdom, and perhaps even Ireland, if the woman is to be believed. I don't want to think he's out of my reach, but if he's gone from Mercia, which is what I do want, I can't see that I'll ever have the opportunity to seek my vengeance for Icel's death. That burns me, but my concerns are more immediate.

Our captive has been released, but far from our hiding place, and I'm beginning to think the damn horse has no idea how to make it back to the bridge.

I could hardly let her go without her blindfold, and neither could I have her appear from where I hide. The afternoon is growing old, and a flicker of concern that full dark might fall before she returns is plaguing me.

But, I couldn't risk anyone physically returning her to Grantabridge. If we have to wait all night, then that's just what we're going to have to do.

‚I've spent too much of my time hiding behind this damn stone. I know all its dips and curves and sharp edges almost as well as I do my hand.

Haden and Jethson have been left in the woodlands that guard our backs. I'm hoping the two will still be there when we need them. I'm hoping that Jethson behaves himself. I'm not entirely convinced that he will though, but I wasn't going to allow Wulfhere to stay with us again, not this time. It's going to be far too fucking dangerous if my plan actually works.

"I wish the bitch would hurry up," Edmund speaks with more frustration than rancour. He's keen to be gone. So am I, but first, I need to know that the jarls are going to ride out.

Edmund squints into the deepening dusk, and I follow his gaze. There's nothing to see, though. Gyrth, Ordlaf, Beornstan and Oda followed a scouting party to the north, but they really didn't seem to do anything, other than ride along the banks of the Granta. Gyrth did acknowledge that another set of Raiders followed them, on the 'Raider' bank of the Granta. It seems that they're keen to ensure their route of escape back to the sea remains open, even with their ramparts.

I wish I knew if their actions here mirror those taken at Torksey and Repton, but I wasn't there when they first claimed those places. I've no fucking idea. Certainly, they've chosen a river site and one that seems to be defensible when the river is incorporated into the rampart and ditch. But with the rest of East Anglia to escape into, they have more leeway than before, when all they had was the Trent as a means of escape.

I must assume that this is their fall-back position, as Torksey was, but the Raiders are thinking on a different tangent this time around. The only element that seems to be the same is that they want to dominate the surrounding landscape. Why else would they patrol as much as they do?

And why did they choose to reinforce Northampton? It's not close enough to Grantabridge to be a comfortable fall-back position, and of course, the river there is the Nene, not the Granta. The rivers don't meet anywhere along their lengths.

"She's fucking coming," Edmund's words thankfully pull me back from my circular thoughts. I swivel to focus on the ghostly figure, knocking my feet against the ground to encourage some feeling back into them.

The horse's head drags. I pity it for the weight it's had to carry so far. Maybe I should have sent another animal to bring the dead man; it's not as though I was running short of horses.

But while Edmund has noticed her, it seems those on guard duty haven't. Maybe they're not as alert as I thought they were.

Even as a spark of flame flares into life, to push back the darkness, there's no movement to show that the lone horse has been sighted.

"I just hope it stops before the fucking riverbank," Edmund's tone brings a wry smirk to my face.

"Cheery fucker, aren't you?" But he doesn't respond, because we're watching, and waiting, the anticipation almost too much to contain. I hope, for the final time, that I've interpreted the probable response correctly. If not, I've just sent the vast majority of my warriors back to Northampton, and I'm going to have to go and get them back to continue harrying the enemy.

They won't take kindly to such fucking crap leadership.

Hereman will probably refuse to do anything I command, sulking instead.

On heavy legs, the poor white horse meanders into view, and then on again. It's almost so dark by now that the distance has become hazy, obscured by the dying light of the day. The flicker of flame from the fire close to the bridge seems to entice the tired horse. The woman, it seems, has fallen silent on the animal's back. Her head nods forward, and I consider that she sleeps. And then I hope she hasn't died.

I'm almost surprised to see her still there, but then, her hands are bound, her mouth gagged, her eyes hooded, and even her feet are attached to the stirrups. She looks, I imagine, as I did when I was taken into Repton as a captive. The similarity isn't lost on me. I'm assuming that the jarls will be intelligent enough to see the same.

"Come on, come on," Edmund drums his hand on the large stone, his fingers busy, although his gaze never falters. I keep my eyes trained on the flame, sure that any moment some sort of outcry will ripple through the thickening air. Close to the river, a mist is starting to form, and it's soon going to be impossible to tell whether it's rain that dampens my cheeks, or the mist.

I bite down on my frustration, try and hold my hand clear from where the seax rests on my weapons belt. It seems I'm just as impatient as Edmund.

The flame suddenly splits in two, and I know it's happening.

"They've fucking seen her," and Edmund's mouth is open to say the same.

"Let it begin." Once more, his words are doom-laden, although the tone isn't.

"Come on, come on." And then two balls of light separate from the central fire, and begin to make their way across the open ground.

I can hear the men demanding to know who is there. Half a smile plays on my lips. They're in for a shock. I see the actual moment that the Raiders exactly determine who rides, alone and tied tightly to the saddle.

For one long moment, they seem to pause, unsure what to do, only then one of the balls of light is running back to the men on guard duty, the remaining figure left to guide the horse home. He does so with difficulty because the animal is fatigued and terrified of the flame so close to its nose.

My captive stirs, and whatever she says, the Raider quickly throws the flaming brand to the floor, stamps on it in the hope the flames won't catch on the tall, damp grasses, and then reaches up to pull the hood clear from her eyes. Then he pushes the dead body clear, and even from my hiding place, I hear it thud to the floor with a disquieting wet sound.

Then there's a flurry of activity, almost too much for Edmund and I to watch, after such a long period of doing nothing. One of the guards rushes over the bridge to summon the jarls, who've grown tired of their vigil and departed. Someone is sent to aid the other man, and a line of flares spring to life on the far side of the river. I appreciate that they've been placed there for just such an emergency.

In the growing light, I watch, hungry to see what the reaction will be to this most provocative of attacks.

First, a horse races from across the river, streaking out toward the white horse. Then another joins it, and another, and finally a riderless mount. Behind them, I can see one of the jarls issuing instructions, and hastily, twenty or so warriors appear, weapons ready, and troop across the bridge as well. There's such a press of bodies that I think someone will inevitably fall into the rushing river below.

More warriors quickly supplement those on watch duty, and even more flames leap to life, almost rimming the new settlement. I doubt there's anyone now who doesn't know what's happening.

"It's going to fucking work," Edmund's voice thrums with pleasure, but I'm not sure yet. It's too soon. The woman still hasn't returned inside Grantabridge, and only now are the other horses close to her.

Angry words are exchanged between some of the riders, probably, I consider, asking why there's no damn light. Then the original man rushes back, taking the riderless mount with him, and tries to pull the body onto the animal's back.

He stands no chance alone.

The three other riders encircle the woman, and one of them gets close enough to release her hands and legs and then she sags forward, almost colliding with her mount's neck. Another two riders appear, both with brands, and while one of them guides my captive and her guards back toward the bridge, the other goes to assist the struggling man with the dead body.

Across the river, more and more warriors are massing, some clearly ready to defend against the attack, others swaying, as though they've drunk too much. And into the flaming light come women and children as well.

"How many the fuck is there?" I breathe the question, and Edmund makes no reply. I imagine he's busy counting.

Our captive makes it to the bridge, is halted by the guards, and then with the flick of an angry head, is allowed to cross. The three other horses escort her, leaving only the enlarged collection of guards and the horseman with the dead body, and the other guard, who sprints beside him.

They make it the guard post and are allowed through with the most cursory of examinations.

On the other side, the horses are led away, the stumbling

woman surrounded by the three jarls, their angry stances easy to read. Even more people quickly gather around her, obscuring her so that she's lost to my sight. Warriors stand in the bright light of the fires, gazing out across the wide river, weapons in hand as though to threaten the empty river. I'm beginning to agree with Edmund that the half-cocked plan is about to work.

Only then, between one breath and the next, every single flame is extinguished. The entire riverbank is plunged into darkness apart from the solitary fire close to the bridge.

Silence rings out, louder than the bloody fury of battle, and absolutely fuck all happens.

"What the fuck?" Edmund whispers his question to me as he blinks, trying to clear his remaining eye from the fug of too many bright lights suddenly extinguished. I'm doing the same. Slivers of silver seem to dance on my eyelids.

"Fuck," I hadn't anticipated this. Not at all.

"What are they fucking doing?" he asks without turning. I shrug and then realise he can't see me do so.

"No fucking idea."

"I suppose it is nearly dark," Edmund tries, but my stomach feels leaden. It seems I've taken a gamble and it's failed. Surely, there should be Raiders making ready to mount up, to find who did this. I think back carefully, trying to decide if we spoke about anything we didn't want Jarl Guthrum's sister to know. But it seems not.

"Maybe she's not quite as important as she implied to Pybba and Rudolf?"

"Maybe she didn't even fucking tell them?" I muse, still peering at the blackness before me. I can see nothing. Full darkness has fallen, and there's one single fire to light the night sky. Even the clouds hang heavy, almost touching my face and merging with the mist from the river. All sound is muted in the dense air.

"She didn't exactly have to tell them," Edmund complains. "It was pretty fucking obvious."

"Yes, it was. Wasn't it? Maybe it was too obvious."

"What do we fucking do now?"

I turn aside from peering at the obscured view. No good will come from looking. There's nothing to see.

"We'll have to wait."

"It's a bit risky," Edmund states. We're shoulder to shoulder, leaning against the rock. Deep in the woodland in front of us, Haden and Jethson wait for us. They might have to wait longer yet.

"Go back to the horses. I'll keep watch here," I instruct Edmund, but he shakes his head.

"No, no, that's not a good idea. We should both go. Make our way back to the campsite we used last night."

"It's a bloody long way, in the dark."

"Yes, yes, it fucking is," Edmund concedes unhappily.

"Could we make it back to the ambush site? From there we would still be able to see anyone riding out."

"It's a bloody long way in the dark as well."

"Then we'll stay here," I decide. It's going to be a long, cold night, and we don't have any food.

"What a fucking mess," I grumble, and Edmund's silence tells me that he entirely agrees with me.

"Here, it is then," he acknowledges, allowing his head to rock back against the stone. He promptly closes his eyes, and I could swear he was actually asleep, only his breathing is too rapid.

My stomach growls angrily, and I try to remember when I last ate. It must have been before I mounted up to begin the day's activities, but I can't remember what it was, or even if I ate much. I lick my lips, tasting the salt of the day's exertion, as a spattering of water seems to adhere to my face; the river mist moving to claim the woodlands.

"Fuck." I shuffle, try and get comfortable, but Edmund has taken the only relaxing position, nestled in a smooth hollow in the rock, whereas I have sharp edges digging in my back. It's impossible. I can sleep almost anywhere, but not here.

Annoyed with myself, I stand, and pace ten steps into the woodland, and then ten steps back. It doesn't help, and so I do it again, hoping it will this time. It doesn't. And then again, once more.

"Sit the fuck down," Edmund growls at me through tight lips, but I can't. Instead, I stand and peer into the darkness. For a long time, I can't even see the single fire, and I think they must have extinguished it. Only then, I do finally catch sight of it.

A flicker of shadow moves across it, first one way and then the next.

"Get the fuck up here," I hiss at Edmund.

"What now?" His voice is laced with fatigue, but his response assures me that he wasn't asleep.

"Look," and I point, even though it's too dark for him to see the movement.

Edmund stands and glares at where he knows the bridge stands. Long moments pass, more and more shadows moving before the flame, and then he gasps.

"The fuckers are mounting up," he whispers so quietly that I have to bend close to his mouth to hear him.

"What? Now?"

"Yes, I can hear the jangle of horse equipment."

I listen eagerly, keen to know that the Raiders are going to respond, and frustrated that we'll not know how many ride out, or even, which way they fucking go. We'll be as blind as if we'd gone to Northampton and just waited for them to attack.

"There's a fucking lot of them," Edmund again whispers, but I've managed to determine that for myself. I've lost count of how many times the flames have been shadowed. If each one represents one rider, then the jarls have decided to respond with far more force than I anticipated.

Unease growls in my empty stomach, and again, I curse my ridiculous plan.

"Well," Edmund states, turning to look at me, his remaining eye glinting at me, "it seems you have your wish. The Raiders are about to go fucking hunting."

I swallow the bile in my throat.

For all I know the Raiders could be coming toward us even

now. They might know where we hide. The damn prisoner might have worked out herself that we've been managing to spy on the events taking place in Grantabridge.

"Shush." Edmund really doesn't need to offer the caution. The sound of hooves over the night-damp grass is easy to hear. It takes longer to determine the destination.

"They're taking the route back to Northampton," Edmund announces. I don't question how he can be so sure. The sound could be coming from all around us for all I know.

"How fucking many?"

I don't expect an answer, but I do sense his head turn to gaze at me, and I'm only pleased we're shrouded in darkness. I don't need to see the roll of his eye or the incredulity in it.

"Fifty," he comments, but I know he's just saying it. He has no actual idea.

"What do we do now?"

We're still stuck in our hiding place, the darkness absolute, the mist so thick it coats me. I consider our horses, I contemplate my warriors and hope they're well on the way to Northampton. I told them they weren't to stop and that they had to ride all night. But, I didn't appreciate thick black clouds would shroud the moon and that it would be impossible to see much beyond the end of my nose, or even that the rain would become more and more persistent.

"We find the horses," I stand, the decision made, only for Edmund to pull me down beside him.

He holds his finger to my lips, and I listen carefully, desperate to know what's happening now.

And then it comes to me, little more than a whimper of sound, and it makes no sense.

"Are they leaving?" the words aren't even a whisper.

"Fuck knows."

"Shit." This changes everything. I need to know what's happening in Grantabridge. They've sent warriors to track down the men responsible for apprehending the jarl's sister, but there's something else happening, and I need to know what it is.

"Fuck. We'll have to wait for daylight."

I can tell that Edmund agrees because he doesn't try and argue with me.

I don't want to be trapped between the Raider riding party and Grantabridge when the sun rises, but there's no choice.

And the sound doesn't stop either but rather continues, throughout what remains of the night. I try and rest, but sleep is beyond me. While Edmund manages to fall into an uneasy sleep, his head resting on the unyielding stone, I stay alert, listening, eyes half-lidded as though I can somehow see what's happening along the riverbank even though my back is to it.

There are ships out there, many ships, and the men and women on them must creep, or the rain-heavy clouds do such an excellent job of dampening all sound that it's almost impossible to hear more than the oars rising and falling. Whether they come or go will only become apparent come the morning. It's going to be a bloody long night.

I startle awake some time later. My eyes ache with the exhaustion of a second night with almost no sleep. Edmund still sleeps beside me, but something has woken me.

It's still dark, and the mist hasn't dissipated, but as I turn to gaze at where I know Grantabridge lies, I can see pinpricks of light, many more than just the one that the guards allowed themselves close to the river crossing.

"What?" I try and rub my eyes to full wakefulness, but it's useless. Every time I blink, I have to focus once more, and there's just not enough time to determine what's happening.

I place my hand on Edmund's arm, unsurprised when he grips it tightly, as though to twist it.

"It's me, you daft bastard," I whisper, and he jerks to full wakefulness, noting my position. It seems that the impenetrable black of the night has lifted. I can see him as clearly as if it were daylight.

"What's happening now?" I indicate the new flames along the riverbank, and Edmund turns to peer.

Yesterday, a long line of flames appeared in response to

the arrival of Jarl Guthrum's sister. These lights don't circle Grantabridge, but rather illuminate an area close to the bridge. More than that, though, I can't see.

While Edmund gazes, I reach for my water bottle and swig the fluid around my mouth. My belly rumbles as the water hits it, and I chew my foul tongue.

I don't demand answers from Edmund. If he had them, I know that he'd share them. Impatience gnaws at me. I didn't want to be stuck here all night. I should be on my way to Northampton as well.

"There are seventeen ships," I startle at Edmund's words.

"Seventeen?" I almost can't believe the number.

"They're being loaded up with people. I think one of them might even be Jarl Guthrum's sister, but I can't be sure."

I try and see what Edmund's telling me, but I can't. The flames, yes, the guards at the gate, yes, but ships? No, I can't see those, although I'm aware that people are walking forward and backwards in front of the flames.

"So, they're leaving?"

"No, some of them are leaving."

"But did they come with more warriors loaded on them?"

I chew my tongue, trying to make sense of this new development.

I can't understand why they'd be sending people away. The settlement looks substantial, the defences, while not yet complete, more than enough to allow them to defend it if we did happen to attack.

"They're definitely being loaded with people. Look," and he points, but of course, I still can't see as well as he can.

"It looks like they've been waiting for the darkness to ease, just as we have." And now I realise that the glooming is lifting, and I can see what Edmund's describing. Only my eyes are caught by something else as well.

"Bastards," while Edmund watches the ships being boarded, more mounted warriors are making their way onto this side of the river. It seems that those they sent out last night weren't their entire force, far from it.

"Get down," I pull Edmund down beside me, and he hisses in frustration but hides all the same.

The sound of hooves and harness is suddenly loud in our ears, and I can hear men calling one to another. Although they speak Danish, the malice in the words is easy enough to decipher.

And then the sound is even closer, and I hold my breath, for surely our hiding place has been discovered.

CHAPTER 17

And then Edmund moves. I try and grab him, bring him back to me, but he's scuttling away from the stone almost on his hands and knees.

The sound as he moves over the mass of damp, fallen leaves is so loud I'm sure it must be audible over the noise of the river and inside Grantabridge itself.

I pause, not even breathing, and then I rush after him, grabbing my water bottle as I go, squatting down, trying to make much less noise than he does. I can't hear anything over the crunch of my jagged movements, and although the darkness of the densely-packed woodland calls to me, it feels as though it's an impossible task to reach it before we're discovered.

I fall to my knees, scurrying forward with my hands in the deep-mulch, the fetid smell of the woodland reaching out to snag my senses. I would gag if I could risk making the noise.

I daren't look behind me. I don't want to know that we've been found, that a blade even now hovers close to my neck. Edmund disappears into the obscurity of the trees in front of me, not even bothering to turn.

"Fucking bastard," the words are little more than my mouth forming the shapes but the knowledge that he's escaped forces more speed to my aching knees. A man of my age shouldn't be scuttling around in such a way.

And then I feel the weight of the thick tree canopy above my head, and I rush to my feet, trying to find Edmund but it's as though night has fallen once more.

Instead, I shelter behind one of the trees, the trunk wide enough to hide me, and only then do I risk turning to see if we've been exposed.

I can clearly see the marks in the thick leaf litter where Edmund and I passed by, but the one man standing by the rock, hand on his weapons belt, seems unable to see the clearly defined marks. Instead, he peers into the woodland, and then back towards where his comrades must wait for him. With a shrug of his slim shoulders, the man streaks back toward his discarded horse.

I watch him go, heart pounding loudly in my chest, my stomach churning with more than just hunger, and then there's a hand on my arm, and I'm turning, seax already in my hand, the blade coming to rest against a neck.

"It's me, you fucking idiot." Edmund's words shock me enough that I hold the edge away from him and then meet his gaze.

"That was fucking close," he complains, as I bend, rest my hands on my knees, and just concentrate on stilling my thudding heart.

"Too damn fucking close," I agree when I can.

We share a glance and then we're both running along the little marked path we took to get to our lookout position.

We've lingered too long, and yet we know a great deal more than we did before. But my concerns are with my men. They're being hunted, and by more than double their number. I spare a thought for them, hoping against hope that in my arrogance I've not consigned both Penda and Gardulf to an untimely death.

My steps are even over the mulch, the dampness of the night seemingly percolated deep inside the woodlands, so that even though it doesn't actually rain, moisture drips from the leaves, only to pool down my face or worse, down my fucking neck.

Edmund leads the way, and although it takes longer than I think it should, we're soon reunited with our mounts. Haden glares at me, his eyes telling me too much. Jethson is closer to him than he was the night before, and I'm glad that neither of them can talk to tell me of what's occurred since we left them. The ground between them shows signs of much activity, and I think we should have tied them tightly to a tree branch. Only we couldn't, because if the worst happened, we wanted them to escape.

We left them unsaddled, and now it takes precious time to make them ready to ride, and all the time, Haden is as unhelpful as always. For him, there's no sense of urgency, or a desire to be reunited with the rest of the horses.

Edmund is mounted in record time, but I still fight with my fucking stubborn horse.

"Will you leave it," I eventually huff, as Haden worries at my weapons belt, as though there'll be a treat there for him. I thrust his huge head upwards, run my hand along his black and white nose, the only apology he's going to get from me.

"Come on. We need to fucking leave." I plead with him, and for once, he heeds my words, and stands docile, as I tighten the saddle, ensuring it's comfortable for both of us.

"Which way?" Edmund asks, but I've been considering this since we fled from Grantabridge.

"We're going to Icknield Way."

Edmund startles at the announcement, but then he nods, as though I needed his agreement.

"Come on," I encourage Haden to move out, not toward Northampton, but rather toward the River Granta, and then to Icknield Way. I can't beat the Raiders back to Northampton by following them, but I can arrive by an entirely different route. I only hope it's somehow quicker.

The going is slow as we pick a path through the dense woodland trees. I can feel Edmund growing frustrated, and I'm unsurprised. More than once, I have to bite back on retracting my decision and head for Ermine Street. But no, I'm sure that this way we'll avoid the Raiders and arrive in good time to assist Ealdorman Ælhun and the rest of my warriors in defending Northampton from the coming assault.

I needed to draw as many of the Raiders from Grantabridge as I could. I couldn't fight them from outside trying to get in. I don't have enough men to lay a siege. Now, I need them to be as far away from it as possible as well. I don't want them simply turning and rushing back to the perceived safety of their riverside settlement.

Not for the first time, I wish it wasn't nearly winter, and that I had a force that numbered the same as the Raiders can call on. But I don't.

The Raiders attacks have taken a heavy toll on Mercian warriors. I can't continuously call on reinforcements from another country as the Raiders can.

We emerge from the tree line cautiously. The sun is high in the sky, the dampness all burned away, but the passage of time concerns me.

"It's clear," Edmund beckons me forward, and then we turn Haden and Jethson's head toward the Granta. I know there's a crossing close by, Gyrth told me as much. We just need to find it.

Haden's gait is smooth once we're free from the trees, and whereas before we moved far too slowly, we now move almost too quickly. It's impossible to keep my eyes on where we're going and who might be close to us. Only as we ford the narrow river crossing, raised slabs of well-worn stone pushing up against the flow of the water, do I hazard a glance back toward Grantabridge. But it's too far away, and I see nothing, not even the haze of smoke on the skyline that pinpoints every place of habitation from a good distance away.

"Come on," I lean forward and slap Haden along his right shoulder in appreciation of his decision to just take the river crossing rather than refuse, as he normally would. Perhaps he senses my urgency, or maybe he just wants to be across before Jethson, and able to choose the pace at which we travel. Either way, I welcome it as we seek out the roadway of the ancient Icknield Way.

The ancient road surface is far from complete, not anymore,

but it's wide enough to allow the two horses to ride side by side. With a steadier pace, it's easier to scout for the enemy. Sweat beads down my back and still my stomach grumbles, and I have nothing more to offer it. Anything I did try to eat would turn to ash in my mouth. I'd rather go hungry.

All the same, it's Edmund who sees the cloud of dust in front of us first, and reins in, cheeks blowing hot. Jethson circles, head low, and I appreciate just how quickly we've been riding.

"They've reached Ermine Street."

Not far in front, Icknield Way and Ermine Street cross.

"Only now?" I question. The Raiders have covered far less distance than us. They've only had to go straight through the woodlands, we've taken a far more indirect route.

"If it's fucking them," Edmund cautions, but who else could it be? I pause then, considering. I had intended to take Icknield Way until it met Watling Street, and return to Northampton that way. But if the Raiders are only just in front of us, it might be possible to outrun them first.

"We're more exposed on the ancient roads," Edmund offers, his thoughts instantly following mine.

"But we'll be quicker," I caution. I allow Haden to tug his head low to nibble at some tall grasses growing to the side of the hard-packed road, where the ditches meant to carry the rainwater away have long since clogged with detritus. We might have to cover a far more considerable distance, but it will be along what remains of the roadways. They might not be maintained as well as they could be, but they'll be better than trusting muddy trackways, and the crossing of the River Ouse.

But I don't know if quicker is fucking better. Maybe we could cause the Raiders some problems along the way.

"There are only two of us," Edmund's snapped words quickly dissipate my ideas of plaguing the mounted Raiders.

"Shit, we'll go via the roads," I confirm, already pulling Haden back to attention. Only Edmund is less keen to move. His face twists in thought.

"I wish we knew the landscape better," he complains. "I wish we knew if there was a trackway from here."

"But we fucking don't."

"No, we don't," he agrees. His unease is evident in the way that Jethson keeps moving beneath him. Rider and horse are too well accustomed to each other not to react when the other is troubled.

"Right, let's fucking do this," Edmund finally agrees, and the horses meander to a steady gallop.

Out in the open, the road traffic increases, and we pass a few people, some mounted, others encouraging slow-moving oxen to transport supplies. I don't take the time to speak to them, even though I would prefer to. Perhaps it's better that they don't realise that the new king of Mercia rides with only one warrior as his guard, through potentially hostile land. Certainly, there's unease and fear on the faces that we encounter as men and women carry whatever they can lay their hands on in a threatening manner.

It pleases me to see such bravery and also worries me. How long have we been under attack? Will it ever end?

As we turn the horses along Watling Street, to head towards Northampton, thick clouds begin to gather, and I hunker inside my cloak, as the wind picks up, bringing with it the hint of rain. It also fore-shortens the day.

"Well need to travel more slowly," I call to Edmund. He's stooped inside his cloak, a picture of misery and for a moment I think he'll ignore my words, only he tugs gently on Jethson's reins, and the animal slows.

"It's going to fucking rain." Of all the things Edmund could be concerned with, it almost makes me laugh to hear that it's getting wet, which bothers him the most.

"Aye, it's going to rain. It looks like it might last a while as well," my eyes once more turn to the sky. The heavy clouds feel oppressive; the wind whipping the collar of my cloak into my mouth. If I was into portents, I might be concerned. I might see it as presaging the fucking Raiders pouring into Mercia once more. But I'm not one for such things. Our fate is what we make it, and right now, I'm doing all I can.

"Come on, we'll stop once it gets too bad." I urge Haden on, trusting that somewhere soon we'll find a place to shelter. We're riding further and further into the heartland of Mercia. I'm hoping that the Raiders had only infiltrated as far west as Northampton, but time will tell.

I can only focus on reaching Northampton, and so I slow Haden to little more than a trot, hide my neck deep in my cloak and wish, just like Edmund, that it wasn't compounding my misery by fucking raining.

We finally stop for the night when the horses are dragging their hooves rather than placing them, and I confess, I'd drifted to sleep in the saddle.

It's hardly a steading fit for a king, but the abandoned stone building at least offers some shelter from the lashing rainstorm and tempestuous winds.

"It'll slow them," Edmund assures me, removing Jethson's saddle and placing it on the floor. Half the roof is missing, but half is still intact, keeping the rain from falling in the farthest corner. Haden seems put out by his accommodation for the night. I'm forced to remove his saddle, wipe the sweat from his back, and offer him the last of my water pooled into a half-broken pot on the floor that only works if I hold it at a specific angle. And all this is done in the grey-light of a full-moon obscured by the thick rain clouds overhead.

Only then can I settle to get some much-needed rest, but even that's not enough. Edmund shakes me to full wakefulness, and for another day, my eyes open unwillingly, blinking away the grit of too little sleep.

"Fuck," I croak, and he thrusts his water bottle at me. I sate my thirst, surprised to find that it contains water, and then we mount up and ride.

The roadway is littered with puddles, the long-blocked draining ditches doing more to vomit the water onto the pitted surface than force it away. My cloak remains sodden from the night before, my feet achingly cold, in a way I've only really noticed since my pretend imprisonment at Repton, barefoot. I'm miserable and frozen, and still, rain pours from the clouds overhead. The sun might well be up, but I can't fucking see it.

A shiver of unease runs through me. I can't allow Haden any greater speed than a trot, and even then, I risk him stumbling and going lame. Edmund is silent beside me, but I'd rather he was spouting his usual complaints. Somehow his reticence speaks more of his frustration.

"They won't ride in the rain," is all I can offer, but it's not true. We both know that. The Raiders will force their unwilling mounts no matter the weather. They'll simply leave lame horses behind them, in pain. Bastards.

We meet no one on the road, and I'm unsurprised. If there were a choice, I wouldn't travel in this weather either. But I need to get back to Northampton. I need to be there when my decisions bring this fresh infiltration by the Raiders to its culmination.

But our progress is painfully slow, and only the growing sound of water pushes us on. We need to cross the River Ouse, and then we should, if the weather weren't so terrible, be able to see the hills close to Northampton itself. Only full dark falls just as we near the river.

Without discussing it, Edmund and I wearily dismount and lead the horses forward. They're as exhausted as we are, and only the potential welcome from a solitary light encourages me to even press on into the settlement close to the river crossing.

Our arrival doesn't go unnoticed, as the creak of a doorway greets the sound of damp hooves.

"We are men of Mercia," Edmund speaks for both of us, and I'm pleased he doesn't mention who we truly are.

"Miserable weather," greets our words, rolled around the tongue of a man as though he echoes them himself. I turn to eye the person who watches us from in front of his steading. It seems evident to me that he tends the river crossing, living as close to it as he does, but in the flickering brand he holds, I can also make out the sheen of a weapon. It seems he's used to trouble.

"Have you seen Raiders travel this way?"

He shakes his head, pulling his beard through his large fingers.

"Not recently. Why?" I decide to take a chance.

"We understand they've taken control of Northampton."

The man recoils so sharply at the words that I appreciate that he's heard no such thing. Indeed, his eyes flicker northwards.

"They've been driven out," I hastily assure him, mindful that a small child has slipped through the closed door, and now stands gaping at us from beside the older man.

"By who?" the question is rough and conveys too much fear.

"King Coelwulf and Ealdorman Ælhun." Now confusion wars with fear.

"The new king?" he asks, and a gleam enters his eye. I think the man far too perceptive.

"Then, why are you here?"

Edmund stirs as though to deny the words, but I place a hand on his arm to stay his denial.

"We're drawing the Raiders from Grantabridge. They're locked up tight there. We can't get them out any other way."

I can't tell whether this pleases him or not, but his next words reassure me.

"Come in from the rain. We have extra food, and there's a stable for the horses."

"My thanks," I offer, already turning to follow where the man points.

"Don't let the fuckers come this way," the man mutters, and I echo his desire, as I dismount and lead Haden to the offer of a warm shelter for the night. I'll not let the 'fuckers' get anywhere. They'll have to fight me for every advance they try to make.

CHAPTER 18

"Where are they?" I bellow the question when I finally ride across the heavily protected bridge at Northampton and into the settlement itself. My arrival, Edmund at my side, sparks a flurry of worried glances from those busy about their labours.

"Who?" It's Tatberht who asks, and I gaze at him, confused by the question.

"The others," I finally mutter, when his blank face continues to be as puzzled as mine.

"What others?"

"Where's Hereman?" I ask instead, already moving to dismount from Haden. We're both drenched. The weather has remained cold and bleak, and I'm almost frozen in place.

Only Tatberht's answer arrests my descent, one leg over Haden's back.

"Hereman is with you. Isn't he?" Tatberht moves as though to look behind me, expecting Hereman to be there, sitting on his horse, watching with his half-amused expression fixed in place.

"They're not here?" Edmund joins me now, his question perhaps easier to understand.

"No, he's not here. No one is here, other than you." Ælfgar joins Tatberht, and his words convince me, finally, that my men are missing.

"Fuck," I'm already settling myself back on Haden's back, trying to ignore the squelch of my clothes.

Edmund is doing the same, and then Ealdorman Ælhun joins our strange party, his face as confused as everyone else's. His frost-rimmed beard drips with water, and he shivers into a fur-lined cloak.

"Where are the rest of your force?" worry laces the words, dragging his lips downwards.

"They should be here," I grumble. "The Raiders were following them. We had to travel a different way. Fuck, this wasn't supposed to happen." I'm already turning Haden to leave once more. Only I pause.

"Is the gateway entirely sealed?" I'm speaking of the one that leads out of Northampton, to the far side of the river.

"Yes, the work is complete. The walkway is nearly in place as well." It's Tatberht who assures me.

"What will you do?" I can see that Ealdorman Ælhun has quickly realised the peril my missing warriors face.

"Find them, bring them home."

"What, just two of you? That's not enough."

"No, it probably fucking isn't. But what's the point in completing the work on the defences if no one is inside Northampton to make use of them. Edmund and I will find the others. Bring them back. If we can. If we can't, you'll have to take charge of ensuring Northampton stays intact, because as bloody inconvenient as it now is, the Raiders are coming, and my warriors are missing."

A spasm of worry seems to settle over Ealdorman Ælhun but then he nods, as though resolved.

"I'll do as you order."

Now it's my turn to look surprised. How quickly I forget that as the king, my word is now the law.

"Thank you," I mutter, but now Tatberht's hand snakes onto my reins.

"I'm coming with you," he announces. "Give me a few moments, and I'll be ready."

I want to shake my head, deny his request, but Tatberht is old enough, and stupid enough, to make such a decision for himself. If he wants to come, then he can come. Maybe, after all, he misses the excitement.

Ælfgar nods. "I'm coming as well."

"Allow entry to no one but us." More and more of Ealdorman Ælhun's warriors are flooding from the hall, no doubt informed of my arrival, and my eyes settle on Wulfsige. There's something in his eyes that I don't like. I wish I had the time to consider what he hides behind his façade, but my men are potentially in need of my assistance.

I won't abandon them, not when I stirred the hornet's nest and sent the Raiders rushing after them.

As we make our way back to the bridge, I catch the eye of the seven men there. I only just rode passed them, words of welcome on their lips. I recognised them but not enough to ask the critical question. And in all honesty, I didn't think it needed to be asked. I wrongly assumed that my warriors would be here.

"Keep fucking alert," I bellow to them, Haden picking his way with some care onto the first piece of wooden planking that runs the length of the bridge. "The Raiders will be coming. They might be close to me when they appear. If you believe that they'll get across the bridge before we do, then hack it down. Have axes ready, just in case. Keep Northampton safe, and the people inside, no matter what happens."

Two of the men startle at my words, while another, nods sagely, and the remaining four simply grin at me, ready to savour the battle, even though it's not even upon them yet.

Tatberht and Ælfgar have joined us quickly. Tatberht rides his mount comfortably, as though his age and infirmities are banished by the prospect of what must come. I only hope I have his thirst for battle when I've seen as many decades as he has. Ælfgar has a tight grimace on his face. He might not want to be here, but he's fucking coming all the same.

Over the bridge, we quickly turn our horses, not back to Watling Street, but instead along the Nene. There's a river crossing further along. Much further to the south but I don't have the time for that. Instead, I lead my three men along the river, noting as I do that the repairs on the ramparts of Northampton have been made, while the ditch flashes wetly at me. I imagine it's almost as deep as the river in places, but deadlier, with its wooden stakes sticking up at strange angles.

The rain continues to fall, a flood of cold water across my legs, sinking into Haden's coat, making the black shimmer, while the white has turned a murky grey. When this is over, both of us are going to need a good bath.

Through the lurking river mist, I pick out a potential crossing place. The river flows thick and sludge-like, and the riverbank is thick with gleaming plants, all waiting to trip me. But, my men are to the far side of Northampton, and the only way to find them is to cross the river.

Haden belatedly realises my intention, and while Edmund, Ælfgar and Tatberht hold their tongues, he stops, one hoof hovering over the slick greenness of the riverbank.

"Come on," I urge him, but my voice is soft. Now isn't the time for bellicose complaints. I need him to obey me, and I need it to be quickly done.

"Rudolf is there. He needs you." I doubt the words will have the desired impact, but maybe Haden is just as intelligent as I think he is because he immediately crashes down the riverbank. The wetness of the thick grasses quickly covers my legs, the damp and wetness sinking ever closer to my skin, and then Haden is in the water. I lift my body as clear from the saddle as possible, keen to redistribute my weight as much as I can.

The water swirls perilously close to the top of my legs, and for a moment, I think we're sinking, only then we're not. With sure movements, Haden makes the short passage across the river, his head fixed on the point he's chosen to disembark at, and I allow it. If the rain continues to fall like this, then I'm unsure how we'll make it back inside Northampton.

I ordered the landward-side gateway sealed and closed for a good reason. But, I confess, I didn't expect to need to make a potentially quick entrance, and that possibility now makes me consider the deep ditch and tall rampart in an entirely different way.

I fear I may have directed that Northampton be made so secure it will lead to the deaths of my warriors rather than those of the Raiders.

Behind me, I can hear Edmund, Ælfgar and Tatberht following through the water. And when Haden rears clear of the water, his back legs dripping with a deluge of water, I don't even take the time to check they've successfully managed the same.

There's no choice. They have to, or they'll get left fucking behind. I need to find my men. Nothing else matters.

And yet, a cry from the rampart at Northampton forces me to turn and look at it. There, suspended perhaps from several spears, both ends held tightly, is the bleached-white banner my Aunt made me, festooned with gold and red thread. I take it for the promise of success that it is.

The cry of a cheer greets me, and I wave my sodden arm in appreciation for the act. The cheer reverberates even louder, and a tight smile touches my worry-stained face.

Ealdorman Ælhun and the warriors of Mercia will be waiting for me. I just need to find Hereman, Rudolf, Pybba and the others first.

Fuck, I hope I'm not too late.

Not that we make quick progress. When we rode from Northampton, days before, the earth was hard-packed, almost frozen, the promise of winter to come evident in the plume of my heated breath. But all that is gone now.

Instead of my breath appearing before me, it's as though we've been enveloped in cloud. The rain is so thick that I can taste it. Fuck, I can see the raindrops falling they're so damn big. And it's not warm rain either, but cold, as though laden with the weight of ice. Not the sort of weather to be riding to war, and that's what we're doing. I could have allowed the Raiders to see out the winter inside Grantabridge. Perhaps I should have done, but I want them fucking gone.

I could, if I needed to, make an argument that Grantabridge is part of East Anglia, and that kingdom fell long ago to the

Raiders. I want them gone from Mercia. Forever. I don't want them in East Anglia, but if that's all I can manage until the fighting season next year, then that's what I'll accept.

In the dank gloominess, it's more difficult to retrace the path we took on first leaving Northampton. I don't want to veer to either side. I'm hoping that my warriors will simply have been waylaid, perhaps by a lame horse and that they're rushing this way even now. I banish my fears that the Raiders have captured them. Such thoughts do no justice to their cleverness.

They wouldn't have allowed themselves to be caught. They'd have died trying to evade capture, and it's that worry that niggles the most. So honourable, so fucking proud. I only hope it's not made them arrogant of their abilities against a vastly superior force.

"Will it ever stop sodding raining?" Edmund's complaint is loud enough to reach my ears, even if he speaks to Jethson. I share his frustration. If it weren't for Haden's sure-footedness, we would have stumbled into a muddy hole more than once by now. I can see so little. If it's not the thick rain hanging in the air, then it's the abundant rain drumming into my eyes, forcing me to blink time and time again. My hands are slick on the reins. If we do happen to come upon the Raider force, I'm not at all convinced I'll even be able to hold my seax without it slipping from my grip.

The only consolation is that the light is so weak, it's more than likely that we'll crash into each other without even realising the other is there. The element of surprise might help all of us.

In no time at all, the bank of grey before me materialises into the start of the woodlands to the west of Ermine Street.

Here, I pull Tatberht, Ælfgar and Edmund to my side, jumping clear from Haden and allowing him to drink from the small beck flowing between the thick tree trunks.

"We need to be alert from now on," I caution, but even before I've finished speaking the words, I appreciate that I'm trying to lecture three men who've spent all of their lives employing such tactics.

"Apologies," I offer before they can so much as huff with annoyance.

"We'll find them," Tatberht assures, his tone firm, but Edmund's continued silence speaks of his disbelief that everything will be quite so easy. He's seen the Raiders. Tatberht, for all his experience, has been in Kingsholm for the last few years. He's not faced the same threats that we have. Ælfgar grunts once more. He has been away from Kingsholm. He has fought the Raiders, and he's survived. That isn't, perhaps the reassurance that it should be.

I lead Haden through the woodland. I don't want to travel via the well-trodden path, but neither can we be far from it. Instead, I've reconciled myself to keeping it within hearing distance, if not sight. And as we journey deeper and deeper into the tightly packed expanse of trees, I don't really think it would have mattered anyway.

While it rains above us, the trees provide some much-needed protection, but we're plunged into near darkness. Every step is taken cautiously. I would order Edmund, Ælfgar and Tatberht to spread out, to look elsewhere for our lost men, but if I did that, it would be impossible to keep sight of them. It's not entirely black as a moonless night, but it isn't far from being so.

My breath grinds too loudly through my chest. I would quieten it, but as so often the case, attempts to make it quieter serve only to make it louder.

Haden steps softly, despite his size, and I rely more on him than what my eyes are telling me. Really, Edmund should lead, but I won't let him. His soft puffs of displeasure reach my ears time and time again, but I refuse to be baited by him.

My ears strain, desperate to hear anything, hoping that it will be my men and not the Raiders.

The drum of the rain is softer, but insistent beneath the trees, and although the icy cold water is no longer drenching me, I don't feel any warmer. If anything, I feel cold. Too cold.

"Fuck," I turn to meet Edmund's eye, and it seems he's thinking the same thing I am.

"We need to get warm," and he nods, his chin half-tilted to indicate Tatberht and Ælfgar. For all Tatberht's eagerness to venture forth, I'm surprised to find a stark-white face appearing from the gloom.

"Right, we need to move more quickly, and we need to put on warmer clothes."

Tatberht starts to shake his head, but the motion slowly stills, his eyes pooling wider, and I close my eyes, knowing without speaking, what he's just seen. Ælfgar realises quickly as well, his gaze urgently sweeping the expanse before us.

I turn unhurriedly, eyes raking in the gloaming, keen to have my assumption confirmed.

Even Haden lifts his head to scent the air, and I know we're no longer alone. What I don't know is whether these people are our allies or enemies.

"There," Edmund points to my right, his finger almost below my nose. Quickly, I see what he's telling me, and if possible, my skin chills even more.

"Bastards." The word is soft, but audible, as I hold Haden ever firmer on his rein.

"How many?" But Edmund shakes his head, urges me to retrace the last ten steps. I follow him, placing each foot carefully to avoid any crisp, brown leaves, unsure why Edmund is making us move. Surely, he risks us being seen, just because of the movement?

Only then I understand, as the thick branches of the enormous oak tree cover us, and more, the thick trunk allows us all to hide, far from sight. I remember passing the tree, the wide and ancient trunk I didn't notice. How, I'm unsure, but I'm grateful for Edmund's better observations.

"What do we fucking do?" Edmund whispers the question, his hand running along Jethson's nose as he calms the unhappy animal.

"How many are there?"

I'd ask how we even know that they're Raiders, but that much was evident from the glitter of iron around their waists. They are the enemy.

"Impossible to see. At least ten."

I expel my held breath at the announcement. There are four of us. Well, eight if we include the horses, and I'd rather not. The trees are too tightly packed to allow us to ride. What, I consider, would I expect them to be able to accomplish?

"It's only two or three of the fuckers to a man," Tatberht mutters. But his face remains white with cold, and I can see how his left arm tremors even as he holds it firm with the right one.

I glance at Edmund, and his nod is just perceptible.

Without pausing to allow Tatberht time to argue, I grab my shield from Haden's back, Edmund doing the same from Jethson.

"Wait here. Keep the horses safe." My voice is rough as I speak, and I spare a thought for Tatberht and Ælfgar's feelings, but only briefly. They know. They've always known.

I allow Edmund to lead the way. He has the better sight, even with just the one eye. He slips from tree to tree, taking us far away from where we've left the others, using whatever cover he can, and I follow. Our steps are not entirely silent, but I wish they were.

And then the smell of smoke reaches my nose, and I understand more. A camp of Raiders, this close to Northampton.

But Edmund keeps moving onwards, each step placed carefully, even as he keeps his gaze forward. I take the time to make sure we're not being tracked, and thoroughly sweep my eyes behind us. I wouldn't miss the tell-tale glint of iron in a hand.

"Here," Edmund hisses to me, and I realise I've become distracted with what might lurk behind us and forgotten about our actual target. I scamper to the side, hover behind Edmund where he stands using another tree trunk to mask his presence. This one is only just wide enough, and I think, if we joined hand to hand, we might just be able to circle it between us.

"There are twenty of them," Edmund's voice is filled with a warning, as his words reach my ears. I know what he's telling me. I'm just not sure that I'm listening to the caution. He should speak plainly.

Laughter rumbles through the air.

"Arrogant fuckers," I complain, but Edmund shakes his head, as though he can't believe I'd risk giving our presence away. I'm sure they're not going to hear us from here.

His hand grips my wrist then, his eye turning to me, the white the brightest I've ever seen it. And then I understand his concern.

The sound of urine hitting the woodland floor sounds louder than any rainstorm, but I'm already moving. The man has his back to me, just to the left and I can reach him before he's rearranged himself, I know I can.

I ignore Edmund's outraged hiss of annoyance and watch my steps. I don't want any tell-tale sounds of snapping branches to give away my presence. Not that I believe there can be any in the dank conditions, but I'm not about to take the risk.

My seax is already in my hand; my shield left beside Edmund. I won't need it for an opportunistic kill like this.

The man whistles tunelessly, his head turning when another echo of laughter fills the air. Before he can do more, I have my hand on his chin, and my seax cuts deep and quickly, the scent of iron and rust assaulting my nostrils after the dampness of the drying woodland.

Carefully, I lay the body to the floor, feeling the dying trembles as the man tries to open and close his mouth to issue a warning that's never going to be given a voice.

Turning, I grin at Edmund, but he doesn't return my delight. Instead, his face is filled with fury. I trample back toward him, not as careful this time, but still managing not to be too noisy.

"Why did you fucking do that?" Edmund demands to know.

"He was there," I whisper, pointing at the spot where the dead man lies hidden.

"And what happens when the others realise he's fucking gone?"

"They'll look for whoever killed him."

"And?"

"And then we can kill them one by one, rather than attacking them and allowing them to gang up on us."

A flicker of fury touches Edmund's cheeks, but then he surprises me by grinning.

"Shit, I forgot you might actually know what you're doing."

His agreement is only just given quickly enough.

The sound of someone crashing through the undergrowth startles us both, but then we're moving. We've done this before. We'll bloody do it again.

I circle the new Raider, Edmund skips to the side and is quickly subsumed by the encroaching darkness. If I didn't know he was there, I'd have no idea.

My role is to intercept the new Raider before he spies the dead man.

My steps are firm, the warmth of a kill doing more to drive the cold from my body than a raging fire.

I quickly catch sight of my target. I can make out little more than the shimmer of iron on his weapons belt, his clothing flashing as a darker outline against the shadows leaping higher and higher because of the fire.

He's on a direct intercept course for the body, but so am I.

At the last possible moment, he glances upwards, as though sensing me, rather than seeing me, but I'm already behind him, and just as with the first warrior, I hold his bearded chin firmly, while my seax drinks once more.

I lie him down next to the first dead man, my hands quickly reaching down to the weapons belt, keen to see the wealth they claimed.

Sharpened edges greet my quest, and I grunt. These men are well equipped. Neither are they young. These Raiders have lived, and fought, and drawn blood and taken tribute in the past. It's good that I took them so easily. The others will likely be more difficult to fell because one missing man is a cause for concern, two is a sure sign of attack.

But, there's no need to draw attention to what's happening. Not yet.

The next to peel away from the fire comes with his hand resting on his sword.

The garbled words he expels with each stamp of his feet ensures I always know where he is.

This time I expect some sort of attempt at defence, but once more, the warrior, no doubt because of the scent of mead on his lips, lays claim to reflexes that are just too slow. He dies with another slice of his neck, although he does at least almost hold his weapon.

Now, I know that the next to seek out their missing men, will not be alone.

I breathe deeply through my open mouth, the scent of shed blood seeming to desecrate this special woodland place, and that's even with the scent of piss and shit rife in the air.

With my eyes trained on the campfire, I wait for what I know must come next.

The first tell is the silence that emanates from around the fire. Before the Raiders were talking loudly, laughing. Now the camp has fallen completely silent, not even the whispers of worried lips reaching me.

I feel my lips grow rigid, my cheeks, so cold for much of the day, tight against the unexpected movement.

They'll come now. Maybe only two of them, perhaps as many as three. Behind them, the others will cower, hoping against hope that the others are just mucking about. Some will have hands on weapons; others will be belligerent, thinking it just the result of too much mead and too little attention.

Daft fuckers.

I'm not sure exactly where Edmund is, but he'll be close. I have to rely on that.

They come on quiet feet but don't mute their breathing, and it's that more than anything that alerts me to where they are, as I hide, out of sight.

I hold my seax, preparing to meet the warrior to the left of me. He rattles like a damp fire. I close my eyes, focus on where he is, and then I leap from behind the tree, seax already outstretched, my arm firm for what will inevitably come next. The daft fuck just about impales himself. The gargle from his throat is enough to alert his comrade of what's happening, but Edmund is already snaking a hand around the man's chin, and as he pulls him back, blood shimmers through the air, a moment of violent colour in the drab landscape.

And then two more are dead.

But Edmund and I don't so much as look at each other. We take practised moves, find new places to shelter, and just wait.

"Eirikr," the shout shatters the silence, and I grin once more. Bloody fools.

When there's no reply to the cry, I hear a splattering of muted conversation and the footsteps of some other unfortunate bastard making his or her way toward me.

I never fail to be surprised by the failure of men clearly under assault to understand just that. It makes it too easy.

I control my panting, listen as carefully as before, and then I feel my forehead wrinkle. Something's changed.

Crafty bastard.

There's not one warrior coming toward me, but rather more. I crack my neck from side to side, lick my dry lips, and wish I'd taken the time to wipe the slickness from my blade. Not that it matters. The blood will mingle, but everyone will be dead. It hardly matters.

Soft footfalls and I appreciate that the enemy has tried to trick me by shouting for one of their numbers, at the same time as sending two warriors to intercept me. Perhaps they're not quite as untried in this as I thought.

Using the tree trunk as my shield, I peer out from behind it, just enough to know where my opponents are. They come, two almost shoulder to shoulder, their eyes rake in all around them, while the warrior who must have shouted, continues to crash and make as much noise as possible off to the side.

"Clever fucks," I admire. "But not clever enough."

Edmund slips from his hiding place, far to the right, and with no intention of keeping himself hidden any longer, roars at the solitary warrior, his sword ready in his hand to snick out and land a blow to the warrior's weapon hand.

The yelp of surprise, coupled with the sound of the dropped weapon thudding to the floor, echoes loudly through the hushed woodland.

Both of my attackers, swivel their heads to discover the source of the noise, hands tight on their weapons. Just the distraction I needed.

Leaving the safety of the tree trunk, I dash forward, arm raised to combat the first of the men.

With his back to me, curls of dark hair snaking up his exposed neck, I prepare for yet another easy kill. But this warrior is more astute than that.

As I raise my seax to land a strike across his neck, a long sword roars upwards, directing my blow away from its target. Quickly, I double my grip, already reaching for the sword that hangs on my weapons belt. But the other warrior is almost quicker.

Suddenly, I'm facing a flurry of blows, from both an axe and a seax, and it's all I can do to retrace my steps while protecting my body.

"*Skiderik*," the warrior calls, and I grin, my face as exposed as theirs. I can tell then that my attacker is much younger than I, the vagaries of long battle experience missing from his black eyes. I grin, a flash of white to break through the gloom, and then I'm hacking. A war axe is a good weapon, for pulling aside shields, but perhaps not for killing a man without such a weapon.

Edmund's man is dead, I can just see from the corner of my eye, as I slide my seax into the prongs of the axe, forcing it away from my body, and closer, always closer, to the man who wields it. I know I don't have much time before the other Raider recovers his senses, and gets involved as well.

I don't fear being outnumbered, but I do want to kill my opponent as quickly as possible.

The heavy silence thrums with the menace of battle as I swing my sword, left-handed, aiming my blow to impact the dancing seax of my foe. With the longer reach, I want to keep both weapons from me, but of course, with my seax entangled in the prongs of the war axe, and my sword keeping the other seax at bay, I have nothing to level at the panting warrior.

Sweat beads down the man's face, the effort of countering my attack on his war axe, making it that much easier to keep his seax away from me.

"Haflioði," the name is shouted through tight lips, and the other warrior startles, recalled to what's happening around him.

"Shit," I breathe. There's nothing for it, but it's going to hurt me just as much as it is him.

I drop my sword, step ever closer, and then my head juts forward, and the crack of cartilage adds yet another sickening sound to the waking woodlands, sending a pulse down my diminished, but still visible, egg-shaped bump.

In the distance, I know the rest of the warband are springing into action. No longer masking their movements, the host crashes through the trees and wayward branches.

Stunned, my opponent drops his war axe even lower, my seax going with it. Blood floods down his nose and into his drooping black moustache, forcing him to gag because breathing through his nose is beyond him, I take one step back, bring my sword forward in a sweeping movement, that slices easily through the thin fabric of his tunic.

Damn fucker shouldn't have cast aside his byrnie.

He stumbles, his weapons forgotten about as his hand's quest for the gaping wound, but I've forgotten him. My intention now is to end the life of the other warrior.

The man is somewhat older, the wrinkles around his eyes attesting to the passage of years, but he seems no more skilled because of that. There are no scars on his face and none on the exposed forearms that flash before me.

A warrior. Perhaps?

"Amlaib," the name rings from his gaping mouth.

"Not the best warrior," I ridicule, abandoning the dying figure as though he were little more than a sack of grain.

My newest opponent is torn. It's clear he wishes to check on whoever Amlaib was, but equally, he doesn't want to die.

We face each other. I'm calm, even though I catch sight of those coming to join the fight, but Haflioði is unsure and undecided, his hands paused on reaching for his weapons.

An advantage to be exploited.

"I'll make it quick," I promise, my words soft, only they have the opposite of the desired effect.

Resolve settles over the face, hands quickly reach for both the sword and the seax, and two sure steps bring the man close enough for our weapons to touch.

"*Skiderik*," my new opponent spits, but unknown to him, Edmund is behind him, a grimace on his face, and his blade ready to skewer through the back.

I give an imperceptible shake of my head. I'll kill the man fairly. No need to take him in the back. Edmund's eye rolls and both eyebrows lift in frustration, but he knows better than to interfere.

The enemy now moves to my left, an attempt to circle me, or to get closer to the dead man, I'm not sure. Or maybe he's aware of Edmund.

If he thinks his allies will get to me quickly enough to ensure he lives, he's mistaken. They make the noise of a herd of cattle crashing through the trees, but they move no faster than a slug.

I tip my head to the right, consider the best way to end this new battle quickly and cleanly. I'm not about to inflict a lingering wound. The cruelty in such a death has never appealed to me.

My foe's sword flashes through the air, and my seax counters it easily enough although my eyes are arrested by the elaborate carvings on the handle and the flicker of oil that seems to shimmer down the blade.

Perhaps the son of another successful Raider, proud to wield his father's blade. Or maybe just taken from a worthy opponent. Either way, the weapon doesn't quite match the warrior I face. It makes me reconsider. Perhaps the shock of the attack has driven his killer instincts from him.

With my sword, I attempt a slicing motion across his belly, but he quickly skips clear of me. The hand that holds his sword is firm, the pressure against my seax, small but continual. A strong man then, for all he doesn't look like one.

Some warriors are bulky and filled with muscle; others are wiry and sinewy. And yet others are even more deceptive. I would think him little more than a lucky bastard if it weren't for that sword.

My eyes narrow. Perhaps I should have allowed Edmund to kill him.

I risk a glance at Edmund, but his attention is focused on the ten men who are nearly upon us. I need to do this quickly. Two against ten isn't impossible, not when they're so ill-disciplined. But this eleventh man might require all of my attention.

Only my opponent has other ideas, the pressure on my seax arm falling away, as he bends to snatch something from the dead man's neck. I don't see what it is, because the action is too fast but I'm quick enough to drive my seax into his armpit, and the cry of pain that froths from his throat, assures me that the assault is a good one.

I hold the edge firm, even while the man buckles, trying to land a strike with his seax. His sword is forgotten about on the floor, lying next to the dead man, as though ready for the grave. Perhaps the sword wasn't his. My eyes narrow and I lean into my seax, my sword meeting his flailing blade.

"Who is he?" I spit. The warrior's suddenly opening eyes assure me that I've made the correct assumption, but his lips stay firmly flat and I know I'll get nothing further from him.

With a grunt of effort, I force the weapon higher and higher, so high that it erupts through the shoulder of my enemy, and tears sparkle in his eyes as he tries to ignore the pain.

Yanking hard, I palm my seax once more and reversing the hold on the weapon, slide it across the soft skin where his head is thrown back, revealing his throat.

My opponent dies with a soft sigh, as though it's a pleasure, and not pain, and I fumble for whatever he held in his hand.

He relinquishes the item quickly, but I've not the time to examine it. Instead, I thrust it inside my tunic, hoping my byrnie will keep it safe, and race to stand beside Edmund.

"Took your fucking time," he complains, his feet trampling down the leave-strewn surface, kicking aside wet leaves as he goes.

"It took as long as it fucking took," I retort, already sizing up the small force coming against us.

The fire that gave away their presence is little more than a smoking ruin, merely adding an extra layer of gloom, but I can see the weapons easily enough, if not the hands that hold them.

"This should be fucking easy," Edmund mutters, all trace of battle fear gone from him with the kills he's already made. I note the line of blood spatters along his face. A strangely straight line, that runs to the left of his nose, before arching over to the right side of his face. I couldn't have applied anything quite so straight on purpose, let alone by chance.

"Five each," I retort, and he shrugs his broad shoulders.

"I could do eight of the fuckers, and you just the two, if you want." His tone is filled with fierce resolve, even though he goads me.

"I could do all nine, and you just the fucking one," I counter, mirroring his actions in flattening the few remaining tall grasses that surround me. There's no need to approach the Raiders. They're coming for us. Nothing's going to stop them.

I haven't claimed my shield. I need both hands to hold my bloodied weapons. Edmund doesn't have his shield either, and neither do the warriors coming toward us.

I do notice that three of them have taken the time to force dark helms over their heads, while one of the other warriors, fiddles with his weapons belt, pulling it tighter so that it doesn't fall down his legs. Despite their missing men, the Raiders still think this attack a casual one, that they can somehow defeat between eating and sleeping. I'll ensure they sleep, but it'll be for all-time, not just the one night.

They come in a sloppy formation, smirks on tight faces of

those without helms. They think this will be undemanding. After all, we're heavily outnumbered. We might have killed some of their men, but quickly, they'll take their vengeance against us.

I take the time to consider my disappointment that they don't know who I am. I would have thought I might have gained some recognition by now, but evidently not.

"A mancus of gold for each kill you claim," and now Edmund watches me keenly.

"Well, you've just made this a little more fucking interesting," he grins, and then the first of the Raiders is upon us.

They come as though a storm over a rock-strewn beach, their steps flailing, erupting from strange angles, and sending blades careering toward both Edmund and me.

I focus, pick the man who seems the most ill-disciplined although he wears a heavy leather byrnie tightly wrapped around his body. He carries a spear, not a sword or axe, and that makes him dangerous even as it flails in the air.

I duck, but one of his allies is less lucky, and although the weapon leaves no mark, the blow to the man's hand, sends his weapon tumbling to the floor.

Quickly, I aim the edge of my sword at his ink-strew forearm, but the blood that wells is only a stream, and not the flood it needs to be. Yet his eyes are poorly focused, and it's easy to shove him aside. He stumbles, arms flailing, his sword almost slicing another of the men focused on me. When he falls, as he must, he tangles with the spear wielder.

Both men fall to the floor, their cries of outrage overriding all else, and I don't think one of us, Raider, or ally, doesn't watch them with disbelief.

"What the fuck?" Edmund's words echo mine, but it's too good an opportunity to miss.

Quickly, I stab down, my sword impaling the spear-carrier's left arm, with my seax I bend low and aim for the other man's already bleeding arm. Before I can land a blow, the whistle of displaced air alerts me to the fact that the spear is moving toward me.

"Fuck," I complain, thinking a sword through his hand would be enough to dissuade him, but clearly not.

In my peripheral vision, I'm aware that the other Raiders have recovered their wits. Edmund already fights two men, one of them trying to take advantage of his missing eye. They assume it means he can't see, but they're wrong.

Hastily, I slice my seax across the fallen foe's arm, just enough to almost sever it, but enough that it still dangles there, more of a hindrance than if his hand were simply gone.

Then I stand tall, pull my sword loose from where it's embedded in the ground, and use it to counter the reach of the spear.

My opponent both screams in pain and anticipated success, but my seax rams into his open mouth, and the spear falls free from his clutch, landing over the other sobbing man, sitting upright and holding his almost-butchered hand.

I grimace at the mass of grey and white on display. I'd rather be greeted with the torrent of blood. As I turn, I wrench my seax free, taking a dull delight in the grating noise, the unmistakable feel along its edge, and then I have three men menacing me.

These are the three who wear helms, alongside other well-tended battle-gear. It can mark a man as both a coward and incredibly gifted. I'll see what they offer me before any decision is made.

I can see little of them but the flash of alert eyes, chins covered in fine beards, threaded with trinkets—a strange way to wear wealth.

"*Angreb*," it seems that they've decided to work together as one unit, and they advance on me, one in front, and one to the left and the other to the right. They leave my back free. I turn, ensuring that while Edmund battles his enemy, one of the men already mewing on the ground as though a child whose toy sword has been taken from him, he also has my back when he wins free. I know he will. There's no doubt in my mind.

And hopefully, he'll put the crying man out of his misery. No man should live while his splayed guts are clutched in his marooned-hands.

"Right," I face the first man. He comes at me full-on, his teeth bared in a grimace. I don't look at his hands, where he twirls a long war axe menacingly, the sharpened edge gleaming brightly. It's supposed to intimidate, but it does no such thing. I'm surprised that he's not taken his nose off with the fucking ludicrous movement.

But I don't attack him, instead going for the helmed warrior to my left.

The movement is quick, concise, and entirely unexpected. My eyes don't even leave the face of the man in front of me, but the crunch of the blow sounds loudly. I rip my blade back from his heart, considering going for the warrior to my right, but that would be too predictable. Instead, as the dead man crashes to the floor, I leap into the warrior with his spinning war axe. The weapon flies through the air as his slack grip gives way under the onslaught.

I aim for his chest, but I just stab and stab and stab. Whether the wounds I inflict are deep or not matters little to me. I want him to be so confused by the ferocity of the attack, that he forgets all sense of what he should be doing.

His war axe is gone, fallen with a satisfying thud onto the trampled grasses, but he still has a smaller weapon, almost a sharpened knife, and in his left hand it's an impressive weapon. Or it could be if he wasn't so concerned with my concentrated attack.

"*Angreb*," the words spit from his teeth, but the remaining warrior doesn't move, no doubt too stunned by the ferocity of the attack.

"*Angreb*," comes again, but the force behind the words has gone. I'd make the killing stroke, but before I can, the sound of retreating feet reaches my ears.

"Fuck," I don't want anyone to escape.

With a quick movement, I stab my blade deep into the man's flayed chest, his byrnie shedding in the face of the repeated attack. Blood pours from his open mouth, staining his tunic with the hue of a sunrise, but I'm already dashing after the warrior who thinks to flee.

I can't have the figure escaping. I can't allow them to warn the rest of the warriors from Grantabridge that there are figures in the woodland, keen to take their lives.

But the warrior is quick, and already has a head start on me, as I lumber to action.

I spare a thought for Edmund, and resolved that he can handle the two remaining Raiders, I try and sprint after the fleeing shape. They've chosen not to rush back toward the camp, but instead into the darkening shapes of the trees. Only the flash of their helm allows me to keep track of them.

Most would wear a blackened helm, but this warrior's is sheeted in blue. How, I'm unsure, but it makes it easy to keep track of them, even though my steps are slower.

I try and pace myself, breathe already abrasive through my parched throat, but every time I think they might stop, a fresh burst of speed allows them to pull away.

"Bastard," I can't even find the air for the word, but it rings around my head, and it's the chime of failure that keeps me going. I need to find my warriors. I must kill this solitary Raider to ensure my presence remains a secret.

I duck and dodge, avoiding the skeletal reach of those trees who've shed their leaves, adding the mass to the slippery mess that carpets the woodland floor. More than once, I'm surprised by thin branches that slap against my face, and those that try and trip me.

Every time I have to pull my gaze away from the Raider I chase, I struggle to find them again. If it weren't for the halo of blue, they would have long escaped me.

"Fuck," my legs tangle beneath me, and the air explodes from my body as I hit the ground. I consider just staying there, nursing the pain that shudders along my knocked shin, but then I haul my body upright. Of course, the figure I'm chasing has disappeared, but just because I can't see them, doesn't mean that I can't hear them.

Even above the air I suck into my body, the clatter of fleeing feet is easy to hear. I tilt my head to one side, consider the best way to go, and then I'm running once more, not along the path the Raider has taken, but rather to the side of them, at a slight angle.

I can see where they might appear, helped somewhat by a shaft of light that seems to shine directly onto the place I want to be. Some might consider it a God-given piece of luck, but I'm only prepared to admit to it being opportune.

I run faster than I ever have, dodging out of the way of every dip and hollow that tries to trip me. The warrior takes the path I expect them too, and they don't even look up to see me before running onto the end of my blade.

The warrior moves so fast that I'm forced backwards, along with the dying runner, just about able to hold my blade steady, until I hit the ground, forced over by the shambling weight of the dying Raider and his pent-up speed.

"Bloody bollocks," blood pools onto my face, through lips partly open, their last exhalation almost a caress.

My seax hand is pinned, the handle sticking uncomfortably into my byrnie as the weight of the dying Raider settles on me. With my left hand, I scrabble at the sodden mass that covers the ground, a grimace for whatever sordid items I grip in my quest to find something to thrust upwards.

I peer into the staring eyes, noticing for the first time the unusual hue, so dark as to be almost entirely black, against the white of the rest of the eye. A Moor, no doubt renowned for their warrior skills. What they're doing fighting with the bastard Raiders, I don't know. Why men and women used to the warm sun would think to make their home in the frigid northern kingdoms is beyond me.

With a grunt of effort, I force myself upwards, the body falling away, as it rolls almost entirely over, the face buried in the mulch.

I release the grip on my seax and thrust it into my weapons belt. Lurching to my feet, I give the body the most cursory of glances, reaching for my sword, which must somehow have come unfastened in the fall, and lies on the ground.

A cry reverberates through the woods, and I'm reminded of Edmund.

Despite the need to rest, I retrace my steps, pushing myself to run more rapidly as the sounds of iron on iron seem to fill the deadened woodland. There could be a hundred warriors for all I know. Sound travels strangely, my heart thumping loudly, to allow the sound to coalesce, as it did when I first chased the warrior.

The sight that greets me is not the most reassuring.

Edmund still fights. He has a long gash running down his forearm, and he faces not two Raiders, but rather four. Where the others came from, I have no idea, but it's clear that I've only just arrived in time. Edmund is being circled by the four Raiders, all of them with intent expressions, and he can't defend himself from all corners.

I suck a breath.

"Well, that looks like a nice, fucking easy kill," I call, my voice just loud enough to startle the four attackers while allowing Edmund's tense shoulders to settle. He's no longer alone. It's important for him to know that.

A wordless exchange between the remaining warriors and one of them steps toward me, swinging a seax in his right hand. I can see the jagged edge. It looks clean to me.

"Shall I teach you how to use it?" I ask, jutting my chin at the virgin blade.

"I know how to use it, you fucking bastard," the words surprise me, as does the fact that of the four Raiders, only one of them has chosen to face me. The other three redirect their attention at Edmund, and the pressure of too little time, makes me regret my words. I just need to kill the Raider, not belittle them first.

"You better show me then," I call, bending my legs, and ignoring the screech of protest from my back and thighs. I'm no longer young. Age can creep up on me at the most inconvenient of times.

"I will, and then I'll split you from crotch to neck, and we'll see who's so bloody clever then."

"After you," and the Raider, eyes taking in my stance, hesitates for no more than a heartbeat before launching himself at me. The Raider is younger than I am. That much is clear from the lack of lines on his face. Surprisingly, he wears no beard, and I can see the firmness of his chin. He has no battle scars that I can see, but I don't mind giving him both his first and his last.

He aims for my throat with a sweeping blow, and it's almost too easy to duck away from the attack. Or rather, that's my intention, but halfway through the motion, I feel my back-leg tremble, and it takes all of my skill to hold the position. Even so, the blade comes perilously close, and my rage rumbles into being.

"Fucker," and I'm upright, aiming my seax at the man's upper leg, keen to get a quick slice on the artery that's poorly concealed there. I should like him to die quickly, but not too fast. Only the warrior is good, and my blade is deflected, my hand instinctively tightening to keep a firm grip on it.

The warrior leers at me, and rushes forward, his intention communicated by the lowering of his chin.

I turn my back on him, not a move I'd usually make, and then I stab behind, keen to have his headbutt hit the rear of my head, not the front.

His nose explodes in a sea of crushed rose petals as I rear my head backwards.

The sound sends a thrill of satisfaction through me, and I use it to stab into his leg and finally crack open the vessel that keeps the blood in his body.

Terrified eyes look my way, but I kick him away from me as I rush to aid Edmund.

"I need a new fucking opponent," I call hoarsely. I could do with a long drink of water, perhaps as much as a barrel full, but my work isn't yet complete.

Anguished eyes glance at the dying man behind me, and without speaking, one of the warriors comes toward me. Edmund hasn't been so quick to disarm and kill both of his opponents, and I can tell that he's growing tired, his movements weakening, under the onslaught of the men who still face him.

I wish then that I'd not forced Tatberht and Ælfgar to stay behind. I would have appreciated Tatberht's economy with weapons. Tatberht was always able to kill with the fewest strikes. And Ælfgar would be an additional number to confuse the enemy. He can fight, not with much flare, but killing a man doesn't need to be flamboyant. It just needs to be accomplished.

Maybe I should even have rushed the three men—better two of us against three, than one of us against two.

I spit and clear my throat, wrinkling my nose at the taste of yet more blood in my mouth. It's not mine. I'm sick of tasting every Raider that I kill and yet no matter how closely I clamp my mouth shut, blood always gets inside.

"Come on then, you fucker," my new opponent seems to be my equal in build and muscle, but he's not been running and killing and stalking the Raiders, as I have. So, he's fresher, for all a thin trail of blood seems to have attached itself to his byrnie. It's a flash of colour on an otherwise drab man. He carries no silver arm-rings or trinkets around his neck, and his weapons belt is purely functional. I approve of such restraint.

The man clamps his lips tightly together as we both move toward one another. My arms ache, my legs as well, but Edmund is in peril. I push all of my discomforts aside and focus on what must be done.

But again, the warrior surprises me.

"Why are you here? Why are you killing us?" I pause, seax ready to strike, confusion knitting my brow.

The warrior continues, his accent is hardly audible even as he speaks my language.

"You are from Northampton? We've been waiting here, as you commanded us."

For a long moment, I hardly know what to say, and the Raider seems to understand that I'm ignorant of what he speaks about, a slow smirk touches his cheeks, a knowing look in his eyes, and before I can recover, he lunges toward me, blade outstretched.

Hastily, I try to parry the blow, but it's too well-timed, and my response is just a fraction too slow, and I know he's going to claim first blood. Only then he doesn't.

An arc of warm fluid arches through the air, landing on my face, my lips, even up my nose. I'm choking on it even while I wave my seax in the air. But there's no need.

My opponent has fallen to the side, or rather, some of him has fallen to one side.

"What the fuck?" and I'm looking into Tatberht's amused eyes as he crows over his kill.

"Stupid fucker," Tatberht announces, already turning to assist Ælfgar and Edmund against the two remaining men. I'm motionless, my eyes blinking and yet my vision refusing to clear. I bend low, see something shimmering beneath the man's tight byrnie, and when I pull it free, my head pulses with fury.

"What the fuck?" I exclaim, only no one answers me. Belatedly, I sweep my gaze to my three warriors, reassure myself that the enemy are all dead, and then I'm stamping to the campsite. I need to see. I need to understand.

CHAPTER 19

"What the fuck is it?" Edmund shouts the words to me, his voice fatigued, but I don't answer. Instead, I'm riffling through the saddlebags of the Raiders who made this camp their home, and clearly for some time. How, I consider, did we not see them when we first went this way? How long, I consider, have they been here?

The horses all watch me with dulled eyes, and I'm unsurprised, their coats are ill-kept, and their saddles haven't been removed for so long, I can see red, angry welts where they've broken through the skin.

As I hunt, I unbuckle and cast each saddle to the floor, only just missing the fire in my haste. With gentle hands, that belie my fury, I undo harness and allow the animals to crop at the grasses on the edges of the campsite. These warriors have been hiding here for weeks, perhaps ever since we came to Northampton, perhaps ever since I left Torksey.

Whatever they've been doing, it's been long planned, and my thoughts turn to Ealdorman Wulfstan, and then to Wulfsige. Surely, he must have a part to play in all this. Who else could it be?

"Look?" Edmund is beside me, and before he can show his anger at my inexplicable actions, I thrust what I found into his hand.

It's a small silver piece. I know what it is. I've seen it before, or rather, something similar.

"Why the fuck would they have one of these?" Edmund turns it in his hand. He's pulled his gloves clear, but even so, his hands carry the shade of red it's almost impossible to scrub away entirely. The lives of our enemy are never lightly taken, and they linger on us for longer than others might realise.

"It's obvious," I fume, still working my way down the line of horses. Tatberht, although still pleased with his kill, has begun the process, only from the other end of the line of mounts. He and Ælfgar work together to make an ally of the horse, remove the saddle and then dive for treasures in the saddlebags.

They, like me, only know to look for something. What it will be should be apparent.

"They meant to use it to gain admission somewhere, that must be why the man spoke our tongue so clearly."

I nod, pleased I don't have to explain. My suspicions are well and truly roused, and yet I'm sure there must be something else as well. I need more. Only the saddlebags give up nothing, and I'm suddenly exhausted and can't face walking back to investigate the bodies of the dead.

Tatberht has flung a discarded log onto the embers of the fire, and quickly, flames leap higher. I'd question why he does so, but the dampness of my clothes, reminds me of our journey here, under a dense bank of grey cloud filled with the menace of the heavy, and icy cold rain. We need to get warmer. We may as well do it with the fire that's already there.

I slump to the ground, only as I do, the crackle of something in my byrnie calls to me, and I reach and pull out both the item I took from the man who tried to run away, but also the parchment from the attack close to Grantabridge. I'd forgotten I even had it.

"What's that?" Tatberht notices my movements, but I'm shaking my head.

"I don't fucking know yet, give me a moment."

I unfold the parchment on my knee, trying to force back the creases so that I can see it. I'm not sure what I expect to see, and it certainly isn't what seems to be some sort of depiction of the landscape. Perhaps around Grantabridge, or maybe not.

Edmund has come to look over my shoulder by now, and while I squint at the green-tinged ink so carefully etched into the small piece of vellum, no larger than my hand, I'm trying to decide just what it is before me.

"Well, Coelwulf," and his tone has turned icy cold. "It seems to me that you have enemies everywhere and that they work to undermine what you do." I grunt. The map, because that's what it is, of the main roads and rivers close to Northampton is the surest indicator yet that once more, men and women work against Mercia, not for her.

"It seems we didn't need to go to Grantabridge," my words are heavy, the realisation that we've been enticed here, purposefully, weighing me down. I don't like being manipulated. I don't fucking like it at all.

"No, they were coming for you anyway." I turn to meet the eyes of Tatberht and Ælfgar.

"Fucking bollocks. You've brought us into the mouth of the wolf willingly." I hear the rage in Edmund's voice. "And they have a double-headed eagle sigil to ensure they make their way to your side." Now his voice quivers with fury, but I don't think it's directed at me anyway.

"There's a fucking target on your back, and it's even bigger than we thought. Even the fucking Mercians mean to betray you." And Edmund stalks away. He wasn't exactly effusive with me becoming king. He thought I should only concern myself with the ancient kingdom of the Hwicce, the land my father ruled over. I can't help thinking that he's right.

Not that I'm about to fucking tell him that.

"What do we do now?" Tatberht's words force me to think about my perilous situation.

"We go after the others."

"You can't," Edmund explodes from behind me. I thought he'd fucked off somewhere to glower but apparently not.

"We came out here to find them. We have to go on." I want to remind him that his son is there, but it seems too cruel.

"*We* do, yes. You can get your arse back to Northampton and find out who the fucking traitor is. Although I imagine it's Wulfsige. Crafty fucker. And if it's not him, then it has to be Ealdorman Ælhun."

"So, you think it would be better for me to ride back alone, rather than stay together."

"Yes, I fucking do."

"But you can't be sure there aren't more Raiders close."

"No, I can't. In fact, I know there are Raiders somewhere. Alone, you can evade them. You sure as fuck can't go into yet another battle with them. It's evident they're here for you. That lad, who came to Worcester, he was sent there to tempt you out of the fastness of Western Mercia. They learned in the summer that they couldn't come and get you from there. And you thought you were such a clever fuck drawing the bastards from Grantabridge."

"I'm not abandoning my warriors." I fill my voice with resolve. I'm surprised even to be giving voice to the words. Edmund knows I'll never go back to Northampton willingly. I do not refer to his other words. They're accurate, and I don't have to say they are. Whatever he thinks of me, and however angry he might be, he won't be expecting an apology. That would really unsettle him.

"We're going to find the others," I pierce Edmund with my eyes, daring him to back away, and he doesn't. There's respect on his face, and that surprises me. It probably shouldn't.

"Then we go on, together, keeping each other close. Fuck knows how many Raiders inhabit the land between here and Grantabridge."

I'm pleased he doesn't force me to beg, and I go to stand, only his hand is on my shoulder.

"We can at least get dry," he instructs me, the pressure on my shoulder significant enough that I'm forced to stay where I am, even though I don't want to. As he speaks, Ælfgar hefts yet another discarded log onto the resurgent fire, and the heat washes over me. Even though the flames are orange and not superheated blue, my face feels as though it burns, and it's that which makes me realise just how cold I am, and tired.

"We can have a bit of time," I confirm. "But we need to get the horses."

"We don't," and Ælfgar grins.

"Fucking bollocks." Haden is picking his way toward me, veering aside from the bodies of the dead, his gaze intent. I know what he's thinking. I'm thinking the same.

"What about the horses?"

"They'll either stay here, or they won't. There's more than enough for them to eat. We'll get them when we can."

"What about the dead?" Tatberht juts his chin to where the Raiders are slowly cooling.

"We'll leave them for their 'ally.'"

"Thank fuck for that. I've done enough for one day. I don't want to be digging bloody great big holes for those bastards."

The four of us settle to silence, each thinking our own thoughts. I've berated myself for making some pretty crap decisions of late, but knowing that I've been drawn here by others makes me consider that I've genuinely not done too badly myself. Northampton is mine. They probably didn't expect that. There might be an enemy inside Northampton, but as Edmund says, it is obvious as to who. With that knowledge, we can overcome them all, even with the odds so greatly stacked against us, and that's entirely what I intend to fucking do.

CHAPTER 20

We travel under heavy clouds, although the rain holds off, for now. I don't see that it will for long, but at least I'm dry. Warm as well.

Not that Edmund allows us out to make our way along the track that runs through the least densely populated part of the woodlands. Instead, we remain under the sheltering canopy, only able to see the sky every so often, where a bough has lost its leaves.

The horses somehow sense the need for complete silence, and their hoof falls are quieter than I could manage. I'm impressed, but it only adds to the oppressive atmosphere between us all. I can hear the scampering of the forest animals around us, the birds arcing into the sky from the high branches, but nothing else.

Edmund rides in front, Jethson enjoying the sensation of leading Haden, while Ælfgar and then Tatberht ride behind me. I can see what Edmund is thinking with his instructions. Ælfgar and Tatberht can as well, and yet they don't complain at finding themselves both marked as unimportant next to me, and also not as reliable as Edmund.

I would have commented, reminded Edmund that we're all equal in my eyes, but with a wink, Tatberht took his place, as though relishing the task. Ælfgar made no complaint either. If this is what it means to have men repledge themselves to the kingship, then it sits uneasily with me. My men. Mercia's men.

THE LAST HORSE

They're all worth far more to me than they seem to realise.

We hear nothing further until the trickle of running water percolates my thoughts, and then I startle. I must have dosed in the saddle, and now we're almost at the next river that needs crossing, on the route we previously took to Grantabridge.

Edmund holds his hand up, pausing our forward momentum, and Haden shambles to a halt. Surely, the day must be nearly at an end. I feel as though I've done little but ride and ride. My arse, as used to it as it is, aches, and I need to sleep.

I can see that Edmund is unsure, and so I call to him.

"We should wait here, get some rest. I don't like it either, but there's little to be gained from exposing ourselves now."

Edmund nods, and from behind, I hear a sigh of relief from Ælfgar or Tatberht, and a tight smile slides onto my face. When we left Northampton, we knew the task would be impossible. Now it seems insurmountable.

"We should go back a way, remain hidden from the river. They might have found their fucking ships by now."

Edmund doesn't argue with me, and so I turn Haden aside, meeting the gaze of both Ælfgar and Tatberht. The other men sit rigidly in their saddle. I reconsider then. We need rest, but will anybody get any?

"I saw a likely looking spot," Tatberht offers.

"Show me," and Tatberht turns Wombel smartly. I'm surprised he saw somewhere that would shelter us. I've been looking but seen nowhere. But, true to his word, Tatberht takes us to a long-fallen tree, no doubt ancient before lightning split its trunk and it came crashing to the ground. The place has clearly been used for such a purpose before, and the wood extends along two sides, with just the one open. It'll give us something to guard our backs, while we protect the open expanse. I can't see that anyone will be able to climb the vast trunk without us noticing. They'll make a racket with all the leaves and brittle branches.

"How the fuck did I miss this?" I ask, only then remembering that I drowsed in the saddle.

The four of us dismount eagerly, the horses just as keen to

be free from their burdens. Water has collected along the tree, trickling into a small, natural pool, at the far end, and Haden drinks eagerly, before resolving to pull on the long, damp grasses that almost mask the tree trunk entirely.

I pull my cloak tight, and settle to the ground, back to the tree. We all know they'll be no fire. Not tonight. Not when we're so exposed, and when we know we're being hunted just as surely as the rest of my missing warriors.

Tatberht unearths a loaf of bread from his saddlebags and roughly breaks it into four pieces. I chew absentmindedly, not sure I taste it until I'm handed a pungent cheese to add to it.

"Fucking bollocks," I exclaim, the tartness of the cheese almost making me wish I hadn't bothered.

"Your Aunt was never the best at making cheese," Tatberht offers.

"But it does last a bloody long time," Ælfgar rebuffs, popping a considerable chunk into his mouth. I consider how he can eat so much in one go, but then he chokes, the taste just too potent.

Edmund is moody and silent. He refuses to sit, and instead paces, from the roots of the downed tree to the top of the bough, where little but straggly branches remain, covered in ivy but not leaves.

"Will you sit the fuck down," I'm forced to complain when I've finished eating.

"Someone needs to be alert, you bastard," Edmund retorts, his one eye flashing dangerously at me, as though daring me to argue with him.

"We are alert, but we're alert down here, not up there. If someone comes this way, then we have somewhere to hide."

"And they won't see the horses, but they will see me?"

"The horses aren't patrolling from one side to another. Look, they're still. They're resting, which is what we're all supposed to be doing."

But Edmund refuses to be swayed by my words, and I bite back more. I'll only be wasting my breath.

"Edmund, you take first watch," I order, unsurprised when he startles at my instruction. "I'll take the middle one and Tatberht, you and Ælfgar take the final one. An attack is more likely to come then if there's going to be one."

I can see that Edmund wants to argue with my decisions, but I'm the king, and before that, I was his lord, and he's spent years obeying my instructions. I know what they're all thinking, and I don't much care.

With nothing further to say, I roll my cloak around me and curl tightly against the tree. There might be no end of insects making that decaying trunk their home, but the thick ivy serves to keep the wind at bay, and the wind has a chill edge to it, with the promise of yet more rain to come.

Tatberht and Ælfgar continue to murmur to each other for some time, but soon, all is quiet, apart from Edmund and his continual marching. It irritates, but if I complain, it'll only encourage him to step more heavily, and so I hold my tongue and hope for sleep.

A hand on my shoulder and my seax is in my hand, ready to strike.

"Your watch," Edmund's voice is laced with fatigue. "I've seen and heard nothing above the snoring and farting." As I stagger upright, Edmund tumbles to the ground, and I appreciate that he's not about to say anything else to me.

I shiver, climb to my feet, and quickly move to empty my bladder, away from the slumbering horses, so that the wind doesn't drive the stream back on my men.

The feel of cold air on my body wakes me immediately, and I peer into the shadowed murkiness. Overhead, thick clouds skid across the sky, driven by a fierce wind, and I hope that the wind takes the clouds elsewhere. I've had enough of being wet, even though I can smell it in the air.

For all I told Tatberht and Ælfgar I expected an attack to come with the dawn, I truly anticipate it will come while I stand, hidden behind a sea of long, dead, brittle branches, the moon hooded but giving a glimmer of light that just about illuminates the near-distance.

The sound of the river is a constant in the distance, and I wrap my cloak tightly around my body, stamping my feet to keep some warmth in them. I blank my thoughts, think only of the night noises, and any sound that's out of place, surprised when I realise that it's time to wake the others.

Tatberht is a bastard to wake, Ælfgar much easier, and the two shamble away from where Edmund sleeps. I curl into the warmth of the ground where they've been sleeping. I don't imagine that I'll sleep, convinced now that an assault is imminent so that I'm surprised when Edmund wakes me, his voice rough with sleep.

"Where are the fuckers?" It seems I'm not the only one who anticipated a raid during the night.

"Nowhere near here," Tatberht grumbles, lifting his arms high and widely yawning as he stands in front of us. Ælfgar is busy with his horse, and Haden ambles close to me.

"Right, we cross the ford," I instruct. "Stay close, and stay alert." Again, I speak to men who don't need the caution, but I give it anyway.

Edmund leads the way, and I follow behind him. The wind blows fiercely, driving water into our faces, for all it doesn't actually rain.

As we emerge from beneath the protection of the trees, I glance toward the ford, expecting to see the Raiders there. Only it's eerily quiet. Too quiet, and that makes me grip my seax once more.

There are signs of people crossing the wide river where it's shallowest. Not the Roman-made ford I saw at Littleborough, but the elements have conspired to allow carts and horses to cross.

The rain-slick grass is trampled, and there's a pile of flat rocks as well, no doubt collected by traders when their cartwheels grind to a halt over the ragged river floor. But there's no one there now.

Haden stops, turning his nose to scent the air. The wind is so fierce I'm convinced that we could smell a fire from a great distance, but instead, the air is cold, clear and devoid of any suggestion that we're not entirely alone.

Edmund turns to meet my eyes, and I know what he's thinking. Where are the gazes of those who hunt for us? But more, where the fuck are Hereman, Pybba, Rudolf, and of course, his son?

I shrug, indicate the ford with my head, and he moves on. I follow, Tatberht and Ælfgar behind me. Although I keep my head turning, just waiting for someone to try and ambush us, there's nothing. Nothing at all.

Haden picks his way across the water without complaint. The river is deeper than last time we spanned the river, swirling above his three black knees, just the one white, but he picks a path cleanly. With a final glance over my shoulders, we once more slip beneath the sheltering embrace of thick trees. Edmund doesn't choose the regularly taken track but instead merges into the greenery some distance away.

As soon as the trees cover us, I feel my shoulders relax, only for a flash of red to catch my eye. I dismount hastily, bending to look at what's caught my attention. Edmund circles back.

"What have you found?" Edmund's voice is only just above a whisper, but I hear him easily enough.

I swipe my finger through the pool of maroon splattered against a pile of moss.

"Blood," I confirm, sniffing it, just to be sure.

"Reasonably fresh," I almost retch at the scent, but of course, there's no way of knowing whether it came from the Raiders or my warriors. All the same, I feel a stirring of vengeance inside me. Damn the fuckers if they've injured my warriors.

"I wish it told us which fucking way to go." I mirror Edmund's words but merely mount back up.

"We must be close. Keep alert." Again, I know I'm speaking to veterans of our campaign against the Raiders, but I give the caution all the same. Sometimes a man needs to be reminded that he's not invincible.

The trees are packed densely, just as on the far side of the Ouse, and we move only as quickly as the horses can manage, picking a careful path through twisted roots that stick through the spongy layer, covered with brown, crisp leaves and a bed of needles. I almost think it might be better to walk, as we hunt for clues, but then there's no need.

"There's more here," Edmund spots the blood splatters this time, and even I can see where the undergrowth has been beaten back or walked through. I almost don't need the hood prints to assure me that we're tracking someone.

Grim determination settles over me, and I wish Edmund would allow me to go first. I want to know first, I want to see before the others, but Jethson refuses to allow Haden to pass.

I know when we've found who we follow, not because I can see them, but rather because I can't. It's too silent, and it's too still, and then I know why.

"Fuck," I've dismounted before Edmund can even try and argue against it.

"There's been an attack here," what goes unsaid is that it must have been similar to our attack on the Raiders only the day before.

I rush forward, eyes fixed on the first of the bodies, tumbled and twisted on the ground. With hands that almost shake, I turn the body face-up, fearing to look, but it's not one of my warriors.

"A fucking Raider," I call, my voice loud with relief, abandoning the dead and moving to the next bodies. There are three here, and I imagine they died protecting the backs of each other.

"Raiders here as well," I call. I should probably be silent, but the others need to know.

Edmund has encouraged Jethson to the far side of the sudden clearing, to where I can glimpse the marble of more death.

"Here as well," he informs me. I turn then, survey the area. It would have been a good place for an ambush. But I suspect it was where an attack that began at the river ended.

"Are they from Grantabridge?" I muse but have no way of knowing.

"It can't be our men," Edmund states, his voice ringing with conviction. "They wouldn't have left the dead like this."

Normally, I would agree with Edmund, but Haden is nosing something on the ground, and I rush to pull him aside before he can stain himself with the river of ruby.

"Fuck," Edmund is beside me so fast I blink, surprised, as I bend down and delicately turn the body.

"Fuck, fuck, fuck." I tumble to my knees, only aware when the dampness of the ground permeates my trews.

"What is it?" Tatberht calls, but I can't find the words.

The body before me has bled profusely from a wound that flashes whitely, the blood long since leaked onto the ground. The rain of last night has merged with it, trapped as it is on a pile of leaves that have somehow arched upwards, as though to keep the precious offering from draining away.

Eoppa.

"It's Eoppa," I finally manage to say. Those words seem to singe my mouth.

"Fuck," Ælfgar bows his head low, whereas Tatberht remains silent.

"Fuck, he wanted to leave, after all this. I should have sent him back to fucking Kingsholm as soon as he asked me."

Edmund hands me two small pebbles, and I reach out and close the eyes of my warrior. It shouldn't have been like this, and Edmund clearly knows that we can't take the time to bury him properly. Not right now.

"Poor bastard," Tatberht finally mutters.

"What happened here," still kneeling on the ground, regardless of my damp knees, I look around. There are bodies seemingly everywhere, but so far, only one of them belongs to one of my men.

"A bloody great big battle," Edmund states. He's busy walking around, from one body to another, kicking those he knows to be an enemy while turning those about whom he's not yet sure.

"I'd say at least fifteen dead. Maybe more. I think some of them slunk away elsewhere, maybe back to the river."

"Are there any more Mercians?"

"No. Just Eoppa."

It brings me no solace, only worries me further.

"Then, where the fuck are the others?" But of course, Edmund, Tatberht and Ælfgar only know what I do.

"We need to ride on, find the others. They must be somewhere close."

"Or we missed them in the woodlands." I could strangle Edmund sometimes.

"Yes, or we fucking missed them, but we need to be moving and looking for them."

"What about Eoppa?" Tatberht asks the question, and I wish he hadn't.

"We'll come back for him when we can. For now, it's too risky. If our warriors have wounds, then they need our help. We must find them immediately."

Tatberht looks far from happy, and I can't deny that it hurts me to stand, and mount Haden, pulling his nose away from Eoppa.

"He's dead now. What happens to his body won't hurt him anymore," but the words ring empty and my three warriors know that they don't reflect my real opinion.

"Which way from here?"

I only wish it was an easy decision. I consider the river we've just forded. Is it likely that they were attacked there? Is it possible that they stalked the Raiders to this spot? The problem is, every option is a possibility.

"It seems pointless to go back toward Ermine Street when they must have passed this way already. Otherwise, Eoppa wouldn't be here."

There's clearly no denying the logic because my three warriors remain silent, even Edmund, which is always a surprise.

"Right, back across the river. We'll take a different path back toward Northampton, to the south, not the north, as before, and when all this is over, we'll come back for Eoppa and take him back to Kingsholm."

THE LAST HORSE

With the decision made, I mount and direct Haden back along the trampled path we've just taken. Silence descends once more, only to be filled by the sound of the river, as we get closer and closer to it.

But then without even realising, my hand is once more on my seax, and I'm prepared to counter whatever attack might come because I can tell that we're being hunted. Edmund senses it too, and I turn to ensure Ælfgar and Tatberht are just as alert. The two men peer through the trees to either side of the forged path we follow, but I'm convinced that any attack will come from the right.

It seems that Edmund agrees with me. We rode in silence anyway, but now it pulses with the threat. Fuck, there's only four of us, and who knows how many Raiders there are. No doubt, these are the survivors of the battle against the rest of my men. While I've seen many bodies, I know how many Raiders left Grantabridge. There must still be many warriors keen to seek vengeance for the deaths of their comrades.

"Lord Coelwulf," but there's no denying that voice, and I startle on hearing it.

"Rudolf?"

"Thank fuck you've come." A battered and bruised face erupts from the trees to the left, and I meet hooded eyes, rimmed with grief.

Rudolf isn't alone, Wulfhere stands to the side of him, and I've not seen Tatberht move so fast for over a decade. Tatberht sweeps Wulfhere into an embrace, and I can sense Rudolf determining if I might offer him the same welcome. I toy with the idea, but fuck it, I've been worried about the little shit.

Before I can change my mind, I slide from Haden's back, and pull him into my arms, ruffling his hair as I go. I try to be gentle but all the same, I hear him complaining, and I force him backwards, looking at him, trying to assess all his ills just from his appearance, my hands on his shoulders.

"What the fuck happened here?" I demand to know. Rudolf looks shocked at the embrace, in pain, and surprised, all at the same time. It would be comical, only my final question recalls him to what's been happening.

"You better come and see," and his words offer no hope that Eoppa isn't the only casualty. I risk a glance to Edmund, but fierce resolve has settled over his face, Ælfgar's as well. I can hear Wulfhere speaking to Tatberht, the lad looking far too relieved to have someone to look after him, instead of vice versa, and I taste the ashes of grief.

What the fuck have I done?

Rudolf moves quickly through a bank of trees. Here, they're packed together tightly, making it almost impossible for the horses to follow without being assaulted by the tightly woven branches.

I can see why they've chosen such a place to hide, and lick their wounds because that's what's assuredly been happening here.

Rudolf moves with purpose, although he seems to favour his right leg. Tatberht has forced Wulfhere onto his horse and leads the animal. His face is as settled as Edmund's. It seems we're all to be grateful for those who haven't met their death while mourning those who have.

Rudolf whistles a rippling crescendo, and then we're through the trees, and my warriors appear before me, some of them with hands on weapons, others struggling to stand, while at least two lays without seeming to move.

"I found Lord Coelwulf," not that Rudolf needs to explain. A bank of stares meets me, some show the flurry of relief, others a flicker of fury and yet more reveal fierce determination. These men have suffered.

Twenty-two sets of eyes look my way, and I meet them, as fiercely as I can. I want to demand to know what happened to them. I want to know why the fuck they're cowering in the woods rather than returning to Northampton. But there's no need.

"Gardulf?" Edmund's voice is filled with anguish as he glances from where his brother crouches over one of the still bodies, to the body itself. The scent of blood and corruption fills the air, as Edmund rushes to his son's side.

I try and catch Hereman's eye, but it's Pybba who comes to me. He hobbles, a tremor seeming to ripple with each and every step.

"Shit," Rudolf's word informs me that Pybba shouldn't be up and about. The fact that Hiltiberht wavers behind him only reinforces the belief.

But before Pybba can reach my side, Sæbald is there. He, at least, looks hale and hearty, even if his eyes reflect grief.

"Lord Coelwulf. You are most welcome," the formality surprises me, but then, perhaps he needs it to frame his next words.

"I regret to inform you that the Raiders have attacked us. Eoppa died in battle, bravely. Gardulf and Wulfstan are too wounded to move, even if there weren't another host of Raiders over the river."

"What other injuries are there?" It seems formality is to guide our steps.

"Pybba has taken a wound to his leg. Penda has a cut below his right eye. Siric has a broken arm. Beornstan has a deep cut on his neck. Gyrth has knocked his head and remains unsure of who anyone is. Ingwald has lost a toe, and Hereman has deep wounds down the left side of his body from where he went to aid Gardulf. Most have cuts and bruises."

I nod, somehow manage not to say 'fuck,' and grasp his forearm in greeting.

"My thanks," I mutter into his ear, and again, another of my men trembles on seeing me, and I wish, once more, that I'd not left them to travel to Northampton alone. I should have fought with them. They shouldn't have gone through this alone.

"It would have made no difference," Sæbald states, as though reading my thoughts, and then Pybba is before me.

Rudolf hovers close by, as does Hiltiberht. Sæbald opens his mouth to say something further, but Pybba is quicker.

"Where, the fuck, have you been, you arsehole?" Pybba's face is furrowed in fury, the force in his words almost pulling him over. I thrust my arm out to steady him, but Pybba shies away, seemingly preferring to fall rather than accept my help.

"Boys, young boys, you allowed to face the fucking Raiders. The mean fucking bastards wanted to gut them before they've even had a chance to bed a woman. Where the fuck have you been?" The words are so loud, they cause a wood-pigeon to take to the skies, the slap of wings making every warrior there, reach for a weapon to defend themselves.

"Pybba, we've talked about this," Sæbald's voice is weary, and for once, his chin is covered in the bristles of a beard. That tells me more than it should.

"You've fucking spoken about it," Pybba's eyes blaze at me, and although he speaks to Sæbald, he doesn't look away from me.

"We had to come via a different path," I mutter, not liking having my shortcomings so openly acknowledged. This is my fault. I will never deny it.

"Oh, did you now? And obviously, that meant a warm bed and good food in Northampton, while your men were fucking dying in the rain!"

I want to argue. I actually want to tell him to fuck off. He has no idea what I've been doing, where I've been, and his assumptions infuriate me. After all this time, does he genuinely think that I'd be taking my ease while my men were missing? Daft bastard.

"Sit the fuck down before you fall," I instruct Pybba, already moving around him, to reassure myself that my men are as well as can be expected and that their wounds will not prevent us from leaving here. As soon as possible. I know the Raiders on the far bank are dead. It'll give us the chance we need to make it back to Northampton before the rest can catch us.

"Shut the fuck up, Pybba." I don't expect Edmund to leap to my defence, as he checks his son's injuries, speaking hurriedly with Hereman. Neither do I want it.

"Oh, you've changed your fucking attitude, haven't you?" It seems that Pybba is determined to argue. I'm not surprised when I bend down to force Penda's head backwards and look into his eyes. Fear stalks there, and I nod at him, compel him to look into my eyes. Penda has become a man since I last met him, but he's not yet sure that it suits him. The life of a warrior is not for everyone. Perhaps he should follow the path set for him by my Aunt.

But Penda surprises me by gripping my arm, holding my attention.

"He doesn't mean it," but I shake my head.

"He does, and it's his right. Don't make excuses for him."

I've finally made my way to Hereman's side. He breathes heavily, and the side of his byrnie is heavily stained with his blood.

"He'll live," Hereman confirms, but the paleness of Gardulf seems to defy the statement. I look at Edmund, and he nods, his eyes hazed with remorse. He's probably second-guessing himself as much as I am.

"Good. We need to mount up and leave. Find a way to transport him."

And then I'm by the other unmoving mound, gazing at Siric. He isn't pale, but slightly pink, and the heat from him can be felt even before I crouch down next to him.

"We need to get him to your Aunt," Leonath has been tending to him, and his voice is firm. He's not about to accept that Siric won't recover. After all, he's recovered from a similar wound.

"Can we truss him up so that he can ride?"

"Somehow."

"Good, then get it done. Ælfgar will help you."

"But what about the Raiders on the other side of the river?"

"They're dead. All of them." I raise my voice so that everyone can hear.

"We killed them, the four of us. We killed all of them, so we can return to Northampton."

"So, you fucking appear, play the hero and everything will be alright?"

Pybba hasn't sat down, in fact, he's been following me around the makeshift camp, his fury keeping him on his feet, even as he totters from side to side. I feel as though he's become a hound mad for meat, and not likely to be denied.

"I didn't say that, did I? But, Northampton is our destination, and we've killed the enemy over the river. There's nothing to stop you riding on."

"Nothing to fucking stop us? So, the Raiders we slaughtered here, no one's going to come looking for them?"

"I'm sure someone will come for them, but hopefully not yet. We have the time to make it to Northampton." I meet the old fucker's eyes, daring him to argue further. But abruptly, his bile seems to abate, and he slumps to the floor.

I turn, survey the state of everyone once more. I'm not going to hide the truth from them.

"We killed them, the Raiders that blocked your path. There'll be more coming. There are treason and treachery at work against Mercia and her king. But I've come, for all of you, and we'll return to Northampton, recover and resume our fight against the Mercians who want me dead, and the Raiders as well."

A sudden silence falls, and I realise I'm panting, the words seeming to take more effort to give voice to than killing twenty of my opponents, single-handedly. I feel a shimmer of sweat on my brow and would move to wipe it away, but I don't, instead, standing firm, holding my position. I need my men to see that while I might be uneasy about the challenges we face, I won't turn away from them.

I think, just for a moment, that they all might tell me to fuck off, but then, first Hereman, and then Leonath lumber to their feet, only to be followed by more and more of my warriors.

They've been victors here, but in their victory, they've suffered, and they'll endure more hardship yet. But they're my warriors, men of Mercia, and we were born to be persistent fuckers. We're not about to fucking stop now.

CHAPTER 21

Not that it's easy going. Far from it.

Even with the eighteen horses that Wulfhere's managed to round up from the Raiders, and those they've managed to keep from the attacks closer to Grantabridge, it's challenging to find enough that aren't injured to carry my men.

None of the horses is dead, thankfully, although Eoppa's mount, Poppy, has disappeared and Wulfhere is distraught not to be able to find her.

"She'll find her way home," I try and reassure the lad, even while thinking that she'll remain close to Eoppa's dead body. When we come back this way, because we will, I'm sure she'll be there. Waiting. Poppy's a loyal beast.

Hereman proves to be the most difficult to accommodate. Although Billy only carries a slice to his nose, that's already healing well, Hereman simply can't mount the obstinate animal. Gardulf is accommodated on Jethson, the animal able to take the weight of both of them. Siric is slumped on his mount, Leonath riding close to ensure he doesn't fall, and still, I can hear Hereman and Billy arguing.

"You need a fucking smaller horse," I know that Rudolf has been trying to aid Hereman. He stands to the side, eyes flashing, and I can see how much it costs him to keep his temper with the tall warrior.

"I'll manage," Hereman huffs.

"Get on a fucking smaller horse, or we're leaving you here," I make the statement, slapping Billy on his rear so that the animal moves aside. "Here, this one will be better." Wulfhere has found a docile looking sandy-coloured mare, with gentle eyes, and a strong back. I thought to gift her to my Aunt, but first, she has another role to fulfil. At least a third smaller than Billy, I know that Hereman will be able to mount up when he tries.

"My feet will drag on the floor."

"Would you rather have dirty feet or be left fucking behind?"

My temper isn't short, far from it, but I want to be gone, and Hereman seems to have no sense of urgency. None at all. Some daylight remains, and I'm sure it'll be enough to see across the ford. If only Hereman would hurry the fuck up.

I meet his gaze. I can see how much pain he's in, and I appreciate his bravery, even as frustrated as I am.

"Mount up. I fucking need you," I speak persuasively to him, from Haden's back. "I need you to protect us. You know, I do."

"Fine," Hereman eventually huffs and is then mounted in no time at all, the stirrups almost dragging on the ground. He looks a sight, with his feet only just off the ground, but better that than walking.

"Right, you all know you're positions. Stay alert, stay focused, help those who are wounded."

And I lead the way from the camp, and back toward the trackway that I followed only that morning.

Gyrth and Sæbald have staked out the surrounding area while everyone was making ready to leave.

"There are tracks, but the freshest head back toward Grantabridge, not toward the ford."

"Good. Will you ride ahead when we cross the ford?" But before they can agree, I continue.

"If the rest get attacked, and the odds are impossible, you need to get everyone to safety, or as many of them as you can. I'll take the rear." I think they'll argue with me, and in fact, Sæbald opens his mouth to do just that, but Gyrth is quicker.

"You have our word, My Lord King."

I don't fucking appreciate him taking the instruction in such a way, but if that's how it has to be, I'll accept it.

As Haden steps onto the trackway, I look both in front and behind, before I beckon the rest out. Edmund, with Gardulf, slumped against him, comes first. It won't be an easy trip for him, but I appreciate that Edmund won't be told that. He meets my eyes for the first time in days without rancour.

"Don't do anything fucking crazy," he mutters, before encouraging Jethson out into the open. I hold my position, checking once more that all those who pass me have what they need, and if they don't have what they need, that we've accommodated them as best we can.

Pybba grunts at me, finally meeting my eyes.

"Get away with you, you old bastard," I caution him. Now isn't the time for apologies and regrets.

"Stop calling me fucking old," Pybba grumbles, Penda watching us both with wide eyes. And then it's my turn to follow on. Ælfgar and Tatberht ride with me. We three are the ablest to fight, if it comes to it. I don't offer them anything further than my respect. Now isn't the time to be trying to enforce my wishes on them. All three of us know that we're the most likely to be attacked now that the Raiders on the other side of the river are dead. Any attack will come from behind is, not in front.

My seax has been sharpened by an over-eager Hiltiberht, seemingly pleased to have something to still his agitated hands. Between him and Penda, I'm not sure that either of them will ever be genuinely comfortable riding in my war band. Not that they haven't already earned the honour of doing so, but following on from Eoppa's death, I'm no longer sure I want any man to serve me if terror stalks them. The bastard Raiders have somehow become ever more lethal, and I'll protect those that I can.

By the time I reach the ford, Gyrth and Sæbald have already disappeared to scout ahead, and half of the men and horses have crossed without incident.

I wait for Haden to be his usual awkward self, but he eagerly steps into the water, and for the time it takes him to cross, I can hear little above the rush of the water. I'm grateful that Rudolf and Lyfing keep a sharp eye on the trees behind me. If they notice anyone about to attack, I'll know just from their stance. But, we cross without peril.

The day is getting old, but I push the men. I've instructed Sæbald and Gyrth to make a camp when they find somewhere suitable. I really want to be close enough to Northampton that we return by tomorrow, but it all depends on my horses and men.

In front, I spare a thought for Jethson and his double-load, but the horse seems to be managing well. Indeed, it's some of the wounded horses that are struggling the most. Four of them are in danger of going lame, and my men have chosen alternative mounts rather than task with any greater weight. I don't want to leave any man or horse, but the pace feels too slow.

Yet, Sæbald and Gyrth set a good speed, and by the time it's truly too dark to see by, I'm confident that we've covered a good part of the distance, and I'm eager to dismount.

The place Sæbald has found for the night is similar to the enormous oak tree we sheltered under on the way to find my men. The branches hang so low that they all but obscure everyone beneath the long limbs. There's even room for all the horses as well.

"How old is this thing?" I ask of no-one, considering that maybe the men who built the ancient roads might once have sheltered here as well. For a moment, I feel melancholy, the deeds of men forgotten about, and only trees and stone roads to serve as a testament to what was once accomplished.

Ælfgar and Tatberht share their supplies amongst my warriors, and I go to Edmund.

"How is he?"

"No change," Edmund's voice holds a flicker of emotion, and I gaze at his pale son, seeing all the similarities they share, now that Gardulf's face is slack in sleep.

"She'll save him," I advise but Edmund makes no response, as I riffle through his saddlebags and hand him a chunk of bread and cheese as well.

Hereman is already slumped in sleep beside his brother, snoring so loudly, I swear they could hear him in London.

I consider giving him a prod, but he needs sleep to heal.

Sæbald and Gyrth insist on taking the first watch, and so I insist on claiming the second one, Ælfgar and Tatberht again taking the final one.

The night feels long and cold, but at least the wind has died down, and the branches only shiver intermittently. My exhausted warriors all fall asleep quickly, and I'm left with no choice but to follow them or spend all night awake. The conversation is muted, but even Pybba's rage has dispersed and instead, there's a relief in the camaraderie of being together.

Sæbald wakes me with an urgent whisper, and I startle to full wakefulness.

"Your turn," he says, stifling a yawn apologetically.

"Get some rest," I order him, and make my way through the unmoving shapes and then push through the branches that shield us all. I don't expect there to be any trouble, but it doesn't stop me from remaining alert, by pacing from one side of the tree to the other. I'm sure the feeling of being watched yesterday was because we were being watched, only by my men, who couldn't see well enough to know that it was their allies in the woodlands, not their enemy.

Overhead, the moon is a slither, and the cloud cover little, but I'd almost rather rain was threatened, as the temperature plummets and my air plumes before me. In the morning, the ground will be hard. The season is truly on the turn. I want my wounded men behind stout wooden defences as soon as possible.

Nestled inside my cloak, my thoughts turn once more to Eoppa. He might have been a fucking funny bastard, but I'll miss him. I realise I don't like losing my men in battles where I'm absent. I vow then never to separate my men. It brings nothing but death, and I won't allow it. Not again.

Ælfgar doesn't need waking, and I'm pleased when he and Tatberht appear, stifling yawns and emptying their bladders.

I check on both Siric and Gardulf, but in the darkness, it impossible to tell how they fare. I return to my bed, thinking I won't sleep, but of course, I do, despite how cold I've become. And in the morning, the ground beneath that huge oak has stayed warm because of the press of bodies, but beyond the branches, the view carries a haze of white.

"Fuck," Pybba complains, leading Brimman, as he emerges into the bright, but fiercely cold day. "Wrap up warm," I advise him, as I do all of the men. A night on the hard floor has served to bring more twinges to the fore, and I almost laugh to hear even Rudolf moaning about his aching back as though he's a veteran of a hundred skirmishes.

But there's little time for levity.

"Just think of a nice warm bed," I encourage the loiterers, and then Haden, Ælfgar, Tatberht and I, again take the rear of the straggling line of men and horses.

Edmund seems cheered by Gardulf's improving health, and he rides at the head of the line, Hereman behind him. Even Hereman appears to have begun his recovery, and although he still rides the smaller horse, he does so with a straighter back, and his head constantly turns from side to side, far more alert than yesterday.

"It was too fucking quiet last night," Tatberht's words surprise me.

"Too quiet?"

"Yes, it was too quiet," but he offers nothing further, other than to knee his horse just in front of Haden, leaving me as the solitary rider at the rear of my warband.

A shiver touches my spine, and I'd think it was one of foreboding, but I don't believe in that shit.

We make good time, the going easier, and the men and horses better able to manage their ailments now that they've had some practice at doing so. I'm almost beginning to touch the scent of triumph, when the sound I've been hoping not to hear, belatedly infiltrates my thoughts.

I pause Haden, turn him slightly so that I can hear better, but there's no mistaking it.

"Fuck."

"Ælfgar." He rides closest to me, and as he turns his head, surprised that I'm calling his name, he must hear what I do.

"Bastards," he complains, and that alerts Tatberht as well, and his white head swivels, as his shoulders deflate.

"We need to ride faster," Tatberht states, and I'm not about to argue with him.

"Go down the line, encourage the men. We can't be far. There's time to make it. Tell them that."

I watch him go, bending to speak to Rudolf, and then Lyfing and then Ordheah as he goes, and I'm relieved to be left alone with Ælfgar.

"We'll hold them off," Ælfgar assures me, and I find a grin for him.

"Of course, we fucking will," I agree, encouraging Haden to increase his pace. The gap between Ælfgar and I, and the rest of the men, begins to grow, as the horses lumber beyond a trot to a gentle canter.

Ælfgar grins at me in return, and for a time, I try not to focus on the growing sound of pursuit. My men and their horses can only go so fast, and I'm not about to leave them to face the Raiders alone, not again. Never again.

And then I make the mistake of looking behind me, rather than in front, and my hopes crumble away, as though the brittle leaf from the stem.

We're being chased, and there are so many of them, I can't even count them, not in the brief glance I allow myself.

"Hurry up," I bellow. There's no longer any need for silence. The Raiders have seen us, and my men have seen the Raiders. Now, it's all about fucking speed.

CHAPTER 22

I feel him faltering beneath me, and I'm not surprised.

We've been riding for so long, the attackers behind us, fierce and unrelenting. I wish I could jump from his back, allow him the time he needs, but neither of us has that option.

My eyes have been searching the horizon for all that time, just hoping to see the banner displayed so proudly by the men inside Northampton. I need to see it. He needs to see it, but it feels so far away.

Even my warriors are gone, their mounts fresher and more able to take the punishing pace that Edmund has set from the front of the group. Haden and I have been rushing, from one place to another, for days now, with no chance to rest properly. I'm exhausted. I know that he must be as well.

My warriors were lost, but I found them.

I've had no time to mourn the recent losses.

I might never need to.

But no, Haden's gait lengthens beneath me, as the ground suddenly flattens out, and there, before us, I can see the promise of survival and hope.

All of the other horses, riderless or ridden, stream away, far in the distance, spurred on by the scent of safety behind the sturdy barricade and ditch that protects Northampton. I can just determine that Edmund has reached the river crossing. I watch almost despairingly, as Jethson disappears, no doubt taking steady steps down the steep embankment, the promise of a swim perhaps not the temptation it might once have been.

But the sound of the chase reaches my ears, and despite Haden's best efforts, I know I need to stand, I need to face the Raiders. Even if it's for the final time. Even if only to ensure my men and horses make it back to safety.

I should not have stirred the hornet's nest. I should have thought more before I risked everything just to have the comfort of enjoying the coming winter nights without fear of attack.

My tenure as king will have been brief but filled with acts of bravery, or so I hope they might record it.

Others, Edmund and my Aunt amongst them will berate me for my foolishness, and rage will mark their grief, keeping it at bay. That brings me some comfort.

I watch as more and more of the horses disappear down the riverbank, the hope of survival beginning to thrum through my body in time to the elongated stride of my sweating mount. He'll run himself to death, but it still might not be enough.

Horses and men disappear from sight, although for each of my saved warriors, it seems as though more and more men flood onto the battlements of Northampton. Men watch, weapons ready, although there's nothing they can do from such a distance other than encouraging me, their words failing to reach me, even as their intent does.

I strain to hear, but the only sound in my ears is that of the thudding hooves coming from behind. Fucking bastards. I've killed so many of them, and yet it's never enough.

I notice that Haden's ears flicker, he hears as well, only from somewhere he dredges more speed yet and I consider that it's not the pursuers who drive him on, but rather the hope of a warm bed and plentiful hay.

And then I see it. Pybba, not realising quite how far behind I've fallen, turns and falters. Brimman desperate to be with his stable-brothers, even though Pybba tries to pull him back, to come to my aid, rushes onwards. I can see Pybba's mouth opening and closing, no doubt berating those who've gone before him, perhaps even trying to drag them back. But it's too late. I know that, even though Pybba and Haden seem determined to ignore the fucking obvious.

I wish I had the air to shout to Pybba, tell him to get across the river. My death here is almost inevitable, but his doesn't need to be. And even Haden might make it when I'm felled from his back.

I hope he'll leave me. Such constraints have never prevented Hayden from abandoning me in the past. He better fucking not decide to be loyal and protective now. I'll kill him if he does.

From the top of the embankment that surrounds Northampton, I see Ealdorman Ælhun watching me, impossible to miss his bald pate and frost-rimmed beard. He bellows for me to hurry, just as the other people of Mercia do, to survive, to make it to the river, and then inside Northampton itself. The defences will be impregnable if only I can make it inside.

I wish I'd fucking left the gateway open that would have allowed easier access. Perhaps then I'd have stood more chance of survival. Would the Raiders have risked coming close to the gate when there were so many warriors just waiting to take their lives, missiles ready to strike, and hopefully worse, oil to burn?

My gaze flickers over bows and arrows, spears and even rocks and stones, being held menacingly. It makes me smile to see my proud Mercians. Fuck, it makes me so bloody proud.

I didn't make them like this, that part of their nature was always inside them, but I've been the one to unite them to one purpose, to assure them that King Burgred and his craven ways with the Raiders, was not the only way to defeat the enemy.

I hope they carry on when I'm dead. I don't know who will lead them, but it'll need to be a man with the guile to turn every defeat into a victory, to accept mistakes and learn from them.

It will need to be a better man than I.

And then Haden stumbles. I knew he would.

And I'm flying through the air, my feet coming free from the stirrups, my hands hovering above the reins. I'll not take him with me, neither will I wound him when I fall to the frost-hardened ground.

He'll recover his footing, continue his journey to the river. He knows where he wants to go.

For what feels like a long time, I see the darkened earth coming toward me, the recently constructed trackway, already tangled with winter roots and frost. At the last possible moment, when my head flicks upwards, catching sight of Haden, his pace once more stable as he races on to the river crossing without me, I roll myself tightly, hands to either side so that my weapons don't forge the final wound on me. I'll let the Raiders do that.

The air is knocked from my body, but I don't have time for such niceties as worrying about it, as I rush to my feet. I turn, hands raised, weapons ready, to face the Raiders.

And fuck, there are so fucking many of them. I hardly know where to look.

I did this. I forced them from their lair at Grantabridge.

I antagonised them by killing their scouts, one by one. I led them here. I taunted them. I made them worry that they weren't as secure as they thought they were.

I did this.

And I'll meet my death here as payment.

But the warriors of Mercia, behind their newly built defences, will witness it. I'll not die a coward, skulking and hiding from the Raiders.

No, I'm the king of Mercia, and I'll use my death to show just what can be accomplished, even by only one man, against the nearly hundred mounted Raiders who thunder toward me.

I grin, ensure my helm is firmly wedged on my head from my fall, and then, because to be the legend that Mercia needs to survive, I must, I run at the Raiders.

I'll not wait for them.

The damn fuckers.

But I don't determine on the lead rider. He's careering toward me, and I don't much want to be run down, rather than take some of the bastards with me when I die. No, I focus on the warrior just behind him.

The horse the man rides is a good size, but fast, hard muscle bunching with each and every stroke of its surprisingly long legs. But its eyes are wild, and the warrior strikes its rump time and time again, flashes of burgundy flooding the air. The fucking bastard.

The first rider tries to veer toward me, but his mount is too focused on merely galloping. They rush beyond me, buffeting the air, as I brace myself for the next blow. No doubt the first rider will return, eventually, but for now, I dismiss the bastard from my thoughts, and crouch. I have an idea. A terrible one, but I'm going to try it all the same.

Hoping I judge the action correctly, I push upwards, soaring through the air once more. As the horse is forced to an abrupt stop by its less than careful rider, I'm already mounted, sitting proudly behind the Raider, whose head turns from left to right, as though unsure where I've gone.

Before my foe realises, I slice my seax under the padded byrnie, the blade biting deep as the warrior screams in pain.

"That's for abusing a fucking horse," I whisper, almost a caress into the dying warrior's ear, and he's falling to the ground, and it's easy to encourage the movement.

"Come on, beastie," I don't know the horse's name, but it responds to my gentle words, even with the pounding hooves all around. Quickly, I turn the mount, facing the oncoming Raiders.

If I thought my actions would make them reconsider their attack, I'm entirely wrong. If anything, they're even more determined. For the briefest flicker of time, I realise I could escape, even now, with a fresh horse. But then the moment has gone, between one blink and the next, and my seax is high once more.

Two warriors rush toward me, wild eyes on the horses, weapons ready, one a chillingly huge war axe, the other a spear. Both weapons have a much longer reach than my seax. I consider what I should do in the brief respite, and then both warriors are coming for me. They ride so closely together I think their mounts will tangle. Well, I fucking hope they do. But I have no such luck.

Torn, I don't know whether to dismount or merely stoop low and then the decision is taken from me. I feel the probe of the spear, and realise I can't counter it with the weapons to hand. I do the only thing I can. I slither from the horse, easy to do because I've not threaded my feet through the stirrups.

I'm only just in time as the spear passes harmlessly overhead, and I slap the rump of the horse on the bloody gashes her previous rider raised, sending her racing away, desperate to be free from the pain and the hurt. She doesn't need to be involved in this. She's suffered enough. Her whinny of terror startles the warrior with the war axe, and his blow glances to the side of my face.

Both riders are going too fast to stop, and instead, I ready myself for the next of the fuckers. I try not to consider that there are now three Raiders at my back. I can't protect all of me. Not against so many.

The next rider slides from his horse and walks toward me, face compressed into a tight grimace of satisfaction, or what little I can see beneath the helm. I startle, considering whether I know this man or not, but then decide I don't. He merely resembles someone I've encountered before. These fuckers all look the same with a helm on their heads.

I dredge a grin to my face. This warrior thrums with violence. His leather byrnie, while fitting perfectly to his torso, is covered with scuff marks and dents. This man has fought hard and bloodily. His byrnie hangs low, covering the top of his legs, although his arms are exposed to the air and along them dance inkings of ravens. I can tell from the blackened feathers.

The fact he wears gloves amuses me. A man careful of his hands, but not of his arms. An interesting statement to make.

He also carries a shield, and it's this that gives me cause for concern. It's wicked-looking, with more than just the boss jutting from it. This man revels in dealing death, and it seems he has no concerns about his brutality.

I have no shield for defence.

"King Coelwulf." Ah, he means to speak with me. Fucking

wonderful.

"Who are you?" But he shakes his head. His lower face is shaved, although a bushy moustache settles over thick lips—an unusual look for the Raiders.

"I have a message for you before I end your life."

The words send a shiver down my spine, but I eschew the weakness.

"Seems a bit pointless to tell me something if you're only going to fucking kill me."

I focus only on the Raider. To the rear of him, the rest of the riders have slowed their pace. No doubt they expect this man to kill me without their involvement. I peer behind him, try and catch the eyes of a few of the men, but they don't even flinch. Fuckers.

The warrior recovers himself with a jolt, his lips tightening at the realisation of the effect my words had on him.

"You need to know that the Mercians will learn to say your name with derision, to think you little more than our pet."

I tilt my head to one side, suck my bottom lip, and wrinkle my forehead in thought, not that he can see that below my helm.

"Why the fuck would they think that?"

"Because," and he moves toward me, "we're going to fucking tell 'em that, and when we rule Mercia, they'll have no choice but to believe our words."

"Lies," I counter, my tone cool. His words have no impact on me. The Mercians are not quite as gullible as the Raider seems to think they are. Maybe he thinks he's in Wessex. They'll believe anything in fucking Wessex.

"Lies are only ever a lie from one perspective. There's always a slither of truth in them."

I laugh then, the sound loud and rumbling. Once more, I startle my foe and take pleasure in doing so.

"I don't think the men and women inside Northampton will allow your deceits to percolate into Mercia."

"Perhaps, but then, the rest of the jarl's force is coming this way. It will be nothing to overrun Northampton. After all, we built it. We know it's weaknesses."

The words are meant to worry me, but they don't. I know what the perceived weaknesses are, and they've been countered. The Raiders really do give the Mercians too little astuteness.

"Are you going to sprout shit all day. I merely wanted to know your name before I took your life."

A flash of fury crosses the Raiders face, and I'm aware that the waiting riders shift on their mounts. From behind, I can hear the other Raiders returning, and for all my words, I know time is short.

I spare no thought for anyone other than my Aunt. She'll be alone, with no family to support her. I doubt she'll even notice.

I don't even think of Mercia. I've done what I can. My warriors have shed blood for Mercia. Our tactics have driven the Raiders into the extremities of the Mercian lands, some even falling back to attack Wessex in the hope of easy spoils. Just like this warrior before me, the Raiders are all wind and air. They like the sound of their voices far too much.

"Do not fear," the Raider states. "Your name will forever be associated with mine. There's no need for you to know what that is."

Again, I laugh.

"Cocky fucker," I explode, and as the words leave my mouth, I'm already running, closing down the distance between him and me, keen to claim first blood.

My seax whips before his face before he can even raise his lethal-looking shield. For a heartbeat, I think I might even land that blow, but then the shield crashes into my chest and pain explodes from there.

"Filthy bastard," I recoil, bringing my seax in tight, and trying to sidestep the shield that just keeps coming closer and closer to me. I can feel bruises forming on my skin, but at least, he's not forced first blood. There's time yet.

If only he didn't have that fucking shield, I know I'd be able to get beyond his guard and take his life. Or at least make a bloody good effort at doing so. But the shield remains. He holds it in front of him, and it's so huge, it almost covers his body from neck to ankle. It must weigh more than a man. The Raider is strong and sure of himself. Perhaps he has the skills to be so.

I try again, running against him, but his shield blocks me, and this time, my feet scuttle on the slippery ground as he forces me back, and back, my balance compromised, while my seax tries in vain to draw blood from his forearms.

I'm not even aware that his war axe is trying to strike me, until the blow lands on my right side, threatening to drive the air from me if I let it.

"You can't win," my foe calls, his voice high with derision.

He might be right, but I'm not going to give him the satisfaction of capitulating without a fight. I'll extract his blood. I just need to get close enough to do so. And it's his shield which prevents me from doing anything.

Quickly, I reach for my war axe. It's small compared to the one the Raider carries, but it doesn't mean it's ineffectual.

Hastily, I hook it over the top of the man's deadly shield, forcing all my weight behind it, trying to bring it low enough to either swipe a blow against the man's head or force him to drop it at the risk of overbalancing.

I'm sure that the warrior can't be strong enough to hold both my weight and that of his shield in one hand. I feel it give, the strain making my foe blow hot air that almost reaches my face. I endeavour to make my body heavier, swinging low, so that my knees almost touch my nose.

Only then I feel the reach of a spear close to my ear and know the Raiders behind me are back.

I'm torn. Should I turn, should I stay focused on felling this man. Fuck, if I could, I'd take control of his shield, and then they'd all struggle to kill me.

I lower my head further, put all of my weight behind the shield, only the spear aims for my hand, and I can't risk losing it.

Abruptly, I let go, and at that moment, accomplish more than I have by holding on. The warrior overbalances, almost knocking me to the floor, but as he tumbles forward, I stab down on

THE LAST HORSE

his exposed neck with my seax, pleased to see blood welling even as the man's movements become jerky, his body fighting the inevitable.

Only, he's fallen on the shield. So, while he's now dead, I still have only my seax and war axe for protection.

Cold eyes appraise me from the next warrior to take their chance, the spear retracted, but ready to strike once more, when the command is given. But that's not just yet because I recognise the eyes that watch me—Jarl Guthrum's sister. No doubt, she means to toy with me, seek her revenge for what we did to her. Fuck, she's alive, what more does she want?

"The rumours about you are disappointingly wrong," she opines, her voice rich with scorn, as she dismounts.

"Well, at least there are fucking rumours about me," I pant. Around me, more and more of the Raiders are closing in. Ahead, I can still see Northampton and the promise of safety, but in reality, it's getting further and further away. I only hope that Edmund, Hereman, Pybba, Rudolf and the rest don't make it to the ramparts in time to witness my death. That would be too cruel.

My words make her jolt, and I grin once more. The Raiders are all too easy to upset. They're prickly of their reputations. I would have thought them keener to cement their reputations than argue about them, but seemingly not.

"I've demanded the right to kill you, and my brother has given it," she chuckles, the sound a little off, as she tries to reassert her control.

"Then I suggest you fucking get on with it," is my only response, and my nonchalance seems to unsettle her once more. Because I can, I rush against her. It seems to me that the Raiders are too enamoured of their voices. Added to which, these warriors, are too much under the woman's control to do anything without her agreement.

I crash into her with all of my weight, unbalancing her, as her feet are forced backwards. Her sword flutters from her fingers, as I almost run over her, and she falls below my feet. With barely a thought, I slice down, my seax opening up her neck so that she gargles before the spear can get anywhere near me, and I meet her eyes, luxuriating in my triumph, and her death.

I turn, meet the horrified eyes of every single one of those Raiders, a grin splitting my face.

"Tell your fucking jarl what I did. Tell him she died falling over her own fucking feet," I bellow and then I'm running at the next rider. I've only killed two of the bastards. There are many more to go. I have no problem dying here, but I'm not about to let them kill me easily. I can take more of them with me yet, and then there'll be less to terrorise Mercia when I'm gone.

Only this time, the Raiders are far from eager to wait. This time, it seems they all want the opportunity to kill me.

The first Raider dodges the swing of my axe, turning his horse to follow me as I continue to run. I'll make them follow me. I'll cleave through them all and send them crashing into one another. If I'm lucky, a few of the daft bastards will injure one another in the process.

The thud of hooves behind me seems to grow in intensity, and I decide that those on the edges of the group must have rushed to take their place there, perhaps to halt my progress, maybe just to see what's happening, and now they try and follow me once more.

I hope the Mercians inside Northampton are watching and seeing just how easy it is to confuse the bastards.

And then I encounter a warrior, standing, waiting for me on the cold ground.

It brings me up short, and I almost skid across the ground in an effort to come to a stop before his waiting sword can pierce me.

"*Skiderik*," he grumbles at me, and I consider that this might be Jarl Guthrum, perhaps avenging his sister. Certainly, he has the auburn hair and owl tattoos that I recall from our previous meeting. But who knows, maybe there is any number of brothers, uncles and even sons who all look alike.

"Same to you, you fucker," and I launch my seax against his sword, keen to strike the first blow. He rounds on me, batting my seax away as though it were no more than a piece of wicker fencing. I'm forced backwards as he skips into me, sword busy in his hand, able to keep his body away from my seax, as his men close around us, blocking any chance of escape. I think this might be the man who kills me. Only not yet.

I skip out of the reach of his sword, to the right, making a strike against his exposed arms, for all the weapon passes harmlessly. This seems to infuriate him though, and his next two blows are so heavy, my fingers pulse from the crash of iron on iron, and I only just manage to retain my grip on my weapon.

"*Skiderik*," he spits once more, but I'm too busy to respond. The warriors who surround us are closing in, making it challenging to find the space I need to bring my war axe up to speed, so I need to determine on another means of attack. Not that I have the time to think. The blows from my foe's sword ring louder and louder against either my seax or my war axe, and sometimes both of them, as I endeavour to ward off the explosive attack.

I can't move quickly enough to try and attack him myself. I only have time for a defence. Unless.

The touch of his sword on my forearm almost forces a cry of pain, but I bite my lip tightly, tasting my salt and iron, as the warrior grins, for the briefest of moments, dropping his sword, and that's all the opportunity I need.

With quick steps, I'm close enough to hammer my war axe against his twisting tattoos, while with my seax, I draw a welter of blood, nearly all the way down his right arm.

Before he can respond, I hurry, almost getting my seax to his neck, before he rears, desperate to evade my blade. Then I feel the prod of a weapon from behind.

"Bastards," I roar, not appreciating such an action when I thought I fought one on one. I can feel where my skin has been exposed, where no doubt my blood pulses hotly onto the cold ground.

I'm met by a leering face as I round on my attacker, contempt in those eyes, and I can't help myself. I rush forward, aiming for the man's nose, and the impact brings tears to his eyes and sends him staggering to the floor. I have no time to enjoy the moment, because my original opponent is back, and he doesn't come alone.

Four of them menace me, all with blades in their hands, all with malice written on their face. I appreciate that this truly is where it will all end.

All those battles I've fought in, all those skirmishes where I've out-thought my enemy, will end here, on the blade of one of these damn fucking bastards. And while I thought I'd accepted it, suddenly I don't.

Barely aware of my actions, my seax and war axe soar through the air, impacting one or the other of my enemy, little heeding of where I hit, only that I make contact.

But it's not all my success. I'm buffeted from one to another, swords and seaxs, war axes and even fists knocking me, so that whereas to begin with I could see nothing because of the speed of my actions, now I struggle to see because blood sheets my eyes, my broken nose dripping without ceasing, and those are just the most obvious of my injuries.

And yet, for all my struggle, I can still hear the sound of hooves approaching.

"How many of you cunts are there?" I roar, my voice rising above the crush of the warriors who try to hack me down. And the response I get is not at all the one I'm expecting.

"Fifty, My Lord King. Fifty. We'll be with you shortly." And my actions redouble in effort, because somehow, and I have no idea how it seems that I might just live through this uneven match.

CHAPTER 23

Rudolf reaches me first, his forehead furrowed, his eyes rimmed with fear.

"Just a few cuts and bruises," I lift my arms to show him what I mean, but it only seems to increase his worry.

"A few fucking cuts and bruises?" Edmund's voice is filled with awe, and that's something I never expected to hear. Never.

"Yep," and I'm trying to wipe the blood from my nose so that I can taste something other than myself.

Rudolf thrusts a piece of linen at me, and I hold it against my nose, one eye all but closed, my lips throbbing with a blow I've forgotten I even earned.

"How did they do it?" The words are muffled, but Rudolf seems to be expecting the question.

"They sealed the gateway, as you requested, but they've added a double entrance instead, so they came from inside Northampton. The Raiders had no idea."

"So, I owe my life once more to someone who didn't follow my fucking orders." Rudolf grins, no doubt pleased to hear the complaint on my lips.

"You do, yes. Ealdorman Ælhun and that Wulfsige are crafty fuckers."

I'm slumped to the ground, barely able to draw enough air into my body to stop from keeling over. Around me, the dead and dying are far from quiet, but the battle is over, other than for the final few who need killing. Ealdorman Ælhun and the Mercians are busy at their work far in the distance. The Raiders have been beaten back. Jarl Guthrum forced to run for his life when the Mercian horses clattered through to where we fought, one to one, only surrounded by his warriors. I only just managed to avoid being thrown beneath the hooves of Wulfsige's high-stepping white mare.

"So, who was the traitor?" I muse, trying to focus on something other than the fact I almost died only moments ago.

"Did you say something?" Rudolf asks, from where he's picking his way through the sweating bodies, still warm to the touch, his eyes searching for treasurer.

"No, no lad," I confirm, but Edmund hears me and shakes his head, holding his finger to his lips. He doesn't know either. Not yet.

"Did everyone make it?" I demand to know, remembering now why I was so prepared to sacrifice myself.

"Yes, everyone's alive, if not well. Gardulf has woken, Siric is no longer as hot, the wound rot might not have been as bad as we feared."

I don't demand a full accounting of everyone. I'm sure much has been accomplished in a rush. I'm sure that only moments can have passed since they left me alone, but maybe not. Time on the battlefield runs strangely.

"Good." My words sound muffled, and I almost giggle, a sound unbecoming of Mercia's king. "We'll get Siric to my Aunt at Kingsholm, Gardulf as well, she'll know what to do."

And here the two men pause, Rudolf straightening from his interrogation of a dead man's byrnie, looking from Edmund to me, as though unsure which of them is going to answer.

In the end, neither of them do.

"I will know what to do, yes," the strident voice of my Aunt ripples through the air. I'm trying to stagger to my feet, face her, only she brings her horse in front of me, and her face is the sternest I've ever seen.

"What the fuck?" I mutter, too exhausted to mind my words.

"I would ask you the same," she complains, her hands steady

on the reins of her horse, the animal looking at me with just as much disparagement as my Aunt.

"Why are you here?" I demand to know, Rudolf, helping me stand, Edmund to the other side, trying to assist me as well, for all his eye never leaves my Aunt's face. Once more, I consider just what understanding exists between the two of them, only for her words to drag me back to the here and now.

"I brought you something," she states, no trace of warmth in her voice, but there doesn't need to be, not when the warrior escorting my Aunt guides his horse forwards, and thrusts his helm backwards.

And I confess, I'm crying, and I don't even fucking care who sees as I lurch forward and throw my arms around him after he carefully dismounts from his horse.

Icel's arms snake around my shoulders, and then Edmund joins me, Rudolf, as well, and fuck knows who else, and I'm sobbing and laughing, all at the same time.

"In the reign of King Wiglaf, I faced a force of a hundred and one warriors alone," Icel rumbles, his words clear enough for anyone to hear, as Edmund growls in frustration.

I can feel my Aunt watching me, and I lift my eyes to glance at her, noting the bemused expression on her firm face.

Fuck, I dare her to bloody enjoy this victory.

HISTORICAL NOTES

We're told that Guthrum, Oscetel and Anwend went to Cambridge following their defeat at Repton. How they got there has not been conveyed to us through the available sources. I've proposed a sort of running battle from Repton and then a sly cut down one of the many other rivers that dispersed into the North Sea from the East Coast of England. It's equally possible that they just rode to Cambridge or Grantabridge as they called it, from Repton. What is clear is that Halfdan and the three others jarls went their separate ways at this point. Why, would be fascinating to know, although we can never know for sure. I shan't mention further here, as I intend to cover it later.

Cambridge/Grantabridge, to my mind at least, should be firmly a part of East Anglia, the ancient kingdom falling under the sway of the Vikings (Raiders) earlier in the attacks of the 'Great Heathen Army.' But, on some maps, (especially the one used on the archaeological site report from Repton) Cambridge is very much a part of Mercia. I've adopted this convention. It seemed just possible that the Raiders might have chosen Cambridge because it was just incendiary enough to upset the Mercians while allowing them an easy means of escape, along the Cam/Granta or back into the heartland of East Anglia. To reinforce the suggestion, it does appear that the early settlement of Cambridge was to the east of the river, not to the west, as now.

There is no record of an attack on Northampton in AD874

but there are reports that there were defences built there, by the Raiders in AD850. I appreciated the irony that the building of the defensive burhs – accredited to King Alfred – might well have been based on a much earlier idea by the very people he was trying to dissuade from entering the Wessex settlements. There is a document, called the Burghal Hidage, which appears to be a list of how many warriors it took to protect the ramparts of every burh.

It's not necessarily such a straightforward argument to make because the date is suspect, and some of the information doesn't quite correlate. But again, I've used it as a basis for the discussion that Coelwulf has with his men about how to protect Northampton. Nothing would have simply materialised from thin-air, there must have been precursors to the plans laid in place by King Alfred and potentially King Coelwulf as well. We know so little about Coelwulf.

The fascination of the Raiders with Northampton, in my mind at least, serves as a predecessor to the settlement of the Five Boroughs – Derby, Nottingham, Lincoln, Leicester and Stamford some time later.

There is no record of King Coelwulf's coronation that I can find, or where it took place. I must reinforce that he was accepted as king by the bishops and ealdormen. If not, they wouldn't have witnessed the scant few charters available to us (two of them), which are deemed to be authentic by the pre-eminent historians of the period, who know far more than I do, and whose authority I willingly accept.

The events of this time period are incredibly opaque. It's impossible to know for certain what did, and what didn't happen. There will be people keen to argue that giving King Coelwulf any type of acclaim for holding Mercia against the Raiders is incorrect. Again, I'll be addressing how this might have happened, and just what 'proof' there is in later books. There's still a much wider story to tell, but for now, there are battles to be won.

The words of the commendatory oath spoken by Coelwulf's men are those used in all the books I write for this period, and comes from *The Earls of Mercia: Lordship and Power in Late Anglo-Saxon England* by S Baxter (2007). A fascinating book that has a great deal to blame for my fascination with the period.

A mancus was a coin, or weight the equivalent of 30 silver pence.

As to my map. There is, sadly, not a map that I can direct my readers to that shows all the little details I'm pulling together throughout these stories. The one attached has been a monumental task of cobbling together a great deal of other information. Any mistakes are entirely mine, and I'll own them. Unlike Coelwulf!

On a non-historical note, I've spent much of 'lockdown' walking through the local countryside. I've learned a lot more about the countryside than I thought I needed to know, the sounds, the smells, the heat, the different weather conditions, and perhaps most importantly, and unfortunately, how badly decomposing bodies actually smell, and just how long it lingers for (a dead deer in one of the hedges). I hope that these experiences help the book feel even more realistic.

For those waiting to see what happens between King Coelwulf and King Alfred, I promise it's coming. Watch this space.

CAST OF CHARACTERS

Coelwulf's Warriors

Ælfgar – one of the older members of the warband
Athelstan – killed in the first battle in The Last King
Beornberht – killed in the first battle in The Last King
Beornstan
Coelwulf – King of Mercia, rides Haden
Edmund – rides Jethson, was Coelwulf's brother's man until his death. Brother is Hereman.
Eadberht
Eadulf
Eahric
Eoppa – rides Poppy
Gardulf – first appears in The Last Horse – Edmund's son
Goda
Gyrth
Hereman – brother of Edmund, rides Billy
Hereberht – dies at Torksey, in The Last Warrior.
Hiltiberht - squire
Ingwald
Icel – rides Samson
Leonath – first appears in The Last Horse
Lyfing – wounded in The Last King, now back with the warband
Oda
Ordheah
Ordlaf
Oslac

Penda – first appears in The Last Horse – Pybba's grandson
Pybba – loses his hand in battle, rides Brimman (Sailor in Old English)
Rudolf – youngest warrior, was a squire at the beginning of The Last King, rides Dever
Siric – first appears in The Last Horse
Sæbald –
Tatberht – first appears in The Last Horse, normally remains at Kingsholm. Rides Wombel
Wærwulf – speaks Danish
Wulfstan
Wulfhere – a squire, grandson of Tatberht, rides Stilton
Wulfred – rides Cuthbert

Bishop Wærferth of Worcester
Bishop Deorlaf of Hereford
Bishop Eadberht of Lichfield
Bishop Smithwulf of London
Bishop Ceobred of Leicester
Bishop Burgheard of Lindsey
Ealdorman Beorhtnoth – of western Mercia
Ealdorman Ælhun – of area around Warwick
Ealdorman Alhferht - of western Mercia
Ealdorman Æthelwold – his father Ealdorman Æthelwulf dies at the Battle of Berkshire in AD871
Ealdorman Wulfstan – dies in The Last King
    His son – (fictional) dies in The Last King
    Werburg – his daughter
Ealdorman Beornheard – of eastern Mercia
Ealdorman Aldred – of eastern Mercia
Lady Cyneswith – Coelwulf's (fictional) Aunt

Raiders

Ivarr – dies in AD870
Halfdan – brother of Ivarr, may take his place after his death
Guthrum - one of the three leaders at Repton with Halfdan

His sister
Oscetel – one of the three leaders at Repton with Halfdan
Anwend – one of the three leaders at Repton with Halfdan
        Anwend Anwendsson – his fictional son
Sigurd (fictional)

The royal family of Mercia

King Burgred of Mercia
    m. Lady Æthelswith in AD853 (the sister of King Alfred) they had no children
Beornwald – a fictional nephew for King Burgred
King Wiglaf – ninth century ruler of Mercia
King Wigstan – ninth century ruler of Mercia
King Beorhtwulf – ninth century ruler of Mercia

Misc

Cadell ap Merfyn – fictional brother of Rhodri Mawr, King of Gwynedd (one of the Welsh kingdoms)
Eowa, forest dweller
Coenwulf – Coelwulf's dead (older) brother
Wiglaf and Berhtwulf – the names of Coelwulf's aunt's dogs, Lady Cyneswith
Sigtryggr, Avarr, Gofrith, Barðr – Raiders
Eirikr, Haflioðl, Amlaib – Raiders
Æthelwulf – Mercian warrior under the command of Edwin
Scurfa – Mercian warrior under the command of Edwin
Wulfsige – commander of Ealdorman Ælhun's warriors
Kyred – oathsworn man of Bishop Wærferth of Worcester

Places Mentioned

Northampton, on the River Nene in Mercia.
Grantabridge/Cambridge, in eastern Mercia/East Anglia
Gloucester, on the River Severn, in western Mercia.
Worcester, on the River Severn, in western Mercia.

Hereford, close to the border with Wales
Lichfield, an ancient diocese of Mercia. Now in Staffordshire.
Tamworth, an ancient capital of Mercia. Now in Staffordshire.
Repton, an ancient capital of Mercia. St Wystan's was a royal mausoleum.
Gwent, one of the Welsh kingdoms at this period.
Warwick, in Mercia.
Torksey, in the ancient kingdom of Lindsey, which became part of Northern Mercia
Passenham, in Mercia
River Severn, in the west of England
River Trent, runs through Staffordshire, Derbyshire, Nottingham and Lincolnshire and joins the Humber
River Avon, in Warwickshire
River Thames, runs through London and into Oxfordshire
River Stour, runs from Stourport to Wolverhampton
River Ouse, leads into the Cam/Granta, runs through Bedford (Bed's Ford)
River Nene, runs from Northampton to the Wash
River Welland, runs from Northamptonshire to the Wash
River Granta/Cam, runs from Cambridge to Lena (King's Lynn) (East Anglia)
River Great Ouse, running from South Northamptonshire to East Anglia
Kingsholm, close to Gloucester, an ancient royal site
The Foss Way, ancient roadway running from Lincoln to Exeter
Watling Street, ancient roadway running from Chester to London
Icknield Way, ancient roadway running from Norfolk to Wiltshire
Ermine Street, ancient roadway running from London to Lincoln, and York.

MEET THE AUTHOR

I'm an author of fantasy (viking age/dragon themed) and historical fiction (Early English, Vikings and the British Isles as a whole before the Norman Conquest), born in the old Mercian kingdom at some point since AD1066. I write A LOT. You've been warned!

Find me at mjporterauthor.com, mjporterauthour.blog and @coloursofunison on twitter. I have a newsletter, which can be joined via my website.

Books by M J Porter (in chronological order)

Gods and Kings Series (seventh century Britain)
Pagan Warrior
Pagan King
Warrior King

The Ninth Century
The Last King
The Last Warrior
The Last Sword
The Last Enemy
The Last Sword

The Tenth Century
The Lady of Mercia's Daughter
A Conspiracy of Kings (the sequel to The Lady of Mercia's

Daughter)
  Kingmaker
  The King's Daughter

Chronicles of the English (tenth century Britain)
Brunanburh
Of Kings and Half-Kings
The Second English King

The Mercian Brexit (can be read as a prequel to The First Queen of England)

The First Queen of England (The story of Lady Elfrida) (tenth century England)
  The First Queen of England Part 2
  The First Queen of England Part 3

The King's Mother (The continuing story of Lady Elfrida)
  The Queen Dowager
  Once A Queen

The Earls of Mercia
The Earl Of Mercia's Father
The Danish King's Enemy
Swein: The Danish King (side story)
Northman Part 1
Northman Part 2
Cnut: The Conqueror (full length side story)
Wulfstan: An Anglo-Saxon Thegn (side story)
The King's Earl
The Earl of Mercia
The English Earl
The Earl's King
Viking King
The English King

  Lady Estrid (a novel of eleventh century Denmark) (October 2020)

Fantasy

<u>The Dragon of Unison</u>
Hidden Dragon
Dragon Gone
Dragon Alone
Dragon Ally
Dragon Lost
Dragon Bond

Throne of Ash

<u>As JE Porter</u>
The Innkeeper

The Custard Corpses - a delicious 1940s mystery

ACKNOWLEDGEMENT

I am once more indebted to all my readers, new and old, for allowing me to write about a time period I love, and to share the characters I create with you all.
I would also like to thank my beta readers for their insights. If you follow me on twitter, you might have seen that there was a bit of a problem with a lack of 'ducks' in the first few drafts, or as it was put to me, 'you've gone all polite, again.' That will never do.
So, to call them out, there's EP, ST, AM, CS, AL and CH.
As ever, thanks to my children, AP and MP, for putting up with me, and for answering increasingly random questions about horses and the English language, and for walking with me, even when I didn't bloody want to go!
And thank you to my better half, who is beginning to realise just what I go through with the process of writing and editing each book. It's not always very pretty (and often involves dancing).

Printed in Great Britain
by Amazon